"DO YOU KNOW WHAT YOU ARE DOING TO ME?"

Gabe's hand reached out and touched the line of her jaw. All he knew was how much he wanted her. His hand reached down to cup her breast, and she whispered, "No, Gabe."

It was pure torture, but he pulled away and said, "I won't do anything you don't want me to, Cait."

The trouble was, of course, that she *wanted* him to caress her. She put her hand on top of his and guided it back. He traced her breast gently and cupped it.

"Oh, Gabe . . ." she murmured.

When he lowered his mouth to hers, she let herself fall back on the cot. It seemed their kiss went on forever, but when he pulled away, she realized forever wasn't nearly long enough. . . .

Journey
of the Heart

Marjorie Farrell

A TOPAZ BOOK

TOPAZ
Published by the Penguin Group
Penguin Books USA Inc., 375 Hudson Street,
New York, New York 10014, U.S.A.
Penguin Books Ltd, 27 Wrights Lane,
London W8 5TZ, England
Penguin Books Australia Ltd, Ringwood,
Victoria, Australia
Penguin Books Canada Ltd, 10 Alcorn Avenue,
Toronto, Ontario, Canada M4V 3B2
Penguin Books (N.Z.) Ltd, 182–190 Wairau Road,
Auckland 10, New Zealand

Penguin Books Ltd, Registered Offices:
Harmondsworth, Middlesex, England

First published by Topaz, an imprint of Dutton Signet,
a division of Penguin Books USA Inc.

First Printing, May, 1997
10 9 8 7 6 5 4 3 2

 REGISTERED TRADEMARK—MARCA REGISTRADA

Printed in Canada

PUBLISHER'S NOTE
This is a work of fiction. Names, characters, places, and incidents either are
the product of the author's imagination or are used fictitiously, and any resemblance to actual persons, living or dead, events, or locales is entirely
coincidental.

For "Calico Cait."
And for the rest of the Farrell family:
Jack, Dee, and John. Without the "White Rabbit,"
I never would have gotten to New Mexico
for the first time those many years ago.

ACKNOWLEDGMENTS

For the purposes of my story, I simplified a very complex historical situation, the Lincoln County war. For those who are interested in further background, I recommend Joel Jacobsen's book, *Such Men as Billy the Kid*.

For help with my rusty Spanish, I thank Miguel Martinez and Luisandra Reynoso. All mistakes are mine.

For being my "first readers" and for always giving me encouraging and best of all, honest feedback, thanks, Barbara and Joan.

Prologue

"Gabriel?"

"I'm here, Ma." The tall, thin, fifteen-year-old moved closer to the bed where his mother lay dying.

"You tell your pa I tried to wait till he came home," she whispered, with a tired smile.

"You tell him yourself, Ma," said the boy, leaning forward in his chair and slipping his hand under hers where it lay on the coverlet.

One finger weakly tapped him, as though to say, "You know better."

"Help your pa take care of the young ones," she added. "And Gabriel?"

"Yes, Ma?"

"The good book says it's not good for man to be alone. If your pa should bring another woman here, you be good to her, hear?"

The fever took Mary Ann Hart in three days. It was a week before James Hart returned from driving his cattle up to Abilene and his wife was already buried in the little cemetery outside of town, next to her third child, a daughter who had lived only one day.

"She fought hard, Pa," Gabriel told him as they stood, hats in hand, in front of the new grave.

"She was a fighter, Mary Ann," said Hart in a low, raspy voice. He reached up to put his hand on his son's shoulder. "You take after her, Gabe. And you took good care of her, like a man would do. We'll miss her."

They all did miss her, the tall, freckled, rangy woman who had made their small cabin a home.

"I would have thought Pa would miss Ma a bit longer," said twelve-year-old Sadie eight months later when James Hart announced he was bringing home a bride. "A new mother for you all," was how he'd put it. "We don't need no new mother, Gabe. I can take care of the little ones just fine."

"Shore you can, Sadie. Ben and Jamie are doing fine. I suspect it's Pa that's not doing so well. Ma wouldn't have wanted to see him lonely, you know that."

"But May Lockridge? Why, she's not that much older than you, Gabe."

"She's twenty-three if she's a day, Sadie."

"And Pa's near forty, Gabe!"

"Well, there ain't much to choose from around here, Sadie. Would you rather Miss Parker from the dry goods store?" Miss Parker was fifty and had three black hairs growing out of a bump on her chin, so Sadie knew her big brother was joking her. Sadie signed. "I *miss* Ma, Gabe," she said, her voice quivering.

"So do I, Sarah Ellen, so do I."

James Hart brought home his new bride a week later and for the first few months things seemed to go well. May was young and pretty and energetic and made an obvious effort to win the hearts of the little ones. Ben, who was five, was easy. He missed his mother so much that any woman who had shown him affection could have won him. Jamie, at eight, was a little harder, but after a few weeks he couldn't resist her charm either.

Gabe couldn't blame them, or his pa either, for that matter. She was a charming little thing. Real different from his ma, of course. His ma had pitched in like a partner on their small ranch. She wasn't above doing anything outdoors, unlike May, who confined her energy to the house. It wasn't that she acted weak so much, or reluctant to pitch in on rougher chores. It was as if the idea had never entered her mind. She didn't *have* to say anything about not wanting to get her dress muddy or hands too raw; you just knew she wouldn't ever consider feeding the calves or chopping wood.

James Hart was a taciturn man, but it was clear to his children how taken he was with May. It was in the way he looked up from his coffee in the morning, appreciating her trim waist and curved bosom. It was in the way he hurried her off to bed at night, just after the little boys had been put down to sleep but before Gabe and Sadie went up to the loft space they shared.

"I don't like her, Gabe," Sadie whispered one night after they'd climbed up to bed.

"Now, Sadie," he drawled.

"And you don't either; you can't fool me!"

Gabe was silent. She didn't miss much, Sarah Ellen. Just like Ma: smart as a whip about people and animals. And with the same ability to put her feelings into words. He shared that sixth sense, but not the words. "Well, Sadie, I don't know that it matters so long as Pa likes her. And the boys."

"Maybe you're right, Gabe. Anyways, you'll be out of here soon enough, and I'll just have to find me someone to marry real quick."

"Marry! Who's going to marry a scrawny thing like you, Sarah Ellen Hart! Why you ain't even got a curve yet."

Sadie scooted over from her side of the loft and pinched her brother in the ribs. "I'll get curves faster than you think, Gabe. Faster than you fill out, boy!"

It took three years, but by the time she was fifteen, Sadie Hart was quite pleased with her figure. She was tall, like her mother, it was true, but a little less rangy. Gabe had filled out too. He was a long and lean young man, but his thighs and his butt filled his denims very well, thought Sadie one hot afternoon, and his muscles rippled quite satisfactorily across his back as he chopped wood. She grinned when he turned around and looked at her inquiringly.

"You might haul your little butt over here and take in this wood, Sarah Ellen."

"I'm too busy looking at yours," she teased.

At that moment, May came out of the cabin, her hand shading her forehead. Making out like she's looking for Pa, thought Sadie, when she's really admiring Gabe. It was one thing for his little sister to objectively admire his good points. It was another for their father's wife to be looking at him the way she did. Too often for comfort, thought Sadie. She wondered if Gabe had noticed his stepmother's attention.

Gabe was well aware of it and very glad he no longer slept in the house. When Sadie began filling out her overalls and dresses, he'd gone to his father and suggested they turn the last stall in the barn into a room for him. James had blushed and nodded when he understood the reason and at least Gabe was out of the house. It had grown uncomfortable this year, what with his pa and May not retiring early like they used to. Not that his pa didn't want to occasionally. But May, she seemed to have lost some of her desire to please him. She acted put upon when he got up from his chair early and where before she'd be saying in front of him, "Why, James, he's the strong and silent and handsome type, isn't he?" now she'd complain behind his back about him. "Your pa, he never has two words to say to me at dinnertime."

Gabe reckoned she was getting bored of her older, quiet husband. Pa *didn't* say much, and Gabe could understand that. But Ma had known how to read his silences. Not that she let them wear her down. Not Ma. She understood James Hart and loved him for what he was.

Pa hadn't noticed anything yet, Gabe was sure. And Gabe didn't intend for him to notice. He kept out of May's way, volunteering to ride fence as often as possible, though he'd much prefer working the horses and cattle over mending barbed wire. But one day he was well and truly caught.

Sadie had taken the two boys to town to outfit them for the fall and Pa had ridden out to the east pasture. Before he left he'd called Gabe over to him. "I want you to ride that little bay mare, Gabe. She needs some more gentlin' before we can give her to Sadie for her birthday."

He could hardly refuse. And he loved nothing better than working a green horse. He worked them slowly and gently, unlike many horse breakers who just got on an unbroken horse and rode it hard till it stopped bucking. Or till the wrangler was thrown. Gabe could ride a mean one as good as any, but he'd never seen the point to it.

Sadie had had her eye on the mare since they'd gotten her some months ago. She'd been hinting six days to Sunday that she wanted the bay for her own. Short of outright begging, she'd made her preference for her birthday gift clear. But James had merely turned his head and winking at Gabe, said: "She's too good a mare to be wasted on riding to school and back, Sarah Ellen."

Gabe had been working her on a lunge line with the saddle on but the stirrups tied up. Today he was going to let them hang free so she'd get used to something bumping her sides. The mare was sweet-tempered, but had spunk too. At a walk, she merely shook her head a few times at the unfamiliar weight brushing her sides. But at a trot, she stopped short and gave a pretty demonstration of bucking while Gabe urged her on with his voice and light touches of his whip.

"You have a way with horses, don't you, Gabe?" said a voice behind him.

"I guess I do," he said, his voice flat.

May stood next to him, not so close that they were touching, but close enough that he had to watch out that their arms didn't brush when he flicked the whip.

"She's a pretty little thing, isn't she?" May whispered softly.

Somehow Gabe was sure she was angling for him to say something like: "And so are you, May." He just grunted and urged the mare into a canter, which set her to bucking again and required him to shorten the line and walk toward her and away from his father's wife. He brought the mare down to a trot and then a walk. She was high-stepping and shaking her withers as though she wanted to shake the saddle off.

"Do you think she'll be ready in time for Sadie's birthday?"

"I'll be sure she is," Gabe replied as he approached the mare's head. He pulled her nose down to his chest and scratched her ears, saying, "That's my good girl. You did real well today."

"Here, let me hold her for you, Gabe." May moved in beside him and her hand covered his before he knew it. He let go of the reins instantly and moved down to unsaddle her. The mare sidestepped a little as he pulled the saddle off, but she gazed at him calmly.

"Here, loop the reins over my arm, May, and I'll bring her into the stable."

"Nonsense, Gabe. You have that heavy saddle to carry. I'll lead her in."

Damn, thought Gabe. He and his pa had been unsaddling and settling down horses for years. Now, all of a sudden, May wanted to be helpful? Not damn likely!

May just hung quietly on the stall gate while Gabe wiped the mare down. He didn't know whether to be grateful or worried. Maybe he was making this all up in his head.

When he finished brushing, May climbed down off the door so Gabe could lock it. The barn was warm and smelled of hay and horse manure, a smell Gabe liked but May had never spent much time appreciating. She was standing in front of him and he tried to go around, muttering, "I have to hang up the brushes."

"Gabe," she whispered, "I am sure you know how I feel about you?" Her arms were snaking around his waist and he raised his own as though she were an outlaw who'd called out "Hands up."

"Put down those brushes, Gabe, and hold me."

Gabe's mouth had gone so dry it felt like cotton wool. "You . . . you shouldn't be doing this, May. What about Pa?"

"Let me worry about what we should or shouldn't be doing, Gabe. Your pa need never know."

"There ain't no *we* here, May," Gabe protested, stepping back. That only pulled her with him. He finally dropped the brushes and put his hands on her arms.

"You have such strong hands, Gabe. And arms. It's been driving me crazy watching them all tanned and sweaty while you chop wood."

Had she been any other woman, perhaps her words might have moved him. He was still young and just coming into his manhood and had only stolen a kiss from Molly Preston at the town dance. And sometimes, when his shirt was stripped off and he'd been sweating, he'd preened himself before an imaginary girl who'd admire him and want to put her arms around him. But this was his pa's wife and a woman he didn't even like very much.

He took her arms and pulled them from his waist and held them tight in front of him before he pushed her away. "This is not going to happen, May."

She rubbed her arms where he'd grasped her and said with a knowing smile: "Maybe not today, Gabe. But it will, believe me it will. I'm too young to be drying up in an old man's bed." She turned and walked slowly out of the barn, leaving Gabe standing there, suddenly very conscious of every mote of dust floating down in the beam of light streaming through the window.

He'd start riding fence more. He'd stay away longer and she'd forget this craziness of hers. It would all blow over in a month or so, he told himself. But that night, she was looking at him again and talking to him in such a way that he was sure his pa would notice her tone and wonder at it.

Sadie noticed it. When he excused himself after dinner, Sadie was right behind him and followed him into his room.

"Don't bother to knock or anything, Sarah Ellen!"

"We have to talk, Gabe."

"What about, Sadie?"

"About May."

"What about May?"

"You know damn well what about May. About the fact that she's always following you with her eyes. About the fact that she sounded like poured honey tonight and Pa right there."

Gabe groaned. "I'd hoped nobody else had noticed."

Sadie's face paled. "You aren't . . . doing anything with her, are you, Gabe?"

Gabe's hand was out and slapping her face before he even realized it. He looked at the red imprint on her cheek and said, "I am sorry, Sarah Ellen. I didn't even know what I was doing. But you shouldn't even think something so shameful."

"Oh, Gabe, it was my fault. I didn't really believe it." She flung herself into his arms and sobbed. "I hate her, Gabe. I always have."

"Now, now . . ."

"She won't let up, you know. Not till she's got you twisted around her finger like she has Pa."

"I know she won't let up, Sadie. She followed me into the barn today."

"The barn! She never sets foot in the barn if she can help it. Too smelly and dirty for her!"

Gabe smiled. "Well, she was in it today. I'd been working . . . on, uh, something." Whatever he did, he would not spoil Sadie's birthday surprise. "All of a sudden, there were her arms around me."

Sadie's eyes flashed. "That bitch!"

"Sarah Ellen Hart, what would Ma think about you using such language?"

"If Ma is anywhere close, she's thinking the same thing, Gabriel Hart!"

Gabe smiled. "I guess you're right." They were both quiet for a minute, remembering their mother, thinking how different things would be if she were still there.

Gabe finally broke the silence. "I have to leave, Sadie."

"No, Gabe," she protested. "What will I do with you gone?"

"Why, turn out to be the best damn schoolteacher in the county, just like you've been planning."

"They haven't given me the job yet, Gabe. And even if they do, who knows if I can do it."

"You'll get it and you'll do it well. Just like Ma did till she married Pa."

"And what will you do?"

"Head west, most likely. Hire myself out as a wrangler."

"You should be raising and training horses for yourself, Gabe, not for anybody else."

"Maybe I will be someday, Sadie. But if I stay here, well, Pa's bound to find out soon enough."

"Let him, Gabe. Let him see who she really is!"

"I couldn't bear to see him hurt like that, Sadie."

"It'll hurt him if you go."

"A little. But nothing like if I stayed."

Gabe kept himself busy the next few weeks and depended upon Sadie to keep an eye on May. Between the two of them, the woman never had a chance to get Gabe alone again. But he walked around as jumpy as an animal that senses the presence of a predator. He felt he was being stalked and he couldn't wait to break away.

He was able to ride the little bay mare the day before Sadie's birthday. The women and boys were in town and his father watched Gabe walk her around, his long legs hanging from the stirrups.

"You've done a good job with her, Gabe. Your sister will have a pretty little horse to take her to and from school. It's too bad I don't have more money to put into horses. You're a fine trainer."

"Thanks, Pa," said Gabe as he brought the mare to a stop in front of his father and slid off. It was rare for James Hart to compliment in words. Usually he only gave a nod of appreciation or a pat on the shoulder. Gabe cleared his throat and said with a smile, "I do think my talent lies with horses more than cows, Pa."

"Well, mebbe in a few years, Gabe." His father took his hat off and ran his hands through his thin gray hair. "With all the work we put into the damn cattle, you'd think we'd be rich twice over by now!"

On the morning of Sadie's birthday, there were several small presents at her place, as was their family custom. She started opening them immediately.

"Aw, Sadie, can't you wait till the coffee's been poured?"

"No, I can't, Gabe. I never did have the self-control you have on your birthdays. Oooh, thank you, Ben. Thank you, James," she said when she had unwrapped their gift, a length of dark green calico. "This will make a pretty dress for schoolteaching."

After a few sips of coffee, Gabe excused himself to "go out back." A few minutes later there was a knocking on the front door.

"Who could that be!" exclaimed James dramatically, a wide grin splitting his face.

"Why, it's Gabe with Sadie's . . ." Ben almost choked when his brother's hand came down over his mouth.

"Go see, Sadie."

There was Gabe, holding the reins of the bay mare, all saddled and bridled.

"Happy birthday, Sadie, from me and Pa."

"Oh, Pa!" Sadie threw her arms around her father, who stood there awkwardly patting her back. Then she turned to her brother. "She's saddle-broke, Gabe? When will I be able to ride her?"

"Why, right now, if you want. But let's start out in the corral, just till she gets used to your skirt."

They all tramped out to the corral and hung on the fence as Sadie put the mare through her paces. "Oh, Gabe, she's as easy a ride as I thought she'd be."

"She's a sweet-tempered thing, aren't you, girl?" said Gabe as he held the mare still for Sadie to dismount. "But she has some spirit too."

"Gabe has been working hard for weeks in training her, haven't you, Gabe," said May. "I'd say he has a special touch for the ladies," she added with a teasing smile.

"I know Molly Preston thinks so," teased James.

They all laughed and trooped back to the house for breakfast.

That night, Gabe sat on his cot, his bedroll half packed beside him. He was heartsick at the thought of leaving his home and family. "I've tried my best, Ma," he whispered. "I've taken care of the young ones, like you said. Sadie's grown now, so she'll do fine. And the little ones, well, they love May . . . and so does Pa and that's why I've got to go." He finished packing up his few clothes and lay back on the bed, using the bedroll as a pillow. He'd have to wait a few hours for the moon to come up before he left. He'd take Jasper, the Roman-nosed dun gelding. He was too big to be a good cow pony, but he had endurance. He'd leave a note for his pa, explaining that he had to be off on his own, that he was sick of cowpunching and mending fences. That he was sorry not to tell him in person, but it was easier on both of them this way.

He'd ride west, toward the New Mexico Territory. He was sure he could find a place without much trouble. Maybe in a few years he'd be able to come home. Surely, with him gone, May would turn back to Pa. Goddamn, but he didn't think he'd ever hated anyone in his life, but he hated his father's wife.

One

Ramah, New Mexico

Night Sky had wandered a few hundred yards from the other horses. It had been a dry summer, with too many promises of rain not kept, and the grazing had taken the herd farther from the ranch than usual. Sky had been led away by a small patch of grass and then another, until he was almost under the branches of an old cottonwood that brooded over a dry stream bed.

He was upwind, so it was the shadow of the big cougar that spooked him and saved his life. Just as he was about to reach for a tasty bit of grass, he saw something move out of the corner of his eye and he lifted his head and shifted backward a few steps. It was an old cat and she wasn't quick enough to adjust for the extra distance he'd put between them. So instead of breaking Sky's neck, she only raked his shoulder. Her claws dug in as she felt herself begin to slide off and Sky screamed as she tore a large flap of skin loose. There was an answering call from the big gray stallion who led the herd and the cat scrambled off and climbed the old cottonwood, reaching the top before the stallion got there.

The younger horse's head was down and after rearing and pounding his hoofs into the ground as though he had the old cat underneath them, the stallion turned and nudged Sky away from the tree and back to the herd. Then the stallion drove his herd slowly but steadily back to their home pasture.

Michael Burke was just sitting down to dinner when Jake, his hired hand, knocked on the door. "Beg pardon, Miz Burke, for disturbing your meal, but the horses are coming in, boss."

"It's early for that and Finn usually waits for us to come after them. I'd better go, Elizabeth," he said apologetically to his wife.

"Of course, Michael. I'll keep your dinner hot."

The mares came in first, colts and fillies clinging to their sides. Finn, the big gray stallion, was far to the rear and seemed to be alternately pushing the two-year-olds along and turning back for a lone black straggler.

" 'Tis Night Sky hangin' back like that," Michael muttered. He crawled through the fence, making his way back through the milling mares. The stallion came right up to him and pushed his head against Michael's chest. Then he wheeled around to nip the black's hindquarters and drive him over to Michael.

"Dear God in Heaven!" he exclaimed. A flap of skin was hanging from the horse's neck and withers and dried blood caked his shoulder. "So this is why you brought them in, boyo," he said to his stallion.

"My Lord, look at him," said Jake, coming up behind Michael.

"Get me a halter, Jake. And some water."

"Right away, boss."

Michael talked soothingly to the black. All the while backing him up toward the fence. He and the stallion worked as a team, for every time the younger horse would try to get away, the big gray would gently crowd him back.

"Here you are, boss."

"Thanks, Jake." Michael took the halter in one hand and holding it down by his side, approached Sky slowly, holding out the bucket of water and sloshing a little over the side. The black's ears pricked up and he let Michael approach, backing up only a little as the man managed to get close enough to touch him.

Michael put the bucket down in front of the horse and Sky took two steps forward, which brought him close enough to dip his head and drink.

Michael squatted down in front of him and mur-

mured softly in Irish and English as the colt drank.
He cupped his hand in the water underneath the colt's
muzzle and when Sky lifted his nose out of the bucket
and then dipped down again, it was Michael's hand
he was drinking from. In one smooth movement, Michael drew the halter over the horse's head and ears.
It was a moment before the black realized he was
caught. When he did, he pulled back and tried to rear,
but Michael held firm, and taking the rope from Jake,
clipped it to the halter.

"Hold him for a minute, Jake."

"Yes, sir."

Michael dipped his hand into the water again and
whistled to the big gray stallion. "Have the rest of
this, Finn. And there will be oats for you and your
mares tonight. Yer a fine horse, boyo, a fine horse,"
he said as he stroked the gray neck. "Ye do your
mother proud."

Elizabeth had watched the whole thing from the door.
She'd held her breath as she watched Michael push
his way through the milling horses, even though she
knew there was no need to worry. Michael had an
almost magical way with his horses, and the bond between him and Finn was as strong as that between
him and Frost, Finn's dam. But there was clearly
something wrong with Night Sky and the two-year-old
was her daughter's own, given to Caitlin by Michael
when the colt was two days old. Elizabeth hurried
down to the barn.

Michael had brought the horse in and had him cross-
tied in the largest stall and was gently wiping the
blood off his shoulder with warm water, taking care
to stay away from the wound itself.

"Oh, Michael, it is Cait's Sky. What happened to
him?"

"It looks like a cougar tried for him and almost got
him. He's lucky he isn't lyin' out there, his bones
picked clean by the buzzards. But maybe it would be
just as well," he added, frowning at the horse's torn
side.

Elizabeth slipped into the stall, and standing beside her husband, gazed at the colt's damaged neck and shoulder. She shuddered as she saw the flap of skin and muscle hanging down. The colt's eyes were dull and now that he was inside and tied, his head was drooping.

"How bad is it, Michael?"

"He's lost a lot of blood, haven't ye, boyo?" said Michael softly, as he sponged the black's leg and side. "But he seemed to be walkin' all right, just a little stiffly. If Finn hadn't gotten him in, though . . . But the nearest horse doctor is three days away."

"Michael, let me try sewing him up."

"Do ye think ye could, *a ghra*?"

"I can try. This is Caitlin's horse, Michael. We have to do something. She'd be heartbroken if we had to put him down."

"I know, Elizabeth, I know."

Elizabeth hurried over to the house and came back with her sewing box. "I'll have to grease the thread, Michael. And use a heavy needle. Will you be able to hold him?"

"He's worn out, and I've hobbled his rear foot, so he can't move much."

Elizabeth shuddered as she lifted the heavy flap of skin and flesh. She stroked the black's muzzle and Michael had his hand on the horse's hindquarters. The horse raised his head to look at her.

"Poor Sky. We'll do our best for you, boy. Michael, you'll have to wash around the wound for me. And I brought some basilicum powder to sprinkle on it."

Michael sponged the edges gently and Elizabeth matched the flesh as though she were mending a sheet. At the first few stitches, Sky pulled back and Elizabeth almost lost her balance following him.

"There, there, boy, if you keep still, this won't take long."

It took a good ten minutes, but at last the wound was closed.

"It looks good, Missus Burke," said Jake, who'd come in to watch. "Better than the doc's stitches."

"You'll have to keep him tied, Michael, so he doesn't roll or rub against the side of the stall," she warned.

Michael reached out and pulled her into his side. "Ye did a fine job, *a ghra*, and I know it wasn't easy."

"No, but I've had a little experience," she said with a smile, reaching over and patting Michael's hand, which had a long, crescent-shaped scar from a wood-chopping accident.

"Do you think he'll heal, boss?" asked Jake.

"With Elizabeth's good stitching and some tonic in his oats, I think he'll come through, Jake. But I doubt he'll ever be of any use to us," he added with a sigh. "After he's had a big cat on his back, he'll never let anyone ride him. And a horse that can't be ridden . . . well, he's no use to Caitlin or to me. Finn might have saved him for a time, but we can't afford to feed a useless animal."

"Oh, Michael, you couldn't destroy him after all this," his wife protested.

" 'Tis the last thing I'd want to do, you know that, Elizabeth."

"Caitlin will be home from school in a few months. Why, Sky used to follow her around like a puppy when he was little. And surely you can work with him after he heals?"

"If I can find the time. And don't worry, we won't be doin' anything without Cait's knowin'."

The colt began to heal, and by the end of a week, Michael was able to let him out into the small pasture next to the corral.

"His gait is a bit stiff, but I think that will wear off soon, don't you, Michael?" said Elizabeth as they watched Sky trot slowly around the pasture, his nose lifted, smelling the wind.

"They're all back in the far pasture, Sky," Michael told him as he rattled a bucket of oats. The black approached him skittishly at first, but when Michael put the bucket down, the horse started eating immediately.

"He's a beautiful animal, Michael. Just look at how he's filled out in the past week."

Michael stroked his muzzle. "That's because he's been eatin' oats and molasses and not scrub grass, isn't it, boyo?"

The horse lifted his head and turning to Michael, rested his muzzle on Michael's shoulder for a moment, leaving a scattering of oats when he dipped back into the bucket.

"He's so gentle, Michael. Are you sure he won't let himself be ridden?"

"He's tame enough like this, Elizabeth. After all, Caitlin worked with him when he was a colt. And I'm the one who's been feedin' him so well. But under a saddle?" Michael ran his hand lightly near the stitches and the black shuddered and pulled back, knocking over the bucket and then spooking at the noise, trotting away to the other side of the pasture.

"We'll have to tie him again to get the stitches out, Elizabeth," said Michael with a grin. " 'Tis good to see he has some spirit back. But it will be a good month or so before we can try a saddle on him."

Two

Gabe saw the sheep first, as he came down out of the mountains. It was a large flock, more than he would have expected Mexicans or Indians to own. Certainly more than he would have expected to see in what was known to be cattle country.

After a half mile or so he came to the herder's camp, a small canopied wagon. A black-and-white sheepdog that had been resting in the shade, jumped up and started barking wildly.

"No need to announce ourselves," Gabriel told his horse. His right hand held the reins and his left had dropped down to the worn leather holster strapped to his side. Sheepherders were generally peaceful men, but a stranger appearing out of nowhere would put anyone on guard.

Gabe's hand slid up to the handle of the Colt .45 when he saw an older man emerge from a cluster of piñon pines. He was buttoning up his fly with one hand and in the crook of his other arm rested a shotgun. Anyone who carried his gun just to take a piss was no one to take chances with, thought Gabe.

"*Callate,*" the man told the dog sharply.

"*Hola, amigo,*" called Gabe. "That's a fine dog you have there."

"*Si,* but Chino, he is not too fond of strangers. And neither am I, señor."

Gabe kept his hand on his gun, just in case. "I'm just passing through, *amigo.* And since there aren't likely to be too many strangers out here in the middle of nowhere, I'd say the trouble you seem to be expecting is from someone well-known to you?"

"You aren't working for Mackie, are you?" said the sheepherder, lowering his shotgun and leaning on the stock.

"I'm not working for anyone at the moment. Though I'm hoping to be soon. Who is this Mackie? Is he hiring?"

The Mexican spat his disgust. "He is the biggest cattle rancher in the valley. He's always looking to hire someone quick with a gun," he added, looking pointedly at Gabe's left hand.

Gabe shifted his hand to his thigh. "I'm not looking to be anyone's hired gun," said Gabe.

"You looking to herd sheep, then?" asked the Mexican sarcastically. *"No creo, amigo."*

"I ain't got nothing against sheep myself," said Gabe with a smile. "But I got to admit, I prefer working with cattle or horses. You've got a big flock here."

"It is big, but it isn't mine. My boss, he raises the sheep and horses."

Gabe lifted his eyebrows. "Horses, eh?"

"Mr. Burke, he has a small herd. He breeds a special kind of Indian horse. Appaloosas, he calls them. Sprinkled and dotted on their backsides. They sure are pretty horses."

"Do you think he could use a hand?"

"No se, señor," said the Mexican with a shrug. "But it wouldn't hurt to ask him."

"Gracias, amigo. How will I find his place?"

"It is the first ranch you come to when you reach the valley, about ten miles west of here. Tell him Eduardo sent you."

"Gracias, Eduardo. Hasta luego."

Eduardo just lifted his shotgun and waved it as Gabe rode off, muttering, "What he could use, Mr. Burke, though he doesn't want to hear it, is a hired gun of his own."

The sun was going down by the time Gabe reached the valley. He assumed the pastures he rode beside belonged to this Burke fellow. He was favorably impressed. The fences were well-mended and as he turned down the road that led to the ranch and approached the house and barn, he saw that all was well-maintained.

There didn't seem to be anyone around the corral or barn, so he dismounted, tied his paint, and whacked at his clothes with his hat to get some of the red dust out of them. He smoothed his hair back and giving the horse a pat on the rump, said, "Wish me luck, fella."

Elizabeth was in the bedroom of the ranch house, changing her blouse, when she heard the rap on the screen door and the unfamiliar voice calling out a hello.

"Just a minute," she responded as she buttoned the last button hurriedly and wondered if she was foolish to be a little fearful. She didn't think so; tensions between the sheep owners in the valley and Nelson Mackie were running strong, and although Michael kept reassuring her, she was wary all the same. But Michael would be back from town within the half hour, so surely there was nothing to worry about?

When she pulled the door open, the man on the porch took off his hat and greeted her politely enough.

"Good evening, ma'am. I am sorry if I disturbed you, but there was no one around outside."

"Why, no, my husband and the hired hand are in town. On their way home, actually," she added, thinking, well, that was foolish, Elizabeth, announcing to a complete stranger that you are alone!

"I met your sheepherder . . . if this is the Burke place?"

"Yes, it is."

"Well, Eduardo said for me to tell your husband that he'd seen me. He seemed to think you might want another hand around the place?"

"We're not really shorthanded . . ." Elizabeth started to say.

"That's too bad, ma'am. Eduardo told me Mr. Burke raises horses and I'm good with horses."

"What I was going to say was where the sheep are concerned," said Elizabeth with a smile. "I've been

trying to get my husband to take on more help with
the horses for a while, though.''

"Well, I'd be happy to help you persuade him, Mrs.
Burke,'' the stranger said with a smile.

"Perhaps you would like to stay and talk to my
husband over dinner, Mr. . . . ?''

"Hart. Gabriel Hart. But you can call me Gabe. I
would be right pleased to do that, Mrs. Burke.''

"Supper is in a half hour or so. Whenever my husband returns.''

"Do you need anything, ma'am? Wood? Water?''

"Why, no thank you, Mr. Hart . . . Gabe.'' Elizabeth
peered out the door. "You can unsaddle your horse
if you want and there's hay and water in the barn.
And a pump behind the barn if you want to wash
for supper.''

Gabe looked down at his hands and chuckled. "I
sure do. Thank you, ma'am.''

Elizabeth watched him from the door. He was a tall,
rangy man with silver-blond hair. She wasn't sure if it
was silvered by the sun or whether there was some
premature gray in it, for he wasn't that old. She could
tell from the way he talked to his horse as he walked
him to the barn that he considered him more than
transportation. That's the kind of man Michael needs,
she thought. He seems quiet and steady. And if he
likes horses, he might be into gentling them, not
breaking their spirits, like so many of the wranglers
who had appeared over the years.

After a thorough wash at the pump, Gabe pulled a
clean shirt from his saddle roll. There wasn't much he
could do with his pants, unfortunately, but he did his
best to brush them off. He found a saddle cloth and
gave his boots a good wiping. Just as he came around
the barn, he saw the wagon pull in.

A tall, well-built man with curly black hair liberally
salted with gray climbed down and began to unload
some packages from the back of the wagon. Gabriel
watched as Mrs. Burke came out and greeted her husband. The affection between the two of them was
strong and real, he could tell, not just by the hug they

gave each other but by the way Mrs. Burke quite naturally kept her arm around her husband's waist as they walked up the steps to the porch.

Gabe saw her gesture toward the barn and figured it was time for him to show his face. He slicked his hair back nervously as he walked toward the house. He'd been wandering for the past three months doing odd jobs for anyone who'd hire him, and he could go on doing that. But he sure would like to light somewhere for a while and there was something about this place that called to him.

"This is Mr. Hart, Michael," Mrs. Burke told her husband when Gabe had reached the porch steps.

"My wife tells me yer lookin' for work, Mr. Hart?" said Burke in a soft Irish brogue.

"Gabriel, or Gabe. Well, yes, sir, I am. I met your man Eduardo and he said you might need someone good with horses."

"If it isn't Elizabeth, it's Eduardo," Michael complained with a grin. "Now they're both after me to take someone on. Where are you from, Gabe?"

"From Texas originally, sir. But I've been working in the New Mexico Territory for the past ten years."

"Texas, eh? Are you one of them break 'em or bust riders?"

Gabriel cleared his throat nervously. He could sit and spur a mean horse with the best of them, but that wasn't the way he liked to work. "Well, Mr. Burke, I sure do know how to sit a bronc. And there are some horses that I guess need to be broken, but I prefer to work more gently with a new horse, given the chance. I find it works just as well, though it takes longer."

Michael smiled. "Sure and that's a philosophy close to my own heart, Gabe. I'm willin' to try you out for a while." Michael put out his hand and Gabe shook it firmly. "Now, come on in for some supper and after we eat, I'll show ye around."

"That was the best meal I've had in months, ma'am," said Gabe as he wiped up the last of his green chile stew with a fresh tortilla.

"Why, thank you, Gabe. I like to try my hand at chile from time to time. Would you like a cup of coffee or tea?"

"No, thank you. I think I'll just help myself to more water to cool my tongue!"

"What brings you to this part of the territory, Gabe," Michael asked as they walked down to the corral a few minutes later.

"I've been a bit of a wanderer these past few years, Mr. Burke. Hiring out a few months at a time here and there."

"And do ye like that 'here and there' kind of life?" Michael asked curiously.

"I do . . . and I don't," Gabe answered slowly.

"Do ye still have family in Texas?"

"My father and a sister and two brothers I haven't seen since I left. I do try to write to them though, and Sadie, my sister, she keeps track of me somehow."

"Here's where we work the horses," said Michael as they leaned on the corral fence. "I only have a small herd: Finn, my stallion, six mares, three colts and three fillies and a few yearlings. And three two-year-olds," he added with a heavy sigh.

"The two-year-olds are a problem?"

"Only one. He shouldn't be. He was one of the brightest, sweetest-tempered colts we've ever bred. He belongs to my daughter; he was her sixteenth birthday gift. She had him following her around like a puppy before she left for school."

"Sometimes they do change when they get older. Was he gelded?"

"Sure and I hated to do it, let me tell you," said Michael. "But Finn still has quite a few good years left in him and I can't have two stallions squarin' off at each other, now can I?" he said with a grin.

"No, sir," said Gabe with an answering smile.

"The horses don't run wild, ye understand, but Finn keeps them in the far pasture for the summer, which is way out to the southwest. He brought them in a few weeks ago because of my daughter's horse. The poor bugger had been attacked by a mountain lion.

She must have been an old one or he must have scented her, for he got away, but not without having part of his neck and shoulder torn away."

"And now he won't let you near him," stated Gabe.

"Oh, he'll come to ye for oats or water. Let you pet him. But the slightest move toward his back or neck and he shies away."

Gabe shook his head. "It's that fear of having their necks broken that makes them hard to break in the first place. But if this horse has lived through that nightmare . . . well, I don't know, Mr. Burke, that anyone can tame him."

"I know. 'Tis a damned shame, for he's a beauty. And my Cait will be heartbroken if I have to put him down. She'll not understand that I can't afford to keep him in oats and hay during the winter."

"I'd be happy to work with him, Mr. Burke."

"If you have the time and energy after working the yearlings and the other two-year-olds, ye're welcome to try, Gabe. My daughter will be home soon and though I don't want to upset her, if ye can't do anything with him, well, then, we'll have to deal with it."

"Eduardo said you raise a special kind of horse, Mr. Burke?"

"Appaloosas. Originally bred by the Nez Perces in Idaho. I was lucky enough to win myself a mare many years ago. I started my herd with her. I had no stallion then, so they're not all purebred. But I made a trip out once, years ago, and got me another mare before it was too late."

"Too late?"

"Aye, boyo. Not only were the Nez Perce driven off their land, but the army started killin' their horses, too. So many years to breed them for color and endurance, and then so many good animals destroyed. . . ."

"So yours are the only ones left?"

"Oh, no, there's a few here and there, runnin' wild or kept secret. I'm just glad that by chance I'm part of saving them."

"Who buys them from you?"

"Why, who else but the U.S. Army! They're so

eager to have them now and they don't see the irony atall."

Gabe settled in very easily. He shared the small bunkhouse with Jake, an older man with not much to say for himself. Jake was a kind of jack-of-all-trades, his duties ranging from mending harness to chopping wood to going for the mail, an eleven-mile ride each way. Had the Burkes been running cattle, they would have required more men, but raising sheep and horses took fewer full-time hands, except at shearing and lambing time.

Michael moved Finn and his herd down from the foothills to the lower pasture and set Gabe to work with the yearlings. They were beautiful horses, the Appaloosas, with their unusual markings. The stallion had bred true except for one filly who was probably a throwback to her great-grandsire. She was coal black with no sprinkling of white anywhere. Most were gray or dark brown with a variety of patterns. But the one who stood out was the black two-year-old.

Gabriel saw him the first morning he went out to work the yearlings. The black stood in the far corner of the pasture, his nose up, sniffing the wind. When Gabriel entered with a pail of oats, the black trotted toward him and then shaking his head as if to say, "You're not who I expected," turned and cantered away.

"These aren't for you anyway, Sky," said Gabe with a smile. The black was beautiful and well named, for he had a pattern of small white spots all over his shiny black coat, as though someone had thrown a handful of stars over him.

One of the yearlings approached Gabe curiously and he shook the bucket of oats. "Come on then, sweetheart, and get yourself a treat."

Gabe loved the game: approach, retreat, approach, while the sun shined on him and the glistening hide of a healthy young horse. Finally the little horse came close enough to dip his head in the bucket. When he lifted his muzzle, Gabe quickly and easily slipped the halter on. The yearling backed up and tried to shake the unfamiliar thing off his head. But Gabe held tight to the rope, dipping his hand into the bucket and offering the yearling more oats from his cupped palm, at the same time gently tugging on the rope.

The halter only tightened for a minute, loosening as soon as the horse went for the oats, which was just what Gabe intended. The trick was to time it so the horse thought that *he* was in charge, going for whatever he wanted.

In a short time he had the horse following him and the bucket of oats around the pasture. He ran the same routine with the other yearlings and only ran into problems with one, a small dark brown horse. It looked like this one had been born later than the others. If he had been a dog, Gabe would have called him the runt of the litter.

"So you're not going to play, are you, Shorty?" he said as the horse pulled back as soon as the halter was on. No amount of soothing or coaxing worked. "We'll try again tomorrow, then," Gabe said, slipping the halter off and watching the little horse gallop away on his matchstick legs.

His shirt was soaked with sweat from hours of steady work and he took off his hat to catch the slight breeze that had come up. Night Sky had disappeared to the far corner of the field while Gabe was working, but now he saw the two-year-old come over a slight rise to get a drink from the watering trough in the middle of the pasture.

Gabe only had a handful of oats left in the bucket. He walked slowly toward the black. The horse turned and looked at him and Gabe stooped and dropped down to his knees, rattling the bucket just a little to gain his attention. Gabe could now see the jagged scar that ran down his neck to his shoulder, but as far as he could tell, a saddle wouldn't rub against it. The horse had moved easily, so no permanent damage seemed to have been done. Gabe didn't think it would hurt him to be ridden—just likely spook him to death.

Sky dropped his muzzle back into the trough, all the while keeping an eye on Gabe, who began talking to him in a sort of crooning whisper. "You were real lucky, fella. That cat must have been old or sick or you moved just in time before she landed. Hurt like hell, I bet. And scared you even more. But you are a beautiful horse, aside from that scar." And he was, his black coat shining a deep midnight in contrast to the white spots.

"You look like a smart fella to me, too smart to let yourself be destroyed, Sky. We're going to get to know each other real well, and when the time comes, well, I bet you let me ride you."

Gabe held his hand out and let some oats fall through his fingers. Sky's ears pricked up and he stepped away from the water.

"That's right, you know what these are and you want some, don't you?"

Gabe held his breath as the horse came closer, finally lipping the oats from his hand and then, with a start, jumping back. Gabe gave a low chuckle and stood up. Sky tossed his head and trotted off. "That's all for today, Sky. But I'll be back."

Three

Caitlin Burke looked up from her copy of *Jane Eyre* and over at the calendar that stood on her desk. Only three weeks and she would be home in New Mexico. She looked out the window at the rolling green lawn of the Fayreweather Academy, which was shaded by oak and elm trees. She closed her eyes and tried to summon a picture of the landscape she'd grown up in. Sagebrush, not grass, covered their land. Stunted junipers twisted by the wind. Piñon pines. The only oak trees were gambel oaks and they looked more like bushes. And everything growing out of red dust, not rich black earth.

She had hated leaving it all a year and a half ago. She had thought she'd die of homesickness, not just for her parents but for the land itself. It was six months before she had stopped crying herself to sleep each night. But gradually she had gotten used to it, even come to love the differences. She had made friends. She had discovered literature and writing. And she had met Henry. Now she wasn't sure she wanted to go home.

No, that wasn't true, she thought, as she marked her place and closed the book. Of course she was dying to see Ma and Da and to share with them all that had happened to her in the last six months. She had to admit she was also dying for a good ride, not sitting primly and properly on a sidesaddle, but astride on one of their horses. And there was Heathcliff waiting for her.

She smiled as she remembered her first sight of the little black colt. He'd been born in the early hours of the morning and her da had promised she could see the new baby right after breakfast. Ma and Da exchanged looks over their coffee, but she was so excited that she'd hardly noticed it.

They all went together, but as they stood there, the colt came to her on his wobbly legs and gazed into her eyes as though he already knew her. She'd fallen in love at that moment. "It's like he knows me already, Da," she had whispered.

" 'Tis a good thing he does, since he'll be yours, Cait. Happy birthday, though 'tis two months since ye turned sixteen."

"Oh, Da, do you mean it?"

"It's why you only got a book, Cait," said Elizabeth.

"*Wuthering Heights* was a *wonderful* present, Ma." She was quiet for a minute and then said, "I think I'll call him Heathcliff." It seemed right, for she had fallen in love with the colt instantly, just as Cathy had. And her name was close enough to Cathy, too.

"Heathcliff, is it? I was thinking that he's going to be one of those rare colts with white sprinkled all over him, like the night sky. But he's your horse, Cait," Michael added, his voice strained.

Elizabeth jabbed her husband in the ribs. "Well, sure, 'tis a romantic name," he continued lamely.

Caitlin had to smile herself, two years later. She had been such a romantic sixteen-year-old, identifying with the wild Cathy, imagining the desert landscape to be the moors of Yorkshire as she rode it. Well, the wind was certainly as wild, if a lot hotter and drier. She was much more sophisticated now, not that "green girl from the Wild West" or "Calico Cait" as her classmates used to call her. She didn't even like Cathy much anymore. She had been foolish and faithless and stupid to marry Lynton. Jane Eyre had more integrity and certainly as much passion, though she kept it banked, like a good fire.

And Jane had had a favorite teacher, just like she had. Even in the worst of her homesickness, Caitlin had responded to Mrs. Weld. She was the youngest of the teachers, although a widow, and she was able to understand and empathize with the romantic longings of an adolescent girl. It was she who had pointed out the lack of a real heroine in *Wuthering Heights* when they began studying the English novel. Caitlin hadn't thought much about heroines before. They had a very small collection of books at home, which had grown very slowly over the years, for books were a luxury in New Mexico. Not like in Philadelphia, where families had whole rooms set aside for them.

From that first discussion, Caitlin felt her mind wake up. Now, instead of losing herself completely in a book, she began to think about the characters and what the author might have been trying to do. Mrs. Weld became her model; she wanted to be just like her: a teacher who was able to stimulate her pupils' minds and inspire them to want to do great things.

Well, maybe not *great* things, thought Cait, for women rarely had the chance to perform heroic deeds. But *good* things.

She was excited about her plans for the future. And frightened about returning home only to tell her parents that she had been offered a job at the Fayreweather School as an assistant teacher and that she was unofficially engaged to Henry Beecham.

She'd mentioned Henry in her letters from time to time, so it shouldn't be a complete surprise to them. He was the older brother of her best friend and they had gotten to know each other well the summer she had spent at the Beechams' home. He had graduated from Harvard College and had obtained a clerk's position in a judge's office in Philadelphia. He had visited the school frequently this year, ostensibly to see his sister Susan, but it soon became clear to everyone that he was interested in her roommate, Caitlin Burke.

Henry had asked her to marry him only two weeks ago and she had said yes. It had surprised her that she loved someone like Henry. He was good-looking, certainly, and a brilliant conversationalist, and very passionate about his chosen profession. With his family connections, he would surely be a judge someday himself. But he wasn't the romantic hero she had responded to in novels: dark, brooding, and sensual. Though she had to admit their first few kisses had been very satisfying.

She had said yes immediately and then they had lost themselves in one of their most enjoyable kisses to date. But Caitlin had insisted on an unofficial engagement until she could tell her parents in person and until they had met Henry. So it was agreed that she would go home and prepare the ground, so to speak, and he would arrive later in the summer to get their approval.

Caitlin sighed as she looked out the window. It was all very wonderful, her plans for the future. But would her parents be able to see it the same way?

"Do you think Cait will have changed much, Elizabeth?" Michael asked one night as they were getting ready for bed.

"She has been away for two years, Michael. She is a young lady of eighteen now, not that sixteen-year-old girl who alternated between hoyden and romantic heroine," said Elizabeth with a smile that held a trace of sadness.

"She was a caution, our Cait," admitted Michael. "One day racin' the wildest horse we own, the next moonin' around here like she belonged in a tragic story, exclaiming, 'I cannot live without my life; I cannot live without my soul.' Sure and do ye remember when I caught her givin' a solo performance in the barn?"

"I do, Michael, and you acted with great discretion on that occasion," said Elizabeth, her eyes twinkling. "You backed out like a gentleman and didn't start laughing till you got to the house."

"Sure and the neighbors must have heard me howling."

"Well, I certainly did."

Michael climbed into bed next to his wife and pulled her close. "Ah, Elizabeth, it shouldn't have surprised us, raisin' such a romantic child. I might have laughed at her and that foolish man she named her colt after . . . but 'tis the way I feel about you, *mo muirneach.* . . . I couldn't live without *my* life, I couldn't live without *my* soul." He punctuated his words with soft kisses and with a throaty moan, Elizabeth gave him a passionate response.

Their lovemaking was perhaps less frequent these days than during their first years together, but it never failed to amaze them how deeply they satisfied each other's desires. Just when Elizabeth thought she could not feel any closer to Michael, a night like this would come along and surprise her.

They lay awake in each other's arms for a while afterward. Michael had just begun to fall asleep when Elizabeth shifted, and sitting up against the pillows, said: "What do you think is going to happen with Nelson Mackie, Michael?"

"Ah, Elizabeth," Michael groaned, pulling himself up beside her and putting his arm around her shoulders, "why are ye thinkin' of that *amadan* now?"

"I can't help it. He's bought off two small cattle ranchers and intimidated the Vigils right off their land. He's talked to you twice now, hasn't he?"

"Yes. The first time butter couldn't melt in his mouth. The second, well, he was a bit more 'persuasive,' " said Michael with a touch of sarcasm.

"Eduardo has seen some of his men up in the hills, hasn't he?"

"Just ridin' through, Elizabeth, I'm sure. But he can't intimidate me the way he did the Vigils, and he knows it."

"We have worked so hard these past nineteen years, Michael. But with all that, the valley has been a good place to be and we have good neighbors, whether they are sheepherder or cattle ranchers. Then that snake arrived, bringing his hired guns with him. The only problem we ever had before Mackie was the little bit of rustling people did back and forth, and that's almost over."

Michael smiled. She was right. Fences had gone up slowly in the valley and the small cattle ranchers were always "borrowing" from their neighbors, till their neighbors "borrowed" back.

"It has been good to us, this valley. And it still will be, Elizabeth."

"I hope so, Michael, but I am worried about how far Mackie will go to get his way. From what I have heard about his men, especially Juan Chavez . . . please be careful, Michael," she said passionately.

"I am always careful, *a ghra.* You know that. It won't come to outright violence. Mackie is too smart for that."

"I wish I felt as sure as you do. And if it does, why, he owns the sheriff in Ramah, we all know that."

"I have seen enough fighting to last me a lifetime, Elizabeth, but if it comes to it, I'll fight back. We will call in a Federal marshal if we have to." Michael sighed. "But we are lucky, I'm thinkin', that we have Gabe Hart."

"Gabe? He is so quiet and gentle with the horses. He doesn't say much about himself, but I think he is a good man, Michael."

"Oh, I think he is too. But for a good man and such a hard worker, he surely has wandered a lot. 'Tis odd he hasn't settled down with one outfit."

"Maybe he just never found the right one for him. Maybe he's found it now," she added with a smile. "He should be working with horses, he's so good with them. And you certainly needed the help."

Michael slid down and pulled her in front of him. "You finally got your way, *a ghra.*"

"You work too hard, Michael, for a man your age."

"A man my age! Ye're talking like I'm white-haired already." He was quiet for a moment and then continued. "But you were right, Elizabeth. I did need someone like Gabe around."

Over the next month Michael came to appreciate his new hand even more. The work with the yearlings was proceeding well. They were all broken to the halter except the runt. Gabriel had begun to lunge the two-year-olds, except for Night Sky. But he had finally gotten a halter on the black and was able to lead him around like the yearlings.

Late one afternoon Michael returned from a visit with Eduardo and sat on the corral fence watching Gabriel with Sky. He still needed oats to catch him and halter him, but he did that to the accompaniment of a low, sweet whistle and Michael knew that soon the horse would respond to just the whistle.

When Gabriel had finished walking and trotting him around, he walked over to Michael.

" 'Tis a great thing to have a horse that responds to a whistle, Gabe. It saves a man from chasing the bugger early in the morning."

"I always thought it saved time in the long run," agreed Gabe with his quick smile.

"Caitlin just about had him halter broke before she left, ye know."

"She did a good job with him. He'd be unbreakable now if it wasn't for those early days. She'll be coming home at the end of this week, won't she?"

"She will, thanks be to God. I can't tell you how much her mother has missed her."

Gabe had come to know Michael well enough to tease him a little. "But not you, Mr. Burke?"

Michael laughed. "Even more than her mother! What about your family, Gabe?" he asked after a moment. "Do ye miss them?"

"I do, Mr. Burke. But my sister Sadie has kept me in touch. We write back and forth. If she didn't hear from me every few months, I think she'd come tracking me down till she found me and gave me a good scolding."

"My sister Cait's like that. She makes sure I know what is going on in Mayo and I keep her in touch with what has happened here."

"Women are good at that, aren't they?"

"And thank God they are, boyo. We all need to feel connected, but men don't work at it like they do."

They sat on the fence rail quietly for a minute, watching Sky trot around the corral. Then Michael said, with a studied casualness: "So, ye've never gone home for a visit, Gabe?"

Gabe looked over at his employer, who had a bland look on his face.

"If you mean *could* I go home, Mr. Burke, yes, I could. I'm not wanted in Texas."

" 'Tis a long time not to see your family."

"The problem was, I was wanted in Texas all right," Gabe continued bitterly, "but not the way you mean." Gabe surprised himself. He had never told anyone about May. But there was something about the way Michael had asked him: there was no pressure on him, just an invitation to be forthcoming if he wanted to be. "My stepmother was . . . uh . . . interested in me."

"And how old were ye then?"

"Eighteen."

"That's a hard thing for a young man to deal with," Michael said.

Gabriel was touched by the quiet sympathy in Michael's voice. "I didn't want my pa to know. It would have hurt him too much, so I just ran off. So did she, two years later, with the man they hired to take my place," said Gabe with a bitter laugh.

"Ye never found any New Mexico woman to settle down with?"

"There was one, once."

And it is clear ye're not going to tell me about her, thought Michael. I can't imagine ye trust women much, boyo. But he wasn't going to pry any more than he already had. "You've heard about what's going on in the valley?"

It sounded like a complete change of subject, but Gabriel knew it was not.

"I have. That first day I rode in I could tell there was trouble when I met Eduardo and his shotgun. He wasn't too friendly till he knew I wasn't working for Mackie."

"I'm glad Eduardo sent ye here, Gabe. Elizabeth was right. I needed a man good with horses." He hesitated. "I may be needin' a man good with a gun. And one who isn't running from the law, if we have to call in a marshal," he added in the same matter-of-fact tone he'd been using all along.

"I'm not running from any law, Mr. Burke. I've never done anything they could arrest me for," responded Gabe. "But I guess I'm as good with a gun as I am with horses," he added.

"That's good to know, boyo." Michael slid off the fence. "Well, I guess we'd better be washing up for dinner."

Nothing much had been said, but both men understood what was unspoken: Gabe had thrown in his lot with the Burkes, whatever trouble arose.

Ten years running, thought Michael. If it isn't a woman or the law, then what's kept ye on the move?

Four

"Hurry up, Michael. The train arrives at noon."

"I am hurryin', Elizabeth. Ow! Now I've nicked meself, you've got me rushin' so. We'll be in Grants in
plenty of time."

Elizabeth smiled when she saw the bit of sticking
plaster on her husband's chin.

"You look very fine this morning, me darlin'," said
Michael, exaggerating his brogue as he put his arms
around his wife and gave her a kiss. There was a
knock on the door and Elizabeth tried to pull away,
but Michael kept her by his side as he called,
"Come in."

"Good morning, Mr. Burke, Mrs. Burke. The horses
are all harnessed," Gabe told them.

"Thanks, Gabe. Ye have the supplies all packed
for Eduardo?"

"Yes, sir. I'll start up after I've worked the colts."

"I appreciate it, Gabe. Usually I'd send Jake, but
there's too much for him to do here."

Gabe watched them drive off. They sure were excited to have their daughter coming home. This Miss
Caitlin Burke must be something.

Michael and Elizabeth had an hour to wait in Grants
before the train arrived, and Michael spent it pacing
back and forth on the platform till people started to
look at him strangely.

"Michael, come and sit down next to me," said
his wife.

"I can't sit, *a ghra*."

Thank God they heard the train whistle a few minutes later, or Elizabeth couldn't have stood it much longer.

Two drummers got off and an elderly woman. "Where is she?" muttered Michael.

At last they saw the conductor helping a very sophisticated young lady down the steps. She was wearing a burgundy lawn dress with a chip straw hat charmingly tilted to one side. She took a coin out of her reticule and handed it to the conductor and stood there, calmly waiting for someone to find her.

Elizabeth's throat was aching. It was Cait and how happy she was to see her. And oh, how different she looked from the rough-and-tumble country girl they had sent off to Philadelphia.

Michael went up to her and tipping his hat, said, "May I help you with yer bags, miss?"

"Oh, Da!" cried Cait and flung her arms around her father.

Thank goodness she hadn't changed that much, thought Elizabeth as she hurried over.

Father and daughter pulled away from each other and Elizabeth could see that Michael's cheeks were wet, as were Cait's. She opened her arms and her daughter let herself be enfolded in them. "Oh, Ma," she said shakily, "it's been so long." Elizabeth nodded and hugged her daughter even tighter.

"Well," said Michael, clearing his throat, "is this all ye have?"

"No, Da. There's another valise that the conductor is bringing. I have a few more things coming home than I did leaving."

"I guess so," said her mother, stepping back and looking at Cait's dress. "And all so fashionable they'll put us all to shame, I'll be bound."

Cait blushed. "This was a going-away present from Susan Beecham," she said, smoothing the burgundy lawn. "And I have bought a few dresses with the money I made helping out the younger girls."

"Sure and ye'll be the belle of the valley, Cait," said Michael, picking up her bags. "Just wait till the

next dance. We'll have to drive off all the young men.
Unless there's one you especially like!"

"Now, Michael, we just got her back," scolded Elizabeth. "I want to enjoy her being home first, without
thinking of when she'll be marrying."

Cait felt a pang of guilt as she listened to her parents. It was going to be hard to tell them that they
only had her for the summer and that her marriage
would come sooner than they thought.

When they got to the wagon, Elizabeth said, "You
sit up front next to your Da, Cait."

"I'm fine in the back, Ma."

"No, no," said her mother, climbing into the back
seat, "that way I can enjoy both of you."

Elizabeth was relieved to hear Cait's enthusiasm as
she chatted about her train ride and the terribly
spoiled eight-year-old who'd gotten on at Chicago and
terrorized the train. And the drummers, whose attentions she'd been able to discourage quite well, thank
you. And the antelope she'd seen in Kansas and the
awful smell of Dodge City. "I *am* glad we raise sheep,
Da," she said with a laugh.

"I prefer the woolly buggers meself, Cait."

The sophisticated eighteen-year-old didn't completely disappear, however, thought Elizabeth as she
listened to her daughter chatter on. Cait had matured
and was clearly able to act the young lady, but her
eyes were sparkling as she recognized familiar landmarks on the road and pointed out any changes she
noticed. She was still their Caitlin and Elizabeth
breathed a prayer of thanks that she was home.

They drove through town on their way to the ranch.
There was a group of cowboys standing around in
front of the bank.

"Who are those men, Da? They don't look familiar
to me."

"Those are Nelson Mackie's hands," Michael replied shortly.

"Nelson Mackie?"

"He's been here a little over a year, Cait," said her

mother. "He bought land west of us and runs over five thousand head of cattle."

"Five thousand head! That's a lot of cattle for around here, Da."

"It is, Cait, and he'd be happy to push off any small ranchers he could to make his spread bigger."

Cait heard the anger in her father's voice. Just as she was going to ask him another question, she saw Mr. Turner, the banker, open the door for a short, stocky man in a well-cut gray suit. Mr. Turner shook his hand enthusiastically and Mackie, for that's who she assumed it was, walked over to where his horse was tied. When he saw the Burke family going by he lifted his hat and waving it, started walking over to them.

"Damn the man," muttered Michael. "Can't he be leavin' me alone on a day like today?" He reluctantly pulled the horses up.

"Hello there, Burke. This beautiful young woman must be your daughter just home from school. Mrs. Burke. Miss Burke." He greeted them in a friendly enough manner, thought Caitlin.

"Good afternoon, Mr. Mackie," Elizabeth said politely.

"Nelson Mackie, me daughter, Caitlin Burke."

Caitlin extended her hand and Mackie shook it. "It is a pleasure to meet you, Miss Burke," he said. "I am sure your parents are glad to have you home from . . . ?"

"Philadelphia, Mr. Mackie."

"Ah, yes, Philadelphia. Well, lovely young women are scarce around here, Miss Burke. I am sure you will have no shortage of admirers."

"Thank you, Mr. Mackie," said Cait, with a blush of embarrassment.

"We'd better not keep the horses standing, Michael," said Elizabeth, sensing the anger that was building in her husband. "Good day, Mr. Mackie."

Mackie tipped his hat to them and Michael slapped the reins on his horses' backs.

"He seems like a nice enough man, Da."

"Ay, he *seems* so, Cait. But let's not be spoilin' this beautiful day with talk of the likes of Mackie."

When Cait had arrived in the East, she had felt it to be almost another country. Now, although the train ride had given her another chance to absorb the change in scenery, home seemed the different country. How could one nation hold such extremes? she wondered. And how could she hold on to the memory of Philadelphia as she was claimed by the high desert that held all her memories?

"Look, Da, there's the rock I used to climb with Jimmy Murdoch. And there's the road down to the Begay hogan."

"And here's the turnoff for the ranch," said Michael, "in case ye've forgotten it!"

"Oh, no, I could never forget it. Not after riding out for the mail every week."

When they passed the far pasture, Finn whinnied at the passing wagon and trotted over to investigate.

"Are you busy training the yearlings, Da? And where's Heathcliff? He must be ready to be saddle broke by now."

As Michael hesitated, not wanting to tell her about the black on her first day back, Cait looked over at him and back at her mother and smiled. "It is a rather silly name for a horse, isn't it, Ma? I'm embarrassed at what a child I was when I left."

When you left, thought Elizabeth. And what are you now, Caitlin? She smiled to herself. Her daughter was a young woman, of course. Why was it so hard to accept how a mere two years, though it had felt like forever at the time, had changed her daughter?

"You can always change his name if you want to," said Michael. "He's probably in the near pasture so Gabe can work with him."

"Gabe?"

"Gabe Hart, our new hired hand, Cait," said her mother. "Your Da finally took my advice and got himself some help with the horses. Some *good* help."

"Why, you said you'd never let any bronc buster near your horses, Da!"

"And I wouldn't. But Gabe works them gently, like I do. He's done a fine job, so far, halter-breakin' the yearlings and trainin' the two-year-olds."

Caitlin felt cheated of something she thought was supposed to be hers. Her horse was hers to train. She'd had him following her around before she left. Of course, she hadn't expected her father would actually ignore the horse for almost two years. He would have had to be halter-broke. Maybe lunged a little. But a complete stranger working him? She decided there and then she wasn't going to like Gabe Hart and she most certainly wasn't going to have him training her horse.

"Here we are, Cait."

The long, low ranch house looked the same, with its soft, weathered cedar shingles and bright blue door and window frames. There were chamisa bushes on the side of the house and in the front, a profusion of herbs and flowers that Elizabeth had managed to grow over the years.

Inside the floors were covered with rag rugs and on the wall were hung a trio of Navajo weavings by Serena, Cait's godmother. There was a small piece that Serena had given Caitlin years ago, and two larger ones that were more recent.

There were fresh flowers on the table and Cait turned to her mother and said, "It looks lovely, Ma. I am so glad to be home."

"Thank you, dear, though I'm sure it's nothing to compare to some of those fine houses in Philadelphia you've been visiting."

Elizabeth made the comparison lightly, for she knew she was an inspired gardener and good housekeeper. But Caitlin was ashamed to confess to herself, as she took her bag up to her own room, that she had been making a comparison. How little they had, she thought, as she sat on her bed and gazed around her small room. Her own wall was hung with her mother's watercolors and one of Serena's newer weavings that showed the influence of aniline dyes and store-bought wool. There was a small bookshelf that her father had built that held her cherished three shelves of books, a few pottery shards, and the beaded pouch her father had brought back from his trip to Idaho years ago.

It was very different from Susan Beecham's room. Even the spare room, where Cait stayed when she visited the Beechams', was at least three times the size and luxurious compared to this. The house and her room greeted her, saying you're home where you belong, just like her parents had. And she responded. How could she not? But at the same time, she was seeing it with new eyes. Or as a new person. The young girl she had been rejoiced to be home. The young woman she had become wondered how her mother had lived all these years with so few pretty things. New Mexico was a hard place to live, especially for women, thought Cait. I'm so lucky that I have Henry and the possibility of a richer life.

Five

When Gabe arrived at the sheep camp, Eduardo was out with the flock and so he started unpacking the supplies himself. Within a half hour, the sheepherder had returned.

"*Hola, Eduardo. Usted me recuerde?*"

"*Si, señor, pero donde esta Jake?*"

"Jake is keeping an eye on things at the ranch while the Burkes pick up their daughter in Grants."

"Ah, Senorita Caitlin," said Eduardo, his eyes lighting up. "They will be happy to have her home." He and Gabe began to carry the supplies to his wagon. "So, *amigo*, you must be good with horses or Mr. Burke would not have hired you."

"He likes the way I work them. And I like his horses. I like the Burkes very much too," added Gabe as they got the sacks of flour inside.

"He is a good man, Michael Burke. A good neighbor, too. Do you want something to eat before you head back, Senor Hart?"

"Call me Gabe. And sure, I could use something. I'll be getting back to the ranch after they've finished off supper."

It was the usual beans and biscuits, but Eduardo had added chile to the beans and his wife had sent him some homemade chokecherry jam.

"I don't know if I'll be able to move after all those biscuits, Eduardo," said Gabe, licking his fingers. They sat there, drinking their coffee until Gabe broke the silence.

"Have you seen any of Mackie's men around lately, Eduardo?"

"The other day, *dos hombres* over on that ridge," Eduardo said, gesturing to the southwest. "Will you stay around if there is trouble?"

Gabe swallowed the last of his coffee and stared into the fire. "I suppose so, *amigo.*"

"Are you good with your gun, Gabe?"

"Some might say very good, Eduardo," he said with a wry smile.

"You can't be too good with that Juan Chavez around."

"Tell me something about this Chavez."

"No one knows much about him, señor. He is maybe Mexican, maybe not . . ."

"What do you mean?"

"He could be from one of the older families, with his light hair and green eyes. He speaks Spanish like a Mexican. But he speaks English *sin accento* too. Anyway, Anglo or Mexican, whatever he is, he is one bad *hombre.* They say Mackie hired him because he is so good with a gun."

"Well, you'd better take care of yourself then, Eduardo. Mackie's more likely to go after Burke's sheep than his horses."

"Yo se, Gabe, y tengo una pistola as well as a shotgun," said Eduardo, pointing to the pistol tucked into his belt.

"Thanks for supper, Eduardo. And tell your wife her jelly was the best thing I've had on my biscuits since I left home."

"She'll be happy to hear that, *amigo.*"

"Do you have any children?" Gabe asked as they walked over to the horses.

"Tres hijas y uno hijo," said Eduardo with a proud smile.

"I thought sheepherders didn't get home much," joked Gabe.

"Yes, but those times that I do . . ." Eduardo answered with a wink.

"Adios, Eduardo."

"Adios, Gabe."

He hadn't said much, this Gabe, thought Eduardo

as he watched the man ride off. But somehow he gave the impression that he was damned good with his gun, too.

Gabe rode slowly, the almost full moon lighting his way. It was past midnight by the time he got back to the ranch and he had to unsaddle the horses and water and feed them before he could fall into his own bed.

He didn't sleep well. Maybe it was all the coffee he'd drunk or all the chile he'd eaten. Or maybe it was because of what was going on in this valley, he thought, as he awoke from another dream of Lincoln County.

It had all seemed so clear in the beginning. He'd found a job with John Tunstall, an Englishman who owned a small ranch near Lincoln. Gabe had hit it off with him immediately because of their shared love of horses, and Tunstall had won him over completely when Gabe saw him with Colonel, a chestnut the army had rejected because of blindness. Tunstall had taught Colonel how to obey voice commands and could even make the horse understand when they were coming to an uphill or downhill part of a trail.

After years of wandering, Gabe had thought he'd found a place to call home. He'd fallen in love with the schoolteacher, Caroline Bryce, and joked in his letters to Sadie how he was following in his pa's footsteps. He'd saved a little money over the years and figured he might even be able to buy himself a small spread. Then Tunstall was murdered and all hell broke loose in Lincoln County.

In his grief and fury, Gabe joined a posse led by Dick Brewer, Tunstall's foreman. Brewer was one of the best-liked men in town and when he had himself sworn in as deputy constable, it seemed as if justice might prevail. But the system was corrupt, from the local sheriff all the way up to Thomas Catron, the U.S. attorney, and Gabe found himself riding with a group of men who were now considered vigilantes. At least that's what Caroline had called them. The

Regulators, as they called themselves, had been declared illegal by the legally constituted authorities.

"But those authorities are corrupt!" Gabe protested.

"If they *are* corrupt, then they will be voted out," she would patiently explain to Gabe as though he were one of her schoolchildren and she was giving him a civics lesson.

"And in the meantime, do we let ourselves be taken over by men like John Kinney?"

"He's a Texas Ranger, Gabe."

"Goddamn it, Caroline, he's an outlaw responsible for destroying the peace in El Paso, and now he's going to do it here. The fact that he's wearing a badge doesn't mean shit." Caroline blushed and Gabe apologized, but they quarreled every time they were together.

"I don't know if I can marry someone who chooses violence over the law, Gabe," Caroline finally told him.

"You *know* I'm not a violent man, Caroline."

"I hadn't thought so until now, Gabe," she'd replied sadly. She pulled gently at the garnet ring he'd given her and held it out.

"Caroline, don't do this. You know I love you."

"I am sorry, Gabe, but you're not the man I fell in love with."

"Then you didn't fall in love with Gabriel Hart, but someone you thought I was or would like me to be," he said bitterly.

But when Brewer was killed, Gabe knew things were out of control and he left Lincoln, wandering from job to job, breaking horses when he could, herding cows when he had to. He avoided violence and figured he was just not meant to settle down.

Now here he was, after years of running away from those memories, committed to supporting Michael Burke, with his gun if necessary. "Well, a man has to stop running sometime," he told himself.

* * *

When he got up the next morning, he'd gotten only about three hours of sleep.

"You look like hell, cowboy," he said, groaning as he splashed cold water on his face. He had black circles under his eyes and a bitter taste in his mouth. "And you've got three colts and three two-year-olds to work this morning.

The horses knew how tired he was, of course. They had a sixth sense for these things, always knowing when a man was hung over or just not on top of things. Of course, they took advantage of it, the yearlings acting like they'd never seen a halter before, much less been led around for days, and the two-year-olds refusing to trot in a circle, much less reverse directions or do figure eights for him.

Gabe was so tired and so angry at himself and the horses that he had no idea when he'd gained an audience. He only saw the girl sitting on the corral fence when he was lunging the last two-year-old. Shit. He'd thought the morning couldn't get any worse and here was Miss Burke just home from school back east watching him make a fool of himself.

He felt a little better when he actually got the last two-year-old to reverse and do a figure eight at a walk. Maybe he didn't look like a complete fool.

And maybe he did. The look of disgust on Miss Burke's face was fleeting, but it had been there.

He took off his hat and smoothing down his hair, said: "Good morning. You must be Miss Burke."

"And you must be Gabe Hart, the new wrangler," she said coolly, not bothering to extend her hand. "My father told me about you. He said you were very good with the horses," she added in a tone that was polite enough but held enough skepticism to annoy Gabe, even more than her obvious reluctance to shake his hand. Little snob was what she was, he thought, and he wouldn't have expected it of Burke's daughter.

He only said, "Yes, ma'am."

"My Da says you've been working with Heathcliff." Gabe frowned. "Heathcliff?"

"The black two-year-old," said Caitlin, blushing a little. She *would* have to change his name.

"Oh, Sky?" Gabe hesitated. "What did your father tell you about him?"

"Just that you'd been training him, Mr. Hart. But now that I'm home, I'll be working with him, so you can concentrate on the other horses."

It was clear that Michael Burke had not yet told his daughter of Sky's accident and Gabe certainly didn't think it was his place to enlighten her. He supposed he could understand her desire to train her own horse, especially after seeing him with the others this morning!

"I guess that'd be a decision for Mr. Burke to make," said Gabe quietly, looking up at Caitlin.

His eyes, which were a dark blue, looked up at her steadily. Cait was annoyed that he was trying to make her feel unable to make such a decision for herself, as though she were incompetent. If anyone was incompetent, it was this Gabe Hart. Heathcliff was her horse, after all. Two years ago she would have blurted this all out. But she was eighteen now and a grown woman and could act with as much dignity as this irritating Mr. Hart.

"It is a decision that my father and I will make together, Mr. Hart," she replied.

It was a verbal slap in the face and they both knew it. But Gabe just tipped his hat, saying, "Good morning, Miss Burke," as she climbed off the fence and walked to the house.

He'd put in a lot of time with her horse, he thought, as he went into the barn. He didn't *think* Michael Burke would let her take Sky, not until Gabe had determined if he would ever be ridden. But on the other hand, Burke sure had been looking forward to his daughter's return. If she was the apple of his eye, he just might take the horse away from Gabe. It would be bad for the horse and unfair to Gabe. And what the hell kind of name was Heathcliff for a horse anyway!

*   *   *

Her father was out checking the fences in the southwest field all morning, so it wasn't until lunchtime that Caitlin had a chance to speak with him.

"And what did ye do this mornin', Cait?" Michael asked as they sat down to their midday meal.

"I watched our new wrangler bungle his way through a training session, Da."

Michael lifted his eyebrows and looked over at Elizabeth, who gave a little shrug as though to say: "I don't know what is going on here, either."

"Sure and every man has a bad day with his horses, Cait. Gabe Hart's no bungler."

"Well, be that as it may, I don't want him working with my horse. I told him I would take over."

Michael picked up his coffee mug and cradling it in his hands was quiet for a moment.

"Em, ye did, did ye?"

"I didn't think you'd mind, Da. After all, Heathcliff is mine."

"Nevertheless, Cait," said Elizabeth, "it was your father who hired Gabe and your father who asked him to work Sky in his spare time. You put Gabe in a very awkward position."

Cait blushed. "I'm sorry, Da," she said apologetically. "But I do want to train Heathcliff myself," she added stubbornly. "So would you tell Mr. Hart?"

"I can't, Cait," said her father. " 'Twould not be fair to the horse or to Gabe. He's put in a month's hard work and the horse is just beginning to respond to him."

"Da, I know Heathcliff will remember me. I had him almost halter-broke, remember?"

"Caitlin," interrupted Elizabeth, who could feel the tension building between Michael and his daughter. "Your father has a good reason for giving the horse to Gabe. We didn't tell you yesterday on your first day home, but Sky was injured this spring."

"He's gone lame?" Cait exclaimed.

"No," Elizabeth continued. "He was attacked by a mountain lion and lucky to survive. If it hadn't been for Finn bringing him in, we would have lost him."

"If he isn't lame and he isn't dead, then what is wrong with him?"

"He's recovered physically, as far as we can tell, though he was left with a terrible-looking scar."

"Which would be far worse, Cait, had your mother not been so good with her needle and thread."

"He won't let anyone or anything near his back, Cait," Elizabeth explained. "We don't know if he'll ever be ridden. Your father had no time to work with him, so he gave him to Gabe. Gabe had been making progress and I don't think we should interrupt his training and neither does your father."

"Thank you, *a ghra,*" said Michael, putting his hand over his wife's. "I couldn't bear tellin' ye, Cait."

"I see," said his daughter quietly. "And what happens if he can't ever be ridden?"

"Well, I don't know . . . he's a gelding, ye know, and I can't use him for breeding."

"And we can't afford a useless animal, can we, Da? I've heard you say that often enough."

Michael only looked at her helplessly, his heart resonating to the pain in her voice.

"Then I guess I should wish Mr. Hart luck, shouldn't I? I suppose," she added in a tight voice, "that I am allowed to feed and groom him and let him get to know me again?"

"Of course, Cait," said her father, "so long as ye don't get in the way of Gabe's training."

"Where is he now?"

"Likely in the near pasture."

"I think I'll walk out there to see him. Excuse me, Ma? Da?"

After she left, Michael looked over at his wife and said: "That is one of the hardest things I've ever had to do, Elizabeth."

"I know, Michael. You did it well. And you are right, you know."

"I know. It wouldn't be fair to the horse or the man. But it doesn't make me feel any better, knowing I'm right."

*   *   *

It was not a long walk to the pasture, but Cait was slowed down by her tears and her skirts and shoes. She had dressed without thinking this morning and now realized that her clothes, which would have been casual in Philadelphia, were completely inappropriate for the ranch.

I've been away too long, she thought as she watched her skirt accumulate a layer of red dust. The dress was a light blue cotton and the red dust was stubborn, staining fabric even after hard scrubbing. She'd better dig out her leather riding skirt soon, she realized.

There were a few mares in the pasture and way over in the far corner, a black horse. Her horse.

She whistled the special whistle she'd summoned him with when he was a colt. He only lifted his head and looked around curiously.

She could see a sickle-shaped shadow along his shoulder, which she assumed was the scar. He'd been such a special colt: intelligent, spirited, and full of affection. She'd been sure he'd grow up into something special. And she'd been dreaming so long of riding him and then showing him off to Henry.

She heard footsteps behind her and assuming it was her father, said, with a little sob, "He was such a beauty, Da."

Gabe cleared his throat and said, "He still is, Miss Burke."

Caitlin rubbed the tears off her face quickly and then turned.

"Your father told you about the accident, then? You can't see much from here," said Gabe. "It's a bad scar, but he's still a fine-looking animal," he added reassuringly.

"I owe you an apology, Mr. Hart," Cait said stiffly. "My father explained that since you've won Heathcliff's trust, it is best you continue training him. Although, if it is all right with you, I am to take over some of his grooming."

Gabe was relieved. He'd always had a feel for people as well as horses and he was happy to be right about Michael Burke. His employer had done the right thing, not that Miss Caitlin Burke seemed very happy about it.

"Do you think you can break him, Mr. Hart?" Caitlin tried to keep her voice cool and steady but Gabe could hear the little tremble.

"I sure hope so, Miss Burke. Would you like to see him closer?"

Cait expected that Gabe would go in after the black, but he only gave a distinctive high whistle. The horse turned his head and when Gabe whistled again, came trotting over.

"Hi, there, Sky, want some apple?" said Gabe, holding one out in his open palm. When the horse had lipped it off, he slipped the halter on him easily.

Caitlin didn't know what hurt her the most: the fact that her colt, who had refused her whistle came so easily to Hart, or the ugly scar running down his neck and shoulder.

She climbed through the fence and stood in front of the horse.

"Here, here's another piece of apple, Miss Burke."

Cait wanted to throw it in Hart's face. As though she needed to bribe her own horse to get him to know her again. She whispered softly to him and the black stood quietly. Reaching slowly up to hold the halter, Cait brought his face to hers and breathed a few breaths into his nostrils.

"I've seen your father do that with Finn. He says it's a way of communicating with a horse," said Gabe with a smile.

"May I hold him, Mr. Hart?"

Gabe handed her the halter rope and Cait cupped the black's muzzle, crooning sweet nonsense syllables to him.

She was as good with a horse as her father, Gabe had to admit as he watched her. She was so intent on getting the black to know her and trust her again that she was unaware of his attention. He looked her over from head to foot and aside from the fancy dress and shoes, liked what he saw. She had her hair pulled back and fastened with a beaded leather clasp, but because her hair was thick and curly, a cloud of dark brown framed her face. Her eyes were gray, flecked with green and her eyelashes were almost as long as Sky's, he thought with a smile. She was small, like her mother, but she filled out the light blue dress in a very satisfying way. He was lost in his admiration of her figure and was wondering what it would be like to put his hands around her trim waist when all of a sudden he realized that she'd moved closer to the horse's side and was reaching up to touch the scar.

Sky jerked the rope out of her hand and cantered off, leaving Cait looking down at her palm, which had been scraped raw.

"Damn," muttered Gabe. "It will take me all afternoon to undo that little move."

Cait was furious with herself. She'd rushed the horse, and on her first day back. She knew better than that. But it was as though the scar had drawn her hand to it. She'd wanted to smooth it over, remove the remembered pain, make it go away. And because she knew she was in the wrong, she was even angrier with Gabe Hart. He needn't curse at her like that.

Her face was flushed with embarrassment and anger as she turned to face him. "I don't appreciate being talked to like that, Mr. Hart."

"And I don't like you spooking my horse."

"Heathcliff is *my* horse. You'll do well to remember that."

"Heathcliff! Where in hell did you get a name like that? His name is Night Sky." Gabe was fed up with Miss Caitlin Burke, desirable curves or not.

Cait's face got even redder. "He is named after the hero in one of the great English novels. Someone I doubt *you've* never heard of, Mr. Hart. The man Emily Brontë created had a wild, unbreakable spirit, just like my colt."

"His wild, unbreakable spirit will do him little good on this ranch, Miss Burke. If he is not gentled in a few months, he'll be destroyed."

Now why had he said such a cruel thing? wondered Gabe as he stalked off. He wouldn't let Michael Burke shoot the horse, no matter what happened. He'd grown to love Sky too much for that very spirit he had just mocked. Something called to him in that horse. It was the inner struggle that he sensed every time he worked with Sky. It was a struggle Gabe understood: the fear of being hurt warred with the desire to trust; the determination to remain free warred with the longing to give his devotion. He'd pay for the horse's keep out of his wages, before he'd let him be put down.

Six

"Señor Chavez is here to see you, Señor Mackie," said the housekeeper.

"Thank you, Maria. I'll see him in the library." Mackie pushed back his chair and looked over at his wife. "You'll excuse me, Helen?"

"Of course, Nelson." Helen Mackie was a pale, washed-out woman who answered in the affirmative to anything Mackie asked her, having been bullied into submission over the ten years of their marriage.

Mackie was seated in front of the fire when Chavez appeared in the doorway.

"Come in, Chavez. Would you like a drink?"

The man nodded and sitting opposite Mackie, reached out his hand for the shot glass of whiskey. He drained it in one gulp.

"Another?"

"*Gracias,* señor."

Chavez *sounded* Mexican, thought Mackie, gazing at the puzzle that was his hired gun. But he certainly didn't look it, with his light brown hair and green eyes. Wolf's eyes, thought Mackie.

"So, you visited the Simpsons?"

"Yes," said Chavez, swirling the whiskey around in his glass.

"And?" Mackie demanded impatiently.

"They are very eager to sell, Señor Mackie."

Mackie laughed and poured himself another drink. "Here's to another three hundred acres. You're a good man, Chavez."

A good man was exactly what he was not, Juan Chavez thought ironically as he emptied his glass. A good man wouldn't be suggesting to a small rancher like Simpson that there had been so little rain, señor, and things were so dry that it would not be surprising if, one day, his ranch burned down? It would be better to take Señor Mackie's offer, *si* . . . ? *"Sí,"* said Simpson.

A good man wouldn't be working for Nelson Mackie.

Mackie pulled out a map of the valley. He had traced his own property lines in blue and the other ranchers in red. More and more lines were turning purple, however, as Mackie took over. There were still a few pieces outlined in red on the edges of Mackie's property. And there was one large area that pushed itself into the blue boundaries. That was Michael Burke's spread.

Mackie was tapping his pen right in the middle of Burke's property. "You can spend some of your time with the likes of the Garcias, but Burke's is the one I want to get."

"And he won't sell?"

"I've made him two offers, damned good ones. But he just smiles and gives me that Irish blarney of his. It's bad enough that he owns such a big piece of the valley. But that he's running sheep on it and ruining good grazing land! And the rest of the men listen to him, damn it. It's why I can't get some of them out. So, I'll have to become more, uh, persuasive," said Mackie. "Or rather, you will."

Chavez gave him a bland look. "Just how persuasive?"

"To start with, you will be the one making my last offer. Politely, of course, but let him know it is the last time he'll have a chance to get out with any profit."

"Sí, Señor Mackie. I'll go tomorrow."

Juan Chavez walked slowly back to the bunkhouse. A few of the men were playing poker and invited him to join them, but he said no and pouring himself a cup of coffee walked out and sat on the bench outside, leaning his head against the bunkhouse wall.

He watched the stars come out and silently named the constellations. When he sat like this for a few minutes each evening, he felt free and at peace. He smiled as he remembered when he started stealing this time for himself. He was ten or eleven and had been at the Romero hacienda for three years. The first years of his captivity had been a blur. He'd understood nothing yet was beaten when he didn't obey old Tomas's orders. He'd learned Spanish quickly; he'd had to in order to stop the beatings. Or most of them. One night, after all the fires were banked, he'd snuck out and sat down for the first time that day. When he lifted his head, there they were winking down at him. The same stars his father had named for him. No matter where he was, the same familiar patterns would appear. He got back a little of himself that night. He was Jonathan Rush. From Boston. He didn't remember much more than that and the names of the star patterns and his father's voice. From then on, wherever he was, whomever he was working for, he would take those few minutes of freedom.

In the morning he was up and out early. He went alone. He preferred being alone and he worked better that way. He didn't need any riders to back him up. He was very good at conveying Mackie's threats all by himself.

Elizabeth was watering her flowers when she heard him ride in. She looked up, ready to smile and invite a neighbor in for a cup of tea. It was a warm morning, but she felt herself grow cold when she recognized Chavez. He was alone, thank God. Maybe he was just on his way somewhere and had stopped to water his horse? She put her bucket down and wiping her hands on her apron, walked up the porch steps and called to her husband.

"Michael. We have a visitor."

Jake had gone for the mail yesterday, and Michael was engrossed in the newspaper. "Who is it, Elizabeth?"

"I believe it is Mackie's man, Chavez."

Michael took off his reading glasses and stood up. Chavez. He looked over at the wall where his cavalry pistol hung. He didn't wear a gun regularly, although he always rode with a rifle. He'd worn a pistol long enough in the army, he told anyone who asked. Well, he was not putting it on today, he decided. Not and appear scared of scum like Chavez.

He pushed open the screen door and stood next to his wife.

Chavez had tied his horse and was watching Gabriel work one of the two-year-olds, just as if he were any neighbor here for a visit.

"Wait here, *a ghra,*" Michael told his wife.

"Buenos dias," he said quietly when he reached the corral fence.

"Buenos dias, Señor Burke. Parece que usted se consiguió un hombre que sabe de caballos."

"Yes, Gabe is very good with my horses. Are you interested in buying one, Señor Chavez?"

Chavez laughed and turning to Michael, put out his hand. "I don't think we have ever really met, Mr. Burke."

"No, I haven't had the pleasure of a formal introduction, Chavez. But I feel like I know you," Michael added. He kept his hand by his side and finally Chavez dropped his.

"I am not here for the pleasure of watching your beautiful horses, Mr. Burke. I am here on business."

"And would that be your business or Mr. Mackie's business?" Michael asked caustically.

"Mr. Mackie's business *is* my business."

"Yes, so I thought, Señor Chavez."

"Señor Mackie sent me to tell you that he has reconsidered his offer."

"Em, he has decided that he doesn't want my ranch after all?" asked Michael with dry humor.

"No, he has decided he wants it so much he is willing to give you twenty dollars more an acre."

" 'Tis a more than generous offer," said Michael.

"Yes. It would be to your advantage to take it, Señor Burke."

Michael was silent for a minute and Chavez turned back to watch Gabe.

"Em . . . exactly why would you advise me to accept, Chavez?"

"Because not only is it a more than generous offer, it is Señor Mackie's last offer, Señor Burke."

" 'Tis indeed?" said Michael. "You mean he'll be giving up on me after all this?"

Chavez turned. "Mr. Mackie never gives up on anything he wants, señor. Let us just say it is the last time he will be so generous." Chavez's eyes were unreadable as he continued. "You have a nice place here, Mr. Burke. Beautiful horses. A lovely wife and daughter, I hear."

On the surface, Chavez's words were only a polite litany, but the undertone had nothing of politeness in it.

"Are ye threatening me, Señor Chavez?" Michael asked calmly.

"Why, I am just making an observation, señor. But life is, I am sure you would agree, uncertain. I would urge you to take advantage of Senor Mackie's offer."

"Tell Mr. Mackie I appreciate his generosity, but I prefer the uncertainty of life to being driven off my land by a bully and his hired gun."

Chavez gave Michael an empty smile and said: "I am sorry that is your decision, Mr. Burke. *Hasta luego* . . ."

"You are sorry, my arse," muttered Michael as he watched Chavez ride away. "And I'm sure I will be seeing you again."

Gabe had seen Chavez ride in and had considered interrupting the lunging for a few minutes. But Chavez was alone and Michael right inside, so he decided to go on with his work and just keep his ears and eyes open for trouble.

He ignored Chavez when the man came over to the corral. He couldn't hear what Michael and his visitor were saying, but their faces were calm enough, so he put his attention on the two-year-old. After Chavez had ridden away, Michael stayed by the fence and watched until Gabe had finished.

"She's a sweet-tempered filly, isn't she, Gabe?" he said when his employee led the horse over to the fence.

Gabe stroked the filly's nose. "She is, Mr. Burke." He hesitated and then added, "I saw you had a visitor."

"Señor Chavez, yes."

"I know that this is none of my business," Gabe said hesitantly.

" 'Tis indeed yer business, boyo, if you work for me. Mr. Nelson Mackie had made me another offer. His last offer, so I've been told."

"And you refused," Gabe said quietly.

"I refused," said Michael. "I will not let anyone buy me off a place I've built with me own sweat and hard work. 'Tis my home and my family's and this is one Irishman who won't be driven off his land."

"Good for you, Mr. Burke."

"Well, now, Gabe, I don't know that it will be good for me," Michael responded with a wry smile. "It might be very bad for all of us." He looked Gabe in the eye and said seriously: "Now is the time for lea-vin', Gabe. I'd not think ill of you if ye did."

Gabe returned Michael's gaze steadily. "Why, I haven't finished with these horses, Mr. Burke. And there is still Night Sky to gentle for your daughter."

Michael nodded. "Well, don't say I haven't warned ye, lad. But I can't deny I was hoping ye'd say it. 'Twas a good day for us when Eduardo sent ye here."

It wasn't hard for Elizabeth to guess what Chavez wanted. She didn't have to be there to know Michael's answer: he'd never sell their land. Or be driven off alive. And neither would she. Mackie would have to kill both of them if he wanted the Burke property.

She picked up her bucket to go and fill it again and as it bumped her leg she was suddenly overcome by fear so strong she thought she was going to faint. She set the bucket down and sat on the edge of the porch, leaning back against one of the posts.

"Are ye all right, *a ghra*?" asked Michael as he walked toward the house.

The fear had risen and washed over her like a wave, leaving her drenched in a cold sweat. She shivered, even though it was a hot day. "I just felt a bit faint, that is all, Michael," she said in a low voice.

Michael sat down next to her and put his arm around her. "You are shaking, Elizabeth."

She was and she couldn't seem to stop. Michael pulled her closer and his body heat and the reassuring feel of his arm around her gradually relaxed her.

"Is it Chavez, *a ghra*?"

"I don't know, Michael. Something just . . . came over me when I went to fill the bucket. I am not really that frightened of him, though I suppose I should be with his reputation. I can guess what he came for."

"And ye know my answer?"

"It is mine, too, Michael, you know that."

"Mackie is not going to be such a gentleman now, Elizabeth. No, I am wrong," he continued, with an ironic laugh. "He'll act the gentleman as usual and let his hired wolf do the dirty work. Chavez looks like a wolf, with those green eyes of his. There seems to be no feeling in the man, Elizabeth, or else he couldn't be doing his job."

Elizabeth had finally stopped shaking. "Are ye feeling better, *a ghra*?"

"I am, Michael. And what about Gabe? Will he stay, do you think?"

"He'll stay, Elizabeth. And we are lucky he will."

That night, Elizabeth dreamed of her family. Her father was lying there, that black-red rose of blood on his white shirt. Her mother was on the ground, skirt above her waist. And she, Elizabeth, was walking up the bank, her bucket full. "Here's the water you wanted, Ma." But Jonathan, her little brother, was gone.

She awoke with a start, her chest aching with unshed tears and she felt Michael's solid warmth next to her. She burrowed into his arms and let the tears fall.

Michael woke immediately. "Elizabeth, what is it?"

"I had a dream, Michael. A nightmare about my parents."

"Oh, *muirneach*," he whispered and he stroked her hair gently.

"I used to dream of it every week," she whispered, "but that was long ago in Santa Fe. Before I married Thomas. When I became his wife, I guess I felt safe again."

"And are ye feeling unsafe now, Elizabeth?" asked Michael with pain in his voice.

"Oh, I feel safe here with you, Michael," she protested, reaching up to stroke his cheek.

"I know ye do, but with Chavez riding in like he did . . ."

"I suppose he reminds me of the Comancheros," she said after a moment. She shuddered and her voice broke. "They were lying there, Michael, just like they were that day. My father and my mother. I was coming back with the bucket of water they sent me for. I had wanted my little brother to go, you know. If he had, Michael, then he'd be alive today and I'd be . . ."

"But thank God, ye're alive here with me, Elizabeth, for what would I have done without ye all these years, *muirneach*." He kissed her gently on the lips and she responded with an almost desperate passion. "Make love to me, Michael," she whispered.

Their lovemaking usually began slowly and tenderly and built to a crescendo. Tonight, however, Elizabeth was ready for him almost immediately and Michael entered her after only a few kisses. He could feel his body respond to her need and he drove into her as deep as he could as she raised herself to meet him.

"Oh, Michael," she whispered as she lay there afterward, her head cradled on his chest, "If anything happened to you . . ."

"*Whist*, my dear one, nothing will."

But he lay there after she fell asleep, wondering if he would be able to keep his promise.

Seven

The mail had contained not only Michael's newspaper, but a letter for Cait from Henry. Her mother had handed it to her, noticing only the surname and the postmark and said, "Here is a letter from Susan Beecham, Cait." Neither her mother nor her father noticed her quick blush when she saw Henry's initial.

He was arriving in three weeks and would stay ten days on his way to visit a classmate in California. "I can't wait to meet your parents, my dear," he wrote, "and get their permission to make our engagement official. We can travel back together, just as we planned."

She should be ecstatic, she thought, as she reread the letter. She couldn't wait to see him, that was true. But his imminent arrival meant she had to tell her parents her plans. They assumed she was home for good. That she would be looking for a position teaching school in the county, and eventually marry someone from the valley. She had to tell them soon. Tonight.

She went out for a long ride with the letter tucked inside her blouse. She picnicked in the little canyon east of the ranch and reread the letter several times and daydreamed of Henry. He was very handsome with his brown hair and brown eyes and patrician nose. On her first visit to the Beechams he had overwhelmed her with his brilliant conversation that ranged from politics to literature. At first, she had only listened shyly. Then, with his encouragement, she'd ventured her own opinions. He had listened to them, supported her in them, for he was nothing if not forward-thinking about the position of women. And then one night as he and Susan and Cait had strolled the rolling lawn together after dinner, Susan had excused herself. And Henry had slipped his arm through Cait's and continued their walk down to the small lake at the foot of the hill.

They watched the moon make a bright path across the water and then Henry had turned to her and putting his finger under her chin, tilted her face for his kiss. It was a gentle, tender kiss and Cait felt her mouth open naturally to it. But Henry pulled away and stroked her cheek with his finger.

"I do think that I am falling in love with you, Caitlin Burke," he said with a winsome smile.

Caitlin was thrilled. Susan's handsome, brilliant, sophisticated brother was in love with her, "Calico Cait," as the girls at school had called her.

"You don't have to say anything, Cait," he added, amused rather than taken aback by her silence. "It is too soon for you, I know. But I can be patient."

"It is only that . . . I don't know what to say," she stammered.

He kissed her again, on the cheek this time, and taking her arm in his, walked her back up to the house. "I told Susan to give us ten minutes. We don't want to be creating a scandal," he teased, his eyes laughing down at her.

Of course she fell in love with him. How could she not? She could talk to him about all that she was learning and about her new dreams for the future. "I want to teach young women, Henry," she said. "I want to stretch their minds the way Mrs. Weld has stretched mine."

"That is one of the things I love about you, Cait. Your idealism. And when we marry, you can continue to teach for a while."

"*If* we marry, Henry," she said tartly. "Why, you haven't even asked me."

But of course, she knew he would. And he did, a few months later, on her Christmas visit. She'd said yes, but only to an unofficial engagement, for she had to tell her parents in person.

Now here she was, home a week, and had told them nothing!

"Cait, could you slice the corn bread and put it on the table?"

"Yes, Ma."

"And go call your father."

Caitlin went halfway to the stable and called out: "Da, dinner's ready."

Michael was just coming out of the barn and he walked up to her and putting his arm around her shoulders, said, " 'Tis good to be hearin' you shout for me, Cait. Just like ye used to do."

"Elizabeth, I've said this before . . ."

"Only a million times, Da."

"You cook a good meal for a hardworking man. And don't ye be gettin' disrespectful to your Da, young lady!"

Caitlin grinned at him. "There is dried apple cobbler for dessert, Da."

"And I'll have a large slice, Cait. With cream."

Elizabeth poured the coffees and a contented silence fell on the table as they ate dessert.

"Da, Ma," said Cait, after they'd all finished. "I have something to tell you."

"What is it, Cait?" Elizabeth asked curiously.

"The letter I got yesterday. It wasn't from Susan Beecham. It was from Henry, her brother. I have mentioned him in my letters, you know. I told you I'd met him last summer," she added almost defensively.

"Why, yes, you did. He was studying to be a lawyer, I think you told us," said Elizabeth.

"Actually, he has finished his degree and will be clerking for a judge this coming year. We got to know each other quite well, you know, between summer and Christmas and his visits to the school. To see Susan."

Elizabeth, who had gotten up to clear the table,

stopped and Michael looked across at his daughter. "So, ye got to know this young man well, Cait?"

"Yes, Da. Mmm, actually, he has asked me to marry him."

Elizabeth sat down next to Michael who reached under the table to take her hand in his. "Em, he did, did he?"

"But of course, I told him I could not agree to an official engagement until I talked to you and Ma. And until you'd met him."

"Of course," said Michael softly.

"He is on his way to California to visit a classmate and will be stopping here for a week," she said in a rush. "I know you will like him, Da."

"The important thing," said Elizabeth, keeping her voice calm, "is whether *you* like him. Love him. You didn't say that much about him in your letters, you know. Nothing that would have given us a hint. . . ."

"I *do* love him," Cait said earnestly. "He didn't ask me to marry him until Christmas. And I didn't want to write you about him, I wanted to tell you in person."

"Em, this Henry Beecham, is he plannin' to practice law out here, Cait? After he finishes working for this judge?"

"No, Da. We would live in Philadelphia. I have been offered a position as a teacher at the school. It is what I've always wanted," she added, her eyes smiling.

"I thought what you always wanted was to teach in a county school, Cait," said her mother.

"I meant I've always wanted to become a teacher, Ma. Now that I've been East, I know I want to work at a school like Fayreweather. Where I can teach literature, not just the ABC's."

"Children need teachers to learn their ABC's as much as for literature, Cait," said Elizabeth quietly. "You had all spring to write us about this. To prepare us."

"I know, Ma, but I just didn't know how to tell you. I know you and Da expected me home to stay. When I first went away, that's what I expected, too. . . ."

"But this is your home, Cait," continued Elizabeth in a strained voice.

"Now, Elizabeth," said Michael. He squeezed his wife's hand under the table, both to comfort her and to warn her. "Things change. Young women fall in love and move away from their families."

Elizabeth took a deep breath. "Your father is right, Cait. It is just . . . hard to think about you so far away."

"I knew it would be hard for you, Ma. That's why I kept putting off telling you," Cait admitted, her voice trembling.

"We would never want you keepin' anything from us to protect us, Cait," said her father. "We love you too well for that."

"Thank you, Da," she whispered, tears welling up in her eyes.

"Now then, when is this Mr. Henry Beecham arrivin'?"

"In three weeks, Da. He'll stay for a week and then continue on to California." She hesitated. "If all goes well, then I'll return East with him at the end of the summer. If you and Ma agree, we'll marry at Christmas."

"Oh, Michael, I don't think I can bear it," said Elizabeth that night after Cait had gone to bed.

"I know, *a ghra*. But we must. At least, if this Beecham fellow is worthy of our Cait. If he's not . . ."

"If he's not, Michael?"

"I'll kick him off the ranch!"

"Not if Caitlin loves him."

Michael sighed. "Maybe not. But she wouldn't be goin' back East with him at the end of the summer, I can tell you that!"

"It's just too soon. Why she just got home, I haven't seen her for two years and here she is, all set to leave again. And not just *us*, everything she knows."

"We sent her to that school because she had a good mind, Elizabeth."

"Because I inherited that little bit of money from

my grandfather," said Elizabeth bitterly, "and because she wanted to be a teacher. You were too easy on her, Michael. She should have told us sooner."

"I know, *a ghra*. But 'tis too late to be spoiling our short time with her now. I didn't want ye to be driving her away from us."

"Oh, Michael, I know you are right. But it is too much. First Mackie and Chavez and now this."

Michael gave her a wry smile. "This Henry Beecham will be coming in the middle of a stirred-up hornet's nest."

Eight

Cait had always gone for a short ride before breakfast and since she'd come home she'd fallen into the habit again. Early morning was one of her favorite times, not only because it was cool, but because of the desert silence and the clarity of the early-morning light.

The morning after she talked with her parents, she was up and out at sunrise. It was the time of day when the wild things were out and she saw several deer drinking under the cottonwoods by the creek and a coyote loping along the valley. Her horse shied as a jackrabbit exploded out of the brush.

On her way back, she saw another rider, one coming from the ranch. At first she thought it was her father but then the man took off his hat and the sun turned his hair to silver. It was Gabe Hart.

Cait knew that she was being unfair, but she hated it that this man was training her horse. It went beyond that, she realized, being honest with herself. Her father had entrusted his beloved horses to Gabe Hart and treated him almost like a partner. Her father used to talk to her about the horses; now he was talking to this stranger.

When Gabe came up to her, he pulled his horse up and lifted his hat again. The sun was behind him and lit his hair again. The contrast of silvered gold hair against tanned skin and blue eyes was striking and Cait had to admit that as much as he annoyed her, Gabe Hart was a good-looking man. If you liked the silent type, she added to herself.

"Good morning, Miss Burke."

"Good morning, Mr. Hart. It is a beautiful morning, isn't it?"

"Yes, ma'am." He cleared his throat. "I know you've been riding out early every morning, ma'am," he continued in his Texas drawl. "I hope you're not going too far."

"I haven't gone off ranch property, Mr. Hart," Cait responded sharply.

Gabe felt like he had disturbed a porcupine as he felt Cait prickle. It was too bad he couldn't seem to get along with his boss's daughter, but she obviously hadn't liked him from the beginning and there wasn't much he could do about it.

"It's just that after Chavez's visit yesterday, I am sure that Mr. Burke, uh, your father, would prefer you to stay close to home."

"Chavez?" Cait had heard the name, but neither of her parents had said anything about his visit.

"Mackie's hired gun," said Gabe flatly. "Mackie sent him over yesterday to make your father another offer on the ranch."

"Why didn't Da *tell* me?" she exclaimed without thinking.

"You were out riding when it happened. He'll probably tell you today, Miss Burke."

"What did this Chavez have to say?"

"I was in the corral lunging the filly, so I didn't hear anything. But your father told me he made it very clear it was Mackie's last offer."

"Did he threaten Da?"

"I don't suppose Chavez ever threatens directly," Gabe drawled. "Mackie uses him to 'persuade' people. I wouldn't want him persuading Mr. Burke through you."

"I won't ride out again without my rifle, Mr. Hart. I could show Senor Chavez a little persuading of my own," said Cait, flushed with anger. Sensing her mood, her horse shifted sideways and Gabe noted with approval how good her seat was. She sat straight and tall, her legs signaling the horse as much as her hands on the reins. She hadn't worn a hat this morning and her hair was windblown into wild curls around her face. She was wearing her divided leather riding skirt and an old linen blouse. Somehow that shapeless blouse with its top button unbuttoned made Gabe think of the curves it concealed more than any tucked and fitted shirtwaist revealed. Damn, but he'd better stop thinking that way about Miss Caitlin Burke, he thought, as he tipped his hat and said, "Well, I'd better be on my way."

Cait rode home, her anger and her concern having killed her appetite for breakfast. When she had settled her horse in the barn and joined her parents at the table, Michael turned to her and said: "I meant to talk to you last night, Cait, about your morning ride."

"So you *were* going to tell me about Chavez?" she responded tartly.

"Your father hardly had a chance, Cait, we were so taken up with your plans," said her mother with a touch of quiet anger. "Who told you about him?"

"I met Mr. Hart on my way back and he warned me," Cait responded in a softer voice. "He said Chavez is Mackie's hired gun, Da. That he uses him as a 'persuader.' "

Elizabeth was glad to hear the change in Caitlin's voice. Her hand had been itching to slap her daughter for talking to Michael that way, and she had never touched her daughter in anger in her life. She was horrified by her reaction, but she felt herself wanting to say, "You can't have it both ways, Cait. You can't tell us you are leaving and at the same time expect to be a part of things like you always were." She knew her anger was unreasonable and came from her grief over Cait's news, so she held her tongue and let Michael handle it.

"I told Chavez to let Mackie know we wouldn't either be bought or persuaded, Cait. And we won't, will we, Elizabeth?" he added, looking over at his wife and giving her a warm smile. "We're damned lucky to have Gabe Hart here," he added. "I'm glad he gave you the warning."

"I won't ride off our property alone, Da. And like I told Mr. Hart, I won't go anywhere without my rifle."

"Good girl."

"It is my bread-baking day, Cait," said Elizabeth. "Could you help with the wash? And water the flowers with the leftover water for me," she added. For some reason, the thought of that bucket bumping against her leg brought back all the feelings of panic from the nightmare.

"Of course, Ma."

" 'Tis good ye're here to help yer ma, Cait," said Michael after Elizabeth left to gather up the laundry. "She didn't sleep well the other night. Chavez's visit seems to have stirred up memories of her parents' deaths."

When Cait was five, she had asked why she didn't have a grandma or a grandpa. Michael had sat her on his knee and told her that she indeed did have a grandpa far away in Ireland. "That's *my* Da, Cait," he said. "But yer ma . . . well, she lost her mama and papa many years ago when she was only fourteen. Some bad men killed them."

Cait's eyes had filled and her lip had trembled. "You mean Ma has no ma and da at all?"

"No, Cait, she had them for a while. And those bad men are all dead and gone. You will always have your ma and da."

Cait had put her arms around her mother that night and said, "I'm sorry, Ma."

"For what, Cait?"

" 'Cause you don't have your mama or your papa."

Elizabeth had hugged her close. "Oh, but I have you and your Da and that is all I need."

Elizabeth had mentioned her parents occasionally and Cait knew that the little sewing box her mother used had been Cait's grandmother's. It had all happened such a long time ago that Caitlin supposed her mother had forgotten it all. She was a grown woman, after all, with a grown daughter, so she was surprised to hear that her mother's reaction went beyond her immediate fear of Chavez.

"But that was so long ago, Da," she said slowly.

"Some things ye can bury deep, Cait, but ye never really forget them. Yer ma rarely talks about them, I know. And only thinks about it once in a while. But she lost her parents and her brother in a terrible way and Chavez brought it all back, damn him. For that alone, I'd kill him," Michael continued, almost to himself.

Cait was happy to be struggling with heavy wet sheets and clothes that had red dust stains that were impossible to wash out. The activity kept her from thinking too much.

She had expected that she would come home and although *she* had changed, everything else would be the same: the horses, her mother and father, the valley. They were to have had a long, glorious summer punctuated by Henry's visit and then, when he returned from California, she would go back east with him to her new life, leaving her old life behind. Yet not really behind, for the ranch and her parents would always be there for her to come back to.

But it had to stay the same, or how else could she leave it? Yet it was all changing. Three families had been driven out of the valley. Her horse had been attacked, perhaps ruined. Her Da had hired Gabe Hart. And her beloved home, even her family's safety, was being threatened.

She had put on an old calico dress to do the laundry and it was fairly soaked through by the time she finished. After she'd hung the sheets and clothes and emptied the last bucket of dirty water on the flowers, she felt as wrung out as the sheets. She'd intended to go for another ride, but instead, she wandered over to the corral where Gabe was working.

He was just letting the last two-year-old into the near pasture when he saw her sitting on the fence, her wet dress clinging to her legs. She looked tired and somehow defenseless and he felt some sympathy for her, which surprised him. She'd come home to a lot, he thought: her colt injured and her parents facing Mackie's threats.

He slapped the horse's spotted rump and walking

over to her, said, "I was going to work Sky . . . I mean, Heathcliff, Miss Burke."

"Oh, call him Sky, Mr. Burke." she said with a tired smile. "It is a far better name for him and I think we have both outgrown the other!"

They were the first words she'd exchanged with him that didn't have an edge to them.

"I was wondering if you'd like to halter him and lead him out?"

"You don't think it would interfere with your training, Mr. Hart?" she said, with only a trace of sarcasm.

"If I did, I wouldn't have asked you," he answered quietly.

"I am sorry, Mr. Hart, I haven't been very friendly, have I?"

"Not so I've noticed," he agreed with a slow smile.

"It has been hard to come home and I thought it would be so easy," she said with a wistful smile. She started to slip down from her perch on the fence, but her heel caught, throwing her off balance. Without thinking, Gabe reached out and caught her around the waist as she was about to fall and Cait's hands were grasping his shoulders before she knew it. She slid down him slowly and they both stood there, overcome by embarrassment and something else.

Cait stepped back, breaking the tension between them. "Thank you, Mr. Hart. If you hadn't moved so quickly, I'd be facedown in the dirt. I'll go in and get Sky," she added and walked quickly into the barn, leaving Gabe standing there, remembering the feel of that small waist in his hands and the softness of her breasts as they brushed his body.

"What was Burke's answer, Chavez?" Nelson Mackie looked up from the paperwork on his desk at the man standing in front of him. Chavez was a good-looking devil, he thought, not for the first time. No wonder Maria is always eager to bring me coffee when he's here. He smiled at the fresh cup in front of him. And those cold green eyes of his never even flicker in her direction.

"Burke says he's not selling, Señor Mackie."

"There is nothing more stubborn than an Irishman and I should know," said Mackie. "You were persuasive?"

"I was as clear as I could be without directly threatening him, señor."

Mackie looked down at his hands, which were clasped in front of him and tapped his thumbs together. "I think it is a shame, don't you, that Burke is going to lose some sheep to accidental poisoning?"

Chavez didn't even blink, only nodded his head.

"There's a dance in two weeks' time. That pretty daughter of his has just gotten home from school. You might just dance her into a corner and let her know what can happen to young women if they are not careful."

Chavez nodded again.

"Maybe a few warnings like that will do it. But whatever it takes, he'll sell by the time I'm finished with him. You can go, Chavez."

Mackie had hired Chavez away from Diego Navarro three years ago. "El Lobo" was well-known in West Texas. He had a reputation for coldly carrying out whatever orders Navarro gave him, short of killing. No one ever crossed Navarro, because if they did, El Lobo would come visit. He didn't ride in with a troop of men, blustering and bullying. He came alone and quietly enumerated the accidents that could happen to livestock in such a desolate country.

When Mackie heard of him, he knew he had to hire him, for he was determined to expand his own cattle business into New Mexico. It was easy to get Chavez, he only had to offer him more money than Navarro.

Chavez had served Mackie well. He was a good leader of men, for all he was a loner. Perhaps *because* he was. He was good with a gun, but better still, he was so good at intimidation that it rarely came to killing.

Chavez himself would have had a hard time explaining his singular success except perhaps to say that he'd learned to exert his power over others in a hard school. On the Romero hacienda, he'd watched carefully, as he grew older, how Tomas handled others. If you wanted power, you never showed anyone pity or compassion. You maintained a cold distance from anyone weaker than you, whether it be women, slaves, or a man who could not stand up to you.

Chavez didn't gain pleasure from intimidating the weak. It was just that it was something he was good at. He knew how to follow orders and how to make others do the same. It paid him well. And someday . . .

He was always thinking "someday." Someday, when he had enough money, he would buy his own place and be the only one giving the orders. But the truth was, he had enough money in a Santa Fe bank to buy a decent-size spread now. Something kept him from settling down, so he always said yes to the next job.

His reputation and his nickname amused him. People had such a great fear of wolves, though as far as he knew, they never killed human beings, only livestock. He hadn't killed many men, either, despite his reputation. Certainly never unless his own life was threatened. As for what he did: he tended to see it as a culling out of the weakest, the same way wolves did. The big difference between him and most wolves, of course, was that he ran alone. They should have called him *"El Lobo Solitario."*

He didn't think a few poisoned sheep would change Michael Burke's mind. But a frightened daughter might. He hadn't seen the man's daughter yet, but he'd heard she was pretty, so he was looking forward to a dance and a few minutes alone with Miss Caitlin Burke.

It was a long, hard two weeks before Henry was to arrive. It began with Michael's ride up to the mountains to deliver Eduardo's supplies. He discovered that several sheep had been found dead.

"Poisoned, señor," said Eduardo, as they stood over the bloated carcasses.

"Could it have been anything they've eaten?" Michael asked.

"No, señor, there is no jimson weed around here."

"I didn't really think so, Eduardo. It's that bastard, Mackie. Have you seen any of his men around here?"

Eduardo shook his head. "But someone could have done it while I was down at the camp."

"Well, we must all be more careful. Do ye feel safe up here alone, Eduardo? I could hire someone to keep ye company."

"No need, Señor Burke. I will be fine. And I don't think Mackie would risk harming one of your men."

"I am not so sure, Eduardo. I'll try to send Gabe or Jake up more often."

"*Gracias,* Señor Burke."

Michael told them all at dinner and Caitlin saw her mother's face go white and then red.

"It is that bastard Mackie," Elizabeth said fiercely.

"Ma!" Cait had never heard her mother say anything stronger than "damn" and that rarely.

"We have to go to the sheriff, Michael."

"Ye know he will only laugh in our faces, Elizabeth. Mackie had him appointed. And we have no proof."

"We don't need proof, Michael. We both know it was that Chavez. A true wolf in a sheepfold," she added bitterly.

"Let's just hope that this is all he'll try. When he sees we're not budgin', maybe he'll just give up and turn neighborly," added Michael with an attempt at humor.

Elizabeth smiled, but Caitlin could feel their tension and stayed closer to home on her rides than she had done before. When it was time to meet Henry's train, her father told her that he would have to stay at the ranch to take care of things, and so he sent Jake off with them.

Cait was so eager to see Henry that she didn't think she could stand it. He would fold her in his arms and make the fear go away. She didn't think much further than that, for if she did, she started worrying again. For until this was all resolved, how could she think of leaving?

Nine

When Cait saw Henry step off the train, she grabbed Elizabeth's arm.

"There he is, Ma, over there."

Elizabeth saw a slim, handsome man dressed in a dark blue suit step down and shade his eyes from the glare of the sun.

"Over here, Henry," Cait called and she hurried down the platform to hurl herself into his arms.

She wanted him to squeeze her tight, to kiss all the fear of the past week away, but he only laughed quietly and prying her loose, took her hands, saying, "Let me look at you first, Cait. I want to drink in the sight of you."

She had worn her second-best dress from Philadelphia, but also one of her old bonnets to keep off the sun, which had fallen off and was hanging down her back. The sun was in her eyes and she couldn't really see Henry's face. But the feel of his hands on hers was wonderful. And he could hardly have given her the kisses she wanted in public, after all, she thought.

"Welcome to New Mexico, Mr. Beecham," said Elizabeth who had walked up behind them. "I am Caitlin's mother, Elizabeth Burke."

Henry let go of Cait and bowed, saying, "I am so very pleased to meet you, Mrs. Burke."

"Our wagon is over here. Jake will take your bag for you," Elizabeth added. "It is a long way back, so we had best get started."

"Of course," replied Henry. He took Cait's arm and they walked behind Elizabeth. He pressed it close to him and Cait felt that lovely feeling of being cherished and taken care of that she had felt in Philadelphia. Then his strong hands were around her waist, helping her into the wagon. They didn't leave the same strange warmth that Gabriel Hart's had done . . . but why on earth was she comparing the two? There was no comparison. Henry was everything that Gabe was not: well-educated, a brilliant law clerk, and a witty conversationalist, as well as a firm believer in the right of women to expand their horizons. Gabriel Hart was a good man with horses. While she had come to respect him for that, he was hardly a match for the man she loved.

"I am sorry that Mr. Burke was unable to be with us, Mr. Beecham," said Elizabeth after Cait and Henry were settled in the back seat. "But we have had some difficulties with a not very neighborly neighbor and he felt it best he remain at the ranch."

Henry looked at Cait inquiringly, but she only shook her head and said, "Later. Right now, you must give your full attention to New Mexico Territory."

By the time they arrived at the ranch, Henry had learned the names of the pale green shrubbery that all looked the same to him, but was either sage or chamisa, and had had all the local landmarks pointed out to him. He had expected more of a town than Ramah, with its few buildings, but was polite enough not to say anything but, "It is indeed, uh, picturesque, Caitlin."

When they finally reached the Burke ranch, the sun was going down and Henry was relieved to realize that the air was growing somewhat cooler. He had been sweltering in his suit and his face felt tight and hot. As they pulled up in front of the house, a tall man with pepper and salt hair walked over from the barn to greet them.

"Ye made it back safe and sound, Elizabeth," he said in a soft brogue. "And ye must be Mr. Beecham. Welcome to our home," he added, putting out his hand.

Of course Henry had known Caitlin was Irish on her father's side, but Michael Burke was more . . .

well, Irish than Henry had expected. He considered himself to be quite liberal, but was ashamed to realize that for one moment he had felt relief at the thought that his in-laws would hardly be visiting often.

"How do you do, Mr. Burke. I am grateful for your hospitality. Caitlin has told me so much about her home," he added, turning and smiling at her.

"Well, she didn't tell you to bring a broad-brimmed hat, did she, boyo?" said Michael with a clap on Henry's shoulder. "Yer nose has gotten a little sun, I can see. We will have to find you a hat if ye'er going to do any ridin'."

Henry touched his nose and winced and taking off his bowler hat looked at it ruefully. "I would appreciate that, Mr. Burke."

Michael handed Elizabeth down and turning to Henry, said, "There's a pump in back of the barn, if you want to wash the dust off. I'll have Jake bring yer bag up. We'll be eatin' supper in two shakes of a lamb's tail."

"Did you heat the stew, Michael?"

"*And* mixed up some biscuits, Elizabeth," Michael teased.

"Thank you, Michael," Elizabeth answered, putting her arms around her husband's waist. Turning to her daughter, she said: "Cait, why don't you show Henry where the pump is, dear?"

"Yes, Ma."

Supper turned out to be a rather strained affair. Michael and Elizabeth were very conscious that the sophisticated young man would soon be a part of their family. But since they did not know him, they could hardly yet treat him as such. So they asked very politely about his education and plans for the future.

"I hear you attended Harvard College," said Elizabeth. "I am originally from Boston myself," she added.

"Yes, Caitlin told me. I enjoyed my time in Cambridge very much," Henry replied. "It is not so vastly different from Philadelphia, you know. But I am happy to have found a position in my own hometown."

"I spent a little time in the East meself," said Michael, working as a stable lad in New York. From what I've heard, New York would be a bit more lively than Boston or Philadelphia," he added with a smile.

"Caitlin tells me you were in the army, Mr. Burke."

"The U.S. Calvary for many years. 'Twas the army brought me west and I've never wanted to leave."

"Had you considered making a career of it?"

"A career? I suppose I might have made lieutenant or maybe even captain eventually. But I was not interested in gaining my promotions by turning people off their land."

"Ah, yes," said Henry seriously. "The Indian question."

"I don't know that there was any question about it, boyo. It was one fight after another to push them west. Or south, or wherever the government wanted them."

Henry nodded. "I agree that our policy was not always wise. But we are at least making an effort to educate them, and bring them into the mainstream of our society. I am happy to say that my parents were active in establishing schooling for the natives of this country."

Elizabeth could feel Michael's reaction to this statement and put her hand on her husband's knee. "It is always good to hear of the concern good people back east have for the welfare of Indians and freedmen," she said. "I remember my father and mother attending abolitionist lectures in Boston when I was a girl."

"Educating them to join society!" exclaimed Michael later when he and Elizabeth were getting ready for bed. "Cutting off a boy's hair and forbidding any of them, boy or girl, to speak their native language!"

"I just didn't think our first night together was the time to discuss it, Michael,'" said his wife with a wry smile.

"And you were right, *a ghra*," he admitted. "It is just that we have seen some of the results when we've visited Antonio and Serena. Remember her nephew who went back east to school? He came home in a suit and tie and could hardly speak Navajo. He didn't feel at home with his own people and all those well-meaning people back east? Well, they were not interested in hiring him or introducing him to their daughters."

"I know and I am very glad that Serena refused to send their daughter away." Elizabeth sighed. "Maybe we shouldn't have done it, either."

" 'Tis hardly the same."

"Oh, I know that, Michael. But clearly Cait does not see this as home anymore. Once she goes back east, she won't be our daughter in the same way."

"Well, what did ye think of the lad, Elizabeth?"

"He seems very intelligent. He is certainly handsome. And he obviously respects Caitlin as well as loves her. That is very important to me, Michael. That whomever she marries not hold her back out of some old-fashioned idea of what women should do." Elizabeth hesitated. "But . . ."

"But what, *a ghra*?" asked Michael, putting his arm around his wife as she sat up against the pillows.

"It is hard to know much after just one day, Michael. I think he loves Cait. He showed affection to her at the station. It is just that she is such a passionate person and I sense that he isn't." Elizabeth was quiet for a moment. "He is obviously a fine young man, but I want Cait to have what we have, Michael."

"And what is that, Elizabeth?" Michael whispered.

"A love that combines respect and affection with passion, Michael."

"Ye can't always judge by the outside of a man."

"I know. He may very well be Heathcliff underneath his fine blue suit and spotless linen," she said with a twinkle in her eye.

They both looked at each other and laughed.

"Somehow I don't see Henry Beecham as a lad who'd enjoy wandering over the moors in the rain and the wind, me darlin'. And don't ye think Cait has grown up a bit?"

"Of course, but I think she is still our Cait, passionate about horses and books and ideas. She will need to have that passionate self welcomed in her marriage."

" 'Tis too early to tell anything, Elizabeth. And we must assume that she knows what she wants."

Elizabeth slid down and reaching under Michael's nightshirt, ran her fingers down his chest. "I know what I want, Michael," she whispered.

Michael sat up and pulled his shirt over his head. Then he helped his wife off with her nightgown.

"You are as beautiful to me as you were the first time I saw you, *muirneach*," he said softly, and pulled her down on top of him.

The next morning Cait smiled as she watched her parents. Her father came in and put his arms around her mother's waist as she stood stirring the oatmeal. He leaned forward and murmured his good-morning against her neck. As Elizabeth served Michael his breakfast, she leaned against him naturally and unconsciously. They had what Cait called "the look" in their eyes. She had always rested secure in the way they expressed their affection for each other openly. But as she got older, she began to sense a special tenderness on some days. It must be that they have made love, she had decided one day when she was around fourteen. Not that she knew much about making love then.

Or now, for that matter, she thought, though she could certainly imagine it better, now that she knew the physical details. What would it be like with Henry? she wondered, looking over at him. They had had a few more kisses than that first one before she left Philadelphia. But he had always broken them off too early for her liking. She wanted his tongue exploring her mouth. She loved the feelings his kisses aroused. But he seemed to think her soft moan of pleasure was a signal to stop rather than go on. He would tell her that they mustn't get carried away. And he was right, of course. But oh, she wanted to be carried away.

Henry must have felt her gaze for he looked up and

smiled over at her as he buttered his bread. "I was hoping you would show me the horses today, Cait. And perhaps some of the countryside?"

"That's exactly what I'd planned, Henry,'" she replied with a grin.

After a leisurely breakfast, Henry went up to change into his riding clothes. Michael was already gone by that time, and as Cait helped her mother with the dishes, she asked: "Well, what do you and Da think of him, Ma?" She made her voice sound calm, but she was actually very nervous.

"We think him a fine, intelligent young man, Cait. One who obviously respects you and your ambitions and that is very important," replied Elizabeth without hesitation.

Cait was relieved. The understanding and respect Henry had for her was one of the reasons she wanted to marry him. Of course there was more to it than that, but she could hardly expect her mother to address Henry's other feelings for her.

"I had hoped you would like him."

"Well, we do. But the most important thing, of course," said Elizabeth with a smile, "is that *you* do."

"Oh, I do, Ma."

"Then that is all that is needed," said her mother.

Jake had described Henry as a "fine-looking young man, tho' he *was* a tenderfoot," but Gabe was not quite prepared for what he saw when Caitlin introduced him to Mr. Henry Beecham, a friend of hers from Philadelphia. The little hesitation before "friend" told him the whole story, of course.

Mr. Henry Beecham stood there dressed for riding. Well, Gabe supposed it was for riding. He had on winged taupe breeches and a black wool jacket. His cravat was pinned with a gold bar. His black boots had been shined to a high gloss, although just walking across the yard had given them a good coating of dust. Gabe had to turn away for a minute at the sight of the hat on his head. It was an old one of Mr. Burke's, and Gabe had never seen anything funnier than a Stetson topping the Eastern riding clothes.

"Jake is busy, Mr. Hart. I was wondering if you could saddle Snowflake and one of the other horses for us. I want to show Henry the ranch."

Gabe looked at her for a minute and then giving a curt nod, went into the stable. Miss Caitlin Burke had seemed to pride herself on the fact that she groomed and saddled her own horse, but all of a sudden her Eastern "friend" appeared and Gabe became a groom.

Cait had been riding Snowflake, a sweet little mare. There were two other horses available, Red Hawk, an older and rather plodding gelding, and Patch, a three-year-old with lots of fire and a tendency to warm up by bucking the kinks out if you didn't know how to ride him. He could bore Beecham to death with Hawk or watch him be dumped into the dust, thought Gabe with a smile. It was an easy choice, he thought, as he saddled Patch.

Cait had not seen anyone riding Patch but Gabe and since the gelding knew better than to play his tricks on the wrangler, she only knew him as an energetic and pretty goer. She was pleased Gabe hadn't brought out Red Hawk. He had obviously seen that Henry was an experienced rider.

"So this is an Appaloosa," said Henry, when the horses were led out. He approached confidently and Cait began to point out the distinctive markings.

"There are quite a few painted horses in the West, Henry," she explained, "but the Appaloosa is a separate breed, developed by the Nez Perce Indians in Idaho. You can tell them by the white around their eyes and the freckled look of their muzzles . . . and their scraggly tails," she said, pulling Snowflake's ears down as though to keep them from hearing the "insult." "And, of course, the patterns of white on their rumps."

Henry moved around the two animals confidently, getting Cait to tell him more of their history, and Gabe wondered if he'd handle Patch just fine.

They were in the corral, and Cait suggested that they mount there and ride around a little so Henry could get used to the different saddle. She mounted Snowflake and started her off at a walk, looking back over her shoulder at Henry.

"I'd be a mite careful with Patch. He's a little fresh first thing in the morning," Gabe warned as Henry was putting his foot in the stirrup.

"I am sure I'll be fine, man," said Henry, grabbing the saddle horn and swinging his leg over. He had barely gotten his right foot in the stirrup when Patch gave a series of crow hops and then bucked Henry neatly off. Keeping his face straight, Gabe went after the horse, watching Cait dismount and rush over to where Beecham was lying in the dirt.

"Are you all right, Henry?"

"I am fine, Cait," he said, pulling himself up.

"Mr. Hart, I think you have some explaining to do," she demanded as Gabe brought the horse over.

"Now, Cait, Mr. Hart told me the horse might be a bit fresh first thing," said Henry.

"Wal, it was either Red Hawk or Patch, Miss Burke," drawled Gabe. "And Mr. Beecham looked like he could handle a lively horse," said Gabe innocently. "Do you want me to saddle Red Hawk?" he asked.

"Yes," said Caitlin.

"Don't be silly, Cait," said Henry. "Now that I know his little tricks, Patch and I will do fine."

As indeed they did, Gabe had to admit. Beecham was an experienced rider and he conveyed that to the horse this time up. Patch crow-hopped a little, but Henry was ready and controlled him with his legs and hands.

"You can open the corral gate, Hart," Henry called out after a few minutes. "I think we've gotten the kinks out, haven't we, Patch?" he said, patting the horse's neck.

Gabe watched them trot away. Beecham was obviously as good a sport as he was a rider. If he had suspected Gabe of anything, he had not let on.

Gabe was a little ashamed of himself. He had encountered tenderfeet before and like all cowboys, loved playing jokes on them. But Beecham might have been hurt and Gabe hadn't even worried about that. It was that silly outfit that had set him off, he supposed. Or maybe it was that Henry Beecham was obviously someone special to Caitlin Burke.

Ten

Gabe was not able to forget the way Miss Burke's waist felt, so small and soft under his hands. He hadn't felt that way about a woman for some time. After May he had avoided them all, except for the occasional visit to a local whorehouse. He hadn't had much to offer a respectable woman, nor did most cowboys, poorly paid as they were. And he didn't think they had much to offer him. May had doused his kindling interest in women, leaving him distrustful of them and himself. He had always wondered if there had been something he had said or done that had made May think it was all right to approach him.

Then he had finally let someone get past his quiet reserve: Caroline. He had opened his heart to her, had believed in a woman other than his mother and sister for the first time in a long time. She was the good woman he had never thought to find. But that was the problem; she had never been able to see the Regulators as anything but outlaws.

Since Caroline, he'd kept his contacts with women confined to whores. Until now, when here he was, being distracted by a good woman again. And one with Eastern schooling, who was likely going to marry this Mr. Henry Beecham and move away from the uncivilized New Mexico Territory, which demanded more than simple goodness from a man or a woman. He was being ten times a fool to be thinking of the feel of her waist in his hands.

After Henry's first day of desert riding, he appeared at the stable in the same boots and breeches, but minus his stock and wool coat. Gabe was busy with the colts, so Cait and Henry saddled their own horses. Gabe saw them leave and smiled to himself at the change in Beecham's appearance. He had to give the man credit; he learned quickly. Of course being boiled alive in a jacket like he'd worn yesterday would teach any man who wasn't a stubborn jackass.

When they returned, Cait saw that Gabe was just finishing up with the two-year-olds, which meant he would be working with Night Sky next.

"Henry, I want you to meet someone special," she said, leading him over to the corral fence.

"I've already met Mr. Hart, Cait," he said.

"Yes, but you'll see who I mean in a minute." She climbed up to the top rail and reached her hand down, pulling him up after her. Henry didn't need any help climbing fences, of course, but it was an excuse to hold his hand for a minute. She was pleased when he kept her hand in his as they sat there waiting for Gabe to come out.

Cait had imagined this scene many times over during the past six months. But Henry's sharp intake of breath as Gabe led Sky out was not the gasp of admiration of her fantasies. It was a reaction to the scar.

"My God, Cait, what happened to him?"

"That is my horse, Night Sky. Da thinks he was attacked by a mountain lion. I didn't know about it till I got home. But it has healed very well and doesn't affect his gait at all."

Gabe had been working Sky on a lunge line for the past week. He stood in the center of the corral with a long rawhide whip in his hand, snapping it in the ground to keep the horse moving and reinforce his verbal commands.

"He would be a beautiful animal if it wasn't for that scar," said Henry as he watched Sky move from a trot to an easy lope around the ring.

"I think he is still a beautiful animal," replied Cait in a tight little voice. Although she still mourned his unspoiled appearance, Cait had gotten used to Sky the way he was. And every other inch of him was outstanding.

"Why, yes, of course, Cait," said Henry, patting her hand. "He is well-named too," he added, "with that wonderful pattern of white on black."

"It's hard to tell what a colt will look like when he's born, but I was hoping he would turn out like this."

"Is he broken to the saddle yet?"

Cait let go of Henry's hand and gripping the rail on either side of her, said, "The problem is we don't know yet if he can be broken for riding. He is terrified of anyone going anywhere near his back."

After the lunging, Gabe left the whip in the middle of the corral and keeping by Sky's shoulder, walked and trotted him in a circle.

"The horse is very responsive, Cait," Henry reassured her.

When Gabe brought Sky to a halt in front of them, Cait slipped down and pulled a carrot from her pocket. "Here is your treat for the day, Sky."

"He looks about ready to be ridden to me, Hart," said Henry, jumping down next to Cait. Sky took a few steps back, but when Cait reached out her palm, he came up to snuffle at it and then looked at her as if to say: "No more treats?"

"I thought you Western bronc busters just get on and ride till the horse is broke to saddle," continued Henry in a fake drawl.

"Some do," answered Gabe.

"Da doesn't like to break our horses that way, Henry."

"It's quicker, isn't it? And in this case, you'd get an idea if he *can* be broken."

"It may be quicker, but in the long run, you've got a better, more responsive horse if you convince him gently that what you want is really what he wants," Gabe responded, exaggerating his Texas drawl so much that Cait had to bite her lip to keep from smiling.

"Well, I certainly hope he is broken . . . I mean gentled for riding by the end of the summer so we can take him back east with us, eh, Cait? He'll be the talk of Philadelphia," said Henry, putting his arm over Cait's shoulders.

Caitlin had dreamed of bringing Sky back east and riding with Henry down oak-shaded lanes but somehow having him put the dream into words made her feel that the reality would somehow not match the fantasy. For two years she had held Sky in her mind, imagining him growing from colt to two-year-old, and in that dream space he'd been safe. But the real Sky had been running free, had suffered a terrible attack, and might never recover from it. If he could be gentled, did such a creature of the West belong trotting down Eastern bridle paths?

"What do you think, Hart? Can you have Cait riding him by then?"

Gabe looked at Cait and then Henry and said, "I reckon we should know whether he's salvageable by the end of the summer."

Cait hated him for using that word. It reminded her of what was at stake here.

"It would be a shame if we couldn't bring him back with us, Cait," said Henry as they followed Gabe and the horse into the barn.

"Yes, it would, Henry. Why don't you go up to the house while I groom Sky. I'm trying to spend time with him every day to get him used to me again."

"Of course, my dear."

Sky wouldn't allow a brush near his withers or back yet, but by now he would accept a light stroking with a piece of an old shirt of Gabe's. It had taken Gabe hours of patient work to achieve that: holding the cloth out, letting the horse recognize the familiar scent, reaching up, Sky pulling back and then starting all over again.

Cait tried to put all her love and hope in to her brush strokes and the soft touch of the shirt. Had Sky been a complete renegade unable to tolerate anyone, she would almost feel better, she realized. What was so painful was the fact that he did respond to her and trust her and Gabriel Hart . . . but only up to a point.

It was as clear as if he could speak: "I will do this for you and you can come this close to me . . . but not *that*, not that." Cait felt it must be as painful for the horse as for her. She knew he wanted to give in. She believed, with her father, that when a horse and a human worked together in partnership, it was as much a joy for the animal as for the rider.

Gabe Hart was working the way her father would have: giving the horse all the time and space in the world to let him discover that his own need for partnership was stronger than his fear. She could only hope that Sky's desire would be greater than his fear.

"There is a dance in town Saturday, Elizabeth. I was thinkin' that we all might go," said Michael at the supper table that night.

Cait's face lit up. "Oh, Da, that would be wonderful! Henry would get a chance to meet some of our neighbors. We'll dance him off his feet," she added, smiling over at Henry.

"Will Mackie be there, Michael?" Elizabeth asked quietly.

"I suppose he will be. He's made sure that he's welcome in town."

"And his men?"

"I don't think he'll bring them out full force, *a ghra*," said Michael, patting her hand. "I don't know if Cait told you, Henry, but there has been a wee bit of trouble in the valley."

"No, she hasn't mentioned it, Mr. Burke. What kind of trouble?"

"A Mr. Nelson Mackie arrived here from Texas last year. West Texas wasn't big enough for him and he decided he needed some of New Mexico to run his cattle. He's been gradually pushin' the smaller ranchers off one by one. He's after us now."

"How can he get away with that?" demanded Henry. "Surely they would have had some legal recourse?"

"He doesn't do anything that you might call illegal, boyo, not in broad daylight. He offers fair money, people refuse, he offers more, they accept," Michael said dryly.

"What my husband isn't mentioning is what happens between the first offer and the second, Henry," added Elizabeth.

"Of course, Mackie is never directly involved in that," continued Michael. "He just sends his men out to do a little bullying."

"Or he poisons sheep!" said Elizabeth.

"But surely you can complain to the local law enforcement officer," said Henry.

"Em, the local sheriff in this case is owned by Mackie."

"The territorial judges then?"

"Did ye ever hear anything back east of the Lincoln County war, Henry?" asked Michael.

"Yes, it was all over the papers at one point how a group of vigilantes terrorized the county."

"Em, well, ye see, boyo," continued Michael in a deceptively mild tone, "the newspapers didn't always get the story right. Those so-called outlaws were a legally constituted posse."

"But Da," interrupted Cait, "you have to admit that they acted more like vigilantes than lawmen."

"By the end of it, yes, Cait. But when the government is corrupt, even up to the governor's mansion, 'tis a hard thing to know what to do."

"You'd not make excuses for the likes of William Bonney, would you, Da?"

"You know that I am not a violent man, Caitlin. But out here, Henry, sometimes it takes resorting to violence to protect your own."

"Let's not talk of violence, Michael," said Elizabeth. "I doubt it will come to that. And certainly not at Saturday's dance."

"I'm sorry, *a ghra*. I got a bit carried away on the subject."

"I'd like to hear more about your opinions, Mr. Burke. As a lawyer, you can imagine I'm appalled at the thought of lawlessness." Henry paused and cleared his throat. "Perhaps after coffee we might step outside and enjoy a cigar. There is another matter I want your opinion on also."

Cait blushed. Michael glanced over at his wife and then nodded. "I'd be delighted to try a cigar, Henry."

"What do you think of New Mexico now that you've been here awhile?" Michael asked as they walked toward the corral after dessert and coffee.

"It seems like another country," said Henry. "Desolate. But beautiful," he added. "And I am beginning to think that all the stories we hear about the Wild West back east are not that exaggerated."

" 'Tis just not as glamorous as the papers would have ye believe," said Michael with a quick smile.

"I suppose not," Henry admitted. "Especially if men like yourself are unable to get protection from the law when they are threatened. But do you really think it will come to your having to take the law into your own hands? And would you?" Henry asked soberly.

"I hope it will not, for I don't know what I'd be driven to, boyo."

"I hate to think of Caitlin being in danger." Henry hesitated. "It is about her that I wish to speak with you, Mr. Burke."

"I supposed so." Michael lit the cigar Henry had given him and inhaled. The tip glowed red in the dusk. "I don't smoke much," he said as he exhaled a sigh of appreciation, "but I can appreciate a good cigar."

"The fact is, Mr. Burke," Henry began, more nervous than he had expected to be, "that Caitlin and I consider ourselves unofficially engaged to be married."

"So she told us."

"Of course, I wish to make it an official engagement, but that had to wait till I could talk to you." Michael said nothing and Henry rushed into the silence. "I care very much for your daughter, Mr. Burke, and I would like your permission to marry her."

"And take her back to Philadelphia?"

"My work is there, Mr. Burke. And Caitlin's too. I am sure she has told you of her position at the Fayreweather School?"

"She has. When and where were you planning to be married "

"I had hoped . . . we had hoped that Cait could accompany me back in August when I return from California. The wedding would be at Christmastime. We hope that you and Mrs. Burke will be able to come east for it."

"Philadelphia is far away from New Mexico, Henry. This is Cait's home."

"I think she feels equally at home in Philadelphia, Mr. Burke."

"Well, Mrs. Burke and I would never want to stand in the way of my daughter's happiness, Henry."

"Then you give your permission?" asked Henry eagerly.

"If Caitlin loves you and wishes to make her home with you, then Mrs. Burke and I will wish you both happiness," said Michael, extending his hand.

Henry took it and was surprised at what relief he felt.

"Come, lad, let's go in. If I know my daughter, she won't be able to wait much longer."

Indeed, Cait was standing at the door waiting as the two men walked back up to the house.

"Well, Da," she said, giving him a questioning smile.

"Well, Cait, it looks like ye're officially engaged now."

She flung her arms around Michael's neck. "Oh, Da, I knew you'd like Henry."

Elizabeth came up behind her and said: "Now, Cait, don't strangle your father." Cait looked back at her mother with a teary smile. Elizabeth had been teasing her for years for flinging herself at Michael whenever he returned home.

"We must all have a sip of wine to celebrate an occasion like this," said Elizabeth, and Michael looked over at her in warm approval. If it was hard for him to let his daughter go, he could imagine how difficult it was for his wife. Elizabeth took out their best glasses and the small decanter of port they reserved for special occasions.

"To Cait and Henry's happiness," Michael toasted. They all touched glasses and drank down the wine.

"Elizabeth, Henry was tellin' me that he wishes to bring Caitlin back east with him when he returns in August."

Elizabeth lowered her glass and said slowly, "I see."

"And we would marry at Christmas, Mrs. Burke. I hope that you and Mr. Burke can be there. I would expect winter is a quiet time on a ranch."

"Yes," said Elizabeth, "but it is also a hard time to travel because of the weather."

"Then come earlier, Ma," Cait pleaded. "You and Da haven't been east since you came here years ago."

"Not since I was fourteen," Elizabeth replied slowly. "We will see how things go." She paused and then smiled at the two of them. "You can attend this Saturday dance as an engaged couple. The neighbors will be completely surprised."

"Em, maybe the engaged couple would be likin' some privacy, *a ghra*?" suggested Michael. "I am tired from all this excitement. Will ye come upstairs and keep me company?"

Cait blushed furiously as her father led her mother upstairs and Henry laughed as he took her hand and brought her into the parlor. "That was kind of your father, Cait," he said as they sat down on the sofa.

"He may as well have said 'you have my permission to kiss her,'" exclaimed Cait, her protest halfhearted for of course she hoped that was exactly what Henry was going to do.

Henry put his arm around her and drew her closer. Tilting her chin up he leaned down and kissed her. It was a gentle kiss at first, but as Cait responded he made it deeper, pushing her lips apart with his own. Cait opened to him immediately, wanting to drink him in, and he pushed his tongue gently into her mouth. She gasped with surprise and pleasure for this was the longest, most passionate kiss they had shared. It ended too soon when Henry pulled away after only a few moments. Cait gave a sigh of disappointment and Henry smiled down at her.

"We had better be careful, Cait. I don't wish to abuse your parents' trust in us."

Cait respected Henry for his concern, but at the same time wished for more. She might not be that fifteen-year-old who imagined herself as Catherine Earnshaw nor could she quite see Henry as a Heathcliff, she thought, a little smile playing over her lips, but surely one kiss wasn't enough. She felt very bold as she lifted her mouth to his and then a little ashamed when he only brushed her lips lightly and said, with a nervous laugh, "My dear, you are so tempting . . . but we must not."

If she *was* so tempting, then why did he not succumb? she wondered later as she lay in bed remembering their kiss and longing for another . . . and another. Then she chided herself; she respected Henry for his self-control and sense of honor. Her father and mother had trusted them and she admired him for not wanting to betray that trust.

Eleven

All of them headed for town on Saturday: Michael and Elizabeth, Henry and Cait in the wagon and Gabe and Jake riding alongside. The moon was one day short of being full and Henry marveled aloud at how it lit the piñon-covered hills and the road in front of them. The air was redolent with the pungent smell of sage, for it had rained for a short time that afternoon.

Gabe looked around as he heard Beecham's exclamation. He supposed he took it for granted, this unique beauty, now that he had been here for so many years. Maybe because he didn't feel separate from it, but a part of it. For Beecham, it was something to wonder at because he was just passing through. For the Burkes and himself, the country had worked its way into their souls. Though obviously not so deep into Miss Burke's soul if she was able to leave it far behind. He'd heard about the engagement. It came as no surprise, for what else would a man like Henry Beecham be doing at a horse ranch if it weren't for love.

He could understand what Beecham saw in Miss Burke, for she was a very attractive young woman. Gabe shifted in his saddle as he remembered yet again how she had felt under his hands. But what in blue blazes did she see in Beecham, a girl who'd been raised in New Mexico? She'd be leaving at the end of the summer, and with Night Sky, if he was ready. Damn, but he would miss the horse.

Dances were held in the town hall and by the time the Burkes had pulled up, they could hear the sound of the fiddle and the banjo.

"I hope Ramon is here tonight with his mandolin," said Elizabeth as she handed her cake box to Michael and climbed down from the wagon. "I am in the mood for a Spanish waltz."

Ramon was sitting inside and promised Elizabeth several waltzes when she went over to greet him.

Everyone from a thirty-mile radius was there and Cait thought she and Henry would never be free to dance, for once one person had been introduced to him as Miss Burke's fiancé, the news spread and everyone had to come over and check out the Eastern lawyer who was going to take Miss Cait back to Philadelphia.

Finally the fiddle struck up another tune and they all left to form their squares. "Cait, I would ask you to dance," said Henry, "but I am afraid I'd trample all over you. I'd better watch for a while before I risk this."

"The caller gives the directions, Henry," said Cait, trying to persuade him.

"So I have heard. But let's sit out the first one or two, shall we?" Cait hoped her disappointment didn't show. She loved dancing and had looked forward to being swung in Henry's arms.

"Miss Burke, ma'am?"

It was Gabe Hart, who had been just behind them as they tried to make their way through the welcoming neighbors.

"Yes, Mr. Hart?"

"Why don't we show Mr. Beecham how this is done, so's he can join the next set?"

Cait's face lit up. "You wouldn't mind, would you, Henry?"

"Of course not, Cait. I'll watch Mr. Hart and take notes!"

Gabe was dressed in worn but clean dove-colored wool pants and a navy shirt that brought out the blue of his eyes, Cait couldn't help but notice. She soon found out that he was as good a dancer as a rider as they followed the caller's instructions. She was so caught up in the joy of dancing that she only became aware of him when she felt his arm around her waist

for the promenades. And when he swung her. She had
never been swung quite like that before, just about
swept off her feet by his strength. She laughed up at
him at the same time he looked down at her and all
of a sudden it felt like they were standing still while
everything swung around them, the dancers, the floor,
the walls. Cait shook her head to clear it. She was
dizzy from the turning, that was all. Of course that
was all, she thought. But then why did she feel such
a letdown when Gabe returned her to Henry, bowed
and left?

Henry begged to watch just one more before he
attempted anything. He was lucky, for after the next
square came a waltz. Ramon hadn't joined the musi-
cians yet, so it was just the fiddle and a guitar playing
an old Texas waltz.

"May I have *this* dance, Cait? I can promise not to
make a fool of myself with this one."

Cait felt safe in Henry's arms. Although it was a
turning dance, the circles they made were too big to
make her dizzy. And when he pulled her a little closer
and she looked up to smile at him, nothing whirled
around them. All was in the right place, including herself, there in Henry's arms.

"Thank God, Mackie doesn't seem to be here, Michael," said Elizabeth as her husband waltzed her
around the floor.

"Don't be surprised if he makes an entrance later,
Elizabeth," Michael warned her. "Don't worry,
though; he won't be anything but charming in public."

They were lucky that Mackie did not arrive until an
hour later and he was accompanied only by his wife
whom he danced with once and then abandoned in a
corner with some of the wives of his acquaintances
from town. He asked several women to dance and
Elizabeth was fearful he would approach her, but between Michael, Jake, a few neighbors and even a shy
Gabe Hart, she was kept partnered. As was Cait, she
thought with a relieved smile as she watched her
daughter guiding Henry through his first square dance.

Elizabeth hadn't seen Chavez arrive, but she shivered in Michael's arms a few minutes later when she saw him, dressed all in black, leaning against the wall in a corner watching them with those cold green eyes of his. Michael saw him a second later as they turned and he clasped his wife tighter. "Don't ye worry, *a ghra*. He's only here for show, just to remind us."

"I don't know what it is, Michael," said Elizabeth in a low voice as they walked over to the refreshment table after their dance was finished. "It isn't that I am so afraid of him. He is only one man, after all. There is just something about him that brings back the old memories."

Cait pointed out Mackie and Chavez to Henry. "There he is, Henry, with his Mexican hired gun."

Mackie looked like a well-to-do businessman to Henry and it was hard for him to believe that this was the bully who had been terrorizing the valley. Chavez, on the other hand, looked the real villain of the piece.

"Except for his clothes, he doesn't look Mexican, Cait," Henry said after looking Chavez over.

"Maybe he comes from one of the old Spanish families, which would explain his light hair and eyes," Cait explained. "He speaks both English and Spanish perfectly, so maybe his mother was an Anglo," she continued. "Anyway, he is perfectly happy to push any family off their land, Mexican or Anglo."

Chavez didn't join any of the square dances. He wandered over to where Ramon was sitting and chatted with him for a few minutes. And when Ramon picked up his mandolin and motioned for the guitar player to follow, Chavez waited until the waltz had begun before making his move.

Cait had been dying of thirst after all the dancing and Henry had gone to get both of them some punch. The refreshment table was on the other side of the room and once the music started and couples were on the floor, Henry had to make his way around the perimeter to get back to Cait. By the time he did, it was too late. Chavez was already there, bowing politely, taking Cait's hand in his to lead her onto the dance floor.

Cait hadn't known what to do when Chavez appeared in front of her. He was the last person in the world she wanted to dance with. She wanted to refuse him and as rudely as possible. She wanted to spit on his polished boots. But if she gave in to her anger, what might that mean for them afterward? This was a public dance. She could refuse him politely, she supposed. But as she cast her eyes around for Henry and saw how long it would take for him to reach her, she decided she'd rather be on a crowded dance floor with Chavez than alone in a corner with him. So she gave him a cool "yes" and allowed him to lead her out.

"There is something about a Spanish waltz that touches the heart, isn't there, Miss Burke?" said Chavez, breaking the silence she had maintained as they danced.

"I am surprised that you would notice that, Señor Chavez," Cait answered without thinking.

"So you think I am *sin corazon*, señorita?" he said, smiling a smile that did not reach his eyes. "I assure you, I am not."

Cait controlled herself with great difficulty and said with icy politeness, "I spoke without thinking, señor. And I agree with you about the music." She tried to forget about the man who was holding her and imagine it was Henry's arm around her waist, Henry's hand clasped around hers. But oddly enough, it was Gabe Hart who kept intruding. Perhaps she couldn't imagine Henry responding to the sadness in the music, but sensed that Gabe would resonate to it. But she was in the arms of *"El Lobo,"* who had no feelings at all, she remembered as he spoke again.

"You may think me heartless, Miss Burke, but I assure you, the thought of unnecessary suffering troubles me deeply."

The words were innocuous, but the tone in which they were uttered made Cait's blood run cold, and she stumbled, losing her way in the dance.

"Ah, you don't like it either, señorita? I am glad. Perhaps you can convince your father that no one need suffer any accidental harm. I admire your father, you know, señorita."

"Do you, Señor Chavez?" Cait tried to keep her voice from trembling. She would *not* let this man shake her.

"Yes. He is a man who has worked hard for what he has. He has much that he would hate to lose or see come to harm: his land, his horses, his lovely daughter . . ."

Again his words were seemingly only a statement of fact. Her father *had* worked hard. He would hate to lose what he most loved. Any man would. But the undercurrent to Chavez's words was so terrifying that Cait stumbled again and tried to pull herself out of Chavez's arms.

"Oh, no, señorita, our waltz isn't over yet," he said as he held her tight.

Gabe had kept himself away from Caitlin Burke after their first dance. She had felt so right in his arms as he swung her around and their bodies had seemed to fit together perfectly as they'd walked through the "promenade all." He was a fool to be thinking of her. Even if she wasn't engaged to be married, she was still his employer's daughter and he the hired hand.

Of course, to keep away from her he had to know where she was. All evening he had been very aware of her, even when he was flirting with one of the Wilson girls. When Ramon struck up his waltz and Gabe saw Chavez make his move, he abandoned all thoughts of finding himself a partner and stood watching as they danced.

At first, it seemed as if it was harmless enough. Miss Burke had a polite smile on her face and while Gabe didn't think she was enjoying the dance very much, neither did she seem uncomfortable. Then he saw her stumble as Chavez leaned forward to speak to her. Her smile disappeared and Gabe could tell from the way she stiffened in the Mexican's arms that she was trying to control her reaction to whatever he was saying.

He saw Henry with a look of helpless dismay on his face, standing on the other side of the dance floor, holding two glasses of punch. Michael was nowhere to be seen. Gabe didn't think about it, he just made his way over to them and tapped Chavez on the shoulder, saying, "I haven't had a waltz with Miss Burke all night. I wonder if y'all would mind if I cut in?"

Chavez looked at him with those green eyes that revealed nothing and then down at the trembling woman in his arms. "*Muchas gracias,* Señorita Burke. It was a great pleasure to dance with you," he said softly and moved off the dance floor.

Gabe put his arm gently around Cait's waist and taking her hand, wove his fingers through hers without even thinking about it. He could feel her trembling and when she lifted her eyes to his, he could see the mixture of fear and relief. He almost left her there to go after Chavez and beat him senseless for frightening her. He said nothing at first, merely guided her through the waltz, letting the music reach her and relax her.

Cait was shaken to her core. Despite the overt matter-of-factness in his manner, she knew Chavez had been threatening her Da through her. She had never feared anyone before, but Chavez had terrified her. Had he blustered or more obviously bullied, she could have responded. But his subtle innuendoes and the emotionless, cool tone were better weapons than she had encountered before. She had seen Henry standing helplessly by the refreshment table and hadn't seen her parents at all, so she'd had no hope of rescue. When she had heard Gabe Hart's soft Texas drawl, she had wanted to fling herself into his arms. Thank God, she hadn't. She had listened to the music, followed his lead, and let the strains of the guitar and mandolin carry her until her shivering stopped and she could finally look up at her rescuer.

She had found herself gazing into blue eyes that were looking at her with such concern and sympathy that she could have cried right then and there. She lowered her eyes, immediately embarrassed by the intimacy of the moment. It was as if she and Gabe had seen into each other's souls and for a fleeting second of time she felt closer to him than she felt to anyone on earth. Not even with Henry had she experienced such vulnerability.

"I can't thank you enough, Mr. Hart," she whispered so low that Gabe had to lower his head next to hers to hear her. The feeling of his breath on her cheek made her shiver again.

"It looked to me like Chavez was making you mighty uncomfortable, Miss Burke," Gabe drawled.

"He was awful," she said, a sudden surge of anger bringing her back to her old self.

"Was he threatening you?"

"Not directly. So very subtly that one could hardly call it a threat. It is not the words he uses, but his tone and those cold eyes of his. He is very good at what he does, Mr. Hart," she continued with a bitter little laugh. "I can now understand why people have sold out to Mackie."

Gabe said nothing but she could feel his hand press gently against the small of her back and the warmth from his hand radiated through her. She took a deep breath and said: "I don't know what do to, Mr. Hart. If I tell my Da, he will want to go after Chavez. But if I don't tell him . . ."

"I think it best not to, Miss Burke. For now, it is only words and your father is already on his guard. Now it is you that must be on yours."

"I think you are right," said Cait as Ramon struck the last chord of the waltz. "For now anyway."

The other couples were moving off the dance floor, but Gabe and Cait still stood there. His arm was no longer around her waist but their fingers were still interlaced and it was only when Henry came rushing over that they both seemed to realize it and let go.

"Cait, I am so sorry. I could not get over to you to stop that devil. Did he bother you at all?"

"He only said a few words to me, Henry." Which was the truth, she thought ruefully. He didn't need very many. "Truly, it is nothing to be concerned about. And Mr. Hart here came to my rescue."

"Yes, I saw that," Henry replied gratefully. "Thank

you very much, Hart, for taking care of my fiancée when I couldn't.''

Gabe only drawled: "It was nothing. I hadn't had the pleasure of a waltz with Miss Burke and I wanted to congratulate her on her engagement. Congratulations to both of you,'' he added and then, giving Cait a reassuring smile, he left them.

As he walked away, it felt as though all the strength that had been holding her up walked away with him and Cait grasped Henry's arm and said, "Where is that punch you were getting for me, Henry? I am dizzy from all this waltzing.''

"I saw you dancing with Miss Burke, Chavez,'' said Mackie who had followed his man outside after the waltz.

"*Si,* señor. She is a graceful dancer, Señorita Burke. It is too bad we were interrupted by Hart. But not before I had a chance to have a little talk with her,'' he added reassuringly.

"You didn't say anything obvious, did you? Nothing that would implicate me?''

"I am never obvious, señor. I just told her what she already knows: that her father has worked hard for what he has and it would be sad to see anything of his harmed.''

"Good, good, Chavez,'' said Mackie, dropping his cigarette and grinding it out with his boot. "Maybe that is all we will need. A few poisoned sheep and a frightened daughter should convince Burke I mean business.''

"Let us hope so,'' replied Chavez. And oddly enough he meant it, he realized. He wanted Burke to give in to Mackie now. He was a strong man and Chavez admired strong men. But there was a time to bend and this was that time. Bend or be broken, Señor Burke, he thought to himself. I can help break you, but for some reason I don't want to. I just want you gone, together with that wife of yours.

Twelve

Usually Cait slept late on the morning after a dance, but on this Sunday she awoke at dawn after only a few hours of sleep and was unable to go back to sleep. As the sun rose, it threw a shaft of light through her window that fell on one of Serena's weavings. It had been a gift for one of Cait's birthdays. It was unusual in that it was not done in a geometric pattern, but was a picture woven into the wool. There were mountains in the background and in the foreground a small house and three people and a horse in front of it. It was her Da and Ma and herself and Frost, Da's old mare. Serena and Antonio had only visited the ranch once, years ago, and it was after that Serena wove her present. When she was younger, Cait had always knelt to say her prayers at bedtime and she had always looked up at that picture when she prayed for her parents and herself. The picture made her feel safe and it was one of the few things from home that she had brought to school with her. If only she could be that little girl again, the one Serena had woven holding hands with her Ma and Da. Times had not always been easy for them on the ranch, but there had always been enough to eat and she had been surrounded by love.

The love was still there, of course. But could love alone keep them all safe when men like Chavez and Mackie threatened? They'd have to kill her Da to get him off the ranch, she thought, and then said a quick prayer, "Please God, keep my Da safe."

She'd come home thinking she'd found a clear purpose: she would be the best wife to Henry and the best teacher Fayreweather's had ever hired. She'd known it wouldn't be easy to leave, but she'd thought she'd be leaving it as it always was. How could she leave with Henry if nothing was settled? Or even worse, if things were settled the way Mackie wanted them?

They'll have to give it up, she said to herself. Da won't sell and they won't risk out and out murder, please God. Mackie will just have to be satisfied with what he has now.

"You look tired, Cait," said Henry when she came down later for breakfast.

"She looks like a young woman who didn't sit down for one dance, doesn't she, Elizabeth?" joked Michael.

Cait gave him a tired smile and said, "You're right, Da, it was a wonderful evening."

"Except for your dance with that Mexican," said Henry sympathetically.

Cait gave him an angry glance, and his eyes showed his hurt surprise. "I'm sorry, Henry," she whispered. It wasn't his fault, after all, for she hadn't told him to say nothing.

"What Mexican, Cait?" her father asked.

"It was nothing, Da. Señor Chavez surprised me by requesting a waltz. It didn't seem wise to offend him so I said yes. And it was a short dance, because Mr. Hart cut in."

"I was caught by the refreshments or I would have rescued her, sir," explained Henry, his face pink with embarrassment that a hired hand had done what he should have as Cait's fiancé.

"There was nothing to rescue me from, Henry," said Cait, trying to make light of the whole thing. "Señor Chavez was polite and acted the complete gentleman."

" 'Acted' is probably the right word," said Michael, "for there is no one further from being a gentleman than Juan Chavez. You are *sure* he did nothing to upset you, Cait?"

"Absolutely, Da."

"I still don't like it. And I don't want you ridin' alone, even on the ranch. I know ye hate feelin' hemmed in, but humor yer old Da for now, will ye? Ye'll be out of it soon enough when Henry comes back for you."

Michael didn't seem to notice that Cait had not protested, but Elizabeth did and she wondered if her daughter had given them the whole truth. She would happily shoot Nelson Mackie through the heart, right then and there. He represented everything that was wrong in the West: the uncontrollable greed that had forced the Navajo and other tribes off their land. Now that the Indians had been confined to reservations, the likes of Mackie were after the small landholders. She had heard of cattle corporations in Wyoming and Montana and knew that men like Catron and Mackie were not one of a kind. But she had never dreamed their evil would penetrate the peace of the valley.

It was odd, she thought, that it had not been Chavez in the sights of her imaginary rifle. Certainly a man who served evil had to be evil himself. But she was more disturbed by him than furious at him. Her fury was roused more by Mackie's hypocrisy. He loosed men like Chavez on innocent folk and stood back until the dirty work was done. Then he took what he wanted. Well, he was not going to win this time, she thought. The only way he would walk into her home was over her dead body. She had already lost her parents and her brother to such violence and greed. Nightmares or no nightmares, she would not let it happen again.

When Jake handed her their mail two days later, Elizabeth was surprised to find a letter addressed to Gabe Hart. The return address said S.E. Hart, Amarillo, Texas. This must be from his sister, she thought, and was happy to see that Gabe had someone who cared about him. There were so many young men who worked as cowboys and wranglers out west, thought Elizabeth sadly. Making almost nothing in daily wages, riding for one outfit and then another. She and Michael had hired one from time to time when they needed help with the shearing or repairs around the ranch. They'd work hard, say "yes, ma'am, no, ma'am," to her with great respect and ride on. When he had first arrived, Gabe Hart had seemed no different. But as she watched him work with the horses and had gotten used to his quiet ways, she'd begun to think that he was one of the rare ones, who wanted to find a place to settle down. Perhaps even wanted a woman to love.

Elizabeth laughed to herself. Now she was getting carried away by the romantic side of her nature.

Her daughter was out watering the flowers with the last of the dishwater and Elizabeth waved the letter at her. "Cait, could you do me a favor and bring this to Mr. Hart?"

"Yes, Ma." Cait brought the bucket over and wiped her hands dry on her old dress. She took the envelope from her mother and looked it over curiously.

"Now, don't be nosy, just bring it down to him," teased Elizabeth.

"Yes, Ma. Right away, Ma," responded Cait in an obedient child's voice.

"I think it is from his sister," Elizabeth confided.

"Ma! Just who is being curious, I want to know."

"Oh, hush, I just looked at the return address."

Cait read it aloud. "S.E. Hart. Maybe it is not his sister but a wife he left in Texas and never told us about," Cait said, with a laugh and headed for the barn. It was a joke, of course. She was sure Gabe Hart had no wife and he had already talked about his sister. And why should she care anyway, whether Gabe Hart had a woman in his life?

Gabe was in the tack room oiling the bridles. A thin shaft of sunlight made his hair shine that bright silver that was so striking against his tan.

"A letter came for you, Mr. Hart," Cait said from the tack room door.

He looked up from his work with a hunger in his eyes that surprised and moved her. She handed him his letter and watched as he turned it over and read the postmark. A rare smile lit his face. "It is from my little sister," he said. "She always manages to track me down."

"She must have had some help, Mr. Hart, unless she has herself a private detective," Cait teased.

Gabe laughed. "You're right, Miss Burke. I always make sure she can find me." He looked down at the letter longingly and Cait said quickly, "I hope your sister is well, Mr. Hart," and left him to his reading. She was surprised at the wave of sympathy that had come over her when she saw how important his sister was to him.

Sadie was well, thank goodness, thought Gabe. And so were the boys. Though, as she said, they were no longer boys but young men and quite able to survive on their own for a month or so. Which was why she was writing:

> I have saved enough money from my teacher's pay to do a little traveling. I've missed you all these years, Gabe. It isn't right that we haven't seen each other for so long, so I'm coming to visit you whether you like it or not! Well, of course I hope you want to see me as much as I want to see you. I'm planning to take the stage from Amarillo and should arrive in two weeks' time. I can pay for my own room and board, so if you find me a place in town I won't crowd you any.
>
> Your loving sister,
> Sadie

Sadie coming to visit! He hadn't seen her in ten years. She'd be a woman grown now, a woman who'd been working hard, teaching and keeping house for the boys. Did he want to see her as much as she wanted to see him? Lord, did he want to see her. She'd always made him feel that he did have family who cared for him even though he had to leave. Even though he'd never gone home.

And even if he didn't want to see her, it was too late, he realized with a grin. Sadie had sent the letter just so it would reach him ahead of time, but not so as he could write and tell her not to come! So he guessed she hadn't changed much, that little sister of his. Now where was she going to stay? He'd have to get working on that right away.

Elizabeth was just setting her bread to rise when she heard a knock on the door. She put a damp towel over the loaves and wiping her hands on her apron, went to the door.

"Why, hello, Gabe." She was surprised to see him in the middle of the day, for he usually kept himself busy with the horses and other chores until suppertime. Elizabeth fought down her sudden panic. "Nothing is wrong, is there, Gabe?"

"Oh, no, ma'am. I am sorry to disturb you like this, but I need some advice."

Elizabeth, who hadn't even realized she'd been holding her breath, let it out with a sigh. "Of course. Come in, Gabe, and sit down. I was just about to have some lemonade. Would you like some or would you rather coffee?"

"Lemonade sounds just fine, ma'am."

"It's in the cellar. I'll be right back."

Gabe sat down at the kitchen table. There was a jelly glass full of flowers from the garden in the middle next to a brown pottery bowl full of sugar. The smell of bread rising permeated the air and he was reminded of his own mother's kitchen. She hadn't had a garden, but there had always been wildflowers or "weeds," as his father always teasingly called them, on the table.

"Here you are, Gabe. It keeps pretty cool down in the root cellar," said Elizabeth as she poured them both a glass. She sat down opposite Gabe and said, "Now, what can I help you with, Gabe?"

Gabe had just taken a sip of his lemonade which was so tart he thought his lips would be drawn back into his throat. He coughed and without thinking, said, "I'd love some sugar for this, Mrs. Burke."

Elizabeth sipped hers, made a face, and exclaimed, "My goodness, Caitlin made this this morning before her picnic with Henry. Obviously, she was a little distracted," Elizabeth added ironically as she got up and got a spoon. "Here, Gabe, take as much sugar as you like."

"I reckon having a fiancé visit is a little distracting, ma'am," he drawled.

"For all of us! Now, what besides sweetening your lemonade can I do for you?" she asked with a smile.

"That letter I got today, it was from my sister, Sarah Ellen. Sadie."

"Yes, I remember you mentioned a sister back in Texas. And two young brothers."

"Yes, ma'am. My brothers are old enough to do for themselves for a while. And Sadie, well, we haven't seen each other since I left home . . . anyways, it looks like she's coming for a visit!"

"Why, Gabe, that's wonderful," said Elizabeth as a slow smile lit his face.

"Even if it weren't, it's too late to stop her," he said, his smile even bigger. "But I need to find a place for her to stay while she's here and I thought you might have an idea."

"Well, there is the Widow Smith, just outside of town. She takes in boarders . . . but why shouldn't she stay right here with us?"

"Oh, no, ma'am, I can't impose on you like that."

"Nonsense. It's no imposition. And it will be a pleasure to have another woman around. We won't outnumber the men but at least your sister will even the odds!"

Gabe was still hesitant. "It doesn't seem right for me to have my personal concerns intruding on you, ma'am."

Elizabeth put her glass down and looked him in the eye. "Gabe, *our* personal concerns have certainly affected you. This business with Mackie could get dangerous. Michael tells me you are willing to stay no matter what happens. You didn't have to take on our problems. The least we can do for such loyalty is offer hospitality to your sister."

Gabe's face flushed with pleasure and embarrassment. "Thank you, Mrs. Burke." He hesitated and then continued, "Don't make too much of my staying. I love working with the horses and I like working for Mr. Burke."

"And it gives you a chance to stop running?"

"I'm not on the run, ma'am. I told Mr. Burke that right off."

"I know, Gabe, and I shouldn't pry. But from what you've said, you've been wandering for some time."

Gabe was quiet for a minute and then said, "I had planned to settle down some years back, Mrs. Burke. Build up my own herd. Even marry."

"I shouldn't have asked, Gabe," said Elizabeth when she saw how hard it was for him to talk of such matters.

"No, if I am to stay and if my sister is here, then you have a right to know. I worked in Lincoln for Mr. Tunstall."

"I see," said Elizabeth quietly.

"It all seemed real clear in the beginning, Mrs. Burke. And I am not ashamed to admit that I rode with the Regulators for a while. Of course, things weren't so clear by the end."

"So you rode with Billy the Kid," said Elizabeth, horror and awe combining in her voice.

"William Bonney? Yes, ma'am." Gabe gave her an ironic smile. "The newspapers sure did love him! He wasn't that bad to begin with. Real wild, but not real bad."

Elizabeth heard the despair and anger in Gabe's voice as he continued. "They murdered Tunstall in cold blood, Mrs. Burke. And the legally constituted authorities from the governor on down were corrupt." Gabe hesitated. "She could never see that."

"She?"

"The girl I was going to marry. Oh, I guess I can understand it now. Caroline hated the violence. She couldn't really believe that the law could be so corrupt. She came to hate me in the end."

Elizabeth clasped her hands together and trying to keep her voice calm, said, "Do you think it will come to that with Mackie, Gabe?"

"I hope not. Mackie seems the same sort of snake as Thomas Catron, but a smaller one. I think he'll have to be satisfied with the piece of the valley he's already got."

"I love this country, Gabe," said Elizabeth. "There is something about its harsh beauty that speaks to me. But I hate its violence," she continued passionately. "I lost my family in a Comanchero massacre, a husband to the Navajo . . . We've worked so hard here, Gabe. Michael has broken his back to make this place what it is. Things were peaceful, though. But it seems like the attack on Night Sky was the beginning of everything. Perhaps it is best that Caitlin is going back east. She'll be out of this, at least." Elizabeth looked up at him and said with a half laugh, half sob, "I *am* sorry to go on like that."

"It's all right, ma'am. I hate violence myself, believe it or not. One thing I can say, ma'am, is that I am *good* at it when being good is necessary, not that I'm proud of that. If it helps you and Mr. Burke, then I'm glad of it."

"Thank you for staying, Gabe. I hope Sadie's visit isn't spoiled by any trouble."

"Men like Mackie work slow at first, Mrs. Burke. I'll hustle Sadie out of here if it begins to get bad. Thank you for putting her up."

"It is no problem, Gabe. She can have Henry's room; he's leaving for California in a few days."

"He seems like a good man, Mr. Beecham," said Gabe politely as he got up from the table.

"Yes, a man who is committed to the law. Well, back east it is easier to be," said Elizabeth. "Cait will be safe with him."

Gabe walked back to the barn thinking about Henry Beecham and Caitlin Burke. What a difference between mother and daughter, he thought. The East had been home to Mrs. Burke, but she had let her heart open to this bleak and beautiful land. Yet Caitlin Burke who had grown up here was able to leave it in order to be safe with her Mr. Henry. Henry would keep her safe all right, thought Gabe as he grabbed Night Sky's halter and walked down to the near pasture to whistle him in. I'll bet he even kisses safe. Miss Caitlin Burke would not be safe with me and she'd know that right off the first time I ever kissed her.

Thirteen

"The horse seems to be coming along very well, Mr. Hart," said Henry. He and Cait had returned from their ride just as Gabe was finishing up with Sky. He led the horse over to them so that Cait could give him his usual treat.

"He's doing better than I ever thought he might," agreed Gabe. "I've gotten him to stand for a light going over with my old shirt. I can even leave it on his back for a minute or two. Of course, it's as light as a feather, so don't get your hopes up, Miss Burke," added Gabe as he saw Cait's face light up.

"It is a shame I can't see you ride Sky before I leave, Cait," said Henry after Gabe led the horse away. "But I suppose it will take a few more weeks before he'll even take a saddle."

Later, Cait would want to blame Henry for putting the idea in her head. But it really wasn't his fault. It was all hers. That night she dreamed she was riding Night Sky with no saddle or even a blanket. They were cantering down the road toward Oak Canyon and he was as happy to have her on his back as she was to be on it.

When she awoke, she couldn't shake off her dream and Henry's words came back to her. He was leaving the day after tomorrow. Why *couldn't* she ride Sky for him? She knew it was a crazy thought, but she just couldn't get it out of her head. Maybe Gabe was wrong. Maybe he was going too slowly with the horse. He *was* her horse, after all. He knew her and trusted her as well as he did Gabe Hart. It would be risky, of course, but what a glorious risk, if she could ride him for Henry as she had ridden in her dream.

Something had been building in her since the dance. She'd been scared by Chavez, she who had never feared anyone in her life. Henry was going to come back and take her away from all this. He was a good, safe man, was Henry Beecham. She was lucky to have him. Lucky to love him. Yet something in her wasn't satisfied. She wanted something that she couldn't even put a name to. Not danger, exactly, or at least, not the sort that Chavez threatened. She wanted to be one with the wild spirit of Sky, just as she had in her dream. Henry was leaving in the morning. She would spend some time with Sky today, maybe see how he took to her rubbing him down with the old shirt. If this craziness still had hold of her tomorrow morning, well, then, she'd ride him.

Maybe she wouldn't have gone through with it if Gabe hadn't come into the barn while she was brushing Sky. She had the piece of old shirt in her hand and was working her way lightly down his neck. She could feel the shivers that ran through the horse, but Gabe had him gentled enough that he didn't actually step away from her.

"I don't mind you brushing him, Miss Burke, but for now, I think I'm the only one who should be laying that shirt across his back," he said in a low voice.

"Don't worry, I wasn't going anywhere near his back," said Cait self-righteously.

Now that's a damn lie, thought Gabe as he saw her color up. But he didn't want to push her any more than he wanted to push the colt. He could understand her impatience. Somedays, his own threatened to take over and he would be sweating more with the effort to control it than from the work he was doing with Night Sky.

"I know how much you want to see him gentled before you leave, Miss Cait," he said in a sympathetic voice.

"Yes, but I am sure you are right, Mr. Hart. It is better not to rush things," she said sweetly.

It took everything she had to answer him that way. She was annoyed that he had caught her and all her initial jealousy at his position on the ranch flowed back. She didn't know what it was about Gabe Hart, but he raised such *feelings* in her. Feelings that made her want to hit him. Or kiss him. No, of course, she didn't want to kiss him, she thought, appalled at the thought. She didn't want to kiss anyone but Henry. She wanted to kiss Henry wildly and passionately. And she wanted to ride Night Sky.

Cait was up and dressed before dawn the next morning. She crept quietly downstairs in her stocking feet, only slipping on her boots after she sat down on the porch steps. She was shaking inside with excitement and fear and the sense that she might be doing something very foolish. But she was being driven to it by something in herself she couldn't begin to understand, so she just took a deep breath and went into the barn to get Sky's halter and a bucket of oats.

She gave Gabe's distinctive whistle and the horse came trotting over from the back pasture, stopping a few feet away with a quizzical look in his eye as if to say: "You're not Gabe?" but when she rattled the bucket, he came over to her eagerly. She talked to him softly as he ate and scratched his ears and then slipped the halter on before he knew it. She breathed into his nostrils, the way Da had taught her and Sky stood quietly, gazing into her eyes calmly. She led him down to the corral, walking close to his shoulder and felt a great joy as they moved together as one. She could feel the connection with him. He *wanted* to follow her. She was sure he wanted her to be the first one to ride him.

She had decided to do it quickly. No slow strokes with the old shirt. She would lead him to the fence, tie him loosely, climb up on the rails, and then let herself down slowly until she was on his back. If he stood still, she would untie the halter rope and ride him around the corral.

She had him tied and she had just climbed the fence

when she saw the barn door open and Gabe emerge, barefoot and shirtless.

"No," he shouted just as she lowered herself to Sky's back and then the world exploded.

Gabe hadn't slept well that night and he was awake earlier than usual, feeling he'd been run over by a herd of cattle. His mouth was as dry as a bone, and he got up quietly so as not to wake Jake and pulled his pants on over his bare ass. He needed to pee and then he'd get a drink from the pump back of the barn.

Just as he had filled his cupped hand he heard what sounded like a horse moving around the corral. He frowned, still not thinking clearly, but sure that none of them should be there.

He came around the side of the barn slowly and was still so sleepy that he didn't immediately take in the scene in front of him: Night Sky tied to the fence and Caitlin Burke just about ready to slide her leg over him.

He'd never been so angry in his life. Here he'd worked months with the horse and she was going to wreck it all in a few seconds.

But he yelled too late to stop her. As soon as Sky felt her skirt brush across his back, even before he felt her full weight, he went crazy. As he watched, Gabe realized that the horse was not trying to shake off Caitlin Burke. He was back wherever he'd been attacked and was mad with fear, trying to shake off a mountain lion.

It was worse because Cait had tied him and she was lucky that she was bucked off high and to the side, otherwise she might have been caught under his hooves, which plunged down again and again as though he was trampling his enemy into the dirt.

Gabe was frozen for a second and then ran to where Cait lay in the dirt. He was terrified and when he reached her side, knelt down, afraid to touch her in case something was broken. When she opened her eyes, he saw a terrible fear come into them as she struggled for air. At first he thought she had broken a rib and punctured a lung and then he realized she'd just had the breath knocked out of her. All his anger returned, strengthened by his fear.

He stood up and said in a shaking voice, "Damn you to hell and back, Miss Burke, you deserve to have more than the wind knocked out of you." He turned his back on her and went over to see what he could do with her horse.

Cait wanted to cry, but she could hardly get her breath to breathe, much less sob. She felt like a collapsed balloon and was sure she would die before her lungs could expand again. But finally her attempts at breathing succeeded and she sucked in air gratefully. She moved everything gently. Nothing seemed to be broken, so she pulled herself up. At first the ground rocked beneath her feet and she had to drop to her knees until the dizziness went away.

Then she lifted her head and looked at what she'd done. Sky was standing there soaking wet, his ears laid back and his cheeks rubbed raw from where he'd pulled at the halter to get free. Gabe was five feet away from him, holding his hands out as though in supplication, murmuring softly. Every time he tried to get closer, Sky pulled away, trying to break free.

The tears poured down Caitlin's face. What on earth had she done? Whatever had possessed her? She'd known how to handle a horse better when she was ten. For the first time in her life, she had terrified a horse, a horse that she loved, ruined maybe for good and why? She didn't even know the answer to that question.

"Don't come near him," Gabe muttered harshly as she came up behind him. Or me, he wanted to add, or I just might shake you until your teeth rattle.

He tried once more to get close to the horse, but it only made Sky roll his eyes with fear and pull against the rope again. There is no sense in him rubbing his cheeks bloody, thought Gabe, and he turned back to Cait, grabbing her arm and pulling her toward the fence.

"Climb over the fence, Miss Cait, and go get yourself washed up."

He stood there like an avenging angel. But Gabriel was a messenger, thought Cait irrationally as she stared at him from the other side of the fence. His hair was all elf-locks, he was barefoot and barechested. His face was as cold as she imagined the devil's would be.

"I am so sorry, Mr. Hart," she whispered.

"Tell him that, Miss Burke. And hope that sometime soon he'll listen to you," said Gabe, and he walked off into the barn.

Fourteen

Cait was sitting huddled in the kitchen as dirty as she was when she left the corral when Elizabeth came down to stoke the stove. Usually Michael did this for her but he was still asleep and she'd been awakened by the tail end of a nightmare. She was getting more used to them and was only grateful that this one had come early in the morning, for it was hard to get back to sleep with those images playing in front of her eyes.

"Cait! You are up early," Elizabeth said with surprise in her voice, and then concern. "Why is your riding skirt all dirty? Were you thrown?"

"It was Sky." Cait looked up at her mother with such agony in her eyes that Elizabeth's heart turned over.

"Sky? Did he pull you off your feet?" Elizabeth was trying to imagine what the horse could have done.

"I tried to ride him, Ma."

"Why, I didn't think Gabe had him ready yet . . ." her mother said slowly.

"He wasn't ready to be ridden, but I tried anyway and he threw me."

"Are you all right, Cait?"

"I am fine," she replied in a shaky voice. "Just had the wind knocked out of me. And I'm sure that Mr. Hart would like to knock it out of me again."

Elizabeth reached out and brushed some of the caked mud from her daughter's hair. "But why, Cait? You are almost as good as your Da at handling horses."

Cait flung herself into her mother's arms and sobbed out, "Oh, Ma, I don't know. I don't know why

I did it. And I am so sorry I did and I can't tell Sky that, he won't understand that I didn't mean to scare him."

"Come," said Elizabeth and she took Cait by the hand and led her to the parlor sofa where she sat down with Cait next to her. She put her arm around her daughter's shoulders and when she drew her close, Cait's sobs began again.

This time, Elizabeth let her cry. There was something deeper in this than Night Sky, though that mistake was certainly enough to make anyone cry, thought Elizabeth. If Cait had ruined Gabe's weeks of work . . . well, she didn't want to think about it.

Finally her daughter was still. "A lot has happened this summer, Cait," she observed gently.

"Oh, Ma, everything seemed so clear in Philadelphia."

"What seemed clear?"

"That I loved Henry and want to make my home in the East. That I could be as good a teacher as Mrs. Weld."

"And isn't that still clear? You and Henry have seemed happy together."

"I *do* love Henry. But when I came home, everything had changed. Pa had hired Mr. Hart and let him work with my horse. I was so jealous, Ma."

"I know."

"But I thought I was over it. And then Mackie. How can I leave you and Da? I'll worry myself sick back east knowing you are in danger. And then Henry came and I thought that when we were officially engaged, I would feel safe. But nothing feels safe anymore," she cried.

"Do you love Henry, Caitlin?" Elizabeth asked softly.

"I do, Ma. He is smart and easy to talk to. He will probably be a judge himself someday," she added proudly.

"Do you love him because he is a brilliant lawyer?"

"No, he's also handsome and kind, and he loves me. But . . ."

"But what, Cait?"

"We've done some kissing," she said in a low voice.

"I should hope so!" laughed Elizabeth.

"I *love* kissing Henry," she added almost defiantly.

"Thank goodness," her mother teased.

"Ma!"

"You haven't done anything more than kissing, have you?"

"No and that is what confuses me. I *want* to. But I am not sure Henry does. Oh, I guess it is only because he is so much a gentleman and wants to protect me. . . ."

"But you wish he wouldn't."

"I wish . . . oh, Ma, I know this sounds like I am fifteen again, but I wish he had a little more wildness in him."

Elizabeth was quiet, and Cait continued. "It is not Henry's fault, really, it is me. I just am feeling so torn between loving home and loving Henry. Maybe I am just 'Calico Cait.' That's what the girls at school used to call me at first. I just don't know where I belong anymore."

Elizabeth prayed that she would find the right thing to say to her daughter.

"Are you disgusted with me, Ma?" Cait asked anxiously.

"Oh, Caitlin, I could never be that. You were very wrong to ride Sky, but I think I understand why you did it. You have come to one of the most important times in a woman's life, a time when she moves away from all she has known, from her parents and the home of her childhood, and begins to build a life of her own. It is an exciting time, but it is also terrifying, for if you look behind you, you can see everyone and everything that has been a part of your life, but when you look ahead, there you are, standing with your hand in someone else's, with no way of knowing what is to come."

"I think that is what frightens me," whispered Cait.

"So you can't look back and you can't look ahead. You can only look to the one you love who stands next to you, Cait. If you are lucky enough to have found the right person, then he is your home and the future is what you will create together."

"But how can anyone know for sure if it is the right person?"

Elizabeth laughed. "Oh, Cait, I don't know what to tell you. You are different from me so the right person for you would be a very different one than for me." She hesitated, not wanting to influence her daughter, then said: "But I do believe that the love between you should include both affection and passion."

"I certainly have affection for Henry and he for me," said Cait thoughtfully.

"And you are a passionate woman, Caitlin. About everything," added Elizabeth. "Horses, books, the beauty of your surroundings, wherever you are."

Cait was quiet for a moment and then said, with a glimmer of a smile on her face, "Ma, if I had been raised a real Catholic, like Da, I think I'd have to go to confession."

"And what would you have to confess?" asked Elizabeth with an answering smile.

"I love Henry. But I want him to kiss me in a very different way than he does. The way I imagine Gabe Hart might kiss me," she added in such a low voice that Elizabeth had to strain to hear her. "Not that he ever has or would," Cait added quickly. "But I have *wanted* him to. Is that very awful of me? And I don't even know if I like him. He certainly doesn't like me, especially not after this morning."

Elizabeth smiled over her daughter's head, then gave her a hug. "Gabriel Hart is a very handsome man, Cait. If I were twenty years younger and a single woman, I think I'd be wondering what it would be like to kiss him too. There is a touch of wildness in him, I think, though he seems quiet and shy."

"Shy? Gabe Hart wasn't very shy this morning, I can tell you."

"Oh, I can imagine he told you what he thought of you, but I don't think he opens up his heart to anyone. I am glad his sister is coming for a visit," Elizabeth added thoughtfully. "But, Cait, it is quite all right to feel a stirring of desire and curiosity when you see a handsome, interesting man. Even if you are engaged, or even married. The important thing is that you also have that between you and Henry."

"What if I am not sure we will, Ma?"

"Henry is a very proper young man from the East. He is treating you the way he would want his sister to be treated, I am sure that is all. But if it is not . . ."

"If it is not?"

"You know I was married before I met your Da, Cait."

"Yes."

"I've talked a little about Thomas over the years. He was such a good man, Thomas Woolcott, Cait. He saved my life in many ways by marrying me and we had a good marriage. Had he lived and had your Da not come along, we would have continued to be happy with each other. I would never have known how much we both were missing. We had great affection for each other, Cait, but no real passion. One can have a good marriage without it. I know that. But I would like you to have both. I think you will only be happy if you have both."

"How will I know, Ma?"

"You have some time still. Henry will be back from California in a few weeks and you will have three months in Philadelphia before the wedding."

"Oh, Ma, I don't know if I can leave you."

"It is a part of growing up, Cait. And your father and I would never want you to stay only out of fear for our safety. You have to trust that we can take care of our lives just as we trust that you can make the right decisions for yours."

They both heard Michael come down at the same time. "Oh, Ma, what will I tell Da about Sky?"

"The truth. But you know he will be angry."

"He will be furious."

"You have to face him sometime. Come and help me with breakfast, but first go wash your face and change into clean clothes."

Cait slipped up the stairs and Elizabeth went into the kitchen.

"I was wondering where you had gone, *a ghra,*" said Michael, concern in his eyes. "Did you have another nightmare?"

"Yes, Michael, but I woke up before the worst parts, thank God. I came down to start the fire, but I was distracted by Cait."

"Did I just hear her go up the stairs? What is she doing up so early?"

"She will tell you herself, Michael. But I want you to promise me you won't be too hard on her."

"Why, what can she have done that is so bad, Elizabeth?" His eyes widened. "She and Henry . . . they haven't . . . ?"

"No, Michael, they haven't," responded Elizabeth with a soft laugh. "Though I almost wish they had . . ."

"What are ye sayin', *a ghra?*"

"It seems that Henry has been very much the gentleman."

"Thanks be to God for that," said Michael with relief.

"Yes, but I want Cait to have what we have, Michael."

Michael blushed. "Of course, and so do I. I just don't want to be thinkin' about it!"

When Cait came back down, she had scrubbed her face and changed into an old calico dress. Her cheek had been scraped and bruised from her fall, however, and there was nothing she could to do cover it. Her father noticed it immediately.

"Whatever happened to your face, Cait?"

"I took a fall, Da."

"You are all right?" he asked worriedly.

"Yes, Da. I am all right." She took a deep breath. "But I am afraid Sky is not."

"Sky?"

"I tried to ride him this morning, Da. I wanted to show Henry that I could. I guess I wanted to show Mr. Hart and maybe even you that I could. I *wanted*

Sky to let me ride him, Da. I wanted to know that he trusted me more than anyone else."

Michael's face was set and stern as he took in what she was telling him. As he opened his mouth to speak, Elizabeth touched him gently on the arm, as if to remind him of his promise.

"It is not up to a horse to prove that *he* trusts *you,* Cait. It is up to you to prove that you are trustworthy. *That* is what makes him your horse. And only that."

Her father had never spoken so harshly to her, and she felt it deeply. What made it worse was that every word he spoke to her was true.

"I know that, Da," she answered, with her eyes lowered in shame. "I am so sorry."

"Where is the horse?"

"I tied him to the fence, Da, to mount him. Mr. Hart could not get close enough to untie him," she confessed, her face red.

Michael turned on his heel and was out the door before she knew it.

"Oh, Ma, what can I do?"

"I think you must go out and face what you have done, Cait."

She wanted her mother to take her in her arms. She wanted Henry to come down and tell her he understood. She did not want to go out and see her father's face when he saw Sky. It was the hardest thing she'd ever done, but Cait made herself go out the door and down to the corral.

Sky was still where she'd left him but there was a bucket of water and a small pile of hay in front of him, so Gabe Hart must have been able to get close enough to leave them there, thank God, if not to untie him. Michael was standing a few feet from the fence, murmuring to himself and the horse in Irish. Sky's ears would prick forward as if to listen, and then flatten again if Michael tried to come any closer. The horse was still wet with sweat and as Cait got near, she could see how raw the halter had rubbed him.

"*Dia,*" said Michael, with such disappointment in

his voice that Cait thought her heart would break. "Look what you have done, Caitlin."

What was the point of saying she was sorry again? She was determined not to cry, but she couldn't help it and the tears poured down as she tried not to make a sound. But she couldn't help it as a sob escaped her. Michael turned and the sight of his daughter's misery melted him and he enfolded her in his arms and let her cry against his chest.

"The worst thing, Da, is I know I was wrong, but I can't change anything now," Cait said when she finally stopped crying. "Do you think I've ruined him forever?"

"I don't know, Cait."

"I just wish I could *talk* to him, explain that I would never hurt him. Say I'm sorry to him, like I can say I am sorry to you."

" 'Tis only by our actions we can talk to them, Caitlin. Gabe has been having a slow, quiet conversation with Sky for weeks now."

"But I know he trusted me too, Da. I've been grooming him and walking him."

"I'm sure he did. But trust is such a delicate thing, Cait. Especially when you've been hurt as bad as this one was."

The barn door opened and Gabe stepped out, his old shirt in his hand. When he saw Michael and Cait he came out through the gate and walked over to them.

If Cait had wanted to hide before, right then she wished for the power to make herself invisible. Though she supposed she might as well be, for Gabe talked to her father as though she wasn't there.

"Good morning, Mr. Burke. You've heard what happened, then?"

"Yes, Gabe, Cait told me."

Hart's eyes didn't even flick over to her.

"Well, he's let me bring him water and something to eat. I'm going to try to wipe him down now. And maybe even walk him around a little if he'll let me."

He would have had every right to blame her,

thought Cait, but he didn't. He didn't even mention her folly directly and instead went straight to what was important now: Sky.

"Good luck, boyo. Come, Cait, yer ma's probably got breakfast ready for us. 'Twill be easier for Gabe to work alone."

It was almost as hard to go back into the house as it had been to come out. Cait wanted to watch and see if Gabe could get Sky to let him touch him again. Some of her guilt would have lifted if she could have seen that. And now, oh, now she was willing to admit and even be glad that her horse trusted this man. She could only hope that though the trust between her and Sky was broken, Gabe's relationship with the horse was safe.

Fifteen

When Cait and Henry went out later for their ride, she was thrilled to see that Sky was no longer tied to the fence, but out in the far corner of the front pasture. That meant he had let Gabe get close enough to untie him and lead him to the gate.

Cait and her parents hadn't said anything at the breakfast table, so Henry had no idea what had happened. She didn't have to tell him, of course. But something in her made her want to. Henry would understand. Henry loved her, so he would not blame her like Gabe Hart did.

It was their last ride together before he left and Cait had brought a small picnic. Halfway out, they stopped at a small circle of trees and spread an old blanket on the ground. "I hate to leave you tomorrow, Cait," said Henry, putting his arm around her and pulling her close.

"I'll hate to see you go, Henry."

"But I'll be back soon," he promised, dropping a kiss on her forehead, "and then you and I and Sky will be on our way back to Pennsylvania."

"Maybe not Sky, Henry," she whispered.

"Oh, I'm sure you'll be riding him by the time I come back, Cait."

Cait pulled herself out of the circle of his arm. "I tried to ride him this morning, Henry."

"You did! Good for you."

"I wanted to show off for you, Henry. I even imagined I might be riding him now," she added with a bitter little laugh. "Instead, he'll probably not let me

near him again. And even if he did, Gabe Hart probably wouldn't."

"Why, whatever happened, Cait?"

"He was terrified as soon as I went near his back
and he threw me."

"So that is where this bruise came from," said
Henry, brushing her cheek with his finger. "You didn't
walk into the door in the dark. You are not hurt anywhere else, are you?" Henry asked anxiously.

"I'm just a little stiff. But I am so ashamed of
myself."

"Now, now, Cait," said Henry comfortingly, putting
his arm around her again. "You did nothing so wrong.
He is your horse, after all, and you thought he was
ready to ride. You mustn't upset yourself too much
over this."

Cait had thought this was what she wanted to hear:
Henry seeing her side and lifting the blame from her
shoulders. Henry telling her that what she had done
was not really that bad.

Henry lowered his lips to hers and brushed against
them. As her mouth opened under his, his kiss became
more urgent. This was what she had wanted, wasn't
it? Henry's understanding and comfort and Henry's
desire sparking hers? Except that she felt nothing.

Instead of kissing her, he should be . . . what? Yell-
ing at her the way Gabe Hart had done? Was that
what she wanted? She didn't know, but it seemed that
his making excuses for her made her realize that he
didn't understand just what it was she had put at risk.

She let him kiss her. She opened her mouth under
his and admitted his questing tongue. The kiss was
more passionate than any he'd given her so far, and
ironically, right now it didn't matter.

Just as he didn't seem to understand how much she
had hurt Sky, he couldn't seem to tell that she wasn't
really responding to his kiss, only going through the
motions. He finally pulled away, and stood up, saying,
"We really had better be going, Cait, or I'll forget my
resolve to be slow and careful with you."

As they rode back, Cait chattered without stopping,

wondering where on earth the words were coming from. It was as if she was trying to fill the sudden emptiness she felt between them.

Just before they reached the ranch, Henry pulled his horse up and turned to her. "I'm glad you seem to be feeling better about this morning, Cait. You have nothing to blame yourself for, and when I come back for you, if we can't bring Sky back with us, then we will find a horse for you in Pennsylvania. It will be my wedding present for you," he added.

She gave him a grateful smile. He was being so good to her. Offering what he thought would comfort her. So why did she feel so far away from him? she wondered, as they made their way back to the ranch.

Gabe had never felt such anger in his life as when he'd stepped around the barn and seen Caitlin Burke swinging her leg over Sky's back. And he had never felt such fear as when he saw her lying still in the dirt. Fear had replaced his anger and it had seemed an eternity until he saw her catch that first breath. And then the anger flooded back in reaction.

He'd never spoken like that to anyone in his life. He felt his face growing red whenever he thought of how he'd yelled at her. How hard he'd been on her. It was because he'd come to care so much for Night Sky, he told himself. Because he'd worked so patiently to gain the horse's trust and she'd threatened it all in one moment of stupidity.

But it wasn't just that, he realized, as the scene replayed again and again as he went about his work for the rest of the day. When he would see the horse plunge his hooves into the ground, all the anger would rise. But when he saw Cait lying motionless, all the fear came back and he realized that his feelings for her ran deep. He *cared* about her, even though she annoyed the hell out of him and had driven him into a fury that morning.

Of course he cared about her, he would tell himself. She was Michael and Elizabeth's daughter and he cared about them. He felt affection for the whole fam-

ily, that was all it was. He was scared because he knew
what it would have meant to them to lose their daughter. He couldn't care about her in any other way: she
was engaged to be married. She'd be leaving to go
back east in a month's time. He almost had himself
convinced, until she walked into the barn that night
before supper.

Cait knew she had to see Gabe Hart again that day.
It didn't matter to her whether he was still furious or
whether he didn't want to listen to what she had to
say. She had to let him know that she was aware of
the seriousness of what she had done, that she appreciated all he had accomplished with Sky, and that she'd
never go near her horse again if that was what it took
to heal the terror that haunted him. So she had slipped
out of the house while Henry was packing and her
mother was preparing dinner.

Gabe was pitching clean hay into Snowflake's stall
when she entered the barn. He didn't turn around
when she came in and she couldn't tell if he was ignoring her or just hadn't heard her.

"Mr. Hart."

Gabe turned to face her. There was nothing in his
eyes to encourage her. He just stood there, leaning on
the pitchfork, his face wiped clear of all expression.

"I was wondering if I could speak with you for a
few minutes, Mr. Hart?" she asked, her voice strained
and nervous.

"I don't see why not," he said.

He clearly didn't want to, thought Cait, since his
voice was as devoid of feeling as his face. But she was
his boss's daughter, so he'd listen, even if he didn't
care about her or her need to talk.

Cait clasped her hands in front of her. "I just
wanted to tell you how sorry I am about this morning,
Mr. Hart."

He just stood there, giving her no help at all.

"I . . . it is not like me to push a horse like that, I
don't expect you to believe that, of course," she added
with a rueful smile. "I really don't know why I did
it . . . I thought Sky was ready. I wanted to ride him

before Henry left . . . and . . . I think," she continued slowly, her eyes lowered, "I think I was still jealous of you. I wanted to show everyone that Sky was *my* horse. I am so sorry, Mr. Hart. I will do anything you think will set things right; even not go near him at all if you think that would help."

Cait had lifted her eyes and looked right into his as she made her plea for forgiveness and Gabe's heart melted at the anguish he saw there. She really cared what she thought of her, he realized with wonder. And she really cared about her horse, for she was willing to give him up if it was better for Sky, no matter how painful it was for her.

He turned to set the pitchfork down and heard her little gasp of pain. She thought he was turning away from her in anger, ignoring her apology, he realized and without thinking, he turned back and reached out to her. "No, no, it is all right, Miss Cait," he whispered soothingly as he pulled her into his arms. Or maybe she just walked right into them. He didn't know, but he held her tenderly as she sobbed against his chest.

"I'm so sorry."

"I know . . ."

"I don't know if you can ever forgive me?"

Without thinking, he dropped a kiss on the top of her head. "Of course, I forgive you."

"I promise I'll stay away from him, if you think that's right . . ."

Gabe gently released her and stepped back a little. Sweet Jesus, he had better watch himself, he realized. He wanted to kiss her tears away, to touch his lips to that sweet mouth to stop her crying.

"I don't think that's necessary, darlin'," he said without thinking. "Though I doubt he'll let you do too much with him for a while anyway."

"Then you think he will eventually?" she asked, her eyes full of such hope and hurt that Gabe wanted to pull her into his arms again.

He hooked his thumbs into his belt to keep from reaching out to her. "He let me take the halter off. He even let me rub some salve onto his cheeks. He wouldn't let me go near his back, though," Gabe admitted. "It will take a little time before he is back to where he was."

He could see that she was about to give him another agonized apology. "Now, Miss Cait, what's done is done. No use crying or tormenting yourself. Everyone misjudges a horse at one time or another. I know I have rushed one or two in my time."

"I just wish I could explain it better, even to myself," she said with a watery little smile.

"There's some things you just can't put to rest with words." Gabe paused. "I guess I know that because I'm not real good with words myself. Not like my ma or my sister Sarah Ellen. Now they would go on talking forever trying to make sense of something," he added with a grin.

"Sometimes words are the only way to make sense of things, don't you think?"

"Maybe. And those are the times I'd rather be working a horse. I just can't explain myself in words, the way women can," he said with a little tinge of bitterness.

His tone made Cait wonder if he was speaking of a woman other than his mother or sister. She thought probably he was and was surprised at the stab of jealousy she felt for a moment.

"I'm glad of that, if it means you can't say what a little fool I acted or how angry you are with me."

"Was. I *was* angry this morning. But I was worried too," he added.

"I know, Sky could really have hurt himself because I tied him."

It was probably just as well she didn't realize what he'd meant. She didn't imagine he was worried about her safety. That he'd been terrified that he'd lost her. Which was ridiculous, when she wasn't his to lose.

"Thank you, Mr. Hart," she said shyly, putting out her hand.

He took it and squeezed it gently. "Your ma and pa call me Gabe, Miss Cait."

"Thank you, Gabe." She withdrew her hand slowly

and then said nervously, "I'd better get back to the house. I'm sure supper is almost ready and Ma's cooked a special one."

"That's right, it is Mr. Beecham's last night, isn't it?" Gabe observed coolly.

"Yes, he leaves early in the morning with Jake. But he'll be back in a month's time . . ." Cait stopped.

"To take you back east with him."

"Yes," she said with a quick smile. "Good evening, Gabe. And thank you again."

"Good evening, Miss Cait."

Jake and Henry left right after breakfast the next morning. After a tearful good-bye, Cait set herself to do some of the mending that had piled up in her mother's basket.

"Are ye sure ye don't want to ride with us, Cait?" Michael asked.

"No, Da, you and Ma go ahead. You two haven't had any time alone for a while," she added with a teasing smile.

"She's right, ye know, Elizabeth," said Michael as they rode down the road. "Since Cait got home, the only time I have ye to myself is in bed. And while that is always lovely, *a ghra,* I miss you during the day."

They cantered across the sage-covered plain and then climbed one of the small ridges that bordered the valley, stopping at one of their favorite spots, which was shaded by an old twisted juniper.

They dismounted and Elizabeth sat with her back against Michael's chest and looked over the valley. "So, what do you think of our daughter's choice, Michael?" she asked after a few minutes of comfortable silence.

"He seems a fine young man, but . . ." Michael sighed.

Elizabeth laughed. "But what?"

"But I hate the thought of her leaving us, and to go so far away. I know she must, because she loves him. And us maybe not even gettin' to the wedding if it is at Christmastime."

"You are right about Henry, Michael. He is a fine young man. I just don't think he is the man for Cait, however, and I only hope she finds out before she marries him."

"You are serious, Elizabeth, aren't you?" said Michael with concern in his voice.

"I am. I may be wrong, but I think that although she has a lot of affection and admiration for Henry, it does not add up to love, the kind of love I would have her base her marriage on."

"And what of Henry?"

"Oh, I am sure he loves her. But from some things she has said, I think she is a little disappointed in his physical demonstration of his affection. I talked to her a little about my marriage to Thomas. It may be that I am wrong, Michael, for Henry might just be more reserved, especially at her parents' house."

"I hope you are wrong, *a ghra*. And I hope you are right," he said, laughing, "because then she won't want to be leavin' us."

Cait had finished mending the hem of her mother's petticoat and replaced the buttons on two of Elizabeth's shirtwaists when she pulled an unfamiliar shirt out of the basket. It was an old blue denim, worn so soft that one of the cuffs was pulling away from the sleeve. As she turned it inside out, she realized that it was twin to the torn shirt Gabe Hart had used with Sky. It would be just like her mother to notice it and offer to mend it for him.

The shirt had been laundered, but the faint smell of healthy male clung to it and without thinking, Cait buried her face in the soft cotton and drank it in. It brought her back instantly to the moment yesterday when she was held in Gabe Hart's arms. She hadn't been conscious of anything then, except her shame and remorse. But her body must have taken in the way he smelled and the way he felt, for she could once again feel his hard chest under the soft cotton shirt and smell his distinctive scent: a combination of plain soap and healthy sweat. Henry didn't smell like that; he smelled of cologne and hair oil.

Her cheeks became hot as she realized what she was thinking, and she thrust the shirt back under the other clothes. Whatever was she doing, clutching Mr. Hart's shirt and daydreaming of a moment that was nothing more than a gesture of comfort. And why did she keep comparing the two men? There could be no comparison. Henry Beecham was a well-educated, brilliant man whom she could talk to about anything. (If anything meant books and ideas and politics, a little voice in her head reminded her.) Gabe Hart was an inarticulate horse breaker. He himself had said it: he wasn't very good with words, or, he'd hinted, with women. He couldn't be compared to Henry. And yet . . . when he had waltzed her away from Juan Chavez, when he had lifted her down from the fence, and when he had pulled her into his arms, something stirred in her. She tried to summon up a picture of Henry at his most handsome: in black evening dress, with a starched white shirt and elegant pumps. She'd so admired him at Susan's birthday dance. But his picture kept fading and in its place was a tall, lean, blond-haired cowboy in a well-worn blue shirt and denims and dusty boots. His silver hair shone in the sunlight. His blue eyes blazed out of his tanned face.

According to her mother, it was all right to find another man attractive, she reassured herself. It meant very little as long as you were happy with the man you loved. She hadn't met that many handsome men in her life, after all. It was only natural that she'd notice Mr. Hart, even feel a little stir of interest. There was certainly nothing to worry about, for he had no feeling for her. He hadn't even liked her very much in the beginning, she was sure. And when she went back east, she'd never see him again.

Sixteen

Three days later, Gabe knocked on the Burkes' door. "I'm leaving for town now, Mr. Burke. Is there anything I can pick up for you besides the mail?"

"We could use a packet of tea, Gabe. Just don't leave your sister behind," teased Michael.

"You look very handsome, Gabe," said Elizabeth.

"Thank you, ma'am."

He did, thought Cait, who was sitting with her parents at the kitchen table. He was obviously wearing his best clothes, a white shirt and a pair of gray wool pants. Except for the dance, she never saw him out of jeans and chaps. His hat was brushed clean and his boots polished.

"Will she recognize you, Gabe?" asked Elizabeth. "You haven't seen each other in such a long time."

"Well, I've grown a few inches and put on a few pounds and I'm a bit wrinkled, but I reckon I look enough like I did at eighteen for her to know me. I'll know her, for I'm sure she's grown into the image of our ma."

When Gabe reached town, he tied the wagon in front of the telegraph office where the stage would come in and went in to get the mail. In his eagerness, he'd left early and had time to go into the store and shop around. He picked up the packet of tea, and felt his own coins jingling in his pocket. He'd been paid only two days ago and he'd brought a little with him so he could get a thank-you present for Mrs. Burke.

White sugar was always a luxury, so he had the storekeeper wrap up a packet of that. Then he saw the ribbon: it was a deep green velvet and he immediately imagined it tying back Caitlin Burke's dark brown hair. He ran his finger over the soft nap and in his mind, his fingers were tying it around her curls. But he couldn't bring her such a personal present. He had no right to give her a present at all. But then he realized that there were lengths of dark blue and burgundy right next to the green. He *could* get some ribbons for each of the women: blue for Elizabeth, burgundy for Sadie, and the green for Cait. That wouldn't look strange at all.

By the time the clerk had wrapped his ribbon, he heard the rattle of the stagecoach and hurried outside. He had a moment of panic as Elizabeth's teasing words came back to him. What if he didn't recognize her? What if Sadie didn't know him?

Sadie was the first passenger down and as she stepped out all his doubts fled. She was not as tall or rangy as their ma, but her hair was the same reddish-blond and her eyes the same blue. And she had more freckles now than she had when she was fifteen.

The sun was in her eyes and she stood there, looking around when he stepped in front of her.

"Sadie?"

"Oh, Gabe!" She flung her arms around him and he could feel her shoulders begin to shake.

"Now, Sarah Ellen Hart, don't you start crying or you'll have me bawling on the street like a baby," he warned in a choked-up voice. She stepped out of his arms and started fumbling with her reticule.

"Here, Sadie," he said, pulling a handkerchief out of his pocket and wiping her cheeks dry. He ran his hand over his own quickly to erase the evidence of his own emotion.

"It has been such a long time, Gabe," she said softly. "I can't tell you how much I have missed you."

"And I've missed y'all, too, Sadie."

"Well if you did," she said sharply, "why didn't you just come home, damn it! Especially when May ran off."

"I don't know, Sadie," Gabe confessed. "I guess she made home a place where I was ashamed to be. And once I got to wandering, it just became harder and harder to think of it. I always wrote, you know," he added in his own defense.

"Because I threatened to send the Rangers after you if you didn't! And what if Ma hadn't been a schoolteacher and made you do all that reading and writing?"

"Wal, I guess I would have had to send you the occasional telegram then, Sadie," he drawled. "Is this all you have?" he asked, looking down at her worn carpetbag.

"Just that, though it's a heavy one."

"It sure is. Do you want a lemonade or something before we start off?"

"That would be very nice, Gabe," she said, tucking her arm in his. "Did you find me a place to stay here in town?"

"The Burkes insisted you take their spare room. That way we'll see each other a lot more while you're here."

Sadie frowned. "Are you sure that will be all right, Gabe?"

"You'll like them real well, Sadie. I feel . . . well, as close to feeling at home there as I ever have since I left Texas."

Gabe went back to the store and asked for two cups of lemonade. There was a bench outside and he and Sadie sat down and looked at each other and smiled.

"Do you remember when Pa would take us into town?" asked Sadie.

"How could I forget? You'd be begging and whining for molasses candy the whole ride."

"It was good when Ma was alive, wasn't it, Gabe?" she said softly.

"It was."

They were both quiet for a moment and Sadie watched the townspeople go by. There was a good-looking bay tied across the street in front of the bank and she was just about to point it out when she felt Gabe stiffen as a man came out of the saloon next door. He was not a very big man, but he moved with a strength and grace that reminded her of animals in the wild. He was dressed Mexican-style and a sombrero hung down his back.

"Do you know him, Gabe?" Sadie asked.

"I know him," her brother said shortly, his hand automatically brushing his leg where his holster usually hung.

"You clearly don't like him," she said, with a touch of humor. "Who is he? He's dressed like a Mexican, but he doesn't really look like one."

"His name is Juan Chavez. He's a hired gun for Nelson Mackie, the big landholder around here. Landgrabber is more like it."

The Mexican crossed the street and approached them.

"Damn," Gabe cursed under his breath. "Come on, Sadie, let's go."

"Señor Hart. Who is this charming señorita with you?"

The words were polite enough, but somehow the tone was insulting. Even Sadie could tell that. She was tall for a woman and she didn't have to lift her face too much to give him one of her best schoolteacher looks. She almost gasped when she saw his eyes: they were the coldest and greenest she had ever seen.

"This is my sister, Señor Chavez."

"Now that you tell me, I can see the resemblance. *Encantado,* señorita."

Sadie just nodded her head and tried to look through him.

"I hope you enjoy your visit, señorita. I am sure your brother will keep you safe. *Adios.*"

"Come on, Sadie," said Gabe, "the wagon is over here."

Neither spoke until they were on the edge of town.

"Was he threatening you, Gabe?"

"That's what he is paid for, Sadie. He's so good at it, he's managed to drive quite a few ranchers out of the valley."

"I can imagine he's good at it. Those eyes of his. . . ."

"They call him *El Lobo*. It's not a bad name for him," said Gabe, "for he goes right for the weak."

"So is his boss after the Burkes' too?"

"Mackie's made two offers already and sent Chavez out to the ranch." Gabe hesitated. "A few sheep were poisoned, but no one can prove it wasn't jimson weed. If I could have reached you in time, I would have told you not to come, Sadie, much as I missed you," he added, his voice strained and worried.

"I'm glad you couldn't, then," Sadie said matter-of-factly. "I can take good care of myself, Gabe. You don't need to be worrying."

"Whatever happens, I sure am glad you're here," said Gabe, giving her a quick, hard hug.

By the time they reached the ranch, Gabe had told Sadie all about the Burke family, the size of their spread, and the history of their horses. "They are beautiful, Gabe," said Sadie as she admired the horses in the far pasture.

"I'm working the yearlings and the two-year-olds. It's all going well except for one."

"A rogue, Gabe? I hope you have more sense than to think you can do anything with that kind of horse."

"No, just a two-year-old who's been terrified of anything coming near his back since he was attacked by a mountain lion."

They had reached the near pasture and Gabe pulled up. "There he is, Sadie, over in the south corner."

Sadie saw a black horse covered with silver-dollar-size spots look over his shoulder curiously. "He is beautiful, Gabe."

"His name is Night Sky. He was coming along real well until this week," Gabe said with an exasperated sigh.

"Did you push him too fast, Gabe? That's not like you." Sadie knew Gabe had the patience of a saint with horses. On the other hand, if this one was so special, he might well have been tempted to push a little, she thought.

"Not me, Sadie. Sky is Miss Burke's horse. Her fi-

ancé was here and she was a little too eager to show
Sky off."

"She tried to ride him? Is she still alive, Gabe?"
Sadie asked with a teasing smile. Her brother had always hated any interference when he was working
an animal.

Gabe gave her a shamefaced smile. "I did light into
her, Sadie."

"She deserved it, Gabe. I'm sure it set you back
weeks."

"I hope not, but it will take some time before I get
him back to where he was."

Sadie decided there and then that she was not going
to like Miss Caitlin Burke with her Eastern schooling
and her fancy fiancé and her spoiled determination to
show off at the expense of her horse.

She like Elizabeth Burke immediately, however.
Sadie had been "Mother" for so long that she'd forgotten what it was like to be taken care of. Mrs. Burke
seemed genuinely delighted to have her and brought
her up to the spare room. There was a jar of flowers
on the nightstand and the quilt on the bed was
turned down.

"You must be exhausted from your trip, Miss
Hart."

"Please call me Sadie."

"Sadie then. Please make yourself at home. It is a
few hours till supper. If you want to take a short nap,
I've turned the bed down for you."

"Thank you, Mrs. Burke. For everything. I expected
I would be boarding in town."

"Nonsense. My husband keeps Gabe pretty busy,
you know, and you'd have had very little time to see
each other."

"You have a lovely place here, Mrs. Burke. And
the horses are something special."

Elizabeth smiled. "Another horse lover?"

"Not like Gabe, I'm afraid."

"Well, he is something special, too," said her hostess warmly. "Now, I'll leave you to yourself. You can
rest, unpack, whatever you wish."

"Thank you, Mrs. Burke."

There was an old wardrobe in the corner and Sadie hung up her dresses. The bed looked very inviting and though she hadn't intended to, she lay down on it, just to rest for a few minutes. She was awakened two hours later by the sound of laughter coming up from the kitchen together with the smell of a chile stew and lay there for a minute, not remembering where she was. Then it all came back and she was up in a second to wash her face, comb her hair, and put on a new shirtwaist for dinner.

Seventeen

"Here she is," said Elizabeth, as Sadie came into the kitchen. "I hope you had a good rest?"

"I didn't mean to sleep," said Sadie apologetically. "But as soon as I lay down, I was out like a light."

"Then you definitely needed to. Michael, this is Gabe's sister, Miss Sarah Ellen Hart."

"Good evening, Miss Hart," said Michael, clasping her hand in his.

"Sadie, please, Mr. Burke."

"This is our daughter, Caitlin," he added, as Cait came in the front door. "Cait, come here and meet Gabe's sister."

Cait smiled at the tall, rangy woman next to her father. She had a strong face, too strong to be called "pretty" but with her dark blue eyes that were so much like Gabe's and her wide generous mouth, she could not be considered plain, either, despite her sandy hair and freckles. She extended her hand to Cait and said, "I'm very pleased to meet you, Miss Burke."

She said it politely enough, but Cait detected a lack of warmth. For some reason, she was sure Sarah Ellen Hart did not like her. She didn't have much time to think about it, for her mother summoned her to set the table. "Jake refuses to eat in the big house, but Gabe will be joining us while Sadie is here, Cait, so set an extra place."

"Yes, Ma."

When Michael opened the door to Gabe a few minutes later, Gabe just stood there shyly until Michael said, "Come in, boyo. Here's your place next to Cait and opposite your sister so you can feast on her face as well as Elizabeth's food."

Gabe smiled and sat down on the bench next to Caitlin. It was not a very long bench and after serving the food, Elizabeth slipped in next to her daughter on the other side. Cait had to shift a little to make room for her mother and when her leg brushed Gabe's she drew it back quickly as though she'd come in contact with hot coals.

It was strange to have him eating with them, as though he was one of the family. And even stranger to meet one of his family. The fact that he had a sister made him more real to her somehow. It made him something more than just a wandering horse breaker.

Michael politely questioned Sadie on her stage-coach journey.

"It was hot and dusty and boring and long," she said with a laugh. "And wouldn't you know, there was a woman and her ten-year-old boy traveling with us. I can't seem to get away from them! I had four ten-year-old boys this year, Gabe," she said, lifting her eyes to the ceiling in mock despair.

"Gabe told us you are a schoolteacher," said Elizabeth.

"These last ten years."

"Our Cait has been studying to be a schoolteacher, too," said Michael, looking over at his daughter proudly.

"I thought Gabe told me you were engaged to be married?"

"I am, but my fiancé, Henry, is very encouraging of my desire to teach. I have a position in the Fayre-weather Academy for next year."

"No ten-year-old terrors for you, then," said Sadie with a smile.

"No, the youngest girl is twelve. And they all want to be there."

"That's the difference," Sadie admitted with a sigh. "My girls are always happier in school than the boys. By eight or nine the boys want to be outside all day, learning to rope and ride. Most of them leave by eleven or twelve. Their parents need them on the farm or ranch and I can't convince them that learning to read or calculate will be as important to them someday as knowing how to rope a calf."

"Don't you get discouraged?" Elizabeth said sympathetically.

"Oh, yes, but it was like that when I was in school, so I knew what to expect. I teach them the basics and then they are gone. But at least they have *something*. And once in a while, one of them surprises you."

"Like Josh Miller?" asked Gabe.

Sadie's face lit up.

"Sadie wrote to me about him," Gabe continued. "He was fifteen when he moved to town with his folks. Couldn't do much more than his ABC's 'cause they'd traveled around so much."

"Of course, he didn't go much further than the basic primer with me." Sadie laughed. "But, Lord, how that boy could figure. I had to send for books from Austin and we studied them together. I couldn't convince his parents to send him away to school," she added sadly, "but he did get a job as a teller, and if I know him, he'll be president of the bank someday."

Sadie Hart was clearly a natural and dedicated teacher, thought Cait. She had to admire her for that. She was doing the sort of teaching Cait had once planned to do until she got to Fayreweather. But surely it was better to work in a classroom where all the pupils were at the same level and motivated to learn? Surely opening a young woman's mind to great literature in the way hers had been opened was more valuable than providing a smattering of skills to children who would hardly use them anyway?

Everyone else at the table was clearly enjoying Sadie's presence. Her Da and Ma seemed more relaxed than they had in weeks. Gabe was sitting there smiling, appreciating his sister. They were all at home with one another. They all knew who they were and where home *was*. Cait smiled and laughed with them, but felt like the outsider. She was the one who was leaving, who had decided that the East was to be her home. She wished Henry were here next to her, to squeeze her hand and give her reassurance and make all the inner turmoil go away.

"I saw some of your horses, Mr. Burke," said Sadie. "and they are beautiful animals. I've only seen markings like that on one other horse in my life."

Michael's face lit up as his horses were praised. "You'll have to see Finn, my stallion, Sadie. He has a perfect blanket and a handprint on his hindquarters."

"Handprint?"

"It's the way the spots are arranged, Sadie," explained Gabe. "It looks just like someone put his hand in paint and slapped it on Finn's backside."

"We'll have to give you a horse to ride while you are here. What do you think, Cait?"

"Red Hawk?"

"If she likes an old, steady horse," said Michael. "How do you ride, Sadie?"

"As well as I do," Gabe broke in proudly.

"Then maybe it should be Patch. Provided someone rides the kinks out of him first. We don't want Sadie in the dirt like Henry was," added Michael with a broad smile. His smile faded and he said seriously, "Ye'll have to stay on ranch property, Sadie, if ye go ridin' alone. I don't know if Gabe has told you, but we've been havin' a bit of trouble in the valley."

"He's told me, Mr. Burke. In fact, we met a bit of your trouble in town. A Señor Chavez."

"He didn't bother ye, did he, Gabe?"

"No, Mr. Burke, not really. Just gave us one of his innocent-sounding greetings."

"Damn the man! Pardon me, Sadie, but even a saint would wish him in hell," added Michael with a rueful smile.

"Let's not spoil dessert with talk of Chavez, Michael," said Elizabeth from the stove, where she was putting on a pot of coffee.

"Ye're right, *a ghra.* We won't let him in our house in any way, shape, or form."

After dessert and coffee, Sadie offered to help with the dishes. "No, Cait will help me," said Elizabeth.

"You and Gabe go on and take a walk. You must have plenty of catching up to do."

"So, now that you've met them, how do you like the Burkes, Sadie?" asked Gabe as they walked down the road.

"They are wonderful, Gabe. So warm and welcoming that I feel right at home. I am glad you found them. It's time you were in one place for a while. Though I can't say I like the idea of your getting mixed up in another range war," she added, a worried note in her voice.

"I don't think it will come to that," Gabe reassured her. "I'm hoping that if Michael Burke holds out—which he will—Mackie will just have to give in."

"But what about the sheep, Gabe? That was more than threats. And Senor Chavez: he certainly seems capable of violence."

"He may be, but up to now, Mackie hasn't had to do much more than intimidate."

"But what will he do when intimidation doesn't work?"

"I don't know. But I'll be here to help Mr. Burke when and if anything happens."

"Their daughter seems a nice girl, Gabe. I expected someone a bit spoiled after your tale of her and her horse."

"No, she's the apple of her father's eye," said Gabe with a smile, "but not really spoiled. Just young, I guess."

"And eager to get away from home, it seems."

"Well, she's been away two years and met that Beecham fellow and is all excited about being a teacher back east, Sadie." Gabe didn't know why he was defending Caitlin Burke's choices to his sister. He couldn't understand anyone wanting to be anywhere but here, but then, he was only a cowboy.

The next morning after breakfast, Gabe and Michael were off to work and Elizabeth smiled at her daughter and said: "Shall we take Sadie out and show her the ranch, Cait?"

Cait's face lit up. "Will you come too, Ma?" She'd been afraid that she'd have to play hostess to Gabe's sister and the thought was a little daunting. Miss Sarah Ellen Hart seemed quite sure of herself and her place in the world and that made Cait feel young and confused.

Gabe had already saddled Patch and ridden him around the corral to get him ready for Sadie. Elizabeth took Snowflake and Cait had Red Hawk. They rode across the valley and into the hills south of the ranch. Elizabeth pointed out the boundaries of their property and explained that the sheep were in their summer pasture up in the mountains.

"It's unusual to be raising sheep in these parts, isn't it?" asked Sadie.

"The Mexicans and Navajo have been sheepherders for years before any of us arrived," Elizabeth explained. "Michael wanted to put his energy into the horses, but we needed a 'cash crop' as it were. Sheep require less work and fewer hands than cattle. And Michael's convinced, now that we've been here for almost twenty years, that sheep are better for the land. You can already see the results of overgrazing on the property that Mackie bought."

"I'll bet the cattlemen don't agree with you."

"They don't," replied Elizabeth with a smile. "But Michael has studied it very carefully. Sheep don't compete with cattle, like so many people think, though it's hard to convince them of it."

"It is so beautiful here," said Sadie, waving her hand over the valley.

"Is Texas so different?" Cait asked.

"Where I am from, it is very flat," Sadie replied. "There is the hill country, but where Gabe and I grew up, there is only plains and sky. But it is beautiful in its own way," she added loyally.

"What I miss here," said Elizabeth quietly, "is the red rock country. There is a little of it down El Morro way, but nothing like what was around Fort Defiance."

"I saw the pictures hanging in the parlor," said Sadie.

"Those are Ma's," said Cait proudly. "She is a real artist. I can't draw to save my life," she admitted with a laugh.

"And the weavings?"

"My good friend Serena's," answered Elizabeth. "She is Dine, Navajo, and lives in the heart of the red rock country. She is the real artist."

"I saw some hogans from the stagecoach," said Sadie. "I was surprised, because I thought the reservation was north of here."

"It is. But a small group of Dine had made their homes here and were allowed to stay. A few of them live on the edge of Mackie's property, in fact," added Elizabeth. "But since they survived Fort Sumner, I doubt he will succeed in driving them off."

As they came down from the foothills, Cait looked over at her mother, a challenge in her eyes. "What about it, Ma?"

"It's not fair to you, Cait," said Elizabeth, a twinkle in her eye. "You are riding Red Hawk."

Sadie looked from one to the other, wondering what they were talking about, when Cait suddenly kicked her horse into a canter and then a full gallop. Giving a rebel yell, Sadie gave Patch his head and soon caught up with her. Red Hawk did his best, but Elizabeth was on the faster horse, and it came down to a race between Elizabeth and Sadie. Snowflake passed Patch just as they reached the ranch gate.

Elizabeth was laughing as Cait rode up.

"Don't laugh at me, Ma," she protested, trying to keep her face straight. "Next time, I'll take Snowflake and we'll see who comes in first."

"That was fun, Cait," said her mother. "We haven't done that in a long time."

Sadie looked over at Caitlin Burke and envied her her easy relationship with her mother. The girl's face was flushed and her dark hair blown all around it and Sadie wondered if Gabe had ever noticed how pretty she was.

"Gabe was right, Sadie," said Elizabeth as they

walked the horses down the road. "You are an excellent rider."

"I had a good horse, Mrs. Burke," said Sadie, patting Patch on the neck. "I got the feeling he could have gone on even longer."

"That's why Da loves these horses," said Cait, her eyes shining with the joy of exercise and her love of their horses. "Appaloosas were bred for both speed and endurance."

"There used to be regular races at Fort Defiance," Elizabeth told them. "The Dine would ride in—you have never seen such riders, Sadie. Michael won quite a few races on Frost. She was our first brood mare," Elizabeth explained. "Your Da still misses her, Cait." Elizabeth's eyes were soft and dreamy as though she were back twenty years, watching Michael Burke ride his gray mare to victory and Sadie wondered what it would be like to feel so much for a man with whom you had lived for twenty years. Her ma would have felt that way for her pa, had she lived, Sadie was sure. But she herself had never met a man who had inspired those feelings. She didn't know if it was the men she was meeting or something lacking in her, but she'd just about resigned herself to spinsterhood.

For the next few days, Sadie rode out with Cait and sometimes Elizabeth in the mornings. She got to see Gabe at dinner, and in the afternoons, found herself taking a "siesta." "I don't know what's come over me," she said the first day when she came down from her nap. "I never sleep in the daytime. I feel like I should be helping you more around the house," she told Elizabeth apologetically.

"Nonsense. From what Gabe told me, this is your first time off from teaching and taking care of your younger brothers in years."

So Sadie continued to enjoy the leisurely pace of her days there. She usually ended up at the corral just before supper, to watch Gabe work with Sky.

He had patiently gotten the horse to allow him to use the old saddle blanket to rub him down again.

Whenever Gabe invited Caitlin in, Sky would let her feed him treats and lead him around, but the moment she took the blanket from Gabe and tried to go near the horse's back, he would shy away.

"I suppose you heard what happened," said Cait with a disappointed sigh one afternoon as she went back to join Sadie on the corral fence.

"Gabe told me you tried to ride him." It was hard to keep the disapproval out of her voice.

"I know better. I felt like such a fool, Sadie, and Da was ready to kill me. But the worst part was knowing I had set Sky back and ruined all of Gabe's hard work. I offered to stay away from him if it would help," she continued, "but Gabe seemed to think it best for me to continue grooming him and getting as close as Sky lets me."

Sadie was surprised at the rush of sympathy she felt for Cait. She might have made an impulsive mistake, but was clearly suffering for it, and able to take responsibility for it, too. She seemed to feel sorrier for Gabe and Sky than for herself, which proved she was more grown-up than Sadie had given her credit for.

"Gabe's been very nice about it," Cait continued, "though I'm sure he's still upset with me."

Sadie smiled to herself. So Miss Caitlin Burke cared what Gabe thought of her. She was sure the younger woman was trying to find out whether Gabe had said anything to his sister about her. How interesting.

"Oh, I think he's forgiven you," Sadie replied kindly. "He's made some mistakes with horses in his time."

"It's hard to believe, since he's so good with them," answered Caitlin, her relief almost palpable.

"Nobody's perfect, Cait," said Sadie with a touch of dry humor.

Cait blushed. "Of course not. I didn't mean that Gabe was . . . just that . . . I admire him and so does my Da for how he is with horses."

"Gabe has always been able to sense things with animals or people, and work like this shows him at his best. But when it comes to words, well, he hasn't always been so good telling anyone, particularly women, how he feels."

Sadie didn't think Caitlin Burke had thought much about Gabe around women, from the way her eyes opened a little in surprise. Which was probably just as well, since she was engaged and leaving by the end of the summer.

Eighteen

One morning at the end of her first week on the ranch, both Elizabeth and Cait apologized to Sadie after breakfast. "Cait and I must go into town, Sadie, to meet with the dressmaker. Cait will need some new dresses for her trip back east. You are welcome to come with us, of course," Elizabeth added.

"I think I'll stay here, if that is all right with you. May I take Snowflake out?"

"Why, of course. Just be careful not to go too far."

"I think I am pretty sure of my way now," Sadie reassured her.

She knew the boundaries of the ranch and headed up into the hills, the way she and Cait and Elizabeth had ridden. But they had never gone up into the mountains and she could feel them pulling her. Snowflake was fresh and she decided to see if she could find the sheepherder's camp.

It took a good hour to climb to the high meadows, but the mare was surefooted and all Sadie had to do was enjoy the scenery. The first meadow she reached was dotted with sheep and as she rode through them she was met by a black-and-white dog barking furiously.

Snowflake clearly did not appreciate his presence and Sadie had to work hard to keep her going steady. She'd wanted to go farther, but it seemed like the dog might not let her through the meadow.

Suddenly he turned and ran off, only to come back, looking over his shoulder at the gray-haired man who followed him. It must be Eduardo, the Burkes' shepherd, Sadie realized. He was carrying a shotgun and she waved and called to him, hoping he wouldn't feel threatened by a woman, even if she was a stranger.

"*Hola,* Eduardo."

"*Hola,* señorita. Do I know you?"

"I am Sadie Hart, Gabe's sister," she explained.

Eduardo smiled. "I didn't know Señor Hart had a sister."

"I'm here on a visit from Texas," she explained. "Usually Mrs. Burke and Caitlin and I ride together, but this morning they had to go into town and I decided to explore a little farther on my own."

"*Ten cuidado,* señorita," warned Eduardo, his smile fading. "We have had some trouble, as I'm sure you know."

"Yes, Gabe told me about the sheep. But you are the one who needs to be careful."

Eduardo lifted his shotgun. "I am always prepared, señorita. And my dog, he always lets me know if someone's coming. Would you like a cup of coffee?"

"No, *gracias.* I'm going to ride up a little farther before I turn back."

"There's another meadow through the trees, a few hundred feet up."

"Thank you, Eduardo," she said with a wave as she turned Snowflake.

"*Hasta luego,* señorita."

The view from the next meadow was spectacular. Sadie could see the whole valley spread beneath her and off in the distance, the long mesa north of El Morro. She turned back reluctantly, but she didn't want to stay so long that Gabe or the Burkes got worried about her.

When she reached the first meadow, Eduardo and his dog were nowhere in sight so she rode through and started down the mountain. Maybe it was because she was in a hurry and Snowflake could sense it. Maybe the horse was still nervous after encountering the dog, but halfway down the trail she stumbled and Sadie almost went over her head.

"Easy, girl, easy. It's all right."

But it wasn't, for she could see that the mare was

favoring her right foot and by the time they were down to the foothills, she was limping painfully, and Sadie was forced to dismount.

She lifted the mare's foreleg and examined her hoof first. There was no stone caught in the shoe, which was what Sadie had hoped for. She felt up Snowflake's hock. It was warm and a little swollen. She'd probably put all her weight on it when she stumbled.

"Oh, Snowflake, I'm sorry," said Sadie, though she really had nothing to be sorry for. These things happened, but it would be a long walk back to the ranch.

The mare was limping badly and it took a long time to come down the trail out of the hills. They were almost down when Sadie heard a horse trotting down behind her. When she turned, she recognized the rider immediately: Señor Juan Chavez. What was he doing, riding on the Burke property? She could feel her heart beating faster, but she kept her face calm and expressionless. She'd be damned if he would know she was afraid of him.

"It is Señorita Hart, isn't it?"

Sadie gave him a curt nod. "*Buenos dias,* Señor Chavez."

"You remembered my name. I'm flattered."

"Don't be," Sadie replied flatly as she walked on. Maybe if she ignored him, he would just ride on.

"When a pretty señorita remembers me, how can I not be flattered." His words were all charm, but when Sadie looked up, his green eyes were as opaque as ever.

"You are notorious, Señor Chavez, which is why I remembered you. And I am not a 'pretty señorita,' so you can save your charm for someone else." Chavez laughed and Sadie was surprised to realize that his amusement was spontaneous and genuine.

"What happened to your mare?" he asked, dismounting as he spoke.

"She stumbled coming down. I think her hoof caught on a rock and her leg took all the weight."

"Let me take a look." Chavez handed Sadie the reins of his horse and she took them without thinking and then looked down at them, wondering why she was letting him go near one of Michael Burke's horses. He seemed to be examining Snowflake gently enough, but Sadie moved closer, as though to protect the mare.

"Don't worry, Miss Hart. I won't hurt her. She's definitely suffered a bad strain, but I don't think there will be any permanent damage."

Sadie was so relieved to hear that her appraisal was probably correct that she smiled at Chavez without thinking.

"You'll have to ride with me, Miss Hart," he said, as though expecting her to immediately jump into his saddle because he suggested it.

"I most certainly do not have to," Sadie answered in her best schoolteacher voice.

Chavez pushed his sombrero back and smiled at her. Sadie wasn't sure, but she thought his green eyes might even have shared in the smile.

"Señorita Hart, I assure you I mean no harm."

"Not even after your oh so subtly veiled warning in town, Señor Chavez? I hear you have great talents as a bully."

"You've heard the truth, Miss Hart, but I choose the time and the place. And what could be more annoying to Gabe Hart than that I rescue his sister. I am only taking advantage of the situation. He and Burke will be very aware that I could have threatened you but didn't."

"I don't intend to give you that satisfaction, Señor Chavez."

His eyes turned opaque again. "That is a shame," he replied smoothly, "for your sweet, wide mouth looks like it could give me much satisfaction, señorita."

Sadie raised her hand to slap him and he caught it in midair. His hand closed around her forearm like a vise and when she finally relaxed and he let her go, she rubbed it, knowing she would have bruises the next day.

"*Disculpame,* señorita. But I have not let anyone strike me for years."

"You are a common bully, Mr. Chavez. And from what I have heard, you work for an even bigger one. I have no respect for bullies. I've seen too many of them on the school yard," said Sadie, her voice full of contempt.

"Nevertheless, if you won't ride with me, I will have to keep you company for at least part of the way, Miss Hart."

Sadie grabbed Snowflake's reins and started walking. Chavez mounted his black and in a second, was beside her. "Just because you are being stubborn, I see no reason for me to walk," he said with a smile that almost made him look human again.

Sadie looked away and they worked their way silently down out of the foothills. When they reached the valley, Chavez said: "I'll go a little farther with you, señorita. But I doubt I would be very welcome on the Burkes' ranch."

"Why is it that sometimes you sound Mexican and at others, a gringo, Mr. Chavez?" The question popped out before Sadie realized she was asking it aloud. She looked up at Chavez and saw his face looked more closed than usual.

"It is a long story, Miss Hart," he answered. "And I am very sure that you are not really interested in my life history."

She shouldn't be, thought Sadie, but really, the man was intriguing to her. From what she had heard of him, by no stretch of the imagination could he be called a good man, but she had to admit that whatever his motive was, she appreciated his company on the long hot walk. It would have seemed endless without him.

They were within sight of the entrance gate when Chavez finally pulled up his horse. "*Adios,* señorita. I am sure you will be fine from here."

"*Muchas gracias,* Señor Chavez. *Y vaya con Dios,*" she added. She didn't know whether he heard her or not. It had come out spontaneously, but now that she thought of it, if anyone needed to "go with God," it was Juan Chavez, who had the look of one who rode with the devil.

Halfway to the ranch house, Sadie saw a horse and rider cantering toward her. It was Gabe on his own paint and he pulled up suddenly, creating a cloud of dust around them as soon as he saw her.

"My God, Sarah Ellen, we've been worried about you. It is almost dinnertime and you left after breakfast." He dismounted and threw his arms around her in a bear hug.

"I'm all right, Gabe," she reassured him when he let her go, "but Snowflake strained her hock coming down from the mountains."

Gabe knelt to examine it and without thinking Sadie said, "Señor Chavez said he thought that although it was a bad sprain, it probably wouldn't cause lasting damage."

"Chavez! What the hell were you doing with him?" exclaimed Gabe, straightening up and glaring at her.

"I wasn't doing anything with Mr. Chavez, Gabe," Sadie replied coolly. "He met me on the trail down from the sheep camp. He may not be the Burkes' friend, but he offered me a ride and when I wouldn't take it, accompanied me to the gate. I am grateful to him for that, whatever he is."

Gabe took off his hat and ran his hand through his hair. "I'm sorry I snapped at you, Sadie. I guess I'm thankful you met him, too," he added doubtfully. "But what was he doing around the sheep anyway, unless to poison a few more?"

"He hadn't poisoned any today, as far as I know." Sadie wasn't sure why she was coming to Chavez's defense. If he was hanging around the Burkes' sheep, he was likely up to no good. She certainly didn't really like the man, with his cold eyes and threatening manner, but he wasn't the devil incarnate!

"I feel terrible about Snowflake, Gabe. The Burkes have been so good to me, and here I go and lame one of their best horses."

"You weren't riding foolishly. I know you too well for that, Sarah Ellen."

"No, I wasn't. And I didn't go off the ranch, either, Gabe. Just a little farther than we've gone before. It was just that we were coming downhill on a trail with a lot of loose rock."

"It could have happened to anyone," Gabe reassured her. He took a closer look at his sister. She looked on the verge of tears and must be exhausted from her long walk. "You look completely done in, Sadie. Here, you take Buck and ride up to the house and I'll lead Snowflake." She gave him a grateful smiled and mounted his paint.

"Tell Mrs. Burke to go ahead with dinner and I'll be right along."

"Yes, Gabe."

When she dismounted in front of the corral, she heard the front door slam and Elizabeth hurried over to her, with Michael not far behind.

"Sadie! Thank God you are safe. We were so worried about you."

"I am fine, Mrs. Burke," said Sadie and then looked over at Michael. "Oh, Mr. Burke, I am so sorry to tell you this, but Snowflake strained her hock." She gestured down the road. "Gabe is leading her in."

"I was hopin' it was something like that and not that you'd met up with any of Mackie's men," said Michael. "How did it happen?"

"I wanted to get up a little higher than we've ridden before," said Sadie apologetically. "I followed the trail up to the sheep camp. I met Eduardo and rode the meadows. It was when I started down that she caught herself on a loose rock."

"That was a long walk home, Sadie," said Elizabeth solicitously. "Come, I have dinner on the table."

"Gabe said to sit down and eat, Mrs. Burke. He'll join us when he gets Snowflake settled."

"Keep both our dinners hot, *a ghra*," said Michael. "I'll just be walkin' down to meet him."

Sadie gulped down a glass of lemonade before she even looked at her food. "Mr. Burke was very understanding," she said, lifting her eyes to Elizabeth. "I feel so bad about the mare."

"It could have happened to any of us, Sadie," Elizabeth reassured her.

"But it didn't," Sadie said with a rueful smile. "It happened while I was riding her and you have been so kind to me."

"At least it was an accident, Sadie," said Cait. "Not your own foolishness, like me with Sky. And we're all relieved that you were in no danger."

Sadie gave her a grateful look. "I did meet one of Mackie's men out there, Mrs. Burke," she admitted. "Señor Chavez, as a matter of fact."

Elizabeth paled. "He was not . . . unpleasant to you, was he?"

"No, no, not at all. In fact, he offered to ride double and lead Snowflake. Of course, I said no," she added. "But he stayed with me the whole time and saw me to the entrance gate. I am grateful to him for that."

"I wonder what he was doing up there," said Caitlin, and then wished she hadn't as her mother pushed back her plate.

"I am not hungry after all," said Elizabeth, her voice strained. She was ashamed of her reaction, but Juan Chavez threatened everything she loved. "I think I'll just walk down and meet Gabe and your Da. Will you put the coffee on for us, Cait?"

"Yes, Ma."

Later that evening, Elizabeth put down her book and said to her husband: "Sadie told us about meeting Chavez, Michael."

"Gabe said he accompanied her most of the way home. I must admit I was surprised. I don't see him as the chivalrous sort, do you, *a ghra?*" he asked with a quizzical smile.

"No, I don't, Michael," his wife replied, her voice tight with emotion. "What was he doing up there by the sheep, Michael? Setting out more poison?"

"We don't know that he actually did that, Elizabeth."

"Oh, Michael . . ."

" 'Tis the work of Mackie's men, no doubt about it, but we can't be sure which one."

"There is something about him, Michael. It goes beyond my fear of what he can do to us."

"He can't do anything to us, Elizabeth," said Michael, putting his arm around her and drawing her close. "His talent is bullying people into doing what Mackie wants and I am not a man who's easily bullied."

"Vaya con Dios." Juan Chavez could hear Sadie's clear tones sounding in his head all the way back to the Mackie ranch. He, the man known as "El Lobo," go with God? He hadn't believed in the Almighty since he was ten and finally stopped praying for his parents or sister to come and find him because "they could be alive, God, if you wanted them to be." No one was ever going to come for him, he had realized. He would be a slave for the next eight years and then, if he was lucky, the Romeros might pay him a pittance of a wage. He hadn't felt much for those next eight years, for himself or anyone else. And when he walked out the gate of the hacienda at eighteen, no one even tried to stop him.

He'd worked for men like Mackie ever since. He'd had women, of course, some whores and some who were sorry to see him go, who professed to love him. He believed the whores' moans of delight a lot more than he believed the others. Love him? No, they didn't love *him,* but their manufactured fantasy of him. *El Lobo.* It was one of these women who'd first called him that. He knew once she began using words of love, she believed she could be the one to change him from a lone wolf to one who mated for life. He'd left her brokenhearted.

There were some who would say he used these "good" women. But they used him too. They wanted him for his wildness, his inability to care, for they were the señoritas, Texan or Mexican, who had been gently raised and hemmed in by the conventions of their society and he represented freedom.

Sadie Hart was a "good" woman. A schoolteacher from Texas who'd raised her two brothers, if the gossip he'd heard was correct. He'd renounced good women a long time ago. He was tired of the tears and recriminations.

She certainly didn't seem to fall for his charm or seem impressed by his notoriety as a man who rode the knife edge between respectability and outlawhood. He smiled as he thought of her insistence on walking all the way home rather than take any help from the man who was threatening her brother's employer.

She was no beauty, this Sadie Hart. Too tall and rangy for his taste, which ran to small, plump señoritas. There was no danger there for him, he thought, and then immediately wondered why he had needed to reassure himself.

That evening Mackie called him into the big house after dinner.

"Have your plans progressed any further, Chavez?" he asked bluntly.

"Plans?" Chavez replied mildly.

"I assume you have something in mind for Burke?"

"I think he is aware of the position he is in, señor. I met a houseguest of his coming down from the sheep camp. She'll pass the word that I've been seen around there. He'll know that more of his sheep could become sick."

"And what of his shepherd?"

"The old man, Eduardo? What of him? He is no threat to anyone."

"What if it weren't the sheep who fell victim this time but their shepherd? Burke wouldn't hold out after something like that."

"It might be effective," said Juan slowly as though he was giving the idea his serious consideration. "On the other hand, Burke might be so enraged that he'd dig his feet in more. I think he can be a very stubborn man, Señor Burke." Chavez had killed, but never cold-bloodedly, without provocation. It had always been in self-defense. And he always informed his prospective employers that that was the way he preferred it. Not from any tenderheartedness, he would assure them, but because it was best to stay on the side of the law, if possible.

"I think hitting Señor Burke in the pocketbook will be more effective in the long run," he said without inflection.

Mackie, who was drinking whiskey, pointed his finger at Chavez and gestured with his glass, slopping some of the whiskey on his employee's boots. "I know, I know. You told me you don't shoot unless you're shot at. You'd rather intimidate people."

"I'd rather keep my neck out of a rope, señor."

"All right, for now, we'll do it your way, Chavez," said Mackie, turning his back and dismissing him with a wave. "But your way better work soon. Send Wilson in to see me, will you," he added.

"*Si*, señor."

"How does it look, Gabe?"

"Still a little swollen, but the arnica wrap is helping. She's even put a little weight onto it, haven't you, girl?" he said as Snowflake whuffled at the back of his neck.

Sadie was perched on a nearby bale of hay and when Gabe was finished, he came and sat next to her.

"So, Miss Sarah Ellen, how are you enjoying your visit?"

"Very much, Gabe. How could I not? The country-side is beautiful, and the Burkes have been so welcoming. And I am liking Caitlin better than I thought I would."

"You didn't like her?" asked Gabe, his surprise evident in his voice.

"From what you told me, she sounded young and spoiled. Marrying an Eastern gentleman and going off to teach in a fancy school."

"Now, Sadie, that doesn't make her spoiled. She fell in love with the man."

"Be honest, Gabe. What was your first opinion?" Sadie asked jokingly.

"Wal," he drawled, "I must confess that she seemed

a mite spoiled to me too. Especially around Sky. But I think it was just hard for her to come home and find someone else working with her horse."

"What is this Mr. Beecham like?" Sadie asked curiously.

"He sits a horse well, even though he's used to a postage-stamp saddle."

"I meant aside from how he is with horses, Gabe," said Sadie, jabbing her elbow into her brother's side.

"I guess women would consider him handsome. He must be smart as a whip, because he's going to be a lawyer."

"Is he right for Cait?"

"I reckon," Gabe replied slowly. "He loves her, that's for sure. They'll go back east and be real happy together." Gabe slid off the bale of hay and said, "There's a dance in town Saturday. I want you to promise me at least one waltz, Sarah Ellen, because I am sure all your dances will be gone with all the men flocking around you. It's high time you found someone to take care of you."

It was almost suppertime and as Sadie walked to the house, leaving Gabe to wash up, she thought about his description of Henry Beecham. His words were certainly all positive, but his tone had seemed a little forced. She decided to keep an eye on her brother when he was around Caitlin Burke, especially at the dance on Saturday.

Nineteen

It wasn't as easy to keep an eye on her brother as Sadie had supposed. Just as they arrived at the dance, an attractive, red-haired cowboy came up to Cait and stood shyly, his hat in his hand. "May I have the first waltz, Miss Cait."

"*Miss* Cait? Jimmy Murdoch, where have you been this past month? Out collecting more freckles?"

The cowboy looked down at her and gave her a wicked grin. "Why, I've only been off on a cattle drive to Dodge City. But you've been away for two years to a fancy school, so I figured I'd better treat you with the respect a proper young lady deserves."

"How many times did we ride for the mail together, Jimmy Murdoch? I didn't notice you treating me with any respect then!"

"Aw, Cait, you know I'm only teasing you. But my broken heart will feel a lot better if you'll only dance with me."

"Broken heart?" she replied skeptically.

"I hear you'll be leaving us soon." Sadie could tell he was only half teasing this time.

"I am, Jimmy. But since you have been loving and leaving girls for years, you have gotten your just desserts. But I will save a waltz for you. Sadie, this is my old friend, Jimmy Murdoch. The Murdochs own the ranch next to ours. Jimmy, this is Sadie Hart, who's visiting from Texas."

"Pleased to meet you, ma'am. Will you be my partner for this dance, Miss Hart?" he immediately asked as the caller summoned the dancers to the floor.

"I'd be delighted."

It was lucky that Gabe had reserved his dance ahead of time, for a new woman in town was never without partners. By the time the first waltz was struck up, Sadie had to turn away three men and gave Gabe a relieved smile when he came over to claim her.

He smiled down at her and said: "See, I told you, Sarah Ellen. You could have your choice of any man here."

"Gabe, those cowboys would flock around any new face, they're so starved for women, and you know it." She smiled as she saw Caitlin and Jimmy Murdoch waltz by them. "There goes one charming cowboy." Gabe glanced over. "I haven't seen him before."

"He's been out driving cattle. Evidently his family owns the spread next to the Burkes'. He and Cait are old friends. You'd think she'd have chosen someone like that, wouldn't you?" she continued.

"Not with her education. She can do a lot better than a cowboy."

"She's such a graceful dancer, isn't she, Gabe? Are you going to ask her for a dance?"

"I might, once I've had my turn with some of the other young ladies here," he replied noncommittally.

"Are you not dancing this one, Sadie?" Michael asked when he came upon their guest sitting out a *schottische*.

"I haven't been off that floor for two hours, Mr. Burke," laughed Sadie. "I'm just waiting for Jimmy Murdoch to bring me a glass of punch."

"Jimmy Murdoch, eh? Now, there's a fine lad. I was hoping once that he and Cait . . . but since they are not suited, maybe he'd be someone for you to consider, Sadie."

"Mr. Burke, you are as bad as my brother! I just got through taking care of my brothers and I am not panting to take on another responsibility."

"Ah, but marriage shouldn't be like motherin', Sadie," he said. "Not if you find the right man. But here comes Jimmy. I'll leave you two alone," he added with a wink.

"Here you are, Miss Hart."

"Thank you, Mr. Murdoch."

There was a stir at the door and Jimmy and Sadie watched as a well-dressed older man and his wife came in.

"Damn Mackie," Jimmy said under his breath without thinking.

"Oh, is that Nelson Mackie?" asked Sadie curiously.

"Beg your pardon, ma'am, for swearing. Yes, it is. He's been after my ma to sell since Pa died last spring."

"And she's refused?"

"She says she'll hold out as long as Michael Burke does."

Mackie settled his wife with the doctor's lady and went over to join the bank manager who was in a cluster of businessmen from town. "He has them all in his pocket," Jimmy muttered.

Sadie was no longer watching Mackie, for her eyes had been drawn back to the door. Juan Chavez was standing there, surveying the room like the predator he resembled, she thought with a shiver. Then their eyes met and he gave her a nod of recognition. She should ignore him, she knew, but no matter what he was rumored to be, he had seen her safely home the other day, and so she gave him a quick smile.

Oh, dear, that was a mistake, she thought, for he started to make his way around the room to where she was sitting. There was a dance already in progress, so she couldn't ask Jimmy to take her onto the dance floor. She was trapped.

"*Buenas noches,* Señorita Hart."

He was directly in front of her and she could hardly ignore him. He would be a hard man to ignore, Juan Chavez, in his dark green shirt tucked into black trousers studded with conchos.

"*Buenas noches,* Señor Chavez," she replied calmly. "Jimmy, do you know Señor Chavez?"

"Can't say that I do," Jimmy answered coldly. "Given who he works for, can't say that I want to," he added, giving Chavez a look of distaste.

"The feeling is mutual, I am sure, so perhaps you would like to get Miss Hart another glass of punch. Her glass is empty." Chavez spoke politely, almost as though they were in someone's drawing room, thought Sadie. But the look in his eyes would have convinced a lesser man than Jimmy Murdoch. Jimmy flushed red and Sadie saw his fists clench. The last thing she wanted, the last thing that was needed, was a fight over her!

"I *am* still thirsty, Jimmy," she said, with a pleading look. "I will be fine here until you get back," she reassured him.

Jimmy's hands relaxed and he told her he'd be back directly.

"I see you made it safely home, Miss Hart," Chavez continued in the same polite voice. "How is the mare?"

"Gabe has taken good care of her. He's sure her leg will heal completely."

"Your brother is very good with horses, isn't he?"

Sadie forgot whom she was talking to for a moment and her face lit up. "Gabe has a real talent. It has always been a joy to watch him with a horse. I still have a mare that he gentled for my fifteenth birthday, though she's getting old, of course."

"That couldn't have been that long ago, surely, señorita," said Chavez politely, but with a glint in his eye. It took Sadie a minute to realize that he was teasing her.

"A good ten years. I'm an old spinster schoolteacher, Senor Chavez."

"Hardly that, señorita." Chavez sat down next to her and Sadie was very conscious of the fact that their shoulders were touching. "Miss Burke is a very good dancer, isn't she?" Chavez observed as Caitlin went by on the arm of her partner. "I had half a waltz with her at the last dance, until your brother cut in. I'm surprised he isn't dancing with her tonight. I had the impression that there was some feeling there."

Sadie wanted nothing more than to ask: "Did you think so? Did you ever meet Henry Beecham?" Oddly enough she almost felt she could ask and Juan Chavez would answer her honestly. But he *was* Mackie's henchman, so how could she be contemplating a good gossip with him as though he were her brother?

"Oh, look, here comes Jimmy with my lemonade," she said brightly, thanking God for Murdoch's approach. She expected Chavez to stand up and yield his seat to Jimmy. Not only did he sit there, claiming his territory, he leaned his shoulder into hers.

"Here you are, Miss Hart." Jimmy stood there awkwardly, aware that the music had stopped, the dance floor was clear and he was promised to Mrs. Burke for the next dance.

"Miss Hart, I promised Mrs. Burke this next dance, but if you want . . . I am sure she'd understand . . ." he said helplessly.

"You can't disappoint Mrs. Burke. I will be fine, Mr. Murdoch."

"Are you sure?"

"Absolutely."

"You are a wise woman, Miss Hart," said Chavez after Jimmy left. "Like all redheads, Murdoch has a quick temper. I'd hate to disturb a pleasant occasion like this. Ah, this next dance is a waltz. I would have had to cut in anyway," he added. He didn't smile, to show he was teasing again. He wasn't teasing, Sadie realized. He was completely serious.

"Do you always bully people into what you want, Señor Chavez?"

"Let us just say I am good at persuasion, señorita. May I have this waltz?"

"Are you asking or telling?" Sadie snapped back at him.

Chavez surprised her by laughing. It was a spontaneous, natural laugh. "I enjoy you, señorita. Do you think I could persuade, no, charm you into a dance with me?"

"You are about as charming as a snake, Señor Chavez," she said with an amused smile. She could have held out. She *should* have held out, for she didn't really believe he would force her. But she realized, with no small surprise that she wanted a waltz with Juan Chavez. Just one.

"It *is* a tempting melody, though, isn't it?" she said, as though she was the one hinting for an invitation.

"Ah, I see that *you* are out to charm me, señorita." Chavez put his arm around her waist and guided her to the floor.

The melody was a lovely one; Sadie had not been lying about that. There was an underlying sadness to it that made her feel that she wanted something that she couldn't have, although she wasn't sure what that something was. They moved well together, as though they had danced many times before and were both so lost in that surprising sensation that they were silent for the first few measures.

Sadie was used to Gabe's relaxed dancing. She wondered if Chavez ever relaxed, even on the dance floor. It was not tension she felt, but an energy that seemed akin to the constant awareness of an animal in the wild. Juan Chavez was present in every cell of his body. And so she couldn't help being aware of him. It was as though a magnetic force flowed between them.

"Your brother is glaring at us, señorita," said Chavez, bending his head next to her ear as though he were whispering to her. His warm breath on her neck made her shiver.

"You are afraid for me, no?" he teased in an exaggerated Mexican accent.

"I am afraid for you, no," she replied tartly. "If I am afraid for anyone, it is me. Gabe won't like it that I danced with you. I can't say I blame him, given who you work for and what you do."

"What do I do, señorita?"

"You frighten people off their land, Señor Chavez, and all for greedy bullies like Nelson Mackie. I may not have been here long, but I recognize his type. We have them in Texas."

"And my type?"

"You are one of a kind, Señor Chavez. Which is probably why I am foolish enough to be waltzing with you!"

She looked up at him and was very surprised to see him smiling down at her. It was a genuine smile, one that reached his eyes, softening them so that they were no longer those of a predator, but of a man who seemed to enjoy her company.

"And will your brother's frowns get you to interrupt our waltz?"

"Gabe is a protective older brother and I love him for it, but no, I will not be rude and create a scene for him or anyone. You were kind to me the other day and I am grateful."

"Ah, and so you are only returning my kindness?" said Chavez with mock disappointment.

"I told you already, Señor Chavez," said Sadie, grinning up at him, "I don't know *what* I'm doing dancing with you."

But she did. She knew that she would waltz until the music stopped because it wasn't only the music that sang to her of wanting what you couldn't have. There was something between them, something that drew her like a magnet draws iron filings. It was something she knew she couldn't have, but she would enjoy the bittersweet waltz whether she should or not.

When Gabe saw Chavez with Sadie, he cursed under his breath and watched them closely. He didn't think his sister would be intimidated by the man, but she might have agreed to the dance rather than risk publicly insulting him. But as he watched, Gabe realized she actually seemed to be enjoying it. And Chavez certainly was! He'd never seen the man smile before.

When the music ended, Chavez took Sadie's arm and had the nerve to walk her over to her brother. "I enjoyed my dance with your sister very much, Señor Hart. *Muchas gracias, señorita.*"

"*De nada,* señor," Sadie replied.

"Well, at first I thought he'd bullied you into it, but you sure seemed to be enjoying your dance, Sarah Ellen," Gabe drawled sardonically after Chavez took his leave.

"I am sure she was just pretending, weren't you,

Sadie?" said Caitlin who had hurried over as soon as she saw Chavez walk away.

"Stop growling at me, Gabe," Sadie told her brother. "I'm old enough to make my own decisions now. And I don't know why I said yes to him, Cait. But I wasn't pretending. Señor Chavez is a very good dancer and I enjoyed my waltz with him," she added defiantly.

Gabe gave an exasperated laugh. "I should know better than to get after you, Sadie. You're the same contrary little sister I remember! Well, I don't suppose you'll listen to me, but I don't think it's a good idea to dance with the enemy, Sarah Ellen."

"I don't imagine he'll be asking me again," Sadie responded tartly.

Gabe was very conscious that Caitlin Burke was standing there, listening to them go at each other. "Don't worry, Miss Cait," he reassured her. "This is just like old times, isn't it, Sadie?"

"Yes, he always did think he could tell me what to do just because he was the oldest."

"Well, there is Miss Louise Taylor just waiting for me to claim my dance," said Gabe. "I'll see you two ladies later."

Cait watched Gabe make his way across the floor and was very conscious of the fact that he had danced with every woman in the room at least once and now Louise Taylor for the second time this evening. Every woman, that is, except Caitlin Burke. He had done a very good job of avoiding her. She and Sadie stood there watching Gabe and then Juan Chavez leading their new partners onto the floor for a *schottische,* each lost in a bittersweet moment of wanting another dance with a man who was not for her.

Twenty

Sunday morning after the dance, Gabe lay in his cot. Sunday's work always started later, for the Burkes often went to mass at the little Spanish church near El Morro. Or at least Michael and his daughter, for as Mrs. Burke had told Gabe on his first Sunday there, her Protestant soul would not allow her to attend too many masses.

He pictured Miss Cait dressed in her Sunday best, that aster blue dress that brought out the color of her eyes, and groaned as he felt himself becoming aroused. Damn. It had been very hard to keep away from her last night. He had been aware of her the whole evening: whom she was dancing with, laughing with, even flirting with. He had wanted a waltz with her, wanted to have his arms around her again, to feel the sweet curve of her waist under his hand. But what was the point of encouraging such feelings when she would be leaving in a few weeks' time? So he had exercised a firm control over himself. Not, of course, he thought, with an ironic laugh, that she would have noticed or cared that he was avoiding her.

He had been almost happy by the distraction Sadie had provided him by dancing with Chavez. Lord, his sister was something, he thought with a smile as he sat up and ran his hand through his hair. Well, since a part of him was already awake and up, he thought ruefully, he may as well get up. After peeing and splashing himself down with lukewarm water from the rain barrel as he always did on Sunday, his desire had subsided. He was just coming in from the back door of the bar, toweling his face and hair, shirtless and his jeans unbuttoned at the waist when he almost ran right into Miss Caitlin Burke.

"Why, uh, Miss Cait. I was just washing up. I thought you and your father were off to church?" He was standing there, jabbering like an idiot, thought Gabe.

"I am sorry I disturbed you, Mr. Hart. I didn't think anyone would be up yet. Da left a half hour ago by himself. I was too tired after last night to go with him. I just came to see how Snowflake is doing." Cait was able to keep her voice calm and even but she couldn't help the slight flush of embarrassment that rose from her neck to her face.

She had seen men shirtless before, of course. Her Da for one. Jake, when he was pounding at fence posts. But this was different, more intimate, because Gabe Hart had obviously just come in from his Sunday washup. He had silvery-blond hair on his chest, she realized, which ran down his flat stomach to the open buttons of his denims. He was built so long and lean, she thought, and blushed deeper as she realized where her thoughts were taking her.

"I'll just go take a look at Snowflake's hock, shall I?" she said brightly, as though they were exchanging polite words in someone's parlor.

Gabe smiled as he watched her scurry off. He finished toweling himself dry and put on his old work shirt that he left hanging in the tack room. He tucked it into his jeans and buttoning up the last button, sauntered over to Snowflake's stall thanking God that Miss Caitlin Burke had not wandered in earlier. A good-morning piss and a wash calmed a man down considerably.

He leaned over the stall door and watched her unwrap the mare's bandage. She ran her hand down Snowflake's leg, a look of satisfaction on her face.

"The arnica wrap seems to have brought the swelling down quickly, Miss Cait," said Gabe.

"Yes. Da has always sworn by it for strains and bruises, Mr. Hart. You've done a good job of taking care of her."

"You can leave her leg unwrapped. I'm going to put on a fresh-soaked bandage today."

Gabe opened the stall door and Caitlin came out. He was standing in front of her, unconsciously blocking her way to the barn door and they stood there for a moment each very aware of the other's presence.

"I was surprised to see you up after all that dancing, Miss Cait," said Gabe, finally breaking the silence. "You were one of the most popular young ladies there," he added with a smile, "dancing with everyone in the room." It was an automatic compliment, given just to break the tension hanging between them.

"Not everyone, Mr. Hart. You never asked me to dance." Cait said it without thinking and now it was Gabe who flushed red with embarrassment. What was he supposed to say? That he had avoided her on purpose because she was too tempting? "Uh, every time I was going to speak to you, it seemed like someone else had got there first," he replied lamely. It wasn't true and both of them knew it. But Cait was too appalled by her own forwardness to do anything but smile brightly and say: "Then it is too bad we were both disappointed, Mr. Hart. Excuse me, but I must get back to help with breakfast."

Gabe backed out of the way and she was gone out the door before he had a chance to say good-bye. Then what she had actually said sunk in and he stood there grinning at the realization that Caitlin Burke had noticed the fact that he hadn't danced with her and had, it seemed, been disappointed. Not that it meant much, he told himself, his grin fading. She was still engaged to her Henry. She'd forget a few missed dances with Gabe Hart very quickly.

After breakfast, Sadie followed her brother out to the corral.

"Can I watch you with the colts, Gabe?" she asked.

"I don't work them on Sunday, Sadie. We take it as a day of rest and only do the necessary chores. But

I am going to work with Sky this morning," he added. "I don't like to leave off with him even for a day."

Night Sky was such a beautiful animal that it would be a shame if Gabe were not successful, thought Sadie as she watched her brother put the horse through his paces on the lunge line. She had seen many a piebald and paint in her time but none of them could compare with Sky's spotted coat. He moved fluidly, too, she thought as she admired his canter. The only thing about him that might be considered less than beautiful was his tail and mane, for all the Appaloosas had this same feature. But then, she realized, as she continued to watch, you kind of got used to the look. It *fit*, somehow, though she couldn't say why.

Gabe had brought out the old saddle blanket and brought Sky over to him. The horse would now allow Gabe to rub him down all over, but whenever Gabe lingered near his back or tried to leave his arm there, Sky would give a few little crow-hops away from him.

"You know, Gabe," Sadie said after he'd released the horse into the pasture and came over to the fence, "I can almost understand Cait's impatience. He is such a beautiful animal and his gaits are just about perfect. I was itching to ride him myself, just watching you."

"Don't think I don't know how you felt, Sadie," her brother said with a rueful grin. "Sometimes I have to work real hard to keep myself from leading him over to the fence and slipping on. I've come to love that horse, you know," he added softly. "That's what patience and holding yourself back leads to, most times: love. But if I'm successful, I lose him when Miss Burke goes back east," he added with a sigh.

"And if you are not successful?"

"Wal, like most ranchers, Mr. Burke can't have a useless animal around," Gabe drawled. "But if it comes to that, I'll offer to buy him."

"A horse you can't ride!"

"He's too fine an animal to destroy, Sadie. And it would give me more time to work with him."

"Then I don't know whether to wish you luck or not, Gabe," said Sadie with a wry grin.

*   *   *

Michael Burke had not returned by dinnertime, although that did not seem to worry his wife too much, thought Gabe as they all sat down for a roast chicken and fresh vegetables from the garden. "Michael told me we should go ahead if he wasn't back," Elizabeth explained as she served them. "He was planning to ride up to Eduardo's camp after mass, just to check on things. Your meeting Chavez up there made him a little nervous," she added, looking over at Sadie. Sadie blushed and felt somehow responsible, though she couldn't have explained why, had anyone asked her. She certainly wasn't responsible for meeting Juan Chavez. Nor for his following her down. She had agreed to dance with him, but one waltz was hardly something to feel guilty about, she told herself.

Two hours after dinner, when Michael still hadn't returned, Elizabeth went over to the bunkhouse to find Gabe. He was sitting on the steps, braiding the reins of a bridle.

"Gabe, I hate to disturb you, for this is usually your time off, but I'm beginning to get worried about Mr. Burke. He said he might miss dinner, but I didn't expect him to take this long."

Gabe looked up at the sun. "I reckon it is almost three o'clock, Mrs. Burke. He might just be having a cup of coffee with Eduardo. And you know how Eduardo loves to talk," he added with a smile. "He's up there by himself for days and whenever I go up with supplies he talks my ear off."

"I suppose you could be right," admitted Elizabeth. "I guess I wouldn't be worried if it weren't for Chavez being seen around."

"No need to apologize for worrying, ma'am. I tell you what," said Gabe, putting the bridle down, "why don't I just saddle up Buck and ride out toward the mountains. I'm sure I'll meet Mr. Burke before I get to the foothills," he added reassuringly.

"Thank you, Gabe. I hate to be so fidgety, but I don't like thinking of Michael out there alone."

Gabe was actually a little worried himself the farther he rode. He'd expected to see Michael before the foothills, as he'd told Elizabeth, but it wasn't until he started climbing that he saw his employer coming down the trail toward him. He was going slowly and at first Gabe wondered if another horse had gone lame. But Patch wasn't limping and then Gabe noticed what was tied behind Michael's saddle.

He spurred his paint and pulled up in front of Michael.

"Who is it?" he asked, gesturing at the oilcloth-wrapped body slung over Patch.

"Eduardo," Michael replied, pain and anger in his voice.

"An accident?" Gabe asked, not very hopefully.

"Only if a man can collect two bullets in the chest and one in the leg by accident," Michael said bitterly.

Gabe rested his hand on Eduardo's body and cursed eloquently and fluently.

"Yes, boyo, that's exactly what I've been thinkin'."

"Goddamn Mackie and his hired killers! His 'wolf.' It must have been Chavez. He was up here skulking around, maybe even intending to kill Eduardo last week when Sadie appeared." Gabe's voice was shaking with fury and fear. His sister had probably just missed being a victim herself and the man had the balls to waltz with her on Saturday!

"We don't know that for certain, Gabe," said Michael. "That it was one of Mackie's men, I am sure, but we have no way of knowing which one," he added with real regret. "For if we did, by God, I'd kill him with my own bare hands. Eduardo has worked for me for sixteen years. *Dia,* and I'll have to tell his wife and children."

They rode on in silence and Gabe remembered his first meeting with Eduardo when he'd ridden into the sheepherder's camp.

"Did he get a chance to defend himself, Mr. Burke?"

"His shotgun was lying next to him, but it hadn't been fired. I'd guess they came up on him suddenly and it was over quickly, thank Christ."

They parted at the road and Gabe watched Michael for a few minutes before he turned his horse toward the ranch. He met Elizabeth halfway down the drive. "I couldn't stand the waiting," she explained. "You didn't find him then?" she added, an agonized look on her face. Without thinking, Gabe laid his hand on her shoulder to reassure her. "I found him, Mrs. Burke, and he is all right."

He could feel the tension drain out of her. "But where is he then?"

"Mr. Burke is all right, but I have bad news. Eduardo has been killed."

"Oh, no," cried Elizabeth. "He has been with us for years. Who could have wanted to hurt him?"

Gabe just looked at her.

"Mackie, of course," she said with heavy irony.

"Mr. Burke and I are sure of it."

"Well, this time he has gone too far. He's finally hurt someone and revealed himself as the criminal he is," said Elizabeth passionately.

"I don't know as there is any proof, ma'am," Gabe cautioned her.

"Proof! His hired animal was out there just last week. It was Chavez," she said with a shudder. "I knew I was right to fear him."

Twenty-one

Michael didn't get back until after dark and they all gathered around the table while he attacked the supper Elizabeth had saved for him. " 'Twas a long day without anything in my belly, *a ghra*," he said. "Thank you for saving something for me."

"What *happened*, Da?" Caitlin asked anxiously.

"The dog came running to meet me, barking like crazy, so I knew something was wrong right away. I thought maybe Eduardo had had an accident. I hoped it was only that."

"But why didn't Chino warn Eduardo? He might have escaped them."

"My guess is that he was up with the sheep, Cait. And even if he had warned him, I doubt Eduardo would have left the flock. He would have stood his ground. No, I think they came on him so quickly that he didn't even have time to fire his gun." Michael took a sip of coffee and was silent for a minute. " 'Twas one of the hardest things I've done, bringing Eduardo to Elena's house. He was a good man and a good friend to me." Cait could see tears in her father's eyes. "Damn Mackie and his men to hell," he cursed softly. "*Dia*, but maybe I should have just given in months ago," he added. "Eduardo would still be alive."

"You made the right choice, Michael," said Elizabeth, reaching across the table and taking his hand in hers. "Eduardo made a choice, too. He knew it was dangerous, but he stayed with us."

"At least you can end it now, Da," said Cait. "You have proof you can take to the sheriff."

"What proof, Cait?" responded Michael wearily.

"Why, Eduardo was murdered, Da! You *know* who did it."

"And who would that be?"

"Why, Juan Chavez, Da. He was up there, probably to kill Eduardo the day Sadie came along."

"The sheriff will have to do something, Michael," Elizabeth added in agreement with her daughter.

"I will go to town first thing in the morning, Elizabeth. I will tell him Eduardo was murdered. I'll even tell him that Chavez was up there last week. But if he asks me, and he will, I'll have to tell him that half my sheep were run off too. And he'll most likely conclude that it was common rustling and that Eduardo died defending the flock."

"But, Da, it is so clear," Cait protested.

"I am sure as my name is Michael Joseph Burke that Mackie is responsible for this, Caitlin," said Michael grimly. "But what *proof* do I have, even for an honest sheriff? Chavez, or whoever it was, was hardly going to leave a polite note, admitting it. No, whoever did it was very smart to run off the sheep."

"I can't believe we can't do anything," Cait protested.

"We can try to push the sheriff to investigate. And we can decide, right here and now, if we want to give in," added Michael, looking at his wife and daughter and then over at Gabe.

"Sell the ranch, Da!"

"It was a good man they murdered, Cait. I'd sell if you wanted me to, Elizabeth, to prevent more bloodshed." He looked over at his wife and Cait could see the pain in his eyes. They had worked so hard for what they had. She couldn't bear the thought of them losing it.

"We'd have the horses and the sheep, *a ghra*," added Michael.

"But no land, Michael. Where would we go? No, this is our home and I will not have a bully like Mackie drive us off it," Elizabeth replied in a voice shaking with grief and anger.

"This could be his last attempt to scare us off,"

Michael speculated hopefully. "Even Mackie would have a hard time explaining an injury to me or my family." He hesitated. "Cait, what do you say?"

"I say we stay, Da," she answered fiercely.

"Gabe? I could well understand if ye wanted to change your mind and leave and I'd not blame you one bit. If he pushes me any further it will come to fighting, for I am not going to take any more from him and his hired dogs," Michael added.

"I'm in, Mr. Burke," said Gabe quietly. "I'm tired of wandering. I want to settle down here. As long as you need a wrangler, I'm yours."

"As long as I've got horses, I'll need you, Gabe," Michael answered with a grateful smile. "Well, Miss Sarah Ellen, we'd better put you on the next stage back to Texas."

"Oh, no, Mr. Burke. Unless I am a burden as a guest, I want to stay till this is all settled. I can't leave now, not knowing what might happen to Gabe," she added.

"You are welcome here as long as you like," said Elizabeth. "We just don't want you to be in any danger."

"I'm not afraid, Mrs. Burke."

"Well, then, that's settled," said Michael. "And a good thing it is and a relief to me, to know that you'll be safe back east, Cait, in just a few weeks."

"Yes," said Elizabeth, giving her daughter a quick hug. "I have been dreading your leaving, but now I am relieved you will be away from all of this."

Cait had been so caught up in her determination that her family not give in to Mackie, she had actually forgotten that she herself was leaving anyway. That in less than three weeks she'd be on a train to Philadelphia with Henry. As she helped her mother with the dishes, she realized that Sadie and Gabe, two strangers, would be here with her parents, taking on a fight that did not really belong to them while she was teaching young women the finer points of English literature. All at once it seemed so unimportant what interpretation one placed on Jane's decision to return to Mr.

Rochester, compared to the life and death reality that she would be leaving behind.

Later, as she got herself ready for bed, she felt almost torn in half. The East was where she had decided to build a new home with Henry. A home where her horizons would be expanded, where she would have access to theater and music. A home that would not be threatened by the harsh realities of life in New Mexico: the constant struggle for survival, the harshness of the desert, brutal men like Mackie.

But to leave it all behind *now,* when the two people she loved most were threatened? How could she do that? This was the home of her childhood: the ranch, the desert, the mountains. She loved it all, even every grain of the red dust that got into everything.

She sat by her window awhile, watching the stars come out, one by one and then in clusters. It was a moonless night, so she could not see the mountains, but she knew they were there. How could she leave them? Yet how could she stay? She was promised to Henry. She loved Henry too, didn't she? Surely a grown-up woman would be able to leave her parents behind, no matter how difficult the situation, if she loved her fiancé?

She closed her eyes and pictured Henry's face. She was sure she could imagine his response to Eduardo's death. He'd want first to protect her, to get her out of there and back east where it was safe, where disputes were settled in court, not with threats and violence. What if she told him she wanted to stay until things were settled one way or the other? That she needed to be with her parents. That this was her *home* and she couldn't leave while it was being threatened. Could he understand? If she loved him, wouldn't she want to be with him, no matter how hard it was to leave? Even her parents wanted her out of it. "Home is where the heart is." The old adage came to her mind. Where was her heart?

She couldn't sleep, not in this state. She threw on her old blue flannel wrapper and tiptoed quietly down the stairs. The nights were growing a little cooler now

as fall approached and the stars burned bright and
clear above her as she made her way to the near pasture where she perched on the fence. She could hear
the horses stirring and without thinking, gave a low-
pitched whistle. It was Gabe's whistle, not hers.

She heard the horse before she could see him. He
gave a little snort as he headed for the fence and
realized there was no Gabe and therefore no oats. Yet
he didn't back away when she held out her hand, but
thrust his muzzle into it hopefully. Cait slipped down
next to him, half expecting him to shy away, but as
though sensing her mood, he came closer and rested
his muzzle on her shoulder, just as she'd seen Finn do
with her father. It was as though Sky was trying to
comfort her and the tears she had been holding back
all evening finally came. She leaned against his shoulder, crying into it and the miracle was that he let her.

"You've forgiven me, haven't you?" she whispered
as her tears finally stopped. He turned his head and
whuffed a few breaths down her neck. She took a
deep shuddering breath and ran her hand gently up
his neck. She expected him to back away, but he
stayed close and butted her with his head as if to say:
"Are you all right now?"

"How can I leave?" she whispered. "I do care for
Henry, but not enough. Not the way a wife should, I
am afraid. I *can't* leave Ma and Da and 'cleave to my
husband,' " she said with a little sobbing laugh.

The word itself was strange. To cleave to Henry, to
unite with him in that profound way seemed to mean
that she must tear herself away from all she loved.
And that felt like taking an ax and cleaving her heart
in two.

"I can't leave," she told Sky quietly. "Not now. I
don't know if Henry can understand. I don't know
that I understand."

Sky nodded up and down as if he had understood
everything she had said. She smiled and then froze as
she heard someone coming up behind her.

"Were you planning to ride him again?" Gabe's

voice came out of the darkness. He said it teasingly, but she was so startled that she couldn't hear that.

"No, Mr. Hart, you needn't worry that I'd do anything so foolish again," she responded in a quiet voice, turning to face him. Gabe was standing on the other side of the fence, his gun in his hand. "I didn't really think you were, Miss Cait," he said apologetically. "But I heard someone out here and thought I'd better check."

He holstered his gun in such an easy practiced movement and Cait suddenly realized that there was a side of Gabe Hart she didn't know at all.

"I couldn't sleep," she explained. "Not after Eduardo."

"Come on, let me get you back to the house," he said, leaning over the fence and extending a hand to her. "You'll catch yourself a death, as my ma used to say," he added as he saw her shiver.

Cait reached out and took his hand, grateful for his support. It was awkward climbing in her wrapper and as it was, her robe caught on the fence and pulled away from her shoulders.

"Here, Miss Cait," said Gabe, as he released it and draped it across her shoulders.

"Thank you, Mr. Hart," she said, pulling it closed.

"It looks like Sky is worried about you," he added as the horse tried to nuzzle Cait's neck through the fence.

"I think we are back to trusting each other," she said gratefully. "Though he was disappointed at first that it wasn't you with a bucket of oats."

"You'd best be inside, Miss Cait. Don't you worry about anything," he added. "Your father and mother will be all right. I am sure this is Mackie's last try and all will be quiet after you leave."

"You can't be sure of anything where Mackie and Chavez are concerned and you know that, Mr. Hart. And I am not leaving," she added quietly. She didn't quite know why she was telling Gabe Hart before her parents, but it was said before she thought it out.

"What do you mean, not leaving?"

"Just what I said, Mr. Hart. I can't go in the middle of all this."

"But Mr. Beecham . . . he'll be back in a few weeks."

"I know, and I hope he will understand."

"You'll put off your wedding then?"

Caitlin stopped and looked up at Gabe. "I am not sure of anything anymore, Mr. Hart. Except one thing: this is my home and I will not leave it while it is being threatened."

Gabe heard both the tears and determination in her voice. It must have been a hard decision for her to make. The girl he had thought Caitlin Burke to be most likely would have been heartbroken, but she would have left with her Henry. But this was not a girl's decision, it was a woman's.

They walked in silence until they reached the house.

"Good night, Mr. Hart," whispered Cait.

"I am glad to hear you are staying, Miss Cait," he whispered back. Cait tiptoed up the stairs, wondering why his words warmed her so.

Twenty-two

Michael was up and on his way to town before anyone else but Elizabeth was up. The sheriff's office was closed when he arrived, so he sat on the bench in front of the jail until he saw Sheriff Butler approaching.

"Are you waiting for me, Burke?"

Michael nodded and watched with barely concealed distaste as Butler wiped grease and crumbs off his mustache with his sleeve. He took his time opening the door and then sat down behind his desk and rummaged through some papers before looking up at Michael and belching.

"Excuse me, Mr. Burke," he said with a grin. "Mary serves a heavy breakfast. Now, what can I do for you?"

"I am here to report the murder of Eduardo Vigil, Sheriff. I don't think his killer or killers will be hard to find. If I were you, I'd go up to the Mackie ranch and start with Juan Chavez."

"Now just sit down a minute, Mr. Burke, and let me take down the details. How do you know Eduardo was murdered?"

Michael gritted his teeth. "Because he had two bullets in his chest and one in his leg, Sheriff. And because my wife and I have been threatened several times by Mackie. You also know that only a short while ago, Mackie poisoned several of my sheep."

"Mr. Burke," said Butler with exaggerated patience, "I told you then and I tell you now, we don't know anything of the sort. Those sheep could have eaten jimson weed for all we know. Mr. Mackie is one of the valley's most distinguished citizens. Just because he wants to buy your ranch doesn't make him responsible for a few sheep getting sick."

"This time it wasn't sheep, Butler! It was a good man murdered in cold blood. And Chavez was seen riding down from the sheep meadows only last week."

"Was there any real evidence to suggest it was Señor Chavez who killed Eduardo?"

"If you mean, did he leave a card with his name on it, Sheriff," Michael replied, "then no. But he is Mackie's man and has bullied several families off their land."

"But not hurt anyone, to my knowledge."

"No," Michael had to admit. "Not until now."

"Tell me, Mr. Burke," said Butler, leaning back in his chair, his hands folded over his big belly, "were any of your sheep missing?"

"About half the flock, but that does not mean anything, Sheriff."

"Not mean anything? Why, Mr. Burke, it means that someone has been stealing sheep. Eduardo likely caught them at it and got killed for his loyal efforts to protect your flock."

"It means that whoever did this wanted it to look like that. Damn you, Butler. Aren't you going to do anything?" Michael demanded, standing up and leaning over the desk.

The sheriff's chair came down with a thud. "I am going to take a deputy and ride out to see for myself, Burke. But I am not going to make a fool of myself charging the most prominent citizen of our town with murder."

"I didn't really think you would, Butler," said Michael with barely disguised contempt.

It was no surprise, of course, he thought as he rode home, that that *gobshite* would do nothing. Mackie was the most powerful citizen in the valley and the sheriff made sure to keep on his good side. They would just have to hope that Mackie would give up when he realized that not even murder would make Michael sell.

He was so distracted by his frustrated fury that he

didn't notice the rider approaching until he was almost upon him. He pulled Patch up when he saw that it was Chavez on his black.

"*Buenos dias,* Señor Burke," said Chavez with the annoying mock polite tone he used with everyone.

" 'Tis not a good day with such men as you and Mackie in it," Michael replied coldly.

Chavez's hand moved toward his gun, but Michael's hand reached out and had the Mexican's wrist in an iron grip.

"Oh, no, boyo, you won't push me to draw on you. I'm slower and you know it and I've no intention of dying at your hands. And even the sheriff would have a hard time explaining my death away, seeing as I've just been to town to report Eduardo's murder." Michael's eyes met Chavez's cold, green-eyed stare and it was the younger man who lowered his gaze first.

"Take your hand off me, Señor Burke. I did not kill your Eduardo. And I am not about to kill you."

Michael released Chavez's wrist but let his own hand rest on his holster.

"It was a cold-blooded murder, Chavez, and you've been hanging around my sheep camp. If ever I have any proof, you can be sure ye'll hang for it, boyo," said Michael and then rode off without a backward look.

Juan Chavez had known that Michael Burke was not easily intimidated. But he may have underestimated him, he thought ruefully as he rubbed his wrist, with his Irish brogue and smiling blue eyes. Those eyes had not been smiling when they looked at him, no, through him. And although it may have been many years ago, the man had been an Indian fighter in the U.S. Cavalry.

Eduardo murdered? Chavez wouldn't go so far as to say that he had liked the old man. But Eduardo had reminded him of Ruben, one of Romero's riders and one of the few men on the hacienda who'd been kind to him. Or at least not slapped him around. Damn Mackie. He must have sent someone up there and there had been no need for it. He wheeled his gelding around and headed back to the ranch.

Mackie was just finishing his breakfast when Chavez was admitted.

"Do you want some coffee, Juan?" he asked, looking up from his plate.

"I don't want anything, señor, except an explanation."

Mackie looked at him coldly. "I pay you to intimidate others, Señor Chavez, not to attempt it with me. Now sit down."

Chavez clenched his hand as though to keep it from reaching for his gun and then relaxed it. There was no sense in antagonizing or killing his present employer, he thought ironically and with a deceptively mild voice said "*Si*, señor," and sat.

Mackie took his time finishing his breakfast and then lighting up a cigar, looked over at Chavez and said: "Now what is it that requires an explanation?"

"I have just met Mr. Burke coming from town and he tells me that Eduardo Vigil was murdered."

Mackie raised his eyebrows. "He wasted no time getting to the sheriff, did he? I'll have to get Butler out here and see what Burke wanted."

"He wants me, señor . . . hanging from a rope."

Mackie laughed.

"It is not so amusing to me, Señor Mackie."

"No one will be hanging from a rope, Chavez. He has no proof."

"He certainly has no proof of my involvement, because I wasn't there."

"Look, Juan, your way worked real well with the other small ranchers. But Michael Burke is a stubborn Irishman who has had the misfortune to meet an even more stubborn one. I want this over with. I want his ranch. So I sent Wilson and Canty out to do a different kind of persuading."

"I see. And so you think killing Eduardo will make Burke give in?"

"I'm sure of it. Why, he'll be knocking at my door today, begging me to take his ranch."

"Senor Burke was not in a begging mood when I saw him, señor," said Chavez, with a thin smile.

"Oh, he's likely angry now. Probably thinks he can get the law after me. But I own the law. Just like I own you, Chavez. *Comprende*?" Mackie looked Juan straight in the eye as he said it but this time, he was the one who lowered his gaze, even as Chavez said submissively, *"Si, señor. Comprendo."*

"Comprendo, señor. I understand, Mr. Mackie. In Spanish or English, no matter who blinked first, what it really meant was "Yes, sir, boss."

He'd been following orders for years, so why should it start bothering him now? Chavez wondered. Mackie was no better and certainly no worse than any of the other men he had worked for. They'd all paid him well and because he did his job better than anyone else, given him free rein. It was the closest he'd ever come to freedom since he was sold to the Romero hacienda. But every now and then he was made very aware that someone else called the shots. "El Lobo" they called him. "El Lobo" was how he thought of himself. But maybe, Chavez realized as he walked away from the ranch house, just maybe, he was only a dog disguised as a wolf. An old dog, at that. Almost thirty-seven and what did he have to show for his life? Nothing. No home, no woman, no children. *Dios,* it had never bothered him before! Why was he thinking like this now? There was something about Mackie and this damned valley. And, he had to admit it, about Michael and Elizabeth Burke. He respected Burke. He respected anyone who stood up to him. And Elizabeth Burke . . . There was something about her that was disturbing, that made him remember things that he didn't want to remember.

"Mierde! I'd rather be working for someone like Burke," he said to himself with a mirthless laugh. But a man like Burke would have no need for a man like me. So, maybe you are only an old dog, Juan Chavez, and you know the old saying: You can't teach an old dog new tricks."

*   *   *

Cait had planned to tell her parents about her decision to stay that evening after supper. But when Michael recounted his meeting with the sheriff, he looked over at his daughter and said, "Now, I don't want ye thinking we want to get rid of ye, Cait, but 'tis glad I am ye'll be off with Henry soon."

Cait was sitting across the table from Gabe and when he looked up at her father's words, met his eyes. He gave her an encouraging nod, and taking a deep breath, she said: "Da, Ma, I have something to tell you. I am not going back with Henry. At least not now."

"But he will be here in two weeks! How can ye not go back?" exclaimed Michael.

"Are you *sure* you just don't want to get rid of me, Da?" teased Cait.

"*Dia,* how could you think that! I hate the idea of you going, but you can't let our troubles stand in your way."

"They are my troubles too, Da," Cait told him quietly. "This is my home and I want to be with you and Ma and help you fight for it."

"I'm hopin' it won't come to that, Cait. It probably won't," said Michael reassuringly. "What if ye let Henry go and there is no fighting needed?"

"Then I could always follow him on another train, couldn't I, Da?"

They had all finished their dinner and were just drinking their coffee. "Come, Sadie," said Gabe, "it's a nice evening. Why don't we sit outside to finish our coffee?"

Sadie excused herself and Elizabeth said gratefully, "Thank you, Sadie." She turned back to her daughter as the door closed.

"What are you going to tell Henry, Caitlin?" she asked, placing her hand over her daughter's.

"I'm not sure, Ma. Oh, I will certainly tell him my main reason: that I can't leave you and Da with things so unsettled and dangerous."

"He'll think that all the more reason for you to go, Cait," Elizabeth replied.

"And if this is Mackie's worst, and he gives up when he sees we won't budge, will ye be telling Henry ye'll be on the next train?" asked Michael.

"I don't know, Da," she confessed.

"Ye can't lead the man on, daughter."

"I don't think I can marry him, Ma," she said with a little choke in her voice. "I don't think I love him enough to leave you behind. This is my *home*. . . ."

"When you love someone, then he becomes your home, Cait," Elizabeth said softly.

"You said that about you and Da, Ma, whenever you told me the story of how you left the army to come here. That wherever you went, you had a home in each other."

" 'Tis true, Cait. That's what lovin' someone means," said her father.

"Then maybe I don't love Henry. I *thought* I did," she said, her voice breaking.

"Of course, you did, my dear," said Elizabeth, putting her arm around her.

"I don't want to hurt him . . ."

" 'Twould hurt a man far more to find out later that ye didn't really love him," Michael told her gently.

"You are sure you are not doing this for us, Cait?"

"I am sure, Ma. This is where I belong, not back east."

"Oh, I am so happy not to lose you," whispered Elizabeth.

"And I am so proud of you, Cait," said her father. "I know this was a hard decision to make. This is a woman's decision," he added, reaching over and stroking her hair.

"Well, that was a surprise," said Sadie as she and Gabe walked down toward the pasture. "I feel sorry for this poor Henry."

Gabe only grunted his agreement and Sadie pulled him by the arm. "You don't sound that surprised, Gabe. Or that sorry for Henry," she added with a quick smile.

"She told me about it last night, Sadie."

"She? Caitlin?"

"She couldn't sleep and was out telling Sky all her troubles. I heard the horses stirring and came out to see what it was, is all. So you can stop thinking what you're thinking, Sarah Ellen."

"How do you know what I am thinking, Gabe Hart?"

"She doesn't know I'm alive. And I'm just her daddy's horse wrangler."

"A lot more than a wrangler, Gabe. I'd say that Mr. Burke trusts you like he would a partner. Do you *want* her to know you're alive?" she asked lightly.

Gabe stopped and gave his sister a humorously despairing look. "Wal, Sadie," he drawled, "when I first met Miss Caitlin Burke I didn't like her and she didn't like me. Though I couldn't help noticing what a pretty girl she was, that's all she seemed: a girl, maybe a little spoiled and engaged to someone. Not to mention she was the boss's daughter. But I began to notice that she has some, uh, womanly qualities . . ."

"Gabriel Hart!"

"Only a blind saint wouldn't notice, Sadie. And I'm neither." Gabe's voice became more serious. "I was really angry about Sky, of course. But she surprised me. She apologized and has gone out of her way to help me work with him. And last night, when she told me she was staying, wal, Sadie, she just about took my breath away. I thought she'd be gone and I'd forget her. Now I know I won't be able to forget her," he said ruefully.

"Why do you have to, Gabe? Do you love her?"

"I don't know, Sadie. I can't let myself love her. I can't go through that again, loving some woman who doesn't love me."

"Caroline loved you, Gabe. She just didn't have the courage to go against everything she had been taught."

"I wasn't asking her to, Sadie. I was only asking her to understand, to love me for who I was, not who she wanted me to be." Gabe hesitated. "I've done some killing, Sadie. None of which I am ashamed of, but all of it I regret. And I'm likely going to have to do some more if Mackie doesn't give up."

"Do you think he's accepted that Mr. Burke won't give in?"

"I don't think he'll be satisfied till he's got this piece of land, Sadie. I believe it will come to some sort of fight sooner or later."

They sat there, lost in their own thoughts until Sadie broke the silence. "Do you think it is possible to care for a bad man, Gabe?"

"What do you mean?"

"Oh, I don't know . . . I guess I was thinking of Mackie and his wife. She must love him."

"Maybe she does, but I can't see how any woman can overlook what he is and what he's done."

"There may be something in him that only she sees, Gabe."

"If there is, then she's got damned better eyesight than me," scoffed Gabe.

After Sadie returned to the house, Gabe sat on the corral fence for a while, thinking about their conversation. Although he wasn't that much older in years than Caitlin Burke, she felt young to him in experience. And while he might not be a Mackie or Chavez, the life he had lived was not as simple or uncomplicated as someone like Henry Beecham. In New Mexico, a man was asked questions to which there were no simple answers. If you considered yourself law-abiding, did you stay within the law even if it was corrupt? When you joined a legally constituted posse that was then stripped of its legality, did you continue to ride with them? Henry Beecham would never be faced with questions like that, though every man would have to decide between good and evil sometime in his life, Gabe had to admit to himself. But back east, violent answers to such questions were a damn sight less likely.

Any woman who loved him would have to love him for the choices he'd made in his life and not in spite of them. He just wasn't sure if Caitlin Burke could come to love him enough to do that.

Twenty-three

Now that she had made her decision, Caitlin felt strangely at peace. It was a great relief not to be filled with confusion about her feelings for Henry. All of a sudden, what had seemed so muddy now seemed so clear. She still had great affection and admiration for him, but she could finally see that those together did not add up to a love that could sustain them for the rest of their lives.

She got up in the mornings and welcomed the dawn. She drank in the smell of sagebrush after a thunderstorm and wondered how she had even thought she could leave. She knew it would be painful to tell Henry. She would need to hurt him dreadfully and she could only hope that someday he would understand.

It was harder than she thought. He came in on an afternoon train and Jake picked him up. They only got back to the ranch just before bedtime and there was no possibility to do more than give him a hello and good-night hug in one.

In the morning, Henry gave Cait a questioning look when Gabe came in for breakfast. She was a little surprised because she hadn't thought Henry a snob and on some ranches and farms, hired hands regularly ate with the family, Not back east, of course, she thought, remembering the formality of the Beecham household and how it had intimidated and impressed her at the same time.

When Sadie came down and was introduced, Henry was politely friendly, but later, when he and Cait were out for a morning ride, he commented on it.

"It was very kind of your parents to let Hart's sister stay with you, Cait."

The words were complimentary enough, but the underlying sentiment seemed critical to Cait.

"What do you mean, Henry?"

"Just that she is the sister of your father's wrangler. It would be more usual for her to board in town, wouldn't it?"

"Maybe in Philadelphia, Henry. Out here we care less about such distinctions," Cait replied coolly.

"Now don't prickle up like a cactus, Cait," said Henry. "It is just that I was taught that it is better to maintain some distance between employer and employee."

"Mr. Hart hasn't seen his sister in ten years and Ma thought he would get to spend more time with her if she stayed with us. And he has become more than just Da's hired hand," she added, wondering why she felt so defensive.

They were near one of their favorite spots to picnic and Henry pulled up.

"Shall we stop and rest, Cait?"

Neither of them needed a rest and she knew it, but she nodded, thinking that this was as good a time and place as any to tell Henry about her change of heart.

He spread out the old poncho that was tied to his saddle and they sat down.

"From what you told us at breakfast, you enjoyed your visit to California, Henry."

"I did, Cait, and I am happy to have seen more of the West, but I tell you, I'll be even happier when I am back east. When *we* are back east," he added, turning to her and brushing her cheek with his finger. He leaned down and brushed her lips with his. "I've missed you, Cait."

The look in his eyes almost undid her. Whatever she felt about Henry, there was no question in her mind about him. He loved her. He was a good man and she was about to hurt him deeply. "I have missed you too, Henry," she whispered. It was true, as far as it went.

He put his arm around her, as though to draw her in for another kiss, but she pulled away. "Henry, I must tell you something."

"You can tell me anything, Cait," he replied with a sweet smile.

"You know all the trouble we've been having with Nelson Mackie?"

"Yes."

"It has gotten far worse since you've been away. Last week, Eduardo, our sheepherder, was murdered."

Henry's arm went around her again and this time she didn't have the courage to pull away.

"Thank God I can take you away from all this, Cait. It must be terrifying for you."

"Henry . . ."

"Yes, darling?"

"I can't go back east with you."

"What do you mean, Cait? We are leaving in two days."

"I can't bear to leave my parents to face all this alone. I can't go, not knowing my family and home are being threatened."

Henry, who had stiffened at her first words, relaxed and taking her gently by the shoulders, turned her to face him. "Of course you feel this way, Cait. Anyone would. But if there is so much danger and if Mackie is the sort who would kill to get his way, then the sooner you are out of here the better. I'm sure your parents feel the same way, for they love you too."

There was an easy way to do this, Cait realized. She only had to keep repeating her concerns, promise him that she'd be on the train east in a month's time if Mackie appeared to have given up. It would be hard, but he'd eventually understand and give in. Then all she would have to do is write him a letter explaining the rest. But that was a coward's way. Henry deserved to hear the full reason for her decision now, not later in some version of a "Dear John" letter.

She looked up at his concerned face. Was she *sure* about this? She could join him later, in a month or more if it took that. He wouldn't like it, but he would understand. She did care about him. . . .

"I thought about your family's predicament a lot, Cait," Henry was saying. "I am sure that your father is going about this the wrong way. If the local sheriff is corrupt, then he must seek legal redress elsewhere, especially if he has proof that Mackie killed Eduardo."

"There is no proof, Henry, although we know he did it. Not Mackie himself, of course. He's careful to keep out of it. Chavez, his hired gun, was seen up by the sheep just before Eduardo was killed. But even if there was proof, Mackie has political influence right up to the governor. You don't really understand what it's like out here."

"I understand that it is a territory of the United States with a governor who is responsible to Washington," he replied hotly.

"Let me tell you, Henry, that didn't matter a damn in Lincoln County," said Cait, surprised by the surge of anger that took hold of her. She never swore, not out loud anyway.

Henry gave her a frustrated look. "You are convinced that East is East and West is West, eh, Cait?"

"For now, it is, Henry. New Mexico may be a territory of the United States, but it may as well be a different country."

Henry sighed. "You are right, I don't understand it. But I do understand why you feel you can't leave."

He was giving her the perfect opening for the coward's way out. She couldn't take it.

"Henry, perhaps if all this trouble weren't happening, I would have gone back east with you and we would have lived quite happily together. . . ."

"Of course we would. We still will."

"Let me finish, Henry," she said, pulling out of his arms at last. "I care for you very much."

"You love me, Cait . . . or so you said." Henry started to reach out for her again.

"No, Henry, don't. I thought that my great affection and admiration for you was love, Henry. But I have begun to realize that the way I love you—and I do love you—is not the kind of love you deserve."

"I deserve *you,* Cait. I've loved you since I met you."

"I know, Henry, I know. But you deserve a woman who can give you her whole heart. Can make you her home, forsaking all others. I can't do that, Henry. This is my home and I can't leave it."

"Not even for me?" he pleaded.

"If I felt I *could* leave with you, Henry, I'd know I should leave with you."

"I see," he said stiffly. "But what of your other plans? Teaching at Fayreweather? Will you stay here and waste your talents on farmers' and ranchers' children?"

"At one time, I may have agreed with you, Henry, that it was a waste just to teach a rancher's son to write his name. But Sadie Hart is a teacher—a good teacher—and I am beginning to think that what she does is very important. I would be needed here, Henry."

"You are needed there, too, Cait. I need you. I want a home and family of our own."

When his voice broke on the last words, Cait almost gave in. But she realized again that a man and a woman needed to be drawn to each other by some elemental attraction, the way her parents had been despite their differences. The space between her parents was always charged, as though they lived in their own magnetic field. The space between Henry and her was not alive with that same energy.

"I hate to hurt you, Henry."

"Then don't!" he exclaimed, pulling her into his arms and kissing her in a passion of despair and determination. Cait was in his arms and at the same time, watching herself be kissed from some place outside them. It was the first time she had felt such passion from him. It was what she had thought she wanted, yet now it seemed as if it was not what she wanted after all.

She let him kiss her. She owed him that. But when he let her go at last and looked into her eyes, he knew.

"It would not be fair for me to go with you, Henry," she whispered.

"I think you are right," he responded bitterly.

"I am so sorry," she said softly.

"I know and I don't blame you. But oddly enough, that doesn't help. Come. Let me get you back to the ranch."

They rode home in silence and when they reached the ranch, Henry turned to her and said, "I'll leave this afternoon, Cait."

"But your train isn't for a few days, Henry. You don't have to leave."

"I can't stay here, Cait," he said with a painful smile. "I'll find somewhere in town to stay."

"I understand, Henry."

"I doubt that you do, Cait," he added ironically.

He was gone very quickly, saying his good-byes to the Burkes, receiving their sympathy politely. They were all standing on the porch, watching him walk to the wagon when Cait ran down the steps and threw her arms around him. "Oh, Henry, I wish things were different!"

"I know, Cait, I know. You will write and tell me you are safe?"

"Of course, I will."

"I'll look forward to your letter then. Good-bye, Cait."

"Good-bye, Henry."

Michael and Elizabeth watched her stand there, her arm lifted in a good-bye wave.

"I am proud of her, *a ghra.*"

"So am I, Michael. Oh, but I know how hard it is not to love back in the same way one is loved."

How she got through the rest of that day, Cait never knew. She couldn't cry, she couldn't even talk to her mother about it. There was nothing to do but keep busy. She washed and hung the sheets. She weeded and watered the garden, and when the sheets were dry in the afternoon, she heated up her mother's iron.

"Whatever are you doing, Cait?"

"I'm going to iron the sheets, Ma."

Any other day, and Elizabeth would have laughed. Iron the sheets? As though they'd ever had time for it, or even the desire.

"The Beechams would send theirs out to be laundered and sleeping on a freshly ironed sheet is quite luxurious, Ma."

"I imagine it is, dear."

Elizabeth left quickly and sought out her husband who was down by the near pasture.

"You must promise me something, Michael."

"Anything, *a ghra.*"

"You will *not* comment upon the fact that we will be sleeping on ironed sheets tonight. Our daughter assures me it is a luxurious experience."

Michael chuckled. "I will look forward to making love to you on them, Elizabeth. Who knows, I might like it so much, I'll be havin' you iron them from now on!"

"It isn't funny, Michael."

"I know, Elizabeth. But if it helps her get over this . . ."

Cait was just turning the second sheet when she burned her hand. It was a small, half-moon-shaped weal, but it was deep and red and tears sprang to her eyes as she shook her wrist. She forgot about the iron for a minute when all of a sudden she smelled burning and realized she had just scorched a hole in the sheet.

Ironed sheets indeed! Whatever had she been thinking. Lord, but her wrist hurt and the coldest water came from the pump behind the barn. She was almost glad of the pain, she thought, as she walked out to the barn, holding her arm up in front of her. It distracted her from the pain in her heart. She looked down at her wrist. It was angry and red, but at least it hadn't blistered. But she had forgotten how the smallest burn hurt more than a cut or scrape.

She was almost sobbing from the pain as she turned the corner and only then became aware that someone was ahead of her. Gabe Hart was there, working the pump and as she watched, he cupped one hand and brought the water up to his lips, drinking some and then splashing his face with the rest. She was just turning away, when he looked up and saw her.

"Miss Cait, good afternoon. Did your Da want me?"

Cait shook her head and tried to hold back her tears. She held out her arm and said: "I burned it and was just going to run it under the pump."

"I've heard that some sort of grease is good for a burn," said Gabe.

"Ma says cold water works best," she answered.

"Then come over here, Miss Cait," drawled Gabe. "Hold your hand under and I'll pump."

Cait winced as the water first hit, but then the cold began to bring some relief.

"How did you burn it?"

"I was ironing sheets and I didn't get my hand out of the way quick enough."

"Ironing sheets . . . well, I can't say as I've ever slept on ironed sheets but I imagine it would be real nice," said Gabe politely, thinking that *clean* sheets were a luxury.

Cait looked up into his face and laughed. "Oh, it was ridiculous of me, Mr. Hart. It was just something to do this afternoon to keep me busy. I was through washing and weeding."

Gabe had noticed her reddened eyes and suspected that the tears she had shed were as much over Henry leaving as for the burn.

"Let me see your wrist now," he said, letting go of the pump. Cait held it out to him and he held it as he ran his finger gently next to the angry-looking mark.

"This must hurt quite a bit," he said softly.

"The water helped, Mr. Hart." And it was true. The pain had subsided enough that she was less conscious of it and very conscious of the touch of Gabe Hart's finger on her arm.

"I am sorry to see you in any kind of pain, Miss Cait," he said awkwardly. It wasn't his place to say anything about Henry and her decision to stay, but he hoped she knew that his sympathy included more than the mark on her arm, thought Gabe, as he stroked around it. Or maybe it was just that her underarm was so white and soft.

Without looking up at her he continued. "I think it took a lot of courage to do what you did, Miss Cait. And after all this is over, well, you can join Mr. Beecham back east."

"I won't be doing that, Mr. Hart," she answered, her voice catching on a little sob. He looked up in surprise. Cait gave him a smile, but the tears were spilling down her face again. "It wouldn't be fair to Henry," she whispered.

He felt her sway a little against him and looked around. There was a rough old bench against the barn where a man could sit and pull off his boots. He guided her over to it. "Sit down, Miss Cait. You're likely feeling a little faint, given everything that's happened today."

Cait let herself be led and sank back gratefully against the barn wall. The mad energy that had filled her all day had drained out of her so suddenly that she felt as if nothing was holding her up. Gabe sat down next to her and they sat quietly for a minute, each aware of the other's closeness.

Cait could not help be aware that his thigh was touching hers. She could feel the warmth of his leg through her light cotton dress. She should move, she knew, but it felt so reassuring to have him close that she didn't want to.

"How is you arm feeling now?" Gabe asked, when what he wanted to ask was "*What* wouldn't be fair to Henry?" Did she mean she didn't love Beecham? Or just that she couldn't keep him waiting till things were settled on the ranch?

Cait held her arm out and he very naturally let it rest in his hand as they both looked. "It still looks as red, but it feels better," said Cait.

"It may not heal without a scar," said Gabe, tracing the area around it with his finger again. "It's not that long, but it looks deep."

"Well, the scar will serve to remind me of my foolishness," Cait said lightly.

"Not foolishness, Miss Cait," Gabe said softly, looking up into her face. His eyes were so blue against his tan, she thought. There were thin white lines around them from where he squinted against the sun. It was a strong, weather-beaten face, almost a hard face, except for his mouth. The curve of his lips softened everything.

All of a sudden, the empty feeling was gone and in its place grew an awareness, an exquisitely tuned awareness of a current flowing between them. She was being drawn to him and he to her, she thought, as her face lifted and his lowered to hers and their lips touched.

It was what she had expected to feel with Henry, and never had, this force between them. Then Gabe pulled away and she almost sobbed aloud in her disappointment. But it was only to look into her eyes and give her a questioning look. She looked back a "yes," nodded a "yes," and he ran his finger down her cheek as gently as he had touched her arm. Then he lifted her chin and kissed her.

The first kiss was a gentle brush against her mouth. The second one encouraged her lips to soften and open. With the third, he asked her for all the passionate response she had wanted to give to Henry. It was a long, demanding kiss that took her breath away.

When he pulled away, she wanted to cry out "No, don't stop, don't ever stop." But instead she whispered, her face red with embarrassment, "Oh, Mr. Hart."

"I am sorry, Miss Cait. I had no right to do that. Especially since . . . well, Mr. Beecham may be gone, but he's still your fiancé."

Cait shook her head. "No, I broke the engagement, Mr. Hart. I realized I didn't love Henry, not the way he deserved to be loved. I'm . . . I'm glad you kissed me," she added with a quick smile. "Henry's kisses, well, they never made me feel like yours did, Mr. Hart. I know I made the right decision for both of us," she added.

"It's been a hard day for you," said Gabe, standing up and holding out his hand to her. She took it and he helped her to her feet.

"Uh, I'd better get cleaned up for supper," he stammered awkwardly.

"Yes, and I'd better get in to the house and help Ma."

She could feel his eyes on her as she walked away and she wanted to turn around and walk right back into his arms. But he likely had a great deal of experience of kissing women like that. She had no idea what it had meant for him. Probably very little. And for her it had meant so much.

Gabe watched her go. Lord, he couldn't believe he had lost control like that with Mr. Burke's daughter. Those had been some kisses, though, he thought with a rueful smile and he'd been wanting one for a long time, he had to admit to himself. Her response had been sweet and strong. But that had meant nothing. He'd caught her when she was most vulnerable. As she'd said, they only helped her realize that Beecham wasn't the man for her. Which was not at all the same as saying that Gabe Hart was.

Twenty-four

"Elizabeth? Are ye still awake?"

His wife sighed and stirred. "A little, Michael."

Michael smiled and stroked her hair. He had been sitting down in the parlor after all had gone to bed, trying to imagine an easy way out of his impasse with Mackie. He could think of only one, which was, of course, unthinkable: selling his land.

It was possible Eduardo's murder would be the end of it and Mackie would finally realize he couldn't be intimidated. They could wait and see. But he was tired of waiting for Mackie's next move.

"I am ridin' over to Mackie's in the morning, Elizabeth," he told her as he climbed in next to her.

Elizabeth became more than a little awake when she heard that. "Why, Michael?" she asked. Sitting up against the pillows. "You haven't decided to sell, have you?"

"No, *a ghra.* Unless you want me to? If this is all too much for you, I would, ye know."

"Of course I don't want you to, Michael," she said forcefully.

"I am tired of waiting around to see what the *gobshite* will do next, Elizabeth. I intend to tell him to his face that murdering Eduardo will not make me change my mind. That nothing he can do will change it. He has been running the show long enough."

"You can't just ride in there alone, Michael!" Elizabeth said, reaching out to grasp her husband's hand.

"He can hardly get away with shooting me outright, *a ghra.* I'll be safe enough."

"Please, Michael, ask Gabe to go with you."

Michael patted her hand. "All right, if it will make ye feel any better. And only if Gabe is willing to go."

"But he said he is with us, Michael."

"Well, working for me is one thing. Openly confronting Mackie is another, Elizabeth, should Mackie decide to go further. Which he won't, I am sure," he reassured her.

Michael slid down and pulled his wife in front of him, and spooning against her, fell asleep almost immediately. Elizabeth lay awake for a long time. This country had given her so much, she thought: her first husband, Thomas, Michael, who was her life, Caitlin, good friends in Serena and Antonio. Yet everything it had given had come with the violence that seemed to be a part of this hard land. It had taken her parents and her brother and Thomas. The Dine had suffered greatly for their love for it. And now the killing had started again. She could only hope and pray that Eduardo's death was the beginning and end of it.

Michael was up early the next morning and out to the barn to catch Gabe before breakfast. "I have something to ask you, Gabe," he said, as Gabe finished watering the horses.

"Yes, Mr. Burke?" It was unusual for his employer to be out before breakfast and all of a sudden Gabe wondered if Michael somehow knew what had gone on between Caitlin and him behind the barn. He looked serious enough. But he was sure that Miss Cait would not have told her father.

"I am weary of Mackie always taking the initiative in this. After breakfast I intend to ride over there and tell him that whatever he does, I'm not giving in to him. I told Mrs. Burke and she is a wee bit worried because I planned to go alone. I said I'd ask you. But I know this may put you in a different light with Mackie. 'Tis one thing to be my wrangler. 'Tis another to ride in with me for a confrontation. I want ye to know I have no problem with ye staying here. I'd think no less of ye, especially with yer sister here."

Gabe didn't even have to think about it. It was time

Mackie knew that Michael Burke wasn't alone and high time they pushed back at him. "Eduardo was a friend of mine, Mr. Burke. I told you I was in this with you to the end. I don't like waiting around any more than you do. I'll saddle the horses."

Michael clapped him on the shoulder. "If ye're sure, Gabe, I'll welcome yer company. Elizabeth will have breakfast ready for us, so come up to the house after ye've got the horses saddled. I don't believe in facin' anything on an empty stomach," Michael added with a smile.

Gabe brushed and saddled Patch and Snowflake quickly. It had been foolish of him to think that Caitlin Burke might have mentioned their kisses to her father. There wasn't that much to tell, anyway, and it wasn't likely to happen again.

They rode out after a quick breakfast and Elizabeth and Cait watched them from the porch. The two men were armed, Michael wearing his army revolver and Gabe with a Colt strapped to his left leg. Gabe didn't wear a gun on a regular basis and Cait was a little shocked when she noticed how well-worn the holster was. It hung on his left side; she'd forgotten he was left-handed. "A left-handed gun." The phrase popped into her mind and she gave an involuntary shiver. This was a side of Gabe she'd never seen before. He worked so gently with the horses that it seemed incongruous to think of him as having any talent for violence. But she realized to her own surprise, that she was wishing he had, for then he could help keep her Da safe if it came to a fight. But please God it never will, she murmured to herself.

It was a half-hour ride to the Bar M and they made it in silence. When they reached the main gate, it was Michael who leaned down to open and close it while Gabe kept his eyes open for any sign of Mackie's men.

"I don't like cows, Gabe," he said with deadpan humor as they rode past a part of Mackie's herd.

Gabe laughed. "Then you are certainly in the minority out here, Mr. Burke."

"Oh, I'll admit I don't like sheep too much either. They are silly animals, but look at all this range," he added more seriously, waving his hand in both directions. "It can't support cattle. Not for too long, anyway. At least my silly buggers don't eat that much. A few small ranches aren't bad," he continued, "but these men like Mackie who want to run thousands of cattle . . . the land just can't go on supporting them."

"Is that why you won't sell?"

" 'Tis one reason, boyo. I don't like being pushed is another."

As they rode into the main compound, they encountered a few of Mackie's men who gave them hostile looks, but said and did nothing. "Ye can stay here with the horses, if ye want, Gabe."

"I'll go in with you, Mr. Burke."

They tied their horses to the corral rails and walked toward the house, while several of Mackie's hands, including Juan Chavez, watched.

"Lookee here, Bill," called one of them. " 'Tis the mick and his horse breaker."

Chavez was intrigued and rather amused. It was possible, he supposed, that Burke had changed his mind and was here to sell. But somehow he doubted it. No, he thought that Señor Burke had decided to bring the fight into Mackie's territory. He only wished he could be there to see Mackie's reaction. But he'd hear about it soon enough.

They were admitted by the housekeeper who kept them in the hall until she could find her employer. "Señor Mackie is just finishing his breakfast," she said when she returned, "and he asks if you would like to have a cup of coffee with him."

Michael and Gabe nodded and followed her into the dining room. They stood there in the doorway until Mackie looked up.

"Come in, Mr. Burke, Mr. Hart. Come in. Helen, you know Mr. Burke, of course. Perhaps you could see to Cook getting them some breakfast?"

"No, thank ye, ma'am," said Michael. "We ate before we left."

Mackie gave his wife a quick look and she made her excuses and left the men to themselves. "Sit down, gentlemen. To what do I owe the pleasure of this visit?" he asked blandly as though it were usual for Michael to be making a social call.

"Em, I don't know that ye will be takin' much pleasure in our visit, Mr. Mackie," said Michael with dry humor. "Have ye spoken with Sheriff Butler lately?"

"I saw him just the other day. It was a shame about your sheepherder, Burke. I know what it is like to lose stock to rustlers."

"If ye talked to the sheriff, then ye know that I don't think it was 'sheep rustlers,' Mackie," responded Michael, the humorous tone gone from his voice. "I can't say that sheep-stealing is too common in the territory now. 'Tis usually cattle they are after."

"I know that you think that I was somehow behind this, Burke," said Mackie, in a conciliatory tone. "I suppose I can understand your suspicions. I *am* eager for your land, I won't deny it. I will even admit to a little intimidation in trying to get what I want. But murder?" Mackie wiped his mouth and set his napkin down on the table. Looking directly into Michael's eyes, he said, "I swear I had nothing to do with Eduardo's death, Burke. I have accepted the fact, much as I don't want to, that you are as stubborn a mick as I am," he added with a smile. "I don't believe that anything I say or do will make you sell."

"Sure and I hope ye believe that," Michael said firmly, "for it's true."

"Indeed I do. And now that we've settled that I won't be buying and you won't be selling, maybe we can find a way to get to know each other better as neighbors? You and Mrs. Burke have been in the valley for a long time, but my wife and I are relative newcomers."

"We all need good neighbors," Michael responded blandly.

"My wife's birthday is in a few weeks and I was hoping to invite all our acquaintances from in town and the valley. Will you and your family come?"

"Em, we would be happy to, Mr. Mackie."

"Call me Nelson. And Hart, I'll be sure to invite you and your sister, if she is still here. I noticed that my man Chavez seemed taken with her at the dance. Neither of us is as black as we've been painted, you know, Burke."

" 'Tis glad I am to hear it, Nelson."

Gabe listened to them trading polite compliments and had to concentrate to keep his mouth from hanging open. But he could feel the current between them and realized that underneath the polite fencing, a message was being given and received.

Chavez was waiting by the corral when they came out.

"*Buenos dias, señores.* I see that your mare has recovered, Señor Burke," he added, patting Snowflake's neck.

"Completely, thanks to Gabe's good doctoring," Michael answered in the same tone he'd been using with Mackie.

"I hope your business with Señor Mackie has been concluded satisfactorily, señor?"

"I think we understand each other, Señor Chavez," Michael replied as he mounted Snowflake. "*Hasta luego.*"

Gabe said nothing until they were off of Mackie's land and on the road back home. "Did you believe all that, Mr. Burke?" his own incredulity obvious.

"Sure and why shouldn't I, Gabe?" asked Michael humorously.

Gabe let out a huge sigh of relief.

"You were worrying that I'd be thinking that the fox had suddenly turned into a rabbit?"

"Not exactly."

"Look," said Michael, turning in his saddle to face Gabe. "One thing we hoped was he'd give up when he realized nothing, even Eduardo's murder, would make me sell. Now maybe he has given up. Only time will tell. But ye didn't really expect him to say: 'Yes, Burke, I had Chavez murder Eduardo and I can see it didn't intimidate you so I give up,' did ye, boyo?

How else could he play it but the way he has all along?"

"I guess you're right. Does he believe you?"

"Oh, he believes me, all right. He knows he'll never get my land by buyin' it."

"Well, then," said Gabe with a grin, "you've won, Mr. Burke."

"We'll see, boyo, we'll see."

After Michael and Gabe left, Mackie summoned Chavez.

"You were right, Juan. He is not a man to give in easily."

"Or at all, señor."

"He won't give in even after Eduardo's unfortunate . . . encounter. He went to the sheriff, of course, but Butler is mine, so no one will be accused of murder, as I am sure you are glad to hear."

"Especially since I did not kill anyone, señor," said Chavez softly.

"I think it is time to pull back, Juan. Accept that Burke won't sell. Let all the speculation about Eduardo's death die away. Whatever he believes about Eduardo, Burke won't ever prove anything. I want him to believe I've given up."

"And have you, señor?"

"Burke will never *sell* me that land, Chavez," said Mackie, looking up at his henchman. "So you can lay off your persuasive tactics. We are going to show the townsfolk and the Burke family that we can be good neighbors. Why, you can even go courting that pretty sister of Gabe Hart."

Chavez's mouth tightened and his hands clenched on the chair in front to him.

"Yes," said Mackie thoughtfully, "I think that's just what I want you to be doing, Juan."

"*Si*, señor."

"It shouldn't be a hard job," said Mackie with a smile. "After all, you haven't had a woman since you've been working for me, at least not that I've been aware of."

"No, señor."

"I'm glad we understand each other so well, Chavez," said Mackie, dismissing him.

"What did Mackie say, Da?" Caitlin asked as they all sat down to dinner.

"That he is sorry that a wandering bunch of sheepstealers killed Eduardo. That he realizes I will never sell. And that he wants to be a good neighbor. I think that was it, wasn't it, Gabe?" said Michael, looking over at him with a grin.

"That about covers it."

"Do you believe him, Michael? Has he given up at last?"

"I know in my bones that he was responsible for Eduardo's death, Elizabeth, though I can't prove it. But there is a chance he has given up."

"Well, I for one will never be his good neighbor!"

"It sticks in my craw, too, *a ghra.* I will always see him as a murderin' bastard. But it does no one in the valley any good to have us feudin'." Michael cleared his throat. "He's actually invited us all to Mrs. Mackie's birthday party."

"We won't go, will we, Da?"

"The whole town will be there and many of our neighbors. I think it is a good idea to give this truce a chance, don't you, Elizabeth?"

"I have nothing against Helen Mackie," she replied stiffly. "Except the man she's married to. And I feel more sympathy for her than anger. I doubt that she is involved in any of his scheming."

"Then we'll all show our faces. You were invited too, Miss Sarah Ellen," added Michael, giving Sadie a smile. "And Elizabeth, maybe you can even make your famous black cake?"

"Why, that's more of a holiday recipe, Michael."

"I know, but Mrs. Mackie would appreciate the gesture, I am sure."

"Then I'd better start soaking some raisins! I must say," said Elizabeth ironically, "the last thing I ever thought I'd be doing is baking for Nelson Mackie!"

Twenty-five

Cait avoided Gabe the first few days after his kisses, for she was embarrassed and a little ashamed. What must he think of her, kissing him on the very day she saw Henry off? She had revealed so much . . . well, passion was the only word for it. And when she saw him, would he guess that she desperately wanted him to kiss her again?

After three days of going off for long rides and keeping busy with her household chores, she told herself she was being foolish. After all, she had been watching him train Sky for weeks now. Surely she was making the kisses seem more important than they were if she avoided him completely? She wouldn't want him to think he had offended her. So that afternoon, she walked down to the corral and sat on her usual perch on the fence.

Gabe was just finishing his work and Cait could see that Sky was even further along, for Gabe was actually able to place his arms on Sky's back and rest some of his weight while the horse stood quietly.

"He looks almost ready to ride, Mr. Hart," she called out.

"I think it won't be long before I can give it a try, Miss Cait," Gabe acknowledged. "Would you take him into the barn for me?"

Cait slipped down and after giving Sky his treat, she led him into the barn, and after cross-tying him, began to brush him down. The rhythm of the familiar activity calmed her, and when Gabe came in carrying a saddle blanket, she had lost some of her self-consciousness.

"Why, that's one of the blankets Serena wove."

"Yes, your ma brought it out last week. She told me she thought Sky should have something special for all he's been through. So I've been rubbing him down with it and letting him get used to it."

Cait watched as Gabe slid the red-and-black blanket down Sky's back and legs. "You are so patient with him, Mr. Hart. It almost seems like you know what he's feeling and thinking. I thought my Da was the best man with horses I know, but now I'm not so sure."

Gabe blushed and dropping the saddle blanket over a stall door, leaned back against it. "I wouldn't say that, Miss Cait. Your Da and Finn, why they have something between them that few men achieve with a horse."

"I'd say it is the same with you and Sky, though I hate to admit it, because it still makes me a little bit jealous," she said with an embarrassed smile.

"Wal, I don't know about that," drawled Gabe, "but I've always had a way with horses . . . Uh, I was glad to see you at the corral again, Miss Cait," Gabe continued, his face getting red under his tan. "I was afraid . . . well, I should never have kissed you the other day. I hope we can both pretend that it never happened?"

So that's what he wanted, Cait realized. Those kisses, which had meant so much to her—never mind that they shouldn't have, they did—of course meant nothing to him. He's probably kissed lots of women behind barns!

"There is no need to worry, Mr. Hart," she told him calmly. "It was a momentary foolishness on both our parts." She was amazed she was able to sound so cool. If he wanted to pretend it never happened, then he would hardly want it to happen again, would he?

"I'm glad to hear that, Miss Cait."

He sounded so relieved, Cait thought, as she walked back up to the house. As I should be. But I am only terribly disappointed.

It had worried Gabe when Caitlin seemed to be avoiding him. He'd been foolish to lose control like that and he'd been hoping for an opportunity to apologize. He should be happy, now that it seemed they could go back to being friends. They were both in agreement that those few moments were an isolated incident and that should have set him at ease.

Instead, he kept thinking of the promise of passion in her kisses. But what had he expected? That she'd say, "Oh, Mr. Hart, please kiss me again." Or even more fantastical, "Mr. Hart, I think I am falling in love with you."

Miss Burke, a refined and educated young lady, fall in love with him? Now that was some ridiculous fancy. But those kisses had set something off in him, and by the end of the week, he realized that what he wanted her to say to him was exactly what he wanted to say to her: "Miss Cait, I think I am falling in love with you." Which made him a damn fool.

He hadn't loved a woman since Caroline. She'd hurt him terribly by not even trying to understand him and his actions. Since then, he'd not been any one place long enough to meet any respectable women. He visited whores occasionally. But usually he just stayed away, for some of them reminded him too much of his stepmother, trying to get something for themselves and not caring about him. Most of them, he just felt sorry for, because he was using them, too. And feeling sorry for the woman lying under you was a sure way to interfere with your enjoyment of them.

He'd stolen some kisses from Caroline. But he had felt like a thief, for she was a doctor's daughter and been sheltered from men. When his kisses got too hot, she would pull away and remind him that they weren't even officially engaged. And whores didn't kiss, not that he'd been wanting much to kiss them either.

But with Caitlin Burke . . . well, something had come together for him in those kisses. From the first, he'd found her attractive, but he'd also gradually come to like and respect her. When their lips joined, all the feelings in him seemed to join too.

He was very self-conscious that next week when she came to sit and watch him with the horses, though he tried not to show it. It was hard to be across the table from her at meals and he found himself making excuses and leaving early to get back to work. He was hoping that no one had noticed, but Sadie knew him too well, and one night after supper, followed him out to the barn.

"You are as jumpy as grease on a hot griddle, Gabe," she said as she watched him soaping the reins of one of the bridles. "Is it Mackie that's making you nervous?"

"Mackie doesn't make me nervous, Sadie. Whichever way this goes, a good man is dead and no way to convict him for it, so he just makes me angry."

"Then if it isn't Mackie . . . ?"

"I suppose you won't let me alone till I tell you," said Gabe, looking over at her with a resigned smile.

"We know each other too well, Gabe, even though we've been separated all this time. I can tell when something is bothering you. Is it Caitlin Burke?" she asked shrewdly.

"I *have* come to love her," Gabe said ruefully.

"You do seem to like schoolteachers, Gabe," Sadie teased.

"She's real different from you, Sadie."

"Well, I would hope so, Gabe! A man doesn't want to be marrying his sister! I would guess she's different from Caroline too, Gabe," she added softly.

"I don't know, Sadie, she's had a very sheltered life. And she knows very little about me."

"I think you are underestimating her, Gabe."

Gabe's eyes opened wide with surprise.

"Miss Burke has made a very clear choice, hasn't she? She may have gone to school back east, but her heart is clearly in New Mexico, Gabe. She could have just delayed her wedding, but instead she broke off the engagement. She let Mr. Beecham go. I didn't get to see too much of him, but from what I did see, I'd say she was smart to give him up."

"Smart to give up a rich, handsome lawyer?"

"He's too civilized for her, Gabe, and good for her

that she knows it. She belongs here. And maybe you two belong together," she added lightly.

"I don't think so, Sadie. She's already told me it didn't mean anything," Gabe said without thinking.

"*What* didn't mean anything?"

Gabe's face grew red. "Wal, she burned her wrist and was hurting in other ways and there were a few kisses, that's all. They meant nothing to her."

"And what about you?"

"They meant a lot to me, Sadie, but what could I do but apologize?"

"Oh, Gabe!" exclaimed Sadie in mock despair. "If you apologized for them, then she thinks you didn't mean anything by them, so of course she'd have to say that."

"You're just saying that to make me feel better."

"Maybe so, Gabe. But I'm also a woman and I know how women think. Were the kisses . . . um . . friendly kisses? Or hot kisses?" she asked with a twinkle in her eyes.

"Sarah Ellen Hart, what do you know about hot kisses?" teased Gabe.

"Too little for my liking," Sadie admitted, "though there was one cowboy at a dance back in Texas who stole a few I was very happy to give away."

Gabe was quiet for a minute and then said in a barely audible voice: "I guess those kisses burned my lips enough to leave a scar."

"Then you can't give up," Sadie declared.

"I don't know, Sadie, I promised her it wouldn't happen again."

"And I'm sure you can find a way to convince her to let you out of that promise, Gabe."

"I guess I could try, Sadie."

"Do try, Gabe. You deserve to be happy."

Twenty-six

Mackie's party was to begin at noon and continue through the afternoon and Elizabeth had been busy all morning with the last-minute preparations. She had made a half-dozen black cakes and was also bringing several jars of fresh buttermilk.

"Keep the wrapping around the jars, Cait," she told her daughter as they packed the wagon. "It will help keep them cool."

"Yes, Ma. But I don't know why we're being such good neighbors to Mr. Mackie," she protested.

"It is for Mrs. Mackie, Cait. And your Da. If there is a possibility of living in peace with the man, we must take it."

Elizabeth climbed up on the wagon and taking the reins, waited for Caitlin and Sadie to join her. Michael and Gabe would be riding alongside.

"Sure and aren't we lucky to be escortin' three beautiful women to this party, Gabe?" said Michael as they started off.

"We wouldn't be looking half so pretty without these ribbons you gave us, Gabe," said Elizabeth.

Gabe only nodded and smiled.

"Why, Da, I think we are lucky to have two such handsome escorts," said Cait. She felt it was quite a bold thing to say, but the two men did look so handsome in their own ways. Her father had on his good black coat and his string tie, which was decorated with a chunk of turquoise set in silver that Antonio had given him. She stole a quick glance over at Gabe. He had on a white linen shirt and his gray wool pants.

His black boots were polished well enough to have made a cavalry officer proud.

By the time they reached the Mackie ranch, most of their neighbors and townsfolk had arrived. Nelson Mackie, who was standing with the sheriff and the banker, hurried over when he saw them. "Mrs. Burke, Miss Burke. And this must be Gabe's sister?"

"Miss Sarah Ellen Hart," Gabe said stiffly.

"I am so pleased that you've come," continued Mackie. His pleasure seemed genuine enough, thought Elizabeth. "Come, let me bring you over to my wife."

"I've brought some cake and fresh buttermilk," said Elizabeth, gesturing to the back of the wagon.

"Why, that was very neighborly of you, Mrs. Burke. I'll get someone to take care of that for you," he said, waving to a group of his men. "Chavez, come here and help Mrs. Burke."

Elizabeth shivered as Juan Chavez walked over to them. At least she had a reason for her reaction this time, she thought, since Chavez was most likely the man who had cold-bloodedly murdered Eduardo. He was dressed Mexican-style, as usual, in black pants and a green velvet shirt. He gave Elizabeth a half bow and said politely: "How can I help you, Señora Burke?"

"I think Caitlin and I can handle the cakes, Mr. Chavez, but there are three jars of buttermilk in the back of the wagon. If you could take those to the picnic tables?"

"With pleasure, señora."

Elizabeth and Caitlin took the cakes, which were wrapped in damp cheesecloth and started off.

"I'd better help you with the buttermilk, Señor Chavez," said Sadie. "If you can handle two jars, I'll carry the third."

"*Muchas gracias,* Señorita Hart," said Chavez, smiling down at her. His green shirt made his eyes look even greener, thought Sadie as she took the jar from him. My, but he was a handsome man.

They followed Elizabeth and Cait to the tables in silence but just before he left her with the other women, Chavez leaned down and said: "There will be dancing later, señorita. Will you save a dance or two for me?"

Of course, she should have said no. But his voice was so quiet, so persuasive, that she gave a quick smile and nod without thinking. Now that was foolish, Sarah Ellen Hart, she told herself. But he is good at persuading, she thought, with a wry smile on her lips. No wonder he could talk so many people off their land.

Mackie had set up four large trestle tables to hold the food and drinks and after an hour or so of visiting with his neighbors, he had the cook ring a bell to summon people to eat. There were chairs and benches scattered around the yard and after people had filled their plates they sought out friends and acquaintances to share the meal with.

Elizabeth was friendly with Mrs. Whitefield, the minister's wife and she invited the Whitefields to join them in the shade of an old cottonwood tree.

"I was glad to see you here, Burke," said the reverend. "I was very sorry to hear about Eduardo. I wouldn't want to accuse anyone without evidence," he added, "but I hope this party is a sign that Mackie has given up on trying to push anyone else out."

"And so am I, Reverend," said Michael.

"Cait, I am so pleased to see *you* here," said Mrs. Whitefield. "Your ma has been telling me you have decided to stay in New Mexico."

Cait blushed as she looked up from her plate. "Yes, Mrs. Whitefield. I was sorry to hurt Henry, but I am glad not to be leaving home."

"I am sure that all of the young men are happy about your decision, too," the reverend's wife said with a smile. "Isn't that true, Mr. Hart?"

"Why, uh, yes, ma'am," stammered Gabe, his own face coloring slightly.

"Miss Sarah Ellen, how are you enjoying your visit to the New Mexico Territory?" asked the reverend.

"I confess that I am still a Texan at heart but I do love the mountains and the mesas," Sadie replied.

"And it has been wonderful seeing Gabe after all these years."

"I understand you are a teacher back in Texas," said Mrs. Whitefield.

"Yes, ma'am, for almost ten years."

"Are you still hoping to teach, Cait?" she asked, turning to Cait.

"I haven't had much time to think about it," replied Cait. She was silent for a moment and then added, "But yes, I think if things are settling down, then I'll be looking around for a position."

"I heard the reservation school will be needing a teacher come January," said the reverend.

Cait's eyes widened. "I would be very interested in keeping that little school going. I don't believe in sending Indian children away to boarding schools," she added passionately. "Antonio and Serena have told us that the children they know come home having lost their own language and feeling they belong nowhere."

"I could speak to the agent if you wish, Cait," offered the reverend.

"Oh, I do!" Her pain and confusion about breaking her engagement had distracted her from her other loss. The town and county schools both had teachers who intended to stay, so she had put her desire to teach out of her mind. To have the opportunity to use her training with Navajo children was wonderful and she breathed a silent prayer that the valley remain peaceful.

"There goes Ramon with his mandolin and Bob with the fiddle," said Mrs. Whitefield. "I declare, after all this food, I am ready to dance, Peter," she said to her husband, "Now, Mr. Hart, don't be shy. You take Miss Cait out there and we'll find a partner for your sister. Thank goodness they started with a waltz," she continued, giving her husband her arm. "Anything else on a full stomach would have been most uncomfortable!"

Cait didn't know whether to feel happy or sad as Gabe led her over to the space cleared for dancing.

There was nothing she wanted so much as to be held
in Gabe's arms, but what was the point of torturing
herself with feelings that were not returned? Once he
led her out, however, she just let herself be caught up
in sensation. As he slipped his arm around her waist,
she quite naturally stepped closer and as he took her
hand, without thinking she opened her fingers and he
gently laced his fingers with hers.

They moved so well together that Cait felt she was
floating above the ground and hardly noticed the
bumps and stones through her slippers. She looked up
at his face and met his eyes, and as they circled and
turned, neither's gaze fell. Cait realized that while
their gaze was keeping her from the dizziness of a
turning dance, she was dizzy with something else: delight in the same current of attraction she had felt
with Gabe before.

Mrs. Preston had stopped in front of Charley Wilson
on her way to dance, and nodded toward Sadie.

"It looks like Mrs. Preston has roped me a partner,"
said Sadie with a grin. "Why don't you and Mrs.
Burke go on ahead so you don't miss any of the
waltz," she told Michael.

The Burkes moved off and Sadie was watching
Charley make his way over to her when suddenly out
of nowhere Juan Chavez was standing in front of her.
"You did say you would dance with me, didn't you,
Miss Hart?"

"I suppose I did, Señor Chavez," she said reluctantly.

"Shall it be this waltz?"

"Why ever not," Sadie answered lightly.

They danced as well together as Sadie remembered.
What was surprising to her was how graceful Chavez
was without ever letting himself relax. She thought of
his nickname and realized anew that he combined the
grace of a wild animal with the same moment by moment alertness. Here he was, engaging in a most civilized occupation, yet she felt he was ready to respond
to anything that might happen. He made a very excit-

ing partner, she had to admit, for she was herself made to be awake to every nuance of his movement.

When the music stopped and the fiddle then struck up a reel, Chavez took her hand and led her back to where she had been sitting. No one else had returned and when she sat down, Chavez pulled up a chair next to her.

"You are enjoying your visit with your brother, señorita?"

"I am, señor, despite all that has happened." Just because she had enjoyed her dance didn't mean she had any illusions about El Lobo!, she told herself.

"You mean Eduardo?"

"Yes, Señor Chavez. I met him only once but he was a good man, it seemed to me. We are all sure that someone here is responsible," she added, surprised at her own daring.

"And that someone no doubt is Juan Chavez?" he asked quietly, but with such a steely tone that Sadie was forced to look straight at him. In the shade, his eyes looked more hazel than green and not as shut and cold. She realized the question he was asking: Did she, Sadie Hart, believe he'd killed Eduardo?

"You are Mackie's hired gun, señor. And you have been seen up there more than once."

"So, tell me, Miss Hart, do you normally dance with murderers?" he asked coldly.

She dropped her head. "There is no proof, Mr. Chavez. I guess I do believe a man is innocent until proven guilty."

"And perhaps you like a little taste of danger?" he added ironically.

Sadie looked up at him again and gave him a shamefaced grin. "I should not be dancing with you, señor. And you are right: I like to take risks. But the truth is," she added quietly, "I just do not feel that you are a killer."

"Believe me, señorita, I have killed men."

"Oh, I believe you." said Sadie calmly. "But not, I think, in cold blood."

"What if I told you I did kill Eduardo?"

He was pushing her, she could tell, but she had no idea why. "I would say you were lying, Señor Chavez," she responded, looking straight at him and challenging him with her eyes.

His face softened so that it was hard to believe it was the notorious El Lobo sitting next to her. "I would be lying, señorita. Though how you can know that. . . . But you are right; it is not my way to kill unless threatened. Of course, I would not have you make me out an angel, señorita."

"Don't worry," said Sadie with an ironic smile.

"So, we understand each other? I am a bad hombre, but not so bad you can't dance with me. And you are a good woman, but not so good that you can resist me!"

Chavez had pulled closer while they were talking and Sadie realized his thigh was pressing against hers. She could feel the conchos on his pants through her dress and they were warm from his body heat. She imagined that when she went home, she would find that she carried the impression of one of them on her leg.

Chavez picked up her hand and stroked her fingers gently. "I like you very much, Miss Sadie Hart," he whispered.

Sadie was mesmerized by the pleasure she got from his soft touch and wished the moment to go on forever. She was aware of nothing else and then suddenly Chavez was being pulled out of his chair.

"What the hell do you think you are doing with my sister, Chavez?" Gabe's voice was low, but it vibrated with fury.

"Gabe!" said Sadie, jumping up. "Mr. Chavez and I were merely talking."

Chavez put his hand gently on her shoulders as if to thank her and then moved between Sadie and Gabe. "Your sister is a grown woman, Mr. Hart. Surely she has the right to talk to whomever she wants." Chavez kept his voice low also.

"Well, she sure don't want you either talking to her or pawing her, for that matter," Gabe declared. "Now get the hell away before I do something I'll regret. I'd hate to spoil Mrs. Mackie's birthday."

"Neither of us wants to do that," agreed Chavez with a thin smile. "*Adios, señorita.*"

"*Hasta luego,* señor," Sadie answered emphatically.

"There will be no '*luego*' for either of you, Sadie Hart," growled Gabe. "I'll make sure he doesn't force his company on you again. I know you don't want to cause any trouble for the Burkes, Sadie," he added more gently.

"Actually, Gabe, you don't know anything! I have been taking good care of myself for the last ten years and I don't need my big brother all of a sudden stepping in and telling me what to do. I was enjoying Señor Chavez's company."

"You couldn't have been enjoying his hands all over you!"

"His hands were most certainly not all over me, Gabriel Hart. And if any man's ever are, you can rest easy knowing it's because I want them there. I know how to defend myself very well from unwanted attention."

"Not from a cold-blooded killer, you can't."

"I don't believe Mr. Chavez is responsible for Eduardo's death, Gabe," said Sadie more calmly.

"And pigs can fly," snorted Gabe.

"I did not say Mr. Chavez was a complete innocent, Gabe. But he has told me he has only killed in self-defense and I believe him."

"You really believe that killer, Sarah Ellen?"

"I believe you, Gabe, and you've killed some men in your time."

Gabe stepped back as though she'd slapped him. "The Regulators weren't hired bullies, Sadie, gunning down innocent people. We were fighting against men like Mackie, not working for them."

All the fight went out of Sadie suddenly, like the air out of a balloon, and she sat down, feeling limp and wrung out. "I'm sorry, Gabe. I have no admiration for what Chavez does for a living. But I believe him about this for some reason."

Her brother sat down next to her. "I'm sorry too, Sadie. I'd no cause to light into you like that. When I left Texas, you were still a girl, my little sister. I was just afraid he'd bullied you into letting him touch you."

"Well, he didn't, Gabe." She smiled. "I accept your apology. And they are starting up a reel. Will you dance with me?"

Gabe smiled and offered his arm. As they walked over to the dancing, Sadie realized, confused and conflicted by her reaction, that Juan Chavez had no need to bully her. She had enjoyed his touch, and God help her, whatever he was, she would like him to touch her that way again.

Twenty-seven

Chavez was furious at Gabe's high-handed interference. What did the man think he was going to do: rape his sister in public! Two things El Lobo did not do: kill in cold blood and force favors from women. Any woman who was with him was there because she wanted to be. Miss Sadie Hart was no exception.

Except she was, he thought, with a wry smile on his face. Oh, she was enjoying his company and his touch, no doubt about that. But she should not have been. She should have been frightened and intimidated by the wicked Juan Chavez.

This time his smile was slow and appreciative. He suspected it would take a lot to scare Sadie Hart and for some strange reason that made him feel pleased. Not exactly happy, but then, he hadn't been happy since he was eight years old.

He should want her to feel threatened, he thought, for his attentions to her were part of his job. But at least he had made her brother very angry, and that was certainly part of his responsibilities.

His own anger had faded as he walked across the courtyard and he realized he was in front of the dessert table. On the other side, unwrapping cheesecloth from a rich, dark cake, was Mrs. Burke. There were pieces of pie and cake already sliced in front of him. He could have picked up a plate and gotten out of her way easily. There was something about this woman that disturbed him, and he did not want to spend time around her, though he couldn't have told anyone why, which bothered him even more.

"Would you like some pie, Señor Chavez?" From

the strained tone of her voice, Chavez knew that he had the same effect on Mrs. Burke as she did on him.

"No, *gracias,* señora, but I would like to taste the cake you brought."

Elizabeth picked up a knife and held it in her hand for a moment as though she was speculating what it was good for.

"That is a sharp knife, señora. I hope you are only going to cut cake with it," said Chavez ironically.

Elizabeth looked over at him and as always, was surprised at how much of a gringo he looked despite his name and his fluency in Spanish. The green eyes were somehow familiar, as was the teasing edge to his voice.

"It takes a sharp knife to cut this cake, Señor Chavez, because it is so moist with fruit and brandy," she answered, her voice steady this time. She carefully sliced one of the cakes and putting two thin slices on a plate, offered them to Chavez. She hoped he would just go, once he had what he wanted.

Chavez picked up a slice in his fingers and lifted it halfway to his mouth. As the rich odor of spices and brandy reached his nose he stood very still, as though frozen in place. He wasn't in New Mexico anymore, he was in his mother's kitchen. It was Christmastime and he had snuck in to steal a piece of her black cake. He had just been lifting it to his mouth when his sister caught him. . . .

"Señor Chavez? Is there something wrong with the cake?"

Her voice brought him back. But the disorientation of those few moments left him dizzy and he looked over at Elizabeth Burke as though he'd never seen her before.

"Are you all right?" she asked him gently.

"*Si,* señora." he made himself bite into the cake, though he was terrified that somehow he'd be transported again to the past. It tasted as delicious as it smelled and he complimented Mrs. Burke politely, relieved that nothing more had come back to him.

"It is an old family recipe, señor. I usually only

make it at Christmas, but it seemed appropriate for a birthday too."

"I am sure Mrs. Mackie appreciated your effort, Mrs. Burke."

"Thank you, Señor Chavez."

Chavez took one more bite and then setting his plate down, he turned and left. Elizabeth stood openmouthed in amazement. The Chavez who had come to the dessert table had been the man who frightened and disturbed her. But after that strange moment when he seemed frozen in place, he felt a different person altogether. Almost a familiar one, although that was a foolish thought. How could such a man be familiar to her? But if he was not familiar, he was most certainly more vulnerable in those few moments. Then she almost laughed aloud at her fancies. Juan Chavez vulnerable? El Lobo, Eduardo's probable killer? She must have been imagining things. But why did she suddenly feel a stirring of sympathy for the man? Because, she told herself, he had become real to her. He wasn't just the hired gun or the coldblooded killer. In his eyes, for those few seconds, she had seen something of the boy he must have been, and the man he was, as capable of confusion and fear as anyone.

"*Madre de Dios,*" Chavez whispered as he walked off. What had happened to him back there? He never remembered the time before the hacienda. He couldn't let himself. During the first few weeks of captivity, when he had remembered, he had tried to block the memories, for if he remembered his father and mother and sister alive, then he had to remember them dead. All of them dead, except for him.

Damn Mrs. Burke and her black cake. Somehow the smell of cinnamon and nutmeg had brought back memories of his childhood. Not just a memory; he felt like he'd been there in his mother's kitchen. The present had become the past and it seemed as though the very earth under his feet had shifted.

"Chavez, I saw you chatting with Mrs. Burke. I

hope you convinced her of our desire to be better neighbors?"

It was Mackie who had come up behind him and he hadn't even noticed. "*Si*, Senor Mackie. Mrs. Burke and I had a nice chat about recipes."

Mackie clapped him on the back and laughed. "Recipes, eh? Next thing you know she'll be giving you cooking lessons. Good job, Juan." Mackie slapped him again and moved on.

"Good job." He always did a good job. He always did just what his employers wanted, he thought bitterly. Truly, El Perro might be a better name for you than El Lobo, Juan, *verdad*?

Michael had seen Chavez by the dessert table and when Elizabeth joined him a few minutes later, he took her hand. "I hope that man wasn't disturbin' ye, *a ghra*?"

"Just his presence usually does, Michael, but this time he seemed more human . . . almost familiar," Elizabeth added wonderingly.

"Well, I think we've been here long enough to prove our good intentions. Let's say our good-byes and head home."

On the way back to the ranch, Michael laughed and said to his wife and daughter, "Between Chavez and Mackie's neighborliness, you'd think that nothing a-tall had happened in this valley for the last few months. Maybe Eduardo's murder was their last try."

"I don't believe Senor Chavez had anything to do with Eduardo's death, Mr. Burke," replied Sadie, surprising herself as well as him.

"You don't, do ye? And why is that?"

"He told me he didn't."

Caitlin looked at her in wide-eyed astonishment. "You believed him? What else would you expect him to say, Sadie?"

"I don't know," Sadie confessed. "I'm not saying he never killed anyone. I'm just sure that he is not Eduardo's murderer."

"It will take more than his saying it to convince me," Michael responded flatly.

Later that night, when they were going up to bed, Cait stopped in front of Sadie's door.

"Do you really believe that Juan Chavez is innocent, Sadie? After all that has happened."

"I didn't say he was a good man, Cait. And neither did he claim to be to me," she added with a smile. "Just that I believed him innocent in this one situation."

"Then who did kill Eduardo?"

"Oh, I've no doubt Nelson Mackie had him killed, Cait. But he has plenty of men capable of doing it, doesn't he?"

Cait shuddered. "He certainly does. Some of those men there today were as frightening as Chavez. I guess I would have no problem believing one of them could have killed Eduardo."

"Neither would I," agreed Sadie.

Caitlin bade her a good night and Sadie slipped under the covers. She lay there remembering Juan Chavez's caresses and feeling an aching sadness at the thought that she would not likely be alone with him again.

Twenty-eight

It had been over a week since the Mackies' picnic and things had remained peaceful. Michael had hired a new shepherd and rode up to the meadows regularly to make sure all was well. So far no sheep had wandered away or died, and more important, neither Chavez nor any other of Mackie's men had been seen in the vicinity.

"I don't want to be too quick at trustin' the man," Michael said one day at breakfast, "But I'm beginin' to think he might have given up at last. Nevertheless," he added, "I don't want ye to be ridin' off the ranch alone, Cait. Or you, Sadie. Not yet, anyway."

"Sadie and I were planning to drive into town, Cait. Would you like to come with us?"

"I need to ride over to the reservation to talk to the agent about that teaching position, Ma."

"Gabe, can you ride with Caitlin today?" Elizabeth asked. "Michael, you won't mind if he doesn't work the two-year-olds today?"

"Not at all, *a ghra*. I'd not want ye going alone, Caitlin."

"Da, you don't have to pull Mr. Hart away from the horses. It's only five miles or so," protested Cait.

"I'd feel better if ye weren't ridin' alone yet, Cait. Ye'll go, Gabe?"

"Of course I'll go, sir."

Cait was hanging over the pasture fence looking longingly at Sky when Gabe led their horses out. "I thought I'd be riding him all summer," she said wistfully as she turned and walked over to Snowflake. She rubbed the mare's freckled muzzle. "Don't be insulted, Snowflake, but you are not really *my* horse."

Gabe handed her the reins and after she mounted looked over at her and said, "I think he'll be ready in a few days, Miss Cait. You may well be riding him before the summer is over."

Her eyes lit up. "Do you really think so?"

"I do."

They rode in silence for a while and then as they got closer to the agency, Gabe said: "You really want this job, don't you?"

"Teaching is what I've always wanted to do."

"Yes, but it was a different kind of teaching you were talking about when Sadie arrived, I recall."

Cait was quiet for a moment. "I guess I want to do something that gives to people, Mr. Hart. One of my teachers at Fayreweather was a real inspiration to me. She made me notice the women in the books I was reading, not just the men. I wanted to inspire other girls the way she did me."

"Well, I don't think you'll be doing that kind of teaching here. Most of your pupils won't even understand English."

"No, but they will need to learn it in order to survive. And while I am teaching them my language, I can offer them respect for their ways. If they went away to an Indian school, they would be stripped of all that makes them Dine."

"Dine?"

"That is the Navajo word for the People."

"And we aren't?" asked Gabe with a short laugh.

"Many Indian tribes have named themselves something similar," admitted Cait, "so I guess it isn't just white men they feel superior to. What do you think about Indians, Mr. Hart?"

"I haven't thought too much about them at all," Gabe confessed. "When I was little, Grandpa used to tell stories about fighting the Comanche. They sure seemed a bloodthirsty bunch, from what he told us. On the other hand," Gabe continued thoughtfully, "I remember him telling us about one little boy who was captured when he was five. When they rescued him at fourteen, he was pure Comanche. In fact, Grandpa said he didn't consider himself rescued, but kidnapped, so they must have treated him well."

"My Da fought Indians with the army, of course," said Cait. "But when he came to New Mexico and was made to remove the Navajo from their land, he decided to leave the army rather than continue doing what he felt was wrong. Every few years, when I was growing up, we'd go and visit our Dine friends, Serena and Antonio and their family."

"Then you would be a real good teacher for these Navajo kids, Miss Cait."

"I hope so, Mr. Hart."

When they reached the small agency office, Gabe waited outside. He'd never thought much about Indians before. He was no Indian hater, but he'd pretty much taken for granted that it was destiny that white settlers, who knew how to use the land, had more of a right to it. He suspected that Caitlin Burke would not share this view. She obviously had a more intimate understanding of what it had meant to at least one Navajo family. He admired her determination and idealism. His ma had been like that about teaching and so was Sadie. It seemed very right that he would end up loving a woman so like the strong women in his family.

It had been oppressively hot when they started out, but Gabe realized that a breeze had come up while he was sitting there. He looked east and saw that the sky was getting blacker by the minute over the mountains and the horses were moving restlessly where he had tied them. It was coming to the end of thunderstorm season, but it seemed like one hell of a storm was brewing.

He was just about to knock on the agency door when Cait came out with the agent. They were both looking very pleased, so he assumed she'd gotten the job.

"Oh, Mr. Hart," she said, a big smile on her face,

"Mr. Brookner has just agreed to hire me for the second term."

"That's grand news, Miss Cait, but we'd better be getting back before this storm hits."

Cait's expression changed as soon as she saw the clouds. She knew what was coming. "Thank goodness we're not that far from the ranch," she said. "We've got to be off, Mr. Brookner," she added, turning and shaking his hand.

"Are you sure you both don't want to take shelter here?" the agent offered.

"I think we can outrun it," Gabe replied. "And I want to get back and make sure the horses are all right."

"Good luck, then," Brookner called out as they wheeled their horses and took off at a canter. After two miles, Gabe pulled the horses in. Despite their run, it was hard to keep them to a slow trot as the great claps of thunder grew louder and closer.

"I love thunderstorms," said Cait with a big smile as she turned back and saw a bolt of lightning split the sky and seem to touch one of the mesas.

Gabe looked back and grinned. He could see how quickly the rain was moving toward them. "I like them too, Miss Cait, but I'm not so fond of what they can do. Another few minutes and that rain is going to be on top of us. We'll hold the horses in a few minutes more, but when I say so, ride like hell!" Cait grinned back and when Gabe yelled "Now!" she clapped her heels to Snowflake's sides and the mare took off.

It was a close race. They could feel the cool air behind them and even hear the rain hitting the ground. The storm finally caught them just at the ranch gate and in one moment, they were both drenched.

Cait laughed aloud as the thunder sounded over their heads and the horses flattened out in a run. When they reached the corral, she slid off Snowflake and lifted her face to the downpour. She felt like the rain was washing away all the doubts and guilt that had beset her this summer and she felt free and clear at last.

"Don't be a damn fool, Miss Cait. Get your horse into the barn," Gabe yelled. They all just got inside when a flash of lightning and a clap of thunder seemed to occur simultaneously and the old hitching post next to the corral was split in half.

"Oh my God," exclaimed Cait, her eyes wide in disbelief. "That could have been one of us or the horses!"

"It almost was. What the hell were you doing, just standing out there like it was a shower?" Gabe was shaken to the core at the thought of her reckless behavior. He'd seen a cow struck by lightning once and he shivered at the memory.

"There is no need to yell at me, Mr. Hart. We are all inside and safe," replied Cait, now as angry as he was. "I wasn't standing there that long."

Gabe took a deep breath to calm himself. "I've seen an animal killed in a storm not half as bad as this one," he explained, his anger now under control.

"That must have been a terrible thing," replied Cait. "But the rain felt so good after the heat today. . . ." She stood there, her hair plastered to her head and her shirt sticking to her skin, revealing every lovely curve, and Gabe realized there was more than one way a storm could be exciting.

Cait smiled at him. "Just look at us, soaked to the skin."

"I am trying my best not to look," muttered Gabe, as he turned and busied himself with the horses.

Cait looked down at herself and blushed. She had worn her lightest blouse this morning and the cotton might as well have been gauze, she realized. When Gabe turned, she was still standing there, beginning to shiver a little. "I have a dry shirt in the tack room," he told her. "You look uh, cold, Miss Cait."

"Thank you," she whispered and walked back to the tack room. With shaking hands she unbuttoned her blouse and stripped it off. Her chemise was soaked too, so she pulled that over her head and looked around for the shirt.

"I don't see the shirt, Mr. Hart. Do you remember where you left it?" she called.

"It should be right there. I'll find it," he said and before Cait could think to say anything he was standing in the doorway. She froze like a deer caught in torchlight, her hands across her breasts, trying to keep them hidden.

She thought maybe she knew, after all, what it would be like to be struck by lightning. The force between them was so strong that she was surprised she didn't turn into a pile of ash right then and there. She was as helpless against the pull as she had been before.

Gabe's hand reached out and touched the line of her jaw. Her hands fell from her breasts and she reached out to put her hands on his chest. He couldn't tell if she was pushing him away or holding on for dear life. All he knew was how much he wanted her. There was an old pallet in the corner of the room and he very slowly backed her over to it and sitting down, pulled her after him. His hand reached down to cup her breast and she whispered, "No, Gabe."

It was pure torture, but he pulled away and said, "I won't do anything you don't want me to, Cait."

The trouble was, of course, that she *wanted* him to caress her breast. She put her hand on top of his and guided it back. He traced her breast gently and then cupped it, caressing the nipple with his thumb.

"Oh, Gabe . . ." she murmured.

When he lowered his mouth to hers, she let herself fall back on the cot, for the wood she had been leaning against was rough against her bare shoulders. It seemed their kiss went on forever, but when he pulled away, she realized forever wasn't nearly long enough.

"Do you know what you are doing to me?" said Gabe, his voice low and strained.

"I don't care," she whispered and then moaned with pleasure as he kissed her breast. "But wait, Gabe," she added, and he pulled back again, only to realize that she was reaching up to unbutton his shirt. It was hard, because the material was wet and her fingers were trembling, and when he saw what she was doing he ripped open the last button and pulled it off.

Her hand was at his chest again, but this time there was no doubt; she wasn't pushing him away, but running her fingers through the silver-blond hair and tracing the line that went from sternum down his hard, flat stomach to the waistband of his jeans.

If she went any further, he wouldn't be able to stop himself, he thought in ecstatic despair. When she started to pull the buttons of his pants open, he pushed her fingers away and shifted them so they were lying side by side. He kissed her again, hoping to distract her. But as he was kissing, he could feel her hand running down his chest once again.

This time he helped her. He had to, for he was so hard that his wet pants were uncomfortably tight. It was a relief when they were finally open and he was free of the pressure from the metal buttons.

Cait had grown up on a ranch and she had seen plenty of examples of maleness over the years. So she was not completely surprised at what she felt when Gabe unbuttoned his jeans. Obviously, a man would grow larger, just like other animals. What did surprise her was how lovely and soft something so rigid and male felt under her fingers, and the stirrings of desire in a part of her body she hadn't been much aware of up till now. She wanted to pull him down on top of her, pull him into her, although it wasn't quite clear to her how that might be done. Instinctively, she arched her body up to meet his.

When Gabe felt that soft pressure against him, he finally came to his senses. He pulled back and said: "Cait, I should never have let things get this out of hand." My God, here he was, ready to mount her as though she were just anyone and not the one he loved. Not to mention Michael Burke's daughter. He turned away and tried to get himself back into his pants, but they were so wet he couldn't button them, so he gave up and just pulled his shirt back on.

She lay there, looking so disappointed that he almost laughed out loud. She was a passionate woman, though what good that would do him, he didn't know. Here she was, looking up at him wistfully, as if to say "Why did you stop, Gabe?" rather than being outraged that he'd even begun.

He got up and found the shirt he'd sent her in for. "Here, you'd best put this on before I lose control all over again."

"I wish you would," she whispered as she sat up and slipped her arms into the soft cotton.

"I know, though I can't understand why! Here you are, raised like a lady and about to lose your virginity in a tack room."

He hadn't meant it as a criticism of her, but Cait heard it as a comment on her shameful behavior. Obviously it was all right for him to kiss her passionately and stroke her breasts, but she should have protested and pushed him away. Instead, and she blushed almost purple as she remembered it, she had actually kissed him back as passionately and caressed a part of him she probably was supposed to pretend she didn't know about! She felt utterly humiliated.

"I am not sure what came over me, Mr. Hart," she responded in what she hoped was a dignified manner. "Perhaps it was the storm. It won't happen again, I promise you."

"It can't," said Gabe vehemently. "I can't repay your parents' kindness to me by seducing their daughter! And I can't marry you," he added.

Cait didn't know what she'd been thinking, beyond wanting the incredible pleasure his kisses and caresses had brought her never to end. She certainly hadn't been thinking of marriage. She'd just made one mistake in that direction, thinking she loved a man who could not answer her passion. She didn't want to make another mistake so soon after, thinking she loved a man because he could respond to her. Surely she didn't love Gabe Hart, nor want to be married to him, she told herself. Especially, she thought, her heart sinking, when he said he couldn't marry her. She supposed that meant that he didn't love her either.

"Don't worry, Mr. Hart, marriage to you is the last thing I'd be thinking of." She stood up and with as much dignity as she could muster under the circumstances, said: "It sounds like the storm is over. I'd best get inside and change my clothes. You might want to do the same, Mr. Hart," she added and walked out of the room without looking back.

Gabe stood there feeling utterly ridiculous. Damn it, how had he bungled things so? Not that she could ever care for him, but to get them both so hot and then blurt out a foolish thing like of course he couldn't marry her. Just why had that popped out of his mouth?

He guessed that however stupid he sounded, he had saved them both from further foolishness. He loved Caitlin Burke. God knew he loved and wanted her. But if she wasn't for him, at least this awkwardness would break the attraction that flowed between them.

It took Cait a long time to get to sleep that night because she could not stop thinking of what had happened in the barn. She could feel herself grow warm with desire again as she remembered how Gabe had kissed and caressed her. Then, as she thought of her own behavior, she became even hotter with humiliation. Why was it that Henry, for whom she had felt a great affection, had never been able to give her what she wanted, while Gabe Hart, a man she hardly knew, had her pulling his pants down as though she were the town whore! Whatever must he think of her?

But she did know Gabe, she would remind herself. They had grown to be friends; he had been kind to her. She respected his way with horses and she admired him for his loyalty to her father. But respect and liking and admiration and attraction didn't necessarily add up to love, did they? If only she could talk to her mother about this. But it was one thing to tell her ma that Henry did not meet her need for passion. It was quite another to say: "Ma, I almost let Gabe

Hart make love to me in the tack room. And the only reason we didn't is that *he* stopped us. Does that mean I love him, Ma?"

It had been embarrassing enough to face him after their kisses behind the barn. But today they had become intimate in a way usually reserved for marriage. And Gabe Hart had made it perfectly clear that he was not thinking of marriage. Caitlin wondered what it would be like to be married to him and be free to explore his body and have him explore hers. Then it would start all over again, the cycle of desire, humiliation, and confusion. She didn't fall asleep until at least three in the morning.

"You look tired this morning, Cait," her mother said as they got breakfast ready. "Didn't you sleep well?"

Cait concentrated on placing the silverware on the table just so and said: "I guess I was just too excited about getting the job, Ma."

Elizabeth looked over at her daughter and smiled. "I am so proud of you, Cait. I am sure you will do a wonderful job with those children."

"I hope so, Ma. I guess I'm as nervous as I am excited."

Sadie overheard their exchange as she came in. "I remember my first year teaching, Cait," she said with a sympathetic smile. "I was only sixteen and a half and one of my pupils, Jeb Turner, was a foot taller than me at fourteen! I was sure I'd never get him to mind me."

"How did you handle him?" Cait asked curiously.

"Actually, I didn't have to," Sadie admitted. "He got a huge crush on me so he did everything I wanted. It was the ten-year-olds that had me in tears every day when I came home! But by the end of the year, I'd learned how to keep control."

"I don't know that I have to worry about Dine children misbehaving," Cait said thoughtfully. "More likely the challenge will be getting them to trust me."

Discussing her fears about teaching had distracted her from her dread of seeing Gabe again. But it turned out she needn't have worried after all, for when her Da came in he explained that Gabe had grabbed some biscuits earlier that morning and was riding up to the sheep meadow.

Gabe had had as hard a time getting to sleep as Cait and he knew there was no way he could face her across the breakfast table. As soon as Michael came out that morning he had volunteered to ride up to the sheep camp himself. Everything looked a fresh green after the storm and the pungent smell of sage filled his lungs and seemed to cleanse him of all his worries.

The new shepherd was a younger man, a Basque down from Colorado. He didn't speak much English but knew enough to convey to Gabe that all was well and that Gabe should help himself to coffee while he, Joaquin, went up to the meadow.

The coffee was good and strong and Gabe felt his spirits rise as he sat there at the bottom of the meadow. Maybe things would stay peaceful, he thought. If they did, then he could leave the Burkes without feeling he'd broken faith with them. As he breathed in the scent of piñon and juniper, he even let himself wonder if he could stay. He'd come to love more than Caitlin Burke, he reminded himself. He'd grown to love the horses, especially Night Sky, and it would feel like breaking faith with *him* to leave anytime soon, he realized. There was a bond between them, one formed by patience and trust and even love. He loved that horse for his intelligence and his fear and his courage. It would be almost as hard to leave Sky as it would be to leave Cait behind.

Maybe saving her horse had been a safe way of loving Caitlin Burke. Maybe he was trying to keep himself too safe. And maybe he was misjudging Cait, as Sadie had suggested. She wasn't Caroline, an Eastern girl transplanted West. Cait had been born in New Mexico and though she'd been away from it, she'd loved it enough to stay. He closed his eyes and thought of the way she'd looked when he'd come upon her that evening, talking to Sky. And the way she had felt after the storm.

He loved her far more than he had ever loved Caroline Bryce, he admitted to himself. But could he trust her? She knew he was a good man with a horse. She might even think him a brave man, since he was willing to strap on a gun and face down her father's enemies if he had to. But Gabe wasn't sure how brave he really was. Here he was, asking Night Sky to let go of his fear while he was keeping safe and pushing Cait away because he was afraid to trust his heart to a woman again. To trust himself.

He rode down feeling a lot better than when he'd ridden up. When he got back to the ranch, he saw Caitlin weeding the flower bed in front of the house and he tied his horse and walked over.

"Good morning, Miss Cait. Your ma's flowers are looking a might bedraggled today. I guess the downpour got them as bad as it did us."

Cait was kneeling in the red dirt, trying to lift up some of the petunias and brush the sand off their leaves and petals. She couldn't believe that Gabe would come over and talk to her about yesterday, however obliquely.

"Some of them are more than bedraggled, Mr. Hart," she said quietly. "Petunias are very fragile and most of them won't survive."

"But those spicy smelling red and gold flowers look just fine," he observed.

"The marigolds? They are strong enough to survive almost anything," Cait replied.

"I hope our friendship is more like them, then," said Gabe softly and seriously. "I'd hate to think yesterday would damage it permanently."

"I don't see how we can have a friendship after yesterday, Mr. Hart," said Cait, finally turning and facing him. "Clearly we were both . . . carried away . . . I must beg you to forget my behavior," she added, her voice low and strained.

"I don't know that I can, Miss Cait."

"Oh, but you must," she begged. "I am so ashamed of myself."

"There is nothing for you to be ashamed of," Gabe said, hoping to reassure her when Elizabeth came out onto the porch.

"I am afraid most of the petunias are hopeless, Ma," said her daughter, relieved that her mother's presence had ended the conversation. When Gabe left, however, she realized she was also a little disappointed. Had he really meant it when he said she had nothing to be ashamed of? Unfortunately, he was the only person to whom she could turn for reassurance, she thought ironically.

Twenty-nine

Over the next few days, Gabe could feel a tension building in him as he worked with Night Sky. The horse was ready, he was sure of it. He obeyed voice commands perfectly on the lunge line, going from a walk to a canter, stopping and backing up at the slightest pressure from the hackamore. For the last week, Gabe had been working him with the red-and-black saddle blanket strapped to his back. He'd leaned his full weight on Sky's back, hanging there for a full minute without the horse shying or crow-hopping.

One afternoon toward the end of the week, he decided he would get up before dawn the next day, before anyone else was awake. He could wait a few weeks, letting the horse get used to a saddle, but he was sure once Sky had accepted a rider, he'd take the saddle very easily. And this feeling Gabe had, well, it kept rising in his chest every time he worked with the horse and he could tell from the way Sky responded to him that he was just waiting for the culmination of their work the way Gabe was.

It was the second night after a full moon and when Gabe awoke at four in the morning, the moonlight was still bright enough to light the pasture. He whistled softly to Sky and rattled a pail of oats and the horse came trotting over from the corner. Sky only lipped one handful of oats and then stamped one foot impatiently as if to say: "Come on, let's do it."

Gabe slipped the hackamore on him and led him to the corral, where he tied him to the fence and slipped the blanket on his back. As he smoothed it under the girth, he admired the geometric patterns. It was a beautiful piece of weaving and he surprised himself by saying a little prayer that Mrs. Burke's friend's power was somehow present in the blanket and would help him.

"I'm going to tighten the cinch more than usual, Sky," said Gabe after he'd pulled it to the third hole, which Sky was used to. "Now, don't blow yourself up on me," he warned. The horse merely shifted and gave Gabe a curious look as he hauled at the cinch. Gabe slipped two fingers under it to make sure it wasn't too tight and then untied the reins.

"If I were smart, I'd lunge you for ten minutes, boy," he said as he led the horse to the center of the corral where he'd set up a mounting block. "But it will be getting light soon and I don't want an audience. Especially if you toss me!"

Gabe leaned over the horse's back like he had before, but this time he let Sky take his full weight for a good three minutes. Sky walked forward a few steps and Gabe kept himself hanging there. When he pulled gently on the reins, the horse stopped immediately.

Gabe slid off and brought Sky close to the mounting block.

"This is it, Sky. This is what we've been working for all summer, you and me," he murmured as he stroked the horse's muzzle. "I know I'll feel like that big cat at first, but you should know by now that I won't hurt you."

Gabe stood on the block for a moment. If he was doing this too soon, it would set the horse back once again. But he *knew* he had put enough time in. He *knew* the horse trusted him. But when he felt real weight, with Gabe's legs on either side of him, would it remind him too much of the searing pain of the claws on his neck? Maybe he'd never accept a rider, no matter how much he trusted him.

It was time to stop thinking about it and do it, thought Gabe, and he threw his leg over Sky's back, and using his hand for balance, lowered himself as gently as he could. Sky's head went down and Gabe held himself ready for anything. He'd try to stay on, he decided as he slipped his right hand under the folded blanket and grabbed the wool.

But the horse didn't buck, although Gabe was sure he'd been about to. Instead, as he heard Gabe murmur "Easy boy, I'm not going to hurt you," he started to shudder. The horse was terrified, but because of his trust in Gabe, he just stood there, shaking.

Gabe let the blanket go and leaning forward a little, gently stroked the side of Sky's neck. The shivering didn't stop and Gabe became conscious of the great gift this horse was giving him. Night Sky had given over his heart and his spirit into Gabe's hands. He could feel the horse's fear, but he could also feel the horse's love, for it felt like love to him. His own love for Sky was being given back fourfold. "It may kill me," Sky was saying, "but it is you who asks it, so I will stand."

If Sky didn't throw him, Gabe had originally intended to ride him at a walk around the corral. He changed his mind as soon as he felt the trembling begin. He would sit there as long as he and the horse could bear it. That was enough for this first time.

Gradually, the uncontrollable shivering stopped. Gabe sat for one more minute, murmuring nonsense syllables and stroking Sky's neck and then he slid off. Sky turned and as Gabe approached his head, buried his muzzle in Gabe's shirt, breathing as hard as if he'd been running.

"You are everything I thought you were," Gabe whispered. It took him a minute to realize that both he and the horse were soaking wet. "Look at us, Sky, you'd think we'd just run two miles," he said, laughing shakily, "instead of just standing around for two minutes!"

Caitlin didn't know what woke her. Maybe it was Gabe's whistle, maybe Sky's welcoming whicker, but she lay there for a minute wondering why it was still dark if Gabe was out with the horses. Then gradually it came to her: Gabe had chosen very early morning to ride Sky for the first time.

At first she was angry. She should be there watching because he was her horse. Then as she slipped her feet into her sheepskin moccasins and pulled a shawl around her shoulders, she calmed down. Everyone would have wanted to watch and a crowd may well spook the horse.

Her room was in the front of the house and her window gave her a clear view of the corral. She very quietly pushed it open and watched as Gabe led Sky out. She held her breath as he tightened the girth, for she knew Sky had never felt the full constraint of a cinch yet.

She smiled as she watched Gabe lean his weight on the horse's back. It was going to happen; he was going to ride Sky, she realized, and she held her breath as he led the horse over to the mounting block.

When Gabe let himself down and Sky's head went down, she closed her eyes and felt the bitter taste of despair in her mouth. He'd throw Gabe like he had thrown her, and her father would have no choice but to put him down. But there was no frightened squealing, no thud as Gabe hit the ground, and she opened her eyes again. Sky was standing there and even from her window she could tell he was shaking with fear. But Gabe sat quietly, caressing Sky's neck. From the way his legs hung down and the relaxed way he sat, she could tell he had given himself over to the horse, as though he were saying: "I'm yours, do whatever you want. Just know that I won't hurt you and I won't ask for anything you can't give."

Gabe's hair was glinting silver in the moonlight and Cait thought she had never seen anything as beautiful as horse and rider become one. It was a powerful surrender, for both were strong creatures. Either one was capable of inflicting harm on the other, but Gabe had given up all claim to domination and Sky all opportunities for explosive rebellion.

She wanted Gabe to squeeze his thighs together, lift the reins, and ride around the corral. But clearly he had decided that he'd taken the horse to his limit, so he just slipped off.

Cait pulled back from the window so Gabe wouldn't see her and crawled back in bed. She lay there till dawn, tears slipping down her face. They were tears of relief, for Sky could be ridden, that was clear, no matter how much longer it took to get him used to a saddle. They were also tears of grief, for the little black colt who had followed her around like a puppy and with whom she'd felt such a strong bond, was no longer hers. He had been no one's after the lion's attack, for he'd trusted no one. But now, he was Gabe's, heart and soul. Oh, Cait would eventually ride Sky, she was sure. The horse would always have an affection for her. But Gabe had healed him.

She gradually realized that along with the relief and loss, she was feeling a deep longing. That oneness she had seen, that wordless communication Gabe had achieved with Sky: she wanted it for herself with Gabe. It was what she had wanted the other day. Her feelings for Gabe went far beyond physical desire. She wanted to give her whole self to him and at the same time experience his surrender to her. She wanted his body; she couldn't deny that. But more than that, she wanted his heart and soul so that she could give him hers in return.

There was no way to tell him, of course. But at least she knew he valued their friendship. If she could get over her embarrassment, then friendship was a place to start. Maybe with time and patience, something more would be possible.

Cait had expected that when Gabe came in for breakfast he would be bursting to tell everyone of his success. Instead, he sat quietly at the table letting the conversation flow around him. When Cait glanced over at him from time to time, he looked dazed, as though he was in another world. He probably was, she realized, the private world of himself and his horse.

After breakfast, however, when Michael went out to see the horses in the far pasture and Elizabeth and Sadie went to work in the garden, Gabe stayed behind over a last cup of coffee, while Cait cleared the table and began to wash up.

He came up behind her at the sink and handing her his cup, leaned against the counter. "I have something to tell you, Miss Cait," he said quietly.

So he was going to tell her first, she thought, moved by his thoughtfulness.

"This morning I rode Sky. Wal, maybe rode isn't the right word," he drawled with a self-deprecating smile. "But I was on his back for a full three minutes and I think he would have let me walk him around the corral. I didn't want to push him too far, though."

Cait had already decided that she wouldn't tell Gabe she'd seen him, so she put as surprised and thrilled a look on her face, as if she was finding out for the first time.

"Oh, Mr. Hart, that is wonderful! I can't believe that after all this time it has finally happened."

"He'd come to trust me, but I wasn't sure myself how far that trust would go," Gabe admitted. "Anyway, I wanted to tell you first before I told your Da, because he is your horse."

"Thank you, Mr. Hart. It must have been hard to keep it to yourself this morning," she added with a smile.

"It was all so new, I really couldn't find the words for it, to tell you the truth. I've tamed many horses but never one so badly hurt as Sky nor one that meant as much to me," Gabe confessed.

"When do you think you will ride him again?"

"I'll see what happens when I am on his back tomorrow. If he is calm, then I may walk him a little. Going slow has worked well so far."

"Do you think I will be able to ride him soon?" There was a wistful note in Cait's voice that she tried to keep out but couldn't.

"I'd give it a week or so, Miss Cait. I'd like to start you on the lunge line for I haven't even gotten a saddle on him yet." Gabe hesitated. "I'd like to keep this a secret for a few days. I know everyone will want to be watching and I want him real secure before we have an audience."

"I won't say a word, Mr. Hart. Thank you for sharing the secret with me. I'm sure it meant a lot to you to finally be able to ride him."

"It sure was something, Miss Cait," said Gabe with a wide smile.

"It sure was something." Lord, but he was hopeless with words. But how could he have told her what it felt like to feel so close to the horse? Sometimes there were days when Gabe wished he was one of his horses, so he could communicate their way, and not use words at all. At least she had seemed a little less tongue-tied and embarrassed with him. He'd done the right thing to tell her first.

The next two days he worked Sky in the early morning. The second time he sat the horse, there was the same trembling, but it ended very quickly. Still, he decided to let it go with sitting him. The third morning, Sky stood like any other horse, even looking back at Gabe as if to say, "Okay, I've gotten used to this. What next?"

"All right, fella, let's take a walk." Gabe lifted the reins and squeezed his legs together and Sky started out in a bouncy walk, shaking his head and whisking his tail. His ears moved back and forth as though he was just waiting for Gabe's command to trot, having heard it so many times on the lunge line.

"Oh, no, not yet," Gabe crooned. "We'll just walk this morning," and he kept Sky going around in long slow circles until he moved more smoothly. But the next day, after fifteen minutes of walking, Gabe gave the command to trot and they moved easily and happily around the corral.

By the end of the week, Gabe figured it was time to let everyone know of the horse's progress, so on Friday at breakfast he made the announcement. This time he couldn't keep from grinning.

"Mr. Burke, I have some good news for you."

Michael looked over and grinned back, Gabe's smile was so infectious. "And what might that be, boyo?"

"I think Miss Cait has got herself a very good saddle horse in Night Sky."

"You've ridden him, then?" asked Michael, a look of amazement on his face. "I knew he was coming along, but I was still afraid the feel of someone on his back would be too much for him."

"So was I, Mr. Burke. The first time was hard for him, but now he's trotting around like a circus pony."

"I knew you could do it, Gabe," said Sadie, giving him a quick hug.

"Well, Cait, what have you got to say to all this?" asked her father. "I'd think you'd be doin' a jig, ye'd be so happy."

"I am, Da. But Gabe told me on Monday that he'd ridden Sky," she added shyly.

"That was a thoughtful thing to do, Gabe," said Elizabeth with an appreciative smile.

"I wasn't trying to keep anything a secret, ma'am, but I didn't want too many people around while I was working this week. But this morning, I want you all to come down to the corral," he said, getting up.

"We'll be down in a few minutes, Gabe," said Elizabeth.

Sadie and Cait were on the corral fence when Michael and Elizabeth arrived. When Gabe led Sky out, Elizabeth exclaimed: "Why, he looks wonderful under Serena's blanket, Gabe."

"Yes, ma'am. I haven't put a saddle on him yet. I thought I'd ride him first and then go back to the lunge line to get him used to a saddle."

"Oh, Michael, he has always been one of my favorites," exclaimed Elizabeth as she watched Gabe mount and put Sky through his paces. "Do you remember when he came in last spring all torn and bloody? And look at him now!"

Michael was looking. Sky's head was up and he was walking proudly around the corral. His black coat was gleaming, his hooves were polished, and the white "stars" sprinkled all over were so white they seemed to be shining.

"He's pleased with himself," said Michael, smiling at the sight of him.

"And so he should be, Michael," Elizabeth said. "He's done such hard work with the horse."

"No, *a aghra*, I meant Sky. I've always believed that a horse *wants* to be the best he can be. Frost was that way. She always wanted a challenge, she was always wantin' to work with me, whether it was racin' or paradin'."

"I can't believe Gabe kept this to himself all week. I would have been dying to tell."

"Sure and he did mention it to Cait, didn't he, and wasn't that interesting?" said Michael, a twinkle in his eye.

"It *is* her horse, Michael."

"There is that," he admitted.

"But you think there is something more?"

"I'm not sure what I'm thinking, *a ghra*. But I can't help noticing the way Cait's been watching both horse and rider."

"Do you think Gabe would be a good man for her?" asked his wife.

"If she loved him, I couldn't think of a better. Let's just hope it stays peaceful so she has a chance to find out."

Thirty

"Mackie wants you in the house, Juan," announced Canty as he sat down at the bunkhouse table for supper.

"Now?" Chavez asked calmly as he spooned gravy onto his biscuits.

"He said right away."

"*Mierde*," Chavez murmured as he pushed the bench back.

He was shown into the dining room where Mackie and his wife were just finishing their supper. "Sit down, Juan. There are some enchiladas left and I'm sure they are better than your bunkhouse fare."

"*Gracias,* señor, señora." At least he'd get something hot to eat, he thought as he filled his plate.

"Why don't you go into the parlor, my dear, and I'll join you there for coffee later," Mackie told his wife.

"Of course, Nelson," she said with an obedient nod.

"How about some beer to wash that down?" Mackie called out to Maria to bring them a pitcher of beer and a bottle of tequila. He poured them both a shot glass of the tequila and a mug of beer.

"To the Burke ranch, Chavez, which will sooner or later be mine," he said with a grin. Juan wiped his mouth and lifted his shot glass.

Mackie downed the tequila and took a few swallows of beer. Juan followed suit, though he was careful to take only a small swallow of the tequila. He wanted a clear head.

"So, I saw you followed my orders and kept Miss Hart entertained."

"*Si*, señor."

"I also saw her brother's face when he saw the two of you together," continued Mackie with a satisfied smile.

"Señor Hart does not appreciate my attentions to his sister."

"Good," said Mackie, pouring himself another shot. "We've almost got him where we want him."

"And where is that, señor?" asked Chavez quietly, although he was beginning to think he knew.

"Gabe Hart has a reputation for being good with a gun. In fact, I've heard a rumor that he rode with the Regulators over in Lincoln County. I don't want him getting in my way, Chavez, but another murder would be too suspicious. He's got to be goaded into drawing on you."

"By my attacking his sister?"

"Hardly attacking, Juan. She seems to like you well enough. You just have to make your interest a little more apparent. Push him a little." Mackie gulped down another shot of tequila. "We're all friends in the valley now, so there's no reason you can't just ride up to the Burkes' ranch to do a little courting. Here, have another shot."

This time Juan drained his glass and took a swallow of beer to cool his throat. He was beginning to feel hot, although whether it was from the liquor or Mackie's orders, he wasn't sure.

"I think that if Gabe Hart caught you and his sister in some compromising position, he'd call you out, don't you?" Mackie lifted the bottle of tequila, which was almost empty and shook it. "*Alli esta el gusano,* Juan," he said, pointing to the worm curled in the bottom of the bottle. "Let's see who gets to swallow him." Mackie poured some into his glass, but the worm remained in the bottle. "He's yours then, Chavez." He grinned as he watched the worm fall into Juan's glass. "Bottoms up!"

They both lifted their glasses at the same time and threw their heads back, downing the last of the liquor. Juan could feel the worm going down and it took all his concentration not to gag it right up again.

"Do you think you can take him, Juan?"

"*Si*, señor."

"Good. Once he is out of the way, then we can better deal with Michael Burke."

Juan had gotten the worm before in drinking bouts and it had always gone down easily. He didn't know why it had been so hard to swallow tonight. But maybe it was more than the worm, he thought as he walked over to the corral and leaned against the fence. Maybe it was Mackie's order that just wouldn't go down.

He'd been drawn to Sadie Hart when he met her walking down the trail leading her lame horse. He'd asked her to dance the first time because he wanted to see what she'd do. She wasn't afraid of him at all and she seemed to see him clearly. She had no illusions about him but she also knew he wasn't a monster. At the picnic, although he'd been under Mackie's orders, he'd danced with her because he *wanted* to, not because it was a part of the job.

He wanted to see her again. In fact, he realized, annoyed at himself, he wanted Mackie's pretend neighborliness to be real. He would like to go courting Sadie Hart just for himself. After the picnic, he probably would have started to anyway. Now it had become a part of his job. He was to be the wolf in sheep's clothing. He was to use her attraction to him—and he knew she was attracted to him—against her brother.

This was one order he had a hard time swallowing. He had to, just as he'd had to swallow *el gusano*. But maybe it wasn't just the beer and tequila that wasn't sitting well in his stomach. Maybe it was his orders. Because if he courted Sadie Hart, he'd be courting her for real. He'd be doing what he wanted to do anyway, which should seem like a great joke on his employer. Except the joke was on him, Juan Chavez, for the closer he got to making Sadie care for him, the more he cared for her—and *Dios*, he did care for her—the sooner her brother would react. And if he killed her brother, that was the end of whatever was between them.

*   *   *

Because things had been quiet and none of Mackie's riders had been seen in the vicinity, Michael relaxed his rule of no riding off ranch property. One afternoon, a week after the picnic, Sadie took Snowflake and rode up into the foothills. She didn't want to risk the mare again on the steeper trail, so although it was tempting she turned Snowflake around before they climbed to high ground.

When she heard hoofbeats behind her, her heart started racing and she was cursing herself for going off alone when Juan Chavez pulled up next to her. She let out a sigh of relief.

"Did I frighten you, señorita? I am sorry."

Sadie laughed. "I feel foolish to be frightened. After all, it has been quiet for the last few weeks. But I haven't been off the ranch for all that time."

"It is never foolish to be frightened, *querida*," he said softly. "Señor Mackie's men are not the only rough one's around, you know."

Sadie blushed at the endearment and rode on, tongue-tied, for a few minutes. They would go their own ways, she guessed as soon as they got out of the trees and she realized she hated to see him go.

"Are you thirsty, Señor Chavez? My canteen is full and I brought some cheese and bread with me for a little picnic," she said boldly, pulling Snowflake to a halt.

Chavez smiled down at her. "That's sounds very pleasant, señorita."

They dismounted and tethered the horses. Juan gestured Sadie to the shade of a large juniper. Sadie took a deep breath after they sat down. "I love the smell of the trees here. We just don't have that many where I am from in Texas."

"I know. I've spent some time in Texas."

"Where are you from originally, Mr. Chavez, Texas or New Mexico?"

Sadie had asked the question casually and was startled when she saw the look on his face. He looked both sad and puzzled for a quick moment and then his usual closed look was back.

"I grew up in New Mexico, on the Romero hacienda."

She noticed that he didn't say where he was born, and it felt intrusive to press him further.

"I'm Texas born and bred myself," she said lightly.

"You and your brother?"

"Yes, although Gabe left about ten years ago."

Sadie unwrapped the triangles of bread and cheese. "These are a little dry, so you'll want a swallow of water with it," she said, passing him the canteen after she'd taken a drink. Chavez put the canteen down and reached out his finger and brushed at her lower lip. "You had a crumb there, *querida*," he whispered.

"Why do you call me '*querida*'?"

"Because you are dear to me," he said softly.

Sadie blushed and said: "I don't know why."

"Do you need reasons, señorita? I will give them to you. You are dear to me because of this," he said and lowered his lips to hers. Her mouth opened under his and he took possession of it, exploring with his lips and tongue until he had her moaning with the pleasure of it. "And because of this," he said as he unbuttoned her shirtwaist and cupped her breast and deepened his kiss.

They were alone, where no one could intrude and Sadie knew she should be careful. But she wanted, for once in her life, to let go of her need always to be responsible, and enjoy only the moment. And so when Juan said "and also this" and sought the buttons on her riding skirt, she reached behind and undid them herself and let him ease his hand down and slip it under her drawers.

He pulled her close to him as he found what was waiting for him, moist and warm. She pulled back a little as he began to stroke her and he stopped immediately.

"Don't worry, *querida*. It will feel very good," he whispered.

"I know. That's what I'm afraid of," she said with a shaky laugh.

Her shyness about her own desire and her trust in him almost made him stop. Except it was impossible to stop when she pressed herself against his hand. He caressed her gently, bringing her slowly, slowly to a point where she couldn't have pulled away even if she had wanted to. She arched up and cried out in little gasps as he brought her to a climax and then she clung to him as though she'd never let him go.

Her face was buried in his chest and he dropped soft kisses on the top of her head. *Madre de Dios,* she was unlike any woman he'd ever known: strong and real and unafraid to show him her innermost self.

He himself was aching to be inside her, but he wasn't sure he wanted to push her that far that fast. It seemed as if she might just get him to, however, for as she pushed against him she felt his hardness and lifted her face to his with a winning smile. Then her hand reached down and tentatively stroked him and he groaned. "No, *querida,* no *mas,* or I will lose control."

She didn't say anything, but her hand moved up to his waistband and began to pull at the buttons. "Are you sure about this?" he asked.

Sadie nodded her head and pulling herself out of his arms, stood up, and started to undress. It took forever to get his damned boots off, it seemed, but finally he'd gotten them and his trousers off and then stripped off his shirt. He sat down next to her and put his arm around her shoulders.

"You have never done this before, have you, Sadie?". She shook her head shyly.

"It will hurt a little at first, but I'll try to go as slowly as I can. Just wait here a moment." He walked over to his horse and pulled off his saddle roll and spread his sougan under the tree. "At least you won't have pebbles biting into you," he said lightly as he lay down next to her and pulled her close.

Sadie had seen beauty before, but nothing seemed as beautiful to her as Juan Chavez's body. He wasn't as tall as Gabe, but he was broader and more muscular, with a flat waist and slim hips. His skin felt so soft against her that she had to stroke it and she felt him shiver as she ran a hand down his back. Then he was kissing her, raining little kisses on her face and neck and down her body. *"Si hermosa, querida,"* he whispered.

She smiled as she ran her hand over his shoulder and down his chest. His face and neck were dark from the sun and she'd expected him to be dark all over. Instead, under his shirt he was pale, with light freckles scattered all over his arms and shoulders.

"What are you smiling at, *querida*?" he asked, raising himself on his elbow and running his hand down her belly and along one of her thighs.

"At how pale and freckled you are, Juan," she said. Sadie let her hand slide down his arm and side and then brought it up again, to where he was so big and hard. She had never seen or touched this part of a man before, but her hand seemed to know what to do on its own and Juan groaned again as she grasped him with gentle pressure.

His obvious arousal excited her and deep inside she felt as though she were all warm and liquid. She wanted to have him inside her and she rubbed herself against him. "Are you ready?" he asked quietly as he eased her onto her back and positioned himself on top of her. She nodded a yes.

He was right. It did hurt, more than a little, and she lay there astounded that what she had wanted so much could cause her such pain. He came very quickly, collapsing on her, and she held him close.

As they lay there, she began to feel her desire return and as he shifted a little and pulled out of her, she moaned in disappointment.

"Oh, Sadie, I am sorry," he whispered. "I could not hold myself back."

"Yes, but . . ."

"But what, *querida*?"

It was too embarrassing to ask and besides she didn't quite know what she was asking for, so she just placed her hand on his and brought it down to her. "You learn fast, *querida*," he said with a soft laugh.

As he stroked her, Sadie felt herself drawing up and up and up and then with one final caress of his fingers, he brought her pouring down. She lay shuddering in his arms while he stroked her hair and murmured broken little love phrases in Spanish.

"Next time will be better," he promised.

Oh, God, thought Sadie, please let there be a next time. She felt that all her life had been moving toward this man, this moment. How on earth could she let him go? But what if Gabe was right? she wondered, chilled by the thought. She had given herself in love to a man who was very much a stranger to her. Whatever had happened to no-nonsense, commonsense Sadie Hart? She had given herself body and soul to Nelson Mackie's hired gun. She couldn't let him know she loved him, that much was sure, she thought as she gently pushed him away and sat up.

She looked down and noticed with embarrassment that her thighs were smeared with blood and that there was a stain on his blanket. "I am sorry," she whispered, standing up and looking around for something to clean herself.

"Es nada, querida," he reassured her. "Here, let me help you," he said and walked over to his horse. Reaching into his saddlebag, he pulled out a blue handkerchief and wet it with water from his canteen. "Do you want me to help you or would you rather have privacy?" he asked kindly.

"I'll do it myself," said Sadie. "But thank you." She grabbed up her clothes and went behind one of the sandstone boulders that dotted the hillside.

Juan was dressed and had rolled his blanket up and tied it on his saddle. "I should take that and wash it for you," she said, her face red with embarrassment. "But I'm afraid there would be questions that I couldn't answer."

He came over and put his hands on her shoulders. "It is all right, Sadie. It is nothing to be ashamed of. Unless you are sorry you did this?" he added.

He sounded so caring, thought Sadie. Not repentant,

but concerned, even worried. Would it really matter to him if she had any regrets?

"Perhaps I am . . . a little . . ."

He lifted her chin with his finger, making her look into his eyes. *"Porque?"*

"Because you are Juan Chavez . . . El Lobo . . . and because I don't care who you are, just what you make me feel," she added with a rueful smile. "Surely that is at the very least stupid of me."

"Only if you think more of what others say about me than what you feel about me, Sadie," he responded coolly. "I would like to see you again. I would like you to get to know me better."

"And would you like more of this?"

He smiled. "Of course. It was wonderful, wasn't it? But only if you want to," he added.

"Oh, I'm sure I'll want to," Sadie said with such frustration and humor in her voice that Juan laughed aloud. "You see, that is what I love about you, *querida*. You are honest and open and aren't the least afraid of me, are you?"

"No, I am not afraid of you, Juan Chavez," she said strongly.

But I am afraid of what I feel for you, thought Sadie as they rode away. You may call me *"querida"* all you want, but can a man like you really be capable of love?

Thirty-one

"Señor Burke."

Michael tied his team in front of the mercantile when he heard the call. He turned and watched as Juan Chavez sauntered across the street.

"Whatever does he want, Michael?" asked Elizabeth as she climbed down from the wagon.

"I have no idea, *a ghra,*" muttered her husband.

"*Buenos dias,* señor, señorita," said Chavez, with a sweep of his sombrero. "I wonder if I may ask you a favor?"

Michael gave him a quizzical look. "Ye're askin' me a favor, boyo?"

"We are all good neighbors now, señor, no?"

"No" was what Michael wanted to reply. "I'll believe Mackie and his men are good neighbors when rattlesnakes are!" But he had promised himself that he would act in good faith with Mackie. "So it would seem, Señor Chavez. What can I do for Mr. Mackie?"

"Oh, I am not speaking for Señor Mackie now," Chavez replied, looking a little sheepish, to Michael's surprise. "This is for myself. You see, I have grown very fond of Señorita Hart and would like to spend more time with her. But knowing there have been hard feelings between us because of my job, I did not want to ride out to your ranch unless I would be welcome."

"You wouldn't be very welcome, boyo," Michael answered bluntly. "Especially not by Sadie's brother, I'm sure. But I am a fair man and as you said, we are trying to be good neighbors in this valley. If Miss Hart has no objections, then we don't, do we, Elizabeth?"

he added, reaching for his wife's hand. He could feel her tension, but she came through, as he knew she would.

"If Sadie wished to further her acquaintance with you, Señor Chavez, then you may call on her anytime," said Elizabeth.

"*Muchas gracias,* Señor Burke, Señora. I appreciate your willingness to tolerate my presence even if you can't welcome it," Chavez said with a dry little smile.

"Oh, Michael, must we allow him to come?" asked Elizabeth after Chavez strode away.

"I know he disturbs you, *a ghra,* but I must go along with the game Mackie is playing on the chance that it is not a game."

"It has been very quiet for a while," Elizabeth admitted.

"Yes, but I am taking the biblical advice very seriously, Elizabeth. We will be as wise as serpents even as we act as gentle as doves."

"We met someone in town who wishes to call on you, Miss Sadie," Michael announced that evening at supper.

"Jimmy Murdoch?" asked Cait, giving Sadie a teasing smile.

"No, it was Juan Chavez."

"Oh," said Sadie weakly, paying very careful attention to a slice of tomato on her plate.

"He must have brass balls to think he can come calling on my sister," Gabe exclaimed, and then realized what he had said. "I, uh, beg your pardon, Mrs. Burke. I wasn't thinking where I am."

Michael had a hard time keeping a smile off his face. But he knew Gabe's concern was justified.

"Mr. Burke, Sadie and I have talked about this already, and I've told her there's a good chance Chavez is doing this just for Mackie," said Gabe more calmly.

"Gabe, I am surprised you would insult your sister that way," Elizabeth said sternly. "I am not looking forward to a visit from this man, but to suggest that Sadie might not be attractive to him . . ."

"Begging your pardon, ma'am, but she knows I don't mean it that way. I just can't trust him and I wonder that you can."

"It isn't only a matter of trust, Gabe," said Michael. "We've got to go along in hopes that things stay peaceful. I wouldn't keep Pete Wilson off the place, so how can I keep Chavez?"

"Well, Sadie can keep him off. All she has to do is tell him she doesn't want to see him again." Gabe looked over at his sister, challenging her with his eyes.

"But I do want to see him again, Gabe," Sadie replied in her best schoolteacher's voice.

"Well, Miss Sadie has spoken, Gabe," said Michael. "When Chavez comes calling, there'll be no insults offered the man."

"No, Mr. Burke," growled Gabe. He pushed himself away from the table and excusing himself, stomped out.

"Oh, dear," said Elizabeth.

"Don't worry about Gabe, Mrs. Burke," said Sadie. "He just needs to learn that his little sister isn't so little anymore."

Sadie was in her nightgown and braiding her hair for sleep when she heard a soft knock on her door.

"Come in," she called.

It was Caitlin. "I am sorry to bother you, Sadie. I just wanted to talk for a few minutes."

"Sit down, Cait," said Sadie, gesturing to her bed.

Cait was quiet for a minute as she watched Sadie's deft fingers plaiting her hair.

"I envy you your straight hair, Sadie," she finally said. "I can never get mine to stay in a braid."

"Is that what you came to talk about?" asked Sadie, turning away from the mirror and smiling. Cait ducked her head. "No, I guess I was just wondering why you said yes to Chavez's calling on you. You know it upsets Ma. And Gabe is beside himself."

"Yes and he can stay that way, for all I care. I've already told him I'm free to choose my own company. Though I do not like to upset your mother," Sadie admitted.

"But why would you choose Chavez over a nice cowboy like Jimmy?"

Sadie was tired over all the noses being poked into her business. "Why did you choose Gabe over Henry, Cait?" she asked sharply.

"Why, I didn't choose Gabe, Sadie," she sputtered. "I just decided that I didn't really love Henry the way he deserved to be loved. And that New Mexico was my home."

"That's true, so far as it goes," said Sadie calmly. "But from what I hear, you've got some feelings for Gabe you didn't have for Henry."

"How could he have told you that?" whispered Cait, blushing hotly.

"He didn't volunteer it. I did some good guessing based on what I know of him, Cait. And I don't need to talk about it, because it really isn't any of my business, is it?" she said pointedly.

"No, I guess not, except that he's your brother."

"But I wouldn't presume to tell him what to do. Give advice, maybe, but never orders." Sadie sighed. "I only brought it up so you'd understand. I feel an attraction for Juan Chavez. I know he's done things I wouldn't want to know about. But I don't think he is quite as bad as he's painted. And I don't think it's a good idea to antagonize him or Mackie right now. Though self-sacrifice is surely not the reason I'm seeing him," added Sadie with a grin.

"I apologize, Sadie. I was just worried about Ma."

"If your ma had asked me not to see him here, I wouldn't. Not after all her kindness to me, Cait."

"I just hope you don't get hurt, Sadie."

"Life isn't worth much if you hold back for fear of getting hurt, Cait."

After Cait shut the door quietly behind her, Sadie collapsed on the bed. She had sounded so sure of herself, hadn't she? But it was hard not to let Gabe's words get to her. What if what had happened the other day had meant nothing? But she couldn't believe that, not feeling the way she had with Juan.

* * *

After all the fuss, when Juan Chavez didn't appear for three days, Sadie was ready to believe anything about him. But then, late one afternoon, Elizabeth spied Mackie's buggy driving up to the ranch.

"I wonder what Nelson Mackie wants now," she muttered and then, as it got closer, she recognized the driver. It was Juan Chavez, all dressed up in a suit and tie!

"Sadie, I think you have a visitor," she called into the house.

Sadie and Cait had been cutting up vegetables for stew and Sadie hurried out, forgetting she had her apron on. Juan Chavez stood there looking for all the world as though his name should be John Smith, dressed as he was.

"My lord," said Sadie without thinking.

"I was hoping you would go for a buggy ride with me before supper, Miss Hart," he said formally.

"Why, yes, I would love to," she answered, starting down the steps.

"Sadie."

"Yes, Mrs. Burke?"

"Perhaps you would like to give me your apron. I'll need it to cook supper."

Sadie looked down and grinned. Here she was, acting like a foolish girl with a beau come courting. But she had been waiting for three days! She untied the apron and smiled as Chavez handed her into the carriage. "I won't keep her long, Mrs. Burke," he said.

Sadie was quiet until they reached the road. "Señor Chavez, or should I say, Mr. Chavez, for you don't look at all Mexican dressed like this."

"I thought I should dress respectably when I called upon a respectable woman, Miss Hart," he replied stiffly. She looked over at him in disbelief and saw that Juan Chavez, El Lobo, had a twinkle in his eye.

"My goodness, you actually have a sense of humor," said Sadie, speaking her thoughts aloud.

Chavez laughed. "That is yet another thing I like about you, Miss Hart. You really are not afraid of me."

"Should I be?"

"To tell you the truth, Miss Sadie Hart, I don't know. Perhaps you should. . . ."

"Perhaps I should be more afraid of myself," Sadie told him.

They had turned east, away from town, and after a mile or so, Chavez pulled the buggy off the road and into a cluster of trees. "I thought it would be more comfortable in a buggy, Miss Hart," he said, putting his hand over hers and stroking it as he had the first time they touched.

"What would be?" she whispered.

"This," he said, pulling her back against the seat and kissing her.

Oh, it was as wonderful a sensation as she remembered, the feeling of turning liquid in his arms. She curled against him as he cupped her breast, but after a minute he pulled back.

"You make me feel quite . . . breathless, Miss Hart, but we can't repeat the other day."

"We can't?" Sadie asked, with only partially humorous plaintiveness.

"You know we can't. It was another reason I dressed in a more gentlemanly fashion," he added with a smile.

"I wish we could," Sadie said, sounding shameless but not caring.

"Oh and so do I, *querida*," he murmured, pulling her into his arms for another kiss. She could sense what he was holding back and this time it was she who pulled away.

"It's good I told Mrs. Burke it would be a short ride, Sadie."

"Juan . . ."

"Yes, *querida*," he said, his arm tight around her shoulders.

"Gabe . . . well, you know he is furious about me seeing you . . . he says you are only doing this for Mackie. . . ."

"And what do you think, Sadie?" he asked, stiffening.

"It is hard to know what to think, Juan," she whispered.

"I confess, *querida,* that the first time I danced with you, it was done more to annoy your brother. But by the end of that dance . . ." Juan paused and then continued in a strained voice. "When Mackie gives orders, I obey them. I've been obeying men like him all my life, Sadie. But no one can order me to feel or not to feel. Neither Nelson Mackie nor your brother." He picked up the reins and turned the buggy back toward the ranch. Sadie reached out and put her hand on his and he pulled the horses up.

"I am sorry, Juan."

"*Porqué, querida?* You have every right to ask me what I am doing here."

They rode back in silence, Sadie leaning against his arm. When they pulled up in front of the ranch house, Gabe was leaning against the corral, waiting.

"Oh, dear," said Sadie.

"Never mind, *querida,*" Juan replied as he helped her down. "I will see you again soon?"

"If you want," she said.

"I want." He looked out of the corner of his eye and saw Gabe walking over to them and, leaning down, he gently dropped a kiss on her lips before climbing back into the buggy. By the time Gabe reached her, the buggy was turned around and Gabe could only take his anger out on his sister.

"What were you doing, letting him kiss you like that, Sarah Ellen?"

"I was enjoying it, that's what I was doing, Gabe. I thought you were going to let this go!"

Gabe groaned. "I'm sorry, Sadie, it's just that I don't trust him."

"Then trust me, Gabe."

"I'm trying, I'm trying."

It wasn't until later that night that Sadie realized Juan had never really answered her question. He hadn't denied that his pursuit of her was Mackie's idea. Indeed, he had admitted that his actions were not his own, but dictated by men like Mackie. Only

his feelings were not, he had told her. She would just
have to trust herself to those feelings and if she was
being a fool to do that, well, she guessed she'd find
out soon enough.

Thirty-two

Sky did not mind the saddle the first few days Gabe lunged him with the stirrups tied up, but he showed off his bucking ability as soon as he felt them banging against his sides. Gabe was laughing and cursing him as he tried to make him go in a small circle, and Cait, who had just come out to watch, was taken aback.

"Surely this isn't good sign, is it, Mr. Hart?"

"He's fighting a little just like any newly broke horse would, Miss Cait, rather than standing there shivering, and that's fine with me. But it does mean a little while longer before you can ride him. I'm going to wait a day or two myself," he added with a grin.

Three days later, when Gabe put his foot in the stirrup, Sky only sidestepped a little and then stood quietly while Gabe mounted. Gabe had decided not to use a bridle for a while, so all he had was the hackamore for control. But Sky stepped out quietly enough for his first time under saddle, and Gabe kept him to a walk. After a half hour, he began to work on neck-reining.

If the horse had been a joy to work on the lunge line, he was even more responsive to the direct contact with a rider and by the end of another hour, Gabe had him doing figure eights. He was so intent on what he was doing that he didn't even notice that he'd gathered an audience. It was only when he dismounted that he realized that the whole Burke family as well as Jake and Sadie were watching.

"Ye've worked a miracle, boyo," said Michael when Gabe walked the horse over to the fence.

"Not really, Mr. Burke. He's a *good* horse," replied

Gabe, his love for Sky apparent in his voice. "He should be ready for Miss Cait to ride in a day or two. But she'll have to stay in the corral for a while before taking him out," he added.

Cait gave her congratulations and as she walked back to the house wondered where the eagerness and reckless desire to ride her horse had disappeared. Earlier in the summer, she'd not been able to wait. And now she knew she'd be astride him in a few days and that knowledge meant nothing. Well, not nothing, but she didn't feel the way she'd expected: impatient and excited. But maybe all that would come back.

But two days later, although she'd experienced anticipation and fear, wondering whether he would tolerate a different rider, and a great deal of satisfaction as she walked Sky around the corral, and even got him doing figure eights at a trot, she knew that the bond she had formed with him two years ago wasn't the same. It didn't feel that different riding Sky than to ride any one of their horses and she felt a pang of sadness. And when she dismounted and watched Gabe ride him, taking him from a walk to an easy lope around the corral, she understood. Sky responded to Gabe's subtle signals almost before they were given, as though he and Gabe were in constant communication. The understanding between Gabe and Sky was like that between her father and Finn, and from the stories he'd told, what he had with Frost. In every way except technical ownership, Sky was Gabe's horse.

It hurt for a few moments as she realized it, for Sky had been hers before she went off to school. But time and terror had intervened and it was Gabe who had brought back the horse's trust, not she.

Later that night, she sought out her father. He was sitting on the porch, his chin tilted back, enjoying one of the cigars he'd brought back from town. He didn't smoke often, but when he did, it had to be outside, for Elizabeth would not have the smell in the house.

Cait sat down on the steps and watched the moon rise. It was a three-quarter moon, and its bright light blacked out the stars.

" 'Tis beautiful, isn't it, Cait?" Michael murmured.

"Yes, Da."

"I am very glad you decided to stay."

"So am I, Da." Cait hesitated. "Da, I have something to ask you."

Michael heard something in his daughter's voice and realized she'd sought him out for a purpose. He let the chair's legs down and putting out his cigar, came to sit down on the step next to her.

"Ask away," he said lightly.

"Before I went away to school, there was a way in which Sky was mine, beyond the fact that you gave him to me."

"I remember the day the little bugger walked up the porch and tried to push his way into the house after you," said Michael with a low chuckle.

Cait smiled. "Yes, I'd forgotten to close the corral gate properly." She hesitated and then went on in a shaky voice. "Da, that feeling isn't there anymore."

"He hasn't given you any trouble riding him, has he?"

"Oh, no, he is well-behaved and well-trained. But it feels not so different from riding Snowflake. It's Gabe who Sky would follow into the house now, Da." She was silent for a moment and then said: "Sky is Gabe's horse in every way except one."

" 'Tis true that you can see something special between them," Michael answered slowly, realizing what his daughter was going to say next.

"I want Gabe to have Night Sky, Da."

"Are you sure, Cait?" he asked, putting his arm around her.

"I am, Da. He's worked so long and patiently. And he's been so loyal to you, Da. Oh, I wish Sky still felt the same about me," she added with a little catch in her voice. "But I want Gabe to know that if he should ever decide to leave, he can take Sky with him."

Michael pulled his daughter close to him in a hug. "Ye've a generous heart, Cait."

"But *you* have to be the one to tell him, Da. I don't think he would take Sky from me. And it would be more proper if it were from both of us."

Michael smiled. "I agree. I'll tell him tomorrow."

That night, Michael watched Elizabeth get ready for bed and pulled her close when she crawled under the covers. "Cait came and talked to me tonight, *a ghra*. She wants me to give Night Sky to Gabe."

Elizabeth pulled away and looked up at her husband. "But Sky is *her* horse, Michael. Why, she couldn't wait to ride him. . . ."

"I know, but she recognized what there is between the two of them. You saw it too, Elizabeth. Gabe has given so much of himself to that horse. Cait wants him to know that if he should leave someday, he can take Sky with him."

"Is she going to tell him?"

"Now that is the interesting thing, Elizabeth," said Michael with a grin. "She thinks it would be better for me to do it. 'Proper' was the word she used. What I'm wondering is how proper they have been together!"

"That may be the very reason she wants you to do it, Michael. She wouldn't want him to feel an overwhelming sense of obligation to her, would she?"

The next morning, Michael caught Gabe just before he was going to bring in the colts.

"Can I talk to you a minute, Gabe?"

Gabe closed the pasture gate and walked back to the corral fence. "What is it, Mr. Burke?"

"It is a wonder, what you've done with Sky," began Michael.

"He's been worth every minute of it, Mr. Burke. Miss Cait has herself a great horse."

"Em, well, that is the thing, Gabe. Cait and I have been talking and we both agree that Night Sky should be yours. After all, he already is in every way that counts."

Gabe was stopped dead in his tracks. "You can't do that, Mr. Burke. Why, Miss Cait loves that horse."

"It was her idea, boyo. She wanted you to know that should you ever leave, Sky will go with you."

"I never would have expected . . ." Gabe stammered. "I don't know what to say, or how I can ever thank you."

"You don't need to. Ye've saved a good horse and ye've stayed on during a hard time. Of course, we all hope ye'll be staying for a long time."

"I'm not going anywhere, Mr. Burke, not until we see what Mackie has up his sleeve."

"Well, Sky goes with you, Gabe, if ever you feel you have to leave."

"I can't thank you enough, Mr. Burke. I, uh, I do love that horse," Gabe admitted.

"Sure and anyone could see that, boyo."

Gabe went through the motions of training the colts and then it was time to saddle Sky for Caitlin's ride. As he brushed the horse, he marveled again at the beauty of his markings and the intelligence in those white-rimmed eyes. "You look like a wild one, Sky, but I've never met a horse more willing to work with me," he told the horse who flicked his ears back and forth as he listened to Gabe's murmur.

Cait was waiting by the fence when Gabe brought the horse out and he led Sky over and held him while she mounted. He was too embarrassed even to look at her, so he just said: "Today I think you can try him at a canter, Miss Cait." He watched as she walked and trotted for fifteen minutes and then signaled her to bring him back to a walk.

"When you give him the signal to lope, go around the corral a few times and then we'll try some figure eights."

Riding Sky at a lope was like riding a rocking horse, thought Cait as they cantered around the corral. His gait was so smooth that her bottom never moved from the saddle. After a few circles, she neck-reined him through the figure eights, giving him the subtle signals to change leads that Gabe had taught her. It was as wonderful as she had dreamed it would be, riding her horse. Except he wasn't her horse, she reminded herself.

"Good work, Miss Cait," called Gabe when she brought him down to a walk. "Cool him down and then bring him into the barn." Gabe turned his back and walked into the cool darkness of the barn. She had looked so natural on the horse. How could he take Sky from her? No matter how hard it was to refuse, he could not accept such a gift.

When Cait led Sky in, she saw Gabe sitting on a bale of hay, chewing a piece of straw. He got up and helped her with the saddle, saying gruffly, "After you've wiped him off, I'd like to talk to you about something, Miss Cait. I'll be in the tack room."

By the time Cait had finished with Sky, Gabe had soaped her saddle and moved on to the bridles. When she came in, he gestured for her to sit down and said: "Your father talked to me this morning, Miss Cait. About Sky."

"Oh . . ." Cait felt foolishly tongue-tied.

"He told me you want to give me your horse."

"Sky has really become your horse, Gabe," she said quietly.

"I can't take him from you, Miss Cait. For one thing, there is a connection between the two of you that will only get stronger once you're the only one riding him. For another, he's a valuable animal." Gabe hesitated. "But I am touched by your sweet, generous heart," he added softly. He moved closer and reaching his hand out, smoothed back her hair. Cait could feel a lovely liquid warmth radiate through her, but when she lifted her face for a kiss, Gabe only traced her lips with his finger.

"You see, I can't take such a gift after stealing your kisses," he told her.

"I want you to have Sky, Gabe," Cait said, her voice trembling. "Please let me give him to you."

"All right," Gabe replied slowly and reluctantly. "But I want you to be riding him too. And if you ever change your mind . . ."

"I won't."

"Then I will just say thank you, Miss Cait. Now I'd best finish off my work here," he said, turning away.

Cait whispered a good-bye and left, wanting only to go back and admit to him that she feared he hadn't only taken her kisses but her heart.

Thirty-three

"Chavez?"

"Sí, señor Mackie." Juan was sitting outside the bunkhouse after supper when Mackie approached.

"Walk down to the west pasture with me."

The moon lit the path in front of them.

"How is Miss Sadie Hart, Chavez?"

"She is well, señor," replied Juan, deliberately misinterpreting Mackie's question.

"I mean, how is your 'courting' going? Have you had her yet?"

Juan was surprised at the sudden fierce anger that arose with Mackie's crudeness. "I do not like to talk of the señorita in that way," he said softly but firmly.

"You're not going soft on me, are you, Chavez?"

"Let us just say that the señorita and I have become very friendly. Friendly enough so that her brother is furious, which is what you want, no?"

"I want Gabriel Hart dead, is what I want, so he can't protect Michael Burke when he rides in here to protest your involvement with Miss Sadie."

Juan wasn't really surprised. After all, he had known the whole purpose of his visits to Sadie were to work up her brother. And Mackie wasn't suggesting something he hadn't done before: pushing someone to his limit so that killing him became self-defense. But he hadn't wanted to think about it, he realized as distaste for the task and the man who ordered him filled his mouth.

"You *can* take him, can't you, Chavez?" asked Mackie.

"Sí, señor. I have no doubts about that."

"Good." They had reached the barbed wire fence that demarcated the west pasture from the corrals. "See that, Chavez," said Mackie, waving his arm at the cows and calves gathered by the water trough. "I have only five hundred head on the Rocking M. I will never be a force in this territory until I can run more. I need Burke's land and I am going to get it," he added fiercely. "If you do your job well, you will be highly rewarded, Juan, you know that."

"So you've always said, Señor Mackie."

"You've got to push Gabriel Hart into a fight. Burke won't get any help from the sheriff, of course, so he'll come after me directly. And when he does, I'll be ready for him. I think Michael Burke will be shot down as he threatens the safety of my wife and home. Once he's dead, Mrs. Burke will sell, I'm sure of that. And the important thing is it will have been them who break the peace we've all worked so hard for in this valley, won't it? You will be the innocent suitor of Hart's sister, forced to defend himself. And when Burke comes after you here, well, I can't let him threaten me or my wife, can I?"

"Of course not, señor. But are you so sure Burke will take you on without Hart to back him up? Surely he wouldn't be so reckless?"

"Oh, I think if you do your job right, Juan, we'll see him here within hours of Hart's death."

He'd carried out orders like this before, so why was he all of a sudden questioning himself, thought Chavez as he lay on his bunk unable to sleep. Mackie was no worse than others he'd worked for. He wouldn't really have Hart's death on his conscience, because he would make sure it was self-defense. And he'd never had much of a conscience to begin with. So why all of a sudden was he worried about burdening it? He could make sure he was out of the way when Burke rode in. Mackie had plenty of men to take him down. Let Mackie shoot Michael Burke himself, damn it. Let him do his own dirty work for a change.

It was Sadie, of course. It hadn't been hard to follow

those orders. She was an attractive woman and an unusual one, willing to trust her own judgment of him and look at him through her own eyes, not those of others. She had seen *him* not the hired gun, not El Lobo. And now he was going to betray that trust and she would realize that who she thought she saw wasn't really there. For who was Juan Chavez anyway but the creation of all the men who had ruled his life since the day he was sold to the Romeros. Juan Chavez had no mind of his own and certainly no heart.

Whoever he had been before, that seven-year-old boy who came back in flashes of memory, might have grown up differently had he somehow been rescued from his fate. But then, he wouldn't have survived more than a year had Juan Chavez not taken his place.

It was too late to change now. He'd go calling on Sadie Hart. He'd make sure her brother fought him. He'd kill Gabe and turn his back on Sadie. But he wouldn't take any of Mackie's damn reward. He'd just ride the hell out of this damned valley when it was all over.

Sadie and Gabe had reached an uneasy truce, and aside from commonplaces, hadn't done much talking after Juan's last visit. He hadn't told her directly of Cait's gift, nor whether he'd approached Cait again. And, tell the truth, Sadie, she told herself one morning, you don't care. Let her brother take care of his own problems. Why should I try to help him understand himself or Cait if he won't try to understand me!

All the same, she was glad that Gabe was out riding fence when Juan Chavez rode up a few days after their buggy ride.

"*Buenos tardes,* señorita."

"*Buenos tardes,* Señor Chavez. No buggy today?" she said with a teasing smile.

"I thought you might like to go for a ride this afternoon instead."

"I would love it. Just let me go in and change."

Juan dismounted and sat down on the porch steps. To his right was Mrs. Burke's flower garden, in front of him, the corral. It was a small but well-taken-care-of ranching operation that Burke had here and every time he saw it he was impressed. There was a palpable difference between the Burkes' small enterprise and Mackie's spread and it was the feeling that the Burkes had created something out of their care for each other and the land.

Sadie was down in a few minutes and they walked over to the corral together where Snowflake was tied. "Mrs. Burke said I could take the mare," said Sadie. "She was ridden this morning, but only for a short while." Sadie started to lift the saddle from the corral fence and Juan intervened. "I will do it for you, señorita."

They rode out and turned east toward the mountains. Sadie wondered if they were headed up into the foothills. Did Juan want her again? And more importantly, did she want to give herself? That first time had seemed inevitable and uncontrollable. But was it wise to risk heartbreak, and even more important, a child, with a man she hardly knew?

Evidently he was more interested in riding than kissing, however, for they didn't turn off south toward the mountains but kept on going. There was no easy chatter as there would be with Cait or Gabe. Not that she'd expected it with him. But aside from the joy of a few gallops, the ride was an uncomfortable one and Sadie was almost glad when they turned back to the ranch.

"When will you be going back to Texas, Miss Sadie?" Juan asked, finally breaking their silence. Sadie wondered if this was his prelude to saying good-bye to her.

"Oh, most likely pretty soon, before the weather changes."

"You'll turn into a school teacher again?"

"In January. That will give me enough time to rescue the house from whatever disaster it has suffered since I've been gone. My brothers are not exactly expert housekeepers," she added with a grin.

"I am sure the Burkes will miss you."

"I will miss them," said Sadie. But will you miss me? she wondered, hurt more than she would have thought possible by his casual discussion of her departure.

When they reached the ranch, Chavez noticed that Gabe's paint was tied in front of the house. Good, Hart was back, he thought. After he unsaddled Snowflake and released her into the corral, he turned to Sadie. "I am thirsty, *querida*, but I am not comfortable where I am not welcome. Is there an outside pump?"

"Behind the barn, Juan."

"*Bueno*," he said, looking at her with such intensity that she grew hot all over. When he took her hand in his, she followed without thinking.

They each took a few swallows from the ladle, and then, without any preliminaries, he grabbed her by the shoulders and pushed her against the barn. She was both frightened and thrilled by the hard grasp of his hands, and when he let go, she was almost disappointed. But then he ran both his hands through her hair, cradling her head and tilting it back. When his mouth came down on hers, it was in a bruising kiss, one that took her breath away.

When he finally pulled away, she looked up at him pleadingly, as though for an explanation.

"Oh, *mi corazon*," he whispered, drawing his finger down her cheek. He *did* love her, she thought, and in an instant realized that he indeed had her heart. "Oh, Juan," she said softly.

"It is so cruel that you are leaving, *querida*." He was fumbling with the buttons of her blouse and he gave a satisfied sigh when his hand was finally able to feel her breast. "Your heart is beating like a frightened bird's," he whispered. "Don't worry, *querida*," he said, as he started to unfasten her skirt.

"Juan, we *can't*, not here," she whispered, wanting him terribly but hurt at the same time that he was thinking about taking her up against the barn. Her skirt fell and she stood there in her drawers and he rubbed against her, letting her feel his hardness.

"Juan, *no*," she said a little louder as his hand

slipped down her drawers, exploring her moistness. "Someone might come."

"Yes, I think so," he said with a smile, as he continued to stroke her.

There was something driven about it all, and instead of being able to relax, Sadie pushed him away, saying again, "No, Juan, not here." Then she gasped with horror, not pleasure as she saw Gabe coming around the back of the barn.

Her brother stopped dead and then ran forward, hauling Juan off of Sadie. "Take your filthy hands off my sister, Chavez!"

Sadie's hands were shaking as she tried to button her blouse. Dear God, here she was standing in her drawers. "Gabe," she protested weakly.

"I'll talk to you later, Sarah Ellen." Gabe looked coldly at her and then lowered his eyes to the ground where her skirt was laying around her feet. She bent over and pulled it up, fastening it as quickly as she could. "Gabe, it isn't what you think," she protested as he pushed against Juan's chest, sending him stumbling to his knees.

"Get up, you dirty little murderer. I'm going to kill you for trying to rape my sister so I want you standing."

Chavez got up and moved back, right hand crooked, ready to draw. Sadie wanted to scream, but she felt she was in one of those nightmares where you try to cry and no sound comes out. She started toward her brother, but he just pushed her back and moved out to face Chavez, his left hand hovering.

It happened so quickly that afterward, Sadie wondered if she'd even seen their hands move. Gabe was standing there, blood dripping down his arm, his gun fallen out of paralyzed fingers. She was afraid to look at Juan, but when she turned, there he was, standing there unhurt, staring down at the smoking barrel of his gun as though he'd never seen it before.

Gabe leaned down as though he was going to pick up his gun and Juan said coldly, "Don't even think about it, señor."

Sadie gave him an agonized glance, but Chavez's eyes were now the opaque green of El Lobo's. *"Adios, querida,"* he said softly and walked by them without a backward look.

Gabe had sunk to the ground and Sadie realized that he was losing blood fast. "I'll be right back, Gabe," she said and she ran into the barn to grab a linen sack off the shelf in the tack room, which she tore into strips. Gabe had gotten himself up on the bench and Sadie sat herself next to him, tying the strips around his upper arm to stop the bleeding. Thank God, it did not seem to be a severed artery, she thought. Once the bleeding had finally slowed, she pulled off his shirt and wetting it at the pump, began to clean off the blood.

"Oh, Gabe, I am so sorry, but why did you force him to draw?"

Gabe, who had been leaning back against the barn, eyes closed, sat up and looked at her. "You got it wrong, Sadie. Any man who came upon his sister backed up against the side of a barn would have done the same thing. Chavez was counting on that," he continued bitterly. "Now can't you see that he's been using you?"

"I don't see anything but that you've got a hole in your arm and I don't know if the bullet is still in there or not. We've got to get you to the doctor," she said anxiously. "Can you ride? Elizabeth and Cait took the wagon to town."

"I can ride," Gabe said stoutly. He struggled to his feet, but sank right back down on the bench. "I guess I can't," he told her with a weak smile.

"Then I'll have to ride in for the doctor. Will you be all right if I leave you?"

"Just get me into the tack room and I'll stretch out on the cot." Gabe put his arm around her and leaned heavily as she walked him into the barn.

"I'll be back as soon as I can, Gabe," she said anxiously.

"Don't you worry, Sarah Ellen, I'll be here when you get back," he replied with a grin.

Thirty-four

"Snowflake, I know you've been ridden hard today, but if you have anything left, please give it to me, girl," Sadie pleaded as she kicked the mare into a gallop. Halfway to town, she met Elizabeth and Cait on their way back to the ranch and pulled the mare up.

"Gabe's been shot, Mrs. Burke. I'm going to town for the doctor."

"How bad is it?" Elizabeth asked calmly.

"He's lost a lot of blood, but he's still conscious."

"You go on, Sadie, and we'll take good care of him till you bring the doctor back," Elizabeth replied reassuringly.

"Thank you, ma'am," said Sadie as she clapped her heels to Snowflake's sides.

"Hold on, Cait," Elizabeth told her daughter and slapping the reins on the horses' backs, sent them into a run. Cait gripped the seat tightly and felt she was holding on to more than the wagon. She wanted to jump down and run after Sadie and scream: "What happened?" She wished she'd just taken Snowflake away, so that she could get to the ranch, get to Gabe, pull him in her arms and tell him that she loved him, for God's sake, that he couldn't leave her now, not this way.

Please, God, don't let him die, she prayed over and over to herself as her mother guided the team, expertly avoiding every rut and rock. They reached the ranch just as Michael was tying his horse in front of the house.

"What's happened, Elizabeth?" he cried, running

over to lift her down. "Was it Mackie? I'll kill the *gobshite* if he hurt you in any way."

"No, no, Michael, it's Gabe. We met Sadie on our way back from town. He's been shot and she's gone for the doctor."

"Where is he, *a ghra*?"

"In the barn."

Cait was frozen in place and it wasn't until her father started pulling the barn door open that she was able to move. She climbed down from the wagon on shaking legs and followed her parents.

"It looks like it was only his arm, Michael," Elizabeth was saying as she knelt down next to Gabe. He groaned in pain as Elizabeth loosened the strips Sadie had tied around his upper arm. When he tried to pull himself up, Michael pushed him down gently. "No, no, boyo, you just stay there till the doctor comes." He turned to his daughter, who was standing in the doorway of the tack room. "Cait, get some water."

"Yes, Da."

Cait almost slipped in the pool of Gabe's blood as she ran to the pump and she felt faint at the thought of him losing so much. But she filled the dipper and brought it back to the tack room.

"I think the bullet must have gone straight through, Gabe," Elizabeth was saying reassuringly when Cait returned. "Though I don't know what kind of damage it caused."

"I can't seem to move my fingers much, Mrs. Burke," said Gabe, grimacing in pain as he tried to make a fist.

"It's probably just temporary, Gabe," Michael reassured him.

"Here, Ma," said Cait, holding the dipper out.

"Can you sit up if Michael helps, Gabe?"

Gabe pulled himself up and leaned against the wall.

"Hold it for him, Cait, and make sure he sips it slowly. I'm going to get some old sheets and put them on the sofa so we can move him inside."

"No, no, Mrs. Burke, I don't want you messing up your house."

"*Whist* boyo," said Michael, "and get some water down yer throat before ye dehydrate. Can ye sit alone?"

Gabe nodded.

"Then I'll be going in to help yer mother, Cait."

"Yes, Da."

Cait sat down on the edge of the cot and lifted the dipper to Gabe's mouth. He automatically started to lift his left hand up to take it from her and almost fainted from the pain. "Are you all right, Gabe?" Cait asked, forcing herself not to cry out when he went white. He nodded, his eyes closed. "Stupid," he groaned. "Tried to lift my arm."

Cait sat closer and said: "Just open your mouth, Gabe, and I'll make sure it doesn't spill." She made sure he took slow sips and was so intent on her task that she didn't notice at first when his right hand covered hers. When she finally became conscious of his touch, she looked up into his eyes, which were shadowed by pain and something else entirely.

"Oh, Gabe," she whispered. Cait didn't know what more she might have said had her father not come in to support Gabe into the house.

"The doctor and Sadie are here," called Elizabeth from the porch.

"Thank God," Cait whispered, and then later wondered if Gabe was feeling thankful when the doctor probed his arm.

"You are very lucky, Mr. Hart. The bullet went right through. It did chip the bone and tear some muscle and nerve tissue, however," he added. "You won't be drawing a gun for some time."

Gabe was so pale that he almost matched the sheet Elizabeth had spread on the sofa. "I can't move my hand real well, Doc," he said weakly.

"Nerve damage, Mr. Hart. It will be awhile before we know if it is permanent. But aside from that and barring infection, you should be well on your way to recovery in a few days. Just make sure you drink lots of liquids."

After a cup of coffee and three pieces of corn bread,

the doctor headed back to town and Michael pulled a chair up next to the sofa. "Are ye up to tellin' me what happened, Gabe?"

"I'll tell you, Mr. Burke," said Sadie who had just come in after thanking the doctor and seeing him off. "Señor Chavez called for me today. When we got back from our ride, we were thirsty. For each other's kisses, as well as water, I guess," Sadie added laconically. "Gabe came around the barn just as I was telling Juan I didn't want to be doing anything more than kissing . . . He . . . I mean Gabe . . . misunderstood the situation and forced a fight."

Michael had listened intently as Sadie told her story and she felt she must be blushing purple by the time she got to the end. But he didn't turn away or even look as though he judged her and she blessed him silently for that.

"Is that true, Gabe? You pushed him to draw?"

Gabe groaned and pulled himself up against the cushions. "It depends on how you look at it, Mr. Burke. My guess is that Chavez knew I was around and chose a pretty public place to do his, uh, kissing. I think Mackie put him up to it. I've thought that all along, though I know Sadie doesn't like to hear it. I'm just lucky he didn't kill me."

"He's a professional, Gabe," Michael said thoughtfully. "I'm thinkin' if he intended to kill ye, we'd be waking ye right now."

Gabe frowned. "He was faster than me," he admitted, "but I still think it was a setup. I'm sorry, Sarah Ellen, but I can't trust him or Mackie and that's no insult to you."

"Well, Mackie's not going to get away with this one, by God," declared Michael.

"What do you mean, Michael?" asked Elizabeth from the doorway.

"I mean, I'm ridin' there first thing tomorrow to have it out with him, *a ghra.*"

"No, Michael, you can't go alone," Elizabeth cried.

"He won't have to, ma'am," said Gabe. "I'll go with him."

"Not likely, Gabe," said his employer.

"I can still fire a rifle with my right hand, Mr. Burke. I'm going with you."

"We'll see in the morning, boyo," said Michael, putting his arm on Gabe's shoulder. "But for now, ye just get some rest."

Elizabeth was pacing their bedroom floor when Michael finally came up to bed that night.

"Come to rest, *a ghra*," he said, stepping in front of her and putting his arms around her shoulders. She leaned against him and whispered: "I don't think I can sleep, Michael. I *hate* Nelson Mackie," she said fiercely. "And I knew Chavez would bring disaster; from the very first moment I knew it, Michael."

"So ye did, Elizabeth," he said, pulling her close after they climbed into bed. "But 'tis interesting to me that Chavez, who has such a reputation, missed Gabe. For I'm thinking that Mackie wanted Gabe dead, not alive and able to help us."

"Are you saying that you think Chavez, El Lobo, spared Gabe on purpose, Michael! Out of the goodness of his heart?" she added sarcastically. "The man has no heart."

"I don't know what I'm sayin', *a ghra*. It is only that a woman usually knows, doesn't she, when a man is kissin' her because he wants to?" Michael dropped a kiss on his wife's cheek. "It seems to me that Señor Chavez and Sarah Ellen have done a bit of kissing already," he said ironically. "And Sadie is no naive sixteen-year-old, Elizabeth."

"No, but that doesn't mean she wouldn't be vulnerable to Juan Chavez's charms," said his wife.

"So, ye think Chavez is charming?" teased Michael.

"Like a snake is charming, Michael. No, I think he is a dangerous man, Michael, and I don't want you going after him."

"Oh, I am not going after him, Elizabeth. I am after Nelson Mackie to settle this once and for all."

Sadie lay awake for hours, going over and over every one of her encounters with Juan Chavez. Had anything he'd ever said meant anything? Had he said anything that really indicated he cared about her? His kisses had surely felt real, but maybe, as Gabe thought, his kisses had just been a part of his job, a part that he enjoyed. Was she a damned fool to keep believing that there was something between them, even after what happened today? Gabe might have been killed and all because of her. But then she would think: But Gabe isn't dead and why is that unless he didn't want to hurt me? That would start her agonizing all over again and she finally fell asleep early in the morning.

Chavez had ridden out of the Burkes' ranch cursing himself in Spanish and English. What had *happened* back there? He had intended to force Hart to fight and he'd even figured he'd have to kill him. Then, in the last split second, he'd only shot him in the arm. He hadn't even been conscious of changing his mind. He'd seen nothing but Hart's hand near his holster. His own draw was so fast he was hardly aware of it. And a part of him was surprised to see Hart still standing. But he guessed that most of him was just relieved. How could he kill Sadie's brother in front of her? But if he couldn't, then what did that mean?

He'd never see her again, of course, not after this. Not after pushing her up against the side of the barn and acting like he was going to take her against her will. And especially not after shooting her brother. The pain went deep, right down to a part of himself that he'd shut off for years. He had let Sadie Hart into his heart, almost without realizing it. And what the hell was he going to tell Mackie?

Mackie was leaning against the corral fence, watching one of his cowboys break a new horse when Juan rode in.

"Señor Mackie."

"Chavez. Any news for me?" Mackie asked, keeping his eye on the horse and rider.

"Your plan succeeded, señor." Mackie turned and smiled. "Up to a point," Chavez added.

"What exactly do you mean?"

"Gabe Hart reacted just as you expected. . . ."

"I hope you got a little something out of his sister before he caught you, Chavez," joked Mackie.

Chavez wanted to kill him right then and there and was surprised at the depth of his anger.

"So Hart *is* dead," continued Mackie.

"Not quite, señor. I was faster, of course, but I only managed to get him in the arm. His gun arm," Chavez added reassuringly.

"You only winged him!" Mackie's face was mottled with anger. "El Lobo missed? How could that happen?"

"It puzzles me, too, señor," Juan answered calmly. "I can only think that it is because I am finished with this job and with you."

Madre de Dios, what was happening to him? The words were out of his mouth before he knew he was going to say them. But at the same time, he realized he had never meant anything more. He was through with Mackie and all the men who wanted a heartless animal around to do their bidding.

"I'll be off your property by tomorrow, señor."

"Your damned right you will, Chavez. And Chavez," called Mackie as Juan walked away, "if you are not with me, you're against me. My men will have orders to shoot you on sight."

Juan was up early the next morning and after a quick cup of coffee and a biscuit, packed up his bedroll and mounted his black. One thing he knew, he thought as he looked around him, he wasn't going to miss this place. Or Mackie and his men.

He had no real idea of where he was going, but he figured he'd head west, away from Texas and his past. Toward Arizona and whatever his future was to be. He was only halfway to town, however, when he found himself turning the black around and kicking him into a canter, heading him east.

Thirty-five

Gabe had not slept well, since he'd refused the laudanum the doctor had left for him. He'd dozed off many times during the night, only to be awakened by the throbbing pain in his arm. But at least he wasn't dulled by the drug, he thought as he sat up and lifted his injured arm in front of him. The doctor had also left a large square of linen for him to use as a sling. Gabe folded it into a triangle and tried to tie it around his neck, but found it impossible to do one-handed.

"Damn," he cursed softly as he tried to do it for a third time.

"Can I help you, Gabe?" asked a soft voice. It was Caitlin Burke standing there in her nightgown with only a shawl around her shoulders. Gabe ran his hand over his chin and felt the early-morning stubble. He must surely look like hell, he thought ruefully.

"What are you doing up so early, Miss Cait?" he asked.

"I've been waking up all night and decided I may as well stay up this last time. I came down to light the fire and check on you."

"Wal, I guess that makes two of us who couldn't sleep."

"Were you in much pain, Gabe?" she asked as she walked over to the couch. "I thought the doctor left something for you?"

"He did, but I wanted a clear head this morning. He left this, too, but I can't get it tied one-handed," he admitted.

"Turn toward the wall, Gabe." She slipped the linen under his arm as gently as she could and then brought both ends around his neck. "How high do you want it?"

"A little bit higher, maybe, Miss Cait." Gabe winced as she tightened the sling, but once the knot was fastened and he could relax his arm, it felt much better supported than hanging at his side. He leaned back against the sofa and sighed.

"Maybe you should take some laudanum, Gabe."

"It feels much better now that it's supported, Miss Cait. Thank you." She was sitting on his left side and he wanted nothing more than to pull her against him, but of course he couldn't. And he couldn't exactly ask her to move in closer either, he thought, and a wry smile flitted over his face.

"I'd best light the stove," said Cait, suddenly very aware that she was sitting there in her nightgown.

"Don't go yet, Cait," Gabe asked softly. "There's time before anyone else comes down." He shifted and turned to face her. She looked so sweet and desirable, the dark green shawl across her shoulders, her hair tied back loosely, the dark curls framing her face.

"I must look a sight," she whispered, blushing at the intensity of his gaze. Then her eyes filled with tears. "I am so afraid for Da, Gabe. It's one thing to say 'over our dead bodies,' but I don't think I could face it if something happened to him."

Gabe swung his legs down and patted the seat next to him. "Come over here, Cait, so I can put my good arm around you." Cait sat next to him and he pulled her against his chest. "I've already said I won't let your father go alone, Cait," he reassured her. "I'll be right there with him."

Cait pulled away in amazement. "Are you crazy, Gabe? You're too weak to ride anywhere. And you can't even draw a gun."

"But I can aim a rifle, Cait. Mackie set it up so your father would be alone. But his damned wolf missed, thank God."

"Do you think he missed on purpose, Gabe? Could Sadie be right, that he has some feeling for her?"

"Not you too, Cait!" Gabe said in disgust. "You

women with your romantic dreams. The man is a cold-blooded killer. He killed Eduardo, for God's sake."

"But we don't know that for sure, Gabe."

"*I* know it. And I know he set me up yesterday. And why are we arguing about this?" he protested.

"Because I think you are being unfair to your sister, Gabe Hart," she declared, with more spirit than anger. "And because I don't want to lose Da . . . or you," she added, surprised at her boldness.

"You won't lose either of us, darlin'," said Gabe, sounding more sure than he was. How were two men, one of them wounded, going to take Mackie and his men if it came to a fight? "I promise I'll be back," he added, leaning down and kissing her gently. As she put her arms around him to kiss him back, he groaned.

"Did I hurt you, Gabe?"

"It's more frustration than anything," he told her with a grin. "I'm in no shape for kissing now, so I'll have to come back, won't I?"

By the time Cait got around to lighting the stove, her mother and father had come down, and they were all around the breakfast table, including Gabe, when Sadie joined them. She hardly looked at Gabe when she asked how he was doing.

"Looks like I got more sleep than you did, Sarah Ellen," he answered noncommittally.

They had finished breakfast and Cait was just helping her mother clean the plates when they heard the horse and rider approaching.

"Now who can that be?" Michael asked of no one in particular. He got up and opened the door. "*Dia,*" he said softly. "The man has balls, I have to say that for him."

"Who is it Michael?" Elizabeth asked nervously.

" 'Tis Chavez, *a ghra.*"

"What is he *doing* here, Michael?" she asked, standing next to him. Michael took her hand and squeezed it reassuringly. "I don't know, Elizabeth, but you stay here and I'll find out."

Gabe was halfway out of his chair, saying, "I'll come

with you, Mr. Burke," when Michael turned. "Oh, no, boyo, you just stay here and keep the ladies calm."

Michael's face was set and hard as he nodded to his unexpected visitor. "I wouldn't get down if I were you, Chavez," he said coldly. "What do you want?"

"I came to warn you, señor."

"About what?"

"Señor Mackie. He is expecting you and I would guess that you are not going to disappoint him?"

"I'm leaving in ten minutes. You can ride back and tell him that, Chavez."

"I don't work for Mackie anymore, Señor Burke. Not since he found out I didn't kill Gabriel Hart. I think he guessed that I missed on purpose," Chavez added with a wry smile. "I am on my way to Arizona, but I thought I would warn you."

"If you are on your way to Arizona, then your sense of direction is off," replied Michael.

"*Si*, well, I decided to make a small detour."

"Why should I believe you, Chavez?" Michael demanded.

"I don't know, Señor Burke," admitted Juan. "I surprised myself yesterday and this morning. But I tell you that if you go and offer Mackie the slightest threat, his men will kill you. He doesn't need me for that, señor. He'll just claim you drew on him and then he'll take your land. He doesn't give up until he gets what he wants, Señor Mackie."

"I've known that all along, Chavez." Michael hesitated a minute. "Did you kill Eduardo?" he asked bluntly.

"No, señor," Juan replied quietly. "I've killed many men, but always in a fair fight."

"Which you manage to provoke."

Chavez shrugged. "Sometimes, señor. It's been my job."

"So why is anything different now? Why didn't you kill Gabe yesterday?"

Chavez was silent for moment. "Let's just say my aim was off, señor. I was distracted by . . . other things."

"Well, I thank you for the warning, Chavez," said Michael dismissively.

"Are you going in alone, Señor Burke?"

"No, I'll be with him," said Gabe, who'd just come out, closing the door behind him. "Now get the hell out of here before I blow your head off." Gabe lifted the rifle he'd taken down from the wall.

Michael pushed the barrel down. "Take it easy, boyo."

Chavez had sat there calmly, just gazing at Gabe with his green eyes. "You are well enough to ride, Señor Hart?" he finally asked.

"You just winged me."

He had done more than that, Juan knew, thinking of the blood that had poured down Hart's arm. "I am thinking that three men would be better than two, Señor Burke," he said slowly, looking at Michael and ignoring Gabe.

"You are crazy if you think we'd let you ride with us," Gabe protested.

"I was talking to Señor Burke," Juan replied calmly.

"Why should I trust you, Chavez?" asked Michael.

"I don't know, señor," he said with an ironic smile. "I admit I wouldn't, if I were you. All the same, I am willing to ride with you. I warn you, though, Mackie's men have orders to shoot me on sight," he added with an apologetic shrug.

"All right, Chavez," said Michael flatly. "If you are mad enough to go back under those circumstances, you can come with us. Do you want to come in for a cup of coffee before we go?"

"No, señor, I think I would not be welcomed by your wife and daughter. Or Señorita Hart. I will just wait by the corral."

"You are letting him ride with you, Michael? Have you lost your mind?" cried Elizabeth, when Michael came back into the house.

"After all my years in the army, I know men, *a ghra.* I've been mistaken only once or twice in my trust in one."

"This once could be enough, Michael. I *knew* he would bring pain to this household, I knew what he was the first time I saw him, so why not trust *my* feelings about him?" replied Elizabeth angrily.

"I swear I'll be watching him every minute," Gabe promised her.

Caitlin just sat there, her face pale and expressionless. Her beloved Da couldn't go alone to face Mackie. Yet Gabe couldn't do much to save him, not after losing so much blood. It felt as if something was squeezing her chest, making it hard to breathe. "Take Sky, Gabe," she said quietly.

"I haven't ridden him outside of the corral, Cait."

"But he responds to your voice, Gabe. And he's fast. Take him, please," she pleaded. Suddenly it was of great importance that Gabe take her horse . . . his horse. It felt like a way she could be with him. She had the irrational belief that Sky could protect him.

"All right, Cait, and I promise to bring him back to you safe and sound."

"You just bring yourself back safe, Gabe," she said, almost choking on her unshed tears. "And you, Da," she added, walking over to her father and letting him enfold her in his arms.

"Don't worry, Cait, we'll be back before you even know we're gone. Are you ready, Gabe?"

"Yes, sir."

Just as Gabe was going out the door, Sadie put her hand on his good arm. "You take care, Gabriel Hart," she whispered.

"Don't worry, Sarah Ellen," he answered, smiling down at her.

The three women followed the men to the door and stood there waiting while Gabe and Michael saddled their horses. "Thank God, Gabe rides with his legs," whispered Cait as she watched him mount Sky.

Chavez had mounted his black as soon as the men led their horses out of the corral and just sat there, looking over at the women, his face blank. Cait wasn't sure who she hated more: Mackie or this enigma sitting before them. Chavez had caused most of the trouble in the valley. He had terrified her mother. He had almost killed Gabe. And now he sat there, gazing at them coldly. She heard Sadie take a convulsive breath. How could she have kissed such a man?

Juan watched the three women on the porch, keeping his face expressionless. He'd always thought Burke's daughter a pretty little thing, but it was Elizabeth and Sadie who pulled at him.

He admired Elizabeth Burke and he feared her effect on him. She was as strong as her husband in her own way, standing there waving him off, knowing she could be a widow before noon.

And Sadie? She was not as beautiful as Caitlin Burke, but then, he had never wanted a pretty little thing. He wanted Sadie's down-to-earth strength and humor. Her everyday face with that sweet and enjoyable mouth. He wanted Sadie and he guessed he loved her, which almost made him laugh aloud. He must love her or it wouldn't hurt him so much to sit here, knowing it would be the last time he'd ever see her. Whatever feelings she'd had, she must hate him now.

"Are you ready, Chavez?" Michael asked.

Juan nodded and they wheeled their horses around. Elizabeth and Cait came flying down the steps. "Take care, Michael, I love you," said Elizabeth as he reached down to clasp her hand.

"I will, *muirneach*."

"Da . . ."

"Take care of your ma, Cait."

Caitlin stood there, tears pouring down her cheeks and Gabe couldn't stand it. He was off Sky, handing the reins over to Chavez without thinking, who looked at them with a bemused grin, and had Caitlin in his good arm. "We'll be back, Cait," he promised and gave her a bruising kiss. She flung her arms around his neck. Gabe winced, but it was worth the pain to feel the love and longing she finally revealed to him.

When she let go, he mounted again and they rode off, Michael and Gabe keeping Chavez in front of them. Just as they reached the first barbed wire fence of the south pasture, they heard someone behind them. It was Sadie, standing in the middle of the road, waving and calling: "*Vaya con Dios*, Juan."

Chavez had wanted what the two other men had, he'd realized as he'd watched their loving good-byes. He didn't expect it and most certainly didn't deserve it. But she gave him her forgiveness anyway, if not her love, and he vowed he would keep her brother safe if it was the last thing he did.

Thirty-six

They were quiet until they reached the main road, each one caught up in his good-byes. Gabe was the first to break the silence. "You must be wondering, Mr. Burke, about that kiss. I, uh, want to assure you that after this is all over, I'll make things right."

"And how were ye thinkin' of doin' that, boyo?"

"I am hoping to marry your daughter, Mr. Burke. If she'll have me and if you approve."

"Well, now, Gabe, I'll have to be talkin' to Mrs. Burke about this," said Michael, keeping a straight face. He looked over at Gabe, and seeing the expression on his face, he couldn't keep up his teasing. "I'm only having a bit of fun," he apologized. "Mrs. Burke and I only want Cait to be happy."

"I love her very much," said Gabe in a low voice.

"Ye'd better, after such a kiss," said Michael with a smile. " 'Twas a good day when Eduardo sent ye down to us, Gabe Hart," he added, laying his hand on Gabe's shoulder for a minute.

Sky gave a little crow-hop as Snowflake drew closer. "Do ye think he's ready for this?"

Gabe neck-reined Sky back and settled him down with a few crooning words. "He'll be okay and we're not intending to ride in shooting, are we?" he asked ironically.

"What do you think, Chavez?" Michael asked.

"I wouldn't advise it, Señor Burke," said Juan, turning in his saddle.

"Well, I wasn't contemplating a cavalry charge anyway," said Michael with a grin, "much as I'm used to them. I'm planning to knock on the man's door and talk to him if I can.''

Gabe snorted. "What are you going to say?"

"I am goin' to tell him that he's overstayed his welcome in this valley and it's time for him to move on."

"And if he doesn't agree with you?"

"Then I'll have to insult his wife, though I hate to bring the poor woman into it, or his mother or his manhood . . . whatever will provoke him into a fight."

"But you're no gunfighter, Mr. Burke," protested Gabe.

"Who said anything about guns, boyo. We'll settle this with our fists."

Without thinking, Chavez and Gabe exchanged glances that seemed to hold all the same bemusement at such a quixotic response. Then they both looked away, surprised and uncomfortable with their moment of shared understanding.

"Yer job is to cover me while I'm knockin' him out," Michael told them.

"You'll be lucky to make it to the door, Señor Burke," said Chavez.

"He'll not be shootin' me on sight, Chavez. There's only so much he can cover up. The doctor knows what happened to Gabe. If anything happens to me . . . well, Elizabeth will make sure he does a thorough examination that shows how the bullet went through me back," he said with a quizzical grin.

"There are three men to worry about, Señor Burke. Will Beard, Jim Canty, and Frank Dunn. Not counting Mackie himself," he added. "Though he prefers others to do his shooting for him."

"Maybe there are *four* men, Chavez," said Gabe.

"No, señor," Chavez answered Gabe's challenge softly.

"He's right, Gabe. You have to trust him or ye'll be too distracted to pay attention to the others. What about the rest of Mackie's men?"

"They're just cowboys, señor. These others, they are different."

"Are they the ones who killed Eduardo?"

"I don't know for sure, señor, I wasn't there. But I would guess so."

When they reached the ranch gate, Chavez leaned down to push it open. "Go ahead, señores, I'll close it behind us." He had wondered if Hart would stay back, but he only gave Juan a nervous glance and made sure to be straight behind Michael as they rode through. When they reached the ranch house, everything was quiet and they dismounted quickly, looking around anxiously.

Michael pounded on the front door and when it finally opened, he demanded that the housekeeper inform Nelson Mackie that Michael Burke was here to see him.

"No need to do that, Maria," said Mackie, coming up behind her. "What are you doing here, Burke?"

"You sent your wolf to kill Gabe Hart, Mackie, and I'm not lettin' ye get away with anything more," said Michael. "I had to let Eduardo's death go unpunished because I had no proof. But this time . . ."

"This time you have a witness?" said Mackie, seeing Chavez for the first time and he dismissed the housekeeper and moved closer to the door. "You surprise me, Chavez," he said, ignoring Michael. "I'd have figured you long gone by now. You won't leave this ranch alive, you know," he added conversationally. "What do you mean to do, Burke?"

The sneer on his face infuriated Michael. "I plan to beat the living daylights out of you, Mackie," replied Michael, unbuckling his gun belt and holding it out to Chavez. "Here, hold this for me."

"Are you crazy, Burke?" Mackie asked, looking around him nervously.

"For once, no one is around to help you, señor," said Chavez with a feral smile.

"They *will* be," growled Mackie reaching for the rope hanging from the old brass door bell.

"Oh, no you don't," said Gabe, knocking Mackie's hand down with his rifle.

Michael pulled Mackie out into the yard and then

hit him so hard on the chin that Gabe and Juan could hear the man's teeth hit together.

"You are a fool, Burke," muttered Mackie as he got up and moved his jaw around.

"I don't think so, Nelson. I'm going to beat you till you agree to leave or ye're a bloody pulp, whichever comes first," Michael replied calmly.

Mackie's face turned red with rage and he rushed Michael, driving his head into Michael's stomach and knocking them both down into the dirt. After a rough tumble, they were up again.

It took a good five minutes, but Michael, his own face bruised and bleeding, finally had Mackie where he wanted him: on his knees, just lifting his head and ready for a final cut to the jaw when Gabe yelled a warning. "Three men on their way!"

Mackie had a smile on his face as Michael turned. "Señor Burke!" cried Juan, leaping forward. Michael turned back to see Chavez knock a knife out of Mackie's hand.

"*Muchas gracias,* señor," he said softly.

"*De nada.*"

Mackie struggled up and waved to his men as he stumbled toward the door. There was no sense in trying to stop him, thought Michael, for they had their hands full with the three coming at them. He'd worry about his back later. He smiled gratefully as Chavez threw him his gun.

Two had revolvers and the third a rifle. It was he who started shooting first and Michael yelped as a bullet grazed his cheek. Gabe, who was slowed down by his bad arm, raised his rifle, took careful aim and brought the rifleman down. As he was reloading, Michael shot Dunn in the knee. Juan watched Jim Canty aiming directly at him. It seemed as if everything was going in slow motion: he lifted his gun, but it was too slow, he could tell but then things resumed their normal speed and Gabe took Canty down just in time. Chavez glanced over to give him a grateful smile.

As he did, out of the corner of his eye, he saw the door open and wheeled around just as Mackie emerged, revolver in hand. It's smoking already, thought Juan, a puzzled frown on his face just before he felt the pain in his chest. Why was it so hard to lift his gun? he wondered as he aimed it at Mackie. His fingers could barely squeeze the trigger, but the bullet caught Mackie in the throat and then everything dissolved into a red mist.

Michael and Gabe were frozen. Neither of them had been paying attention to the door and both knew if it hadn't been for Chavez, they'd be dead.

"Dia," Michael whispered, walking slowly over to where Mackie lay, his blood spurting out of him. Gabe knelt down in the dirt and rolled Chavez over. He held his finger to the side of his throat. "He's still alive, Mr. Burke."

"Thank Christ. He saved our lives, Gabe."

"He's bleeding pretty bad, though. It looks like it could have hit his lung."

"Let's get him up on Snowflake."

It was hard work, given Juan's dead weight and Gabe's bad arm, but they finally got him in the saddle and Michael mounted the mare and settled himself down behind Chavez.

"You lead his black, Gabe. And let's get out of here. The rest of Mackie's men may only be hired hands, but I'm not waitin' to find out!"

Once they were out of the gate and well on their way down the road, Michael pulled the mare to a halt. "Can ye spare yer shirt, Gabe? I can feel the blood pourin' out of him."

Gabe lifted the shirt off and together they managed to create a clumsy, makeshift binding that seemed to stop the bleeding a little. Chavez moaned a few times and Michael called his name. "He's out, poor bugger, but that's just as well."

They slowed the horses as they got closer to the ranch. It seemed as if they had been gone for hours, but as they reached the house, Michael realized it was not yet noon. Elizabeth and Cait were at the door and running to meet them.

"My God, Michael, your face! Are you all right?"

"I'm fine, Elizabeth. Help me with Chavez, will ye, Gabe?" Gabe, who had his arm around Cait, let her go reluctantly and they eased Chavez down.

"We must get him into the parlor, *a ghra*."

Elizabeth shuddered.

"I know he frightens you, Elizabeth, but he saved my life. Twice."

"I'll get Jake, Da," said Cait, running toward the barn for the older man. When Jake got there, they were able to carry Chavez in.

Sadie had been standing on the porch, buffeted by conflicting emotions. Her beloved brother was safe, thank the Lord. But the man she loved was being carried into the house, his face white and the makeshift bandage soaked in blood. She stood there alone as they went past, listening to Elizabeth give directions, wondering if she would ever be able to move from that spot. Then she felt an arm around her shoulders. It was Gabe. "Sarah Ellen, are you all right?"

She nodded.

"I am sorry, Sadie, I was wrong about Chavez. Michael Burke would be dead twice over if it hadn't been for him. And I don't think he did it for love of us, Sadie. You judged rightly; he had some feelings for you."

Sadie shuddered and turning into her brother's chest, started to cry in great racking sobs. Gabe just held her and let her cry.

"Oh, Gabe, I was so scared to see you go and with bad feelings between us. What if you hadn't come back? Or came back like Juan? I couldn't have borne it." After a moment, she pulled out of his arms and looked up into her brother's face. "How is he, Gabe?"

"It's a chest wound, Sadie. We can't tell if it hit a lung or not. He's lost a lot of blood. I'm riding for the doctor now."

"I must go into him," said Sadie. "Come back quick, Gabe."

The moment Elizabeth heard that Chavez was responsible for saving Michael's life, she became calm and efficient, spreading a clean sheet on the sofa, getting a basin of hot water from the kitchen, and scissors to cut off Chavez's shirt.

The bullet had gone in low on the right side of his chest. She rolled him over gently to look at his back, but there was no exit wound as she had hoped. "The bullet's still in there, Michael," she said, as she carefully lowered Chavez down again. "The doctor will have to dig for it and he's lost so much blood already. . . . Cait, get a sheet from the linen chest and cut it into strips. At least we can try to stop the bleeding." She took a clean cloth and wet it and cleaned his face. "At least there's no blood from his mouth, Michael, so maybe it just missed his lung. Here, Sadie, you come over and hold this towel to his lips," said Elizabeth, dipping the material into water. "We need to get some liquid back into him."

Luckily the doctor had been in and was back with Gabe in a little over an hour.

"Looks like you're running a hospital here, Mrs. Burke," he joked as he took off his coat and rolled up his sleeves. "You would have made a good nurse," he said approvingly as he loosened the bandages Elizabeth had made. "Has he been conscious at all?"

"No."

"Well, the bullet is still there and must come out. He's too weak for chloroform, so I'll need someone to be ready to hold him down while I probe for it, just in case he comes to. Mrs. Burke? Miss Hart?"

Both women nodded.

Sadie thought she might faint several times as the doctor probed for the bullet. "Shattered a rib," he muttered. "But missed the lung by a hairbreadth. Lucky man. Hmm. . . ."

"What is it, Doctor?" asked Sadie.

"The bullet is lodged in a back muscle next to the spine. This will be tricky."

Juan had been still for most of the doctor's work, but as he went in deeper through the muscle, he groaned and opened his eyes and gasped in pain.

"Hold him down, Mrs. Burke, Miss Hart. I don't want to slip up at this point."

Sadie and Elizabeth gently held Juan's arms and Elizabeth, to her astonishment, found herself crooning to him: "It is all right, Señor Chavez. It will be over soon. It is all right."

"Got it," crowed the doctor, dropping the bullet in a dish. "Now all we can do is wait, Mrs. Burke," he said as he sprinkled sulphur powder into the wound and packed it with clean gauze and wrapped it with his own bandage. "He's pretty young and healthy. Unless an infection sets in, he'll be all right. He'll likely run a fever, though, so I'll leave you some quinine."

"Thank you so much, Dr. Fraser," said Elizabeth as she walked him to the door.

"I hadn't thought you were that fond of Señor Chavez, ma'am," he remarked with a smile.

"He saved Michael's life, Doctor. That is enough to make me care for him," she replied.

Michael was holding the doctor's horse. "I've walked and watered him, so he should be recovered enough from your ride to get you home, Fraser."

"Thank you, Burke. Will I be needed any place else today, do you think?" he asked ironically.

"Nelson Mackie will not be needing you or anything else, Doctor, but there may be one or two of his men who could use your services."

"So Mackie is no longer a threat to you, eh, Burke?"

"Or to the valley. And it was a fair fight on our part, if that is what ye're asking."

"I know you well enough to know that. As a doctor, I'm never glad when death takes someone, but I must confess I have no regrets where Mackie is concerned."

"Nor I," agreed Michael. "Nor I."

Thirty-seven

Chavez lay very quiet that afternoon and evening and as Sadie sat by him, she wondered if he would ever open his eyes again. Perhaps he would just slip away, never having regained consciousness. Never knowing that she loved him. No matter that he didn't love her. He had cared enough about her to spare her brother and save both Gabe and Mr. Burke. Whatever he had been in the past, he had more than made up for it today as far as she was concerned.

Cait and Elizabeth insisted that she get some sleep and sent her off to bed. "I'll take the first shift, Ma," said Cait. "You must be exhausted."

"I'll go up for a little nap, Cait, but call me if anything changes."

"I will."

Cait hadn't wanted to wake her mother, but two hours into her shift, Chavez began tossing and turning and muttering in Spanish and English. When she put her hand on his forehead, she realized he was burning with fever. She crept up the stairs and shook Elizabeth by the shoulder. "Ma," she whispered.

"Umm, what is it, Michael?" Elizabeth groaned.

"It's not Da, it's Cait, Ma. Señor Chavez has a bad fever."

Elizabeth was awake and up in an instant. "Don't wake your Da, Cait. You just go to bed and I'll take over," Elizabeth whispered back, pulling her wrapper around her.

"Are you sure, Ma?"

"Go to bed, dearest," said her mother. "You've done your share."

Elizabeth made her way to the kitchen and poured herself a cup of leftover coffee. It was lukewarm and bitter, but at least it would keep her awake. She poured a little of the powder the doctor had left into a mug and adding water to it, stirring it till it dissolved.

Cait was right; Chavez was burning up, Elizabeth thought. She sponged his face with cool water and dipping a clean cloth in the mug of water, held it to his lips. He sucked at it greedily and she managed to get most of it into him. "Now it is just a matter of waiting," she whispered.

His hand was pulling convulsively at the sheet so she placed one hand on top of it and with the other, stroked his head as though he were a child, saying, "There, there, you will be all right."

When his eyes opened, she drew back in surprise, but then it became clear that he wasn't really seeing her, for he was muttering deliriously. At first, it was in Spanish and he sounded like a frightened child as he said, "*Si*, señor, I will do it. No, no, I don't want to be beaten again."

What kind of childhood had he had? she wondered. He wasn't talking to his mother and father, but only this señor whoever he was. Then he suddenly called out in English, "Don't hurt my ma," and Elizabeth winced as he clutched her hand. His voice lowered and as if he was a little boy convincing himself to be brave, he recited a litany to himself: "My ma is dead. My pa. They killed Lizzie too. I must be brave. I can't cry. . . ."

Elizabeth's hand faltered as she stroked his hot forehead. Why did he speak of his father and mother in English? How had they died? And who was Lizzie?"

She looked into his unseeing eyes. They were green eyes, flecked with brown. The hair she was brushing back with her hand was a light brown. His shoulders were sprinkled with freckles. Like hers. Like her father's had been.

"Who is Lizzie, Juan?" she whispered, but he only continued reciting his dreadful litany.

It *couldn't* be Jonathan. It *couldn't* be, not after all

these years. Lizzie was probably a maid. His mother and father were . . . dead. Killed by Comancheros. He had been hauled onto a horse's back and sold to some Mexican family?

It made sense. Oh, my dear God, it all made sense. How her memories started to come back after she'd seen him. Why he spoke both perfect Spanish and English. Why he was who he was: El Lobo.

"Jonathan," she whispered, cupping his cheek in her hand. "Is it really you, Jonathan?"

His hand tightened on hers and the look in his eyes was that of a tortured child. "Ma? Oh, Ma. I want my Ma . . ."

"Ma's dead, Jonathan," Elizabeth whispered. "But this is Lizzie, and I'm here to take care of you now."

"Mr. Burke?"

Michael stirred and reached his hand out for Elizabeth.

"It's Sadie, Mr. Burke, I'm sorry to disturb you, but I went down to relieve Mrs. Burke, but she won't leave him. She looks awful, Mr. Burke," continued Sadie, sounding shaken.

"Thank you, Sadie," said Michael, raising himself and pushing the hair out of his eyes. "I'll go right down." Jesus, he shouldn't have left Elizabeth alone with him. Not when Chavez disturbed her so. Michael ran downstairs barefoot and in his underwear and stopped at the entrance to the parlor.

His wife was sitting there, stroking Chavez's cheek, whispering to him, calling him Jonathan. Mary, Queen of Heaven, it had been too much for her and she must be off somewhere in the past. Jonathan had been her little brother's name. The one who'd been killed by the Comancheros, along with her parents.

"Elizabeth," he said softly, kneeling beside her and putting his arms around her.

"It's Jonathan, Michael," she said, not turning her head.

" 'Tis not yer brother, *a ghra*. 'Tis Juan Chavez, El Lobo. Don't ye remember?"

She turned to him then and gave him a loving look. "Oh, Michael, I am all right, truly I am. Of course I know who he is . . . now. But once, many years ago, he was just a little boy who'd seen his parents killed. Who thought his sister was dead. He called me Lizzie, Michael . . . Well, that is not exactly true," she admitted, when her husband looked at her in disbelief. "He called for Lizzie. He doesn't know it's me, although maybe we both have known at some level. . . ."

"Maybe Lizzie is just some woman he knew, Elizabeth."

"Michael, he spoke in Spanish to a Señor Tomas who clearly beat him constantly. He never mentioned his parents until he started speaking in English and then he said his ma had been shot, his pa and Lizzie. He even looks like my father, though I never saw it till now."

"Elizabeth, this has stirred up all yer memories. Do you think you just *want* it to be your brother? There is no proof, *a ghra*."

Elizabeth gave a little laugh that ended in a sob. "That may be true, Michael, but I *know* this is Jonathan." She put her hand on Michael's. "He was only seven and sold into slavery, just like Thomas said he might have been. He had most of the good beaten out of him, I'd say. He certainly thinks he is Juan Chavez."

"And that is who he is now, Elizabeth," Michael warned softly. "Even if what you say is true."

"Oh, Michael, I can't bear it," she cried. "Thomas found *me*. And you and I have had each other all these years. I should have tried to find him once we got to Santa Fe," she said, sobbing convulsively.

"But ye thought he was dead."

"Maybe it was easier to believe that, Michael, than to think he was out there somewhere."

"Hush, *a ghra*. Ye were only fourteen. You had no money to search. And the likeliest thing was that the Comancheros killed him."

"I have believed that all these years. But now, to find him and maybe lose him all over again, and he won't ever *know*." She was crying heartbrokenly in Michael's arms and he held her tight until she was finally quiet.

"Look, *a ghra*, he seems less feverish," he said, turning her around. Elizabeth reached out and touched Juan's forehead. It was much cooler. "But there's still the possibility of infection, Michael."

"He'll pull through, *a ghra*. I'm sure of it. Now come up to rest and let Sadie take over."

When Gabe and her Da had come riding in with a wounded Juan Chavez across the saddle, there had been no time for Cait to do anything but register with a heartfelt thank-you that her father and Gabe were unharmed. Things had moved so fast: the doctor's arrival, her mother's insistence on taking over the responsibility for Chavez's recovery, and then Elizabeth's growing belief that Mackie's hired gun was her long-lost brother.

Because Elizabeth had spent so much time in the sick room, Cait had taken over the cooking, although no one seemed to have much appetite for the suppers she prepared.

"I'm sorry, Caitlin," her father said, patting her hand gently as she started to spoon more chile into his plate, "but I'm still too worked up to eat much. I'm sure Gabe will have some more?"

"I'm not that hungry, either," Gabe admitted with an apologetic smile. "I'd best get out and see to the horses," he added as he pushed away from the table.

"How is your arm, boyo?" Michael asked.

"Still hurts, but getting better. I can actually move my fingers again," Gabe added as he slowly and painfully made a loose fist.

"Why don't you give Gabe a hand outside then, Cait? Sadie and I will clean up here, won't we? I don't want Gabe pushing harder than he should."

"Of course, Da."

"I'll do fine," Gabe protested, but he was secretly grateful for the help. Though he would have expected

Michael Burke to be offering himself rather than his daughter.

Gabe pulled the barn door open and was starting for the two saddles on the corral fence when he saw that Cait was already lifting one down. "I can do that, Cait."

"I've been hauling saddles since I was ten, Gabe. Why don't you see to the horses."

Gabe had managed to get Snowflake and Patch fed and watered by the time Cait had gotten the saddles and bridles hung up in the tack room. "Let me take care of Red Hawk, Gabe," she offered.

She filled the horse's trough with fresh hay and was just turning to go for water when she bumped right into Gabe who was coming up behind her with a full bucket. There she was, up against his chest, looking with startled eyes up into his deep blue ones. She heard a clank and felt water splash her feet, so she knew he had dropped the bucket, but all she was conscious of was how he one-handedly pulled her even closer and leaned down to seek her mouth.

"Oh, Gabe . . ." she whispered when they broke apart. "I would have died if you hadn't come back safely."

"And why is that, darlin'?" he asked, dropping a kiss on the top of her head.

"I love you so much and I was afraid I'd lose you before I could tell you." Cait blushed and whispered, "I shouldn't have told you now."

"Why not?" he asked softly.

"Because I'm not sure whether you love *me*," she answered bravely.

"Not love you? Why, I've loved you for weeks now, darlin'."

"Have you, Gabe? Then why haven't you said anything?"

"Why haven't I said anything?" he repeated humorously. "Well, Mr. Henry Beecham for one. And the fact you're Michael Burke's daughter for another," he added more seriously. "And why should I believe you'd love me, a wandering old horse wrangler?"

"Old! Why you are not that much older than I am," Cait protested.

"But years older in experience, Caitlin. I've seen and done things I wouldn't want you to know about."

"I grew up in New Mexico, so don't patronize me, Gabe," she protested.

"I'm not, Cait. It's just that you don't really know that much about me."

"I know that you are wonderful with horses, Gabe. And loyal and brave. Look what you've done for Da."

"I'm also very good with a gun."

"Thank God, or you all might be dead!"

"You have Chavez to thank for that," Gabe corrected her.

"Da told me you killed Beard and Canty, Gabe."

"I've killed others, too, Cait. You know I rode with the Regulators in Lincoln." He was silent for a minute and then continued. "I was engaged to a woman there. Caroline Bryce, the schoolteacher."

Cait pulled back at that. "You loved her?"

"I did," he admitted. "But it was a young man's love, Cait. Nothing compared to what I feel for you," he reassured her.

"Why didn't you marry her?"

"She saw me as a lawless vigilante and hated the violence I was caught up in. She just couldn't see . . ."

"But what choice would any justice-loving person have had there, Gabe? I was only thirteen, but I remember Da and Ma talking about it. Catron owned everyone."

Her response was so quick, so sure, that Gabe felt something open up in him that had been closed off for years.

"I'd be surprised if you hadn't killed, Gabe," Cait continued slowly.

"And it doesn't bother you?"

"Of course, it bothers me. It bothers me that Da has had to kill too. But I've heard enough to know that a man sometimes doesn't have much choice. I don't know what it was like in Lincoln County, Gabe, but Mackie certainly left my Da no choice," she said with suppressed fury. "And if I had been there with you, I would have shot him myself!"

He should have known that despite her time in the East, the daughter of Michael and Elizabeth Burke would have no illusions about life in New Mexico.

"I struggle with the violence here, Gabe," Cait admitted. "I thought I wanted to get away from it. Philadelphia was so civilized and peaceful. I loved school," she continued, a note of sadness in her voice. "But I belong *here*," she added passionately. "Nelson Mackie would have had to kill me as well as my Da to get this ranch, Gabe," she said fiercely.

"Hush, Cait," Gabe said, kissing her gently. "It's all over. Mackie's dead and Chavez . . . well, he might well be your uncle!"

"Whoever he is," whispered Cait, "I am grateful, for he saved the two men I love most in the world."

Juan did not open his eyes again until after noon the next day and when he did, Elizabeth was back by his side. She was sitting there sewing, a small rosewood sewing box on the table beside her. Juan was so weak that even watching the flashing of her silver needle made him dizzy and he had to close his eyes for a moment.

Every time he breathed it felt like someone was sticking hundreds of those needles in his side. But he was obviously alive and in the Burkes' house. But that little rosewood box? He'd seen it before, which was puzzling, since he'd never been inside the Burkes'. He opened his eyes again, this time focusing on the box with the velvet mound that was used as a pincushion. His ma's sewing box had looked just like that. The thought drifted into his mind like smoke and he tried to hold onto it, but like smoke, it drifted right out again.

"You are awake, Señor Chavez?" asked Mrs. Burke in a soft voice. "Do you know where you are?"

Juan nodded. "*Sí,* señora. Your husband and Hart?" he asked in a voice so weak it was hardly a whisper.

"They are safe thanks to you," said Elizabeth with a smile.

Juan tried to pull himself up, but Elizabeth was beside him immediately. "No, no, señor. You've had a high fever and lost a lot of blood. Please lie still."

Juan nodded, sinking back, gratefully obeying her order.

"Let me get you some fresh water." Elizabeth stuck her needle in the velvet and left it on her chair.

He wanted to hold it. For some reason unknown to him he needed to hold that sewing box in his hand to convince himself that it wasn't his mother's. Of course, it wasn't his mother's. How would Elizabeth Burke come into possession of a sewing box that the Comancheros must have destroyed years ago?

This time, he didn't try to get up, but slid over to the edge of the sofa, reaching toward the chair seat. He finally grasped the little box, but he was shaking so hard that it fell out of his hand, hitting the floor and spilling spools of thread.

"*Mierde*," he muttered. He was white with the effort and when Elizabeth returned with the water, his eyes were shut again.

"Be careful, señora. The box . . ." he whispered.

The box? What box? Perhaps he was delirious again? "What box, Señor Chavez?"

"The sewing box." Then Elizabeth realized it was not on the chair but on the floor beside the sofa. She put down the mug and knelt down, scooping the spools of thread and the few pins that had fallen out. "Oh, dear," she said softly.

Juan's eyes opened. "What is it, señora?"

"The box . . . it is broken." Her voice caught as she picked up the top that had split in half.

"I am so sorry, Señora Burke," he said, struggling to sit up. "It is my fault . . . I dropped it."

Elizabeth knelt there looking up at him. "It was my mother's sewing box. . . ."

"It reminded me of my mother's sewing box . . ."

They both spoke at the same time and then fell silent.

Elizabeth spoke first. "You were out of your head with fever last night, Señor Chavez." Elizabeth struggled to keep her voice steady, although her heart was beating wildly. "You spoke in Spanish of a Señor Tomas, who was obviously very cruel to you."

Chavez frowned. "I did? Well, Señor Tomas, he did have his own way of persuading."

"Perhaps that is where you learned yours?"

Juan gave her a bitter smile. "I know it must be hard to have me here, señora. Believe me, I will be gone as soon as I . . ."

"No, no, señor, that is not what I meant," she responded and he gave her a puzzled look. "I only meant that children learn to do what is done to them. If they are treated kindly, they treat others so. If cruelly . . . well, they often grow up to bully others." When Chavez remained silent, Elizabeth continued. "You spoke of your mother last night too, but not in Spanish. And of your father. You saw them killed?"

Juan closed his eyes, once again seeing that blood red rose opening and opening in his father's chest.

"*Si*, señora," he whispered. "I have a few memories that occasionally come back to me."

"You also spoke of someone called Lizzie?" She was too afraid to be more direct.

"*Si*, Lizzie was my sister."

"So you have a sister," said Elizabeth softly.

"No, señora, the Comancheros killed her, too."

"Did you see it happen?" asked Elizabeth so quietly he had to strain to hear her. He closed his eyes again and turned his head away. Why did she ask him these questions and bring it back so clearly? All the fragments fell into place like the pieces of a kaleidoscope and he could remember everything about that morning. His father singing that song they were all tired of. His mother climbing down from the wagon, asking Lizzie to go for water. She didn't want to go for water. And she didn't like him calling her Lizzie and when he did, she stuck her tongue out at him and he was just waiting for her to come back from the creek so he could really get her into trouble when his father's song had been cut off.

"Did you see your sister killed, Juan?" Elizabeth Burke's voice was coming from very far away.

"No, but if they hadn't killed her they would have brought her along to be sold, too."

"What if she was down by the creek and they didn't even know she was there?"

It took him a minute to realize it was Mrs. Burke's voice asking the question, and not his own, inside his head. How could she *know* Lizzie had gone for water? Had he spoken of that in his delirium?

Mrs. Burke put her hand on his and when he turned back to look at her, he was surprised to see tears pouring down her cheeks. "You said my sewing box reminded you of your mother's, Jonathan." He didn't immediately take in what she had called him, but nodded a yes.

"And I said it was *my* mother's."

"What did you call me?" he asked sharply.

"Jonathan. Jonathan Rush."

His hand tightened convulsively. "That is my old name," he whispered.

"They didn't kill me, Jonathan," said Elizabeth. "I was hidden by the creek bank, though I saw it all. I saw them take you, but I couldn't do anything," she told him, her voice breaking. "I am so sorry."

"No, no . . . you can't be Lizzie," he said wonderingly.

"I'm afraid I am," she confessed with a watery smile.

"But how . . . ?" He shook his head as if to clear it.

"How did I come to be Mrs. Michael Burke? It is a long story, Jonathan, for another time. I stayed by the wagon all day and night and the next morning a troop of cavalry rescued me. I wanted them to go after you, but they said it was too late, that you'd been killed or sold. I guess it was easier for me to believe you dead, because the thought of your being alive somewhere would have tormented me. And the last thing I ever did, was to stick my tongue out at you," she said, putting her head down on the sofa and sobbing.

He hadn't really believe her until then, despite all she'd said. "Oh, Lizzie," he said, his voice filled with wonder and pain.

She lifted her head. "I always hated it when you called me that, Jonathan," she said with a heartbroken smile.

It was all too much for him. His head was spinning and his mouth was dry and he felt himself losing consciousness at the same time he felt the gentle touch of his sister's hand.

Thirty-eight

When Michael came in for dinner, he went straight to the parlor and saw his wife sitting beside Chavez as though she'd never left. The man's eyes were closed and he was very pale and Michael had a moment or two of worry until he saw Chavez's chest moving up and down. He walked over to Elizabeth and put his arm around her.

"It *is* Jonathan," she said softly, without looking up.

"Now, *a ghra*, ye don't know that."

"But I do, Michael. He was awake this morning. He wanted to hold my sewing box because it reminded him of his mother's."

"*Dia!*" exclaimed Michael. "That's your mother's sewing box."

"The only thing I have of hers except for a few pieces of jewelry. Chavez had a sister, Michael, whom he called Lizzie. He thought she'd been killed. He'd forgotten that she was down by the creek fetching water."

"I can't believe it, Elizabeth!"

"Neither can I, but it's true. And it all makes sense, Michael. He was treated cruelly as a slave. He'd seen his family massacred. He had none of the love I had. No wonder he ended up El Lobo."

"Not everyone who has a hard time becomes hard," Michael reminded her mildly.

"Oh, I am not trying to excuse him, Michael. I'm sure he has done some awful things. But he was such a little boy, Michael. Only seven," she said, beginning to cry again. "Oh dear, I've been crying off and on all day," she said with an apologetic smile.

"And I am sure you haven't had anything to eat and Cait has prepared a good dinner for us," he said, lifting her to her feet.

"I hate to leave him, Michael."

"He'll not be going anywhere for a while, *a ghra.*"

The next time Juan awoke, it was later that evening. He shifted slightly and then groaned. In addition to the throbbing on his side, he was stiff and sore all over, but this time he was determined to pull himself up.

"Are ye awake, boyo?" Michael Burke was standing over him, holding a kerosene lamp. "Are ye sure ye want to sit up?"

"*Si,* señor," Juan muttered.

"Then let me help ye." Michael's hands were surprisingly gentle as he lifted Juan up and propped another pillow behind his head. "There ye are, not quite perpendicular, but vertical enough to get some broth down yer throat, if ye're hungry?"

Juan was surprised to find that he was and nodded his head.

"I'll get some for ye, then."

But it was not Michael Burke who returned with a small earthenware cup, but Sadie Hart.

"Mr. Burke?"

"Seeing to the horses, Señor Chavez. I offered to bring you this." She set the cup down and tied a napkin around Juan's neck. He became very conscious that he had nothing on above the waist but the silly bib and the strips of bandage around his chest. He tried to pull a sheet up around him and Sadie had to turn her face to hide her smile.

"Here, I think this is cooled off enough," she said, turning back and holding a spoonful of soup to his lips. They both felt so awkward that the first few swallows left more on his chin than in his mouth and Sadie wiped him off with the bib. They did better with the rest, however, and when the cup was empty, Juan whispered, "I didn't realize I was so hungry. Is there any more?"

"No more, for now," said Sadie. "The doctor said go slowly. But I can get you some water."

Chavez insisted on holding the glass himself until he realized that his hands were shaking so much that the water was spilling down his chest. "A good thing I tied that around your neck," said Sadie matter-of-factly as she covered his hand with hers and helped him with the water. "That's enough now," she said after he drained the glass. "I'll get you more later, before you go to sleep."

"I have been sleeping all day, señorita," he said as she leaned over to untie the napkin. As her breast brushed his chest, he smiled at the irony that he was so weak he couldn't even take in the pleasurable sensation, much less take advantage of it. Not that she would want him to, after all that had happened.

"I need to tell you something, Sadie," he whispered as she straightened up. "I wish to tell you I am sorry."

"For what, Señor Chavez?" she asked, her voice steady but her hands shaking. She tried to steady them by folding the makeshift bib as though it had just come back from the laundry.

"I . . . your brother was right, Sadie."

Sadie's heart sank and she prayed she wouldn't disgrace herself by crying.

"Señor Mackie had wanted me to push him into a fight. I made sure that he caught me kissing you under protest. I was rough with you, I think?"

"But never before that, Juan. Are you apologizing for all the other times, too?" Sadie didn't know why she was being such a glutton for pain. It hurt enough to hear him confirm Gabe's judgment. Did she really want to know that nothing between them had been real?

Juan had intended to say yes and set her free. Whoever he was: Juan Chavez, Jonathan Rush, he was not the right man for Sadie Hart. She deserved much better. But when he looked up and saw the pain in her eyes, he whispered, *"Nunca jamas, querida."* He hesitated a little before saying, "It is true that Senor Mackie wanted me to pursue you. But I didn't need his orders after that first time I met you. Everything we did together . . ." Sadie lowered her eyes and blushed at the memory of their lovemaking.

"My heart was in everything, *mi amor*."

"Am I, Juan?"

"Are you what, *querida*?"

"Am I your love?"

"*Si*, Sarah Ellen Hart. *Mi amor sola*. If I wasn't so weak I would show you how I feel instead of telling you." He sighed. "When I leave here I will carry you in my heart always."

"When you leave . . . ?"

"You deserve a better man, *querida*. Not El Lobo. Not someone who almost killed your brother."

"But you didn't, Juan."

"I couldn't," he said simply.

"And you saved him again, at the Mackie ranch. Without you, both Gabe and Mr. Burke would be dead. That makes you a good enough man for me, Señor Lobo," she said, trying to smile.

"Oh, Sadie, you can't . . ."

"But I do," she whispered. "I love you, Juan Chavez. Jonathan Rush," she added softly. "Mrs. Burke told us who you are."

"Ah, but Sadie, that should have convinced you. It is ironic, no, that I was hired to drive my sister off her ranch. Hired to kill her husband. I could have done it too. And I would never have known . . ."

"But I think you did, Juan. I think somewhere, in some way, your heart knew."

"If it did, Sadie, it is only because you gave me back my heart. I have been without one for many years, *querida*," he said, turning away so that she could not see the pain in his eyes.

She knelt down beside him. "Please don't leave me, Juan. Leave here if you must, but take me with you."

He turned back to her, about to protest when she put her fingers gently on his lips. "No, Juan, don't say it."

He reached out and took her hand in his. "I am

too weak to fight you or kiss you, *querida*," he replied with a rueful smile.

"I love you, Juan. I gave you my heart that day in the foothills."

"All right, Sadie. When I leave, if you still wish to go, I will take you with me." He covered her hand in his and held it tightly until he fell asleep.

During the next week, Michael dealt with the sheriff and the town council. Mackie's housekeeper had seen everything from inside the house and was able to give a full account of all that had happened, now that her employer was dead and unable to frighten her. Without Mackie behind him, the sheriff was persuaded to give up his intention to "see justice done."

"Justice has been done, boyo," Michael told him, "Nelson Mackie is dead because he pushed just a little too hard and because he was a murderin' bastard."

"But that Mexican should pay," muttered the sheriff, who was furious that the source of his "retirement" fund was now dead, all due to the sneaking son of a bitch, Chavez, who changed sides at the last minute.

"For what? He didn't kill Eduardo, not that you gave a tinker's damn about that murder," said Michael, looking at him in disgust. "The men responsible are dead. And he saved my life, so Señor Chavez goes or stays a free man. And speakin' of goin', Sheriff, if I were you, I'd be thinkin' of goin' meself. . . ."

"The one person I have sympathy for in all this is Mrs. Mackie, Elizabeth," said Michael at the dinner table that night. "She was not responsible for any of it and she loved the bastard, strange as that may seem."

"I hear she has family in Kansas, Michael?"

"She does, *a ghra,* and once she sells the ranch, she'll not have to worry about being dependent on their charity. She's in a hurry to leave or so I've heard," Michael continued after a moment's silence. "I wouldn't be surprised if she was willing to sell off some of the smaller ranches Mackie bought up," he added, looking pointedly at Gabe.

"The Garcia place is a fine piece of property, with plenty of grass and water," said Gabe thoughtfully.

Cait had not missed her father's hint about the Garcia place and Gabe's interest. She hadn't thought much beyond his declaration of love for her. There hadn't been any time, what with the turmoil of the last ten days. Mackie's death and the violence that had accompanied it made it hard to realize that their ranch was now safe and secure. It had been even harder to grasp that El Lobo was, in fact, her mother's long lost brother and Cait's uncle.

But things were finally beginning to feel closer to normal and the future beckoned to her and so the next day at breakfast, Cait looked across at Gabe and said: "I was wondering if I might ride Sky this morning."

Gabe looked puzzled for a moment as though he was wondering why she needed his permission. It was hard to remember that the horse was his now.

"Of course, Cait. You know you can ride Sky anytime."

"I was hoping you'd accompany me," Cait added. "Just in case I have any trouble with him. I haven't ridden him out of the corral, you know," she said quickly.

"Wal, I guess I could put off working with the two-year-olds till this afternoon," Gabe drawled, looking over at Michael. "If you don't need me for anything else, Mr. Burke?"

"Ye deserve some time off, Gabe. Enjoy yer ride," Michael replied with a wave of his hand.

Sky was only a little skittish as Cait and Gabe rode off the ranch. Once they reached the foothills, he had settled down, but it was clear from the way his ears flicked back and forth and the way he carried his head up that he was curious and happy to be out of the confines of pasture and corral.

Their conversation was limited to comments on Sky or the way the chamisa was beginning to bloom as the autumn approached. Cait was wondering if she would have the courage to suggest they stop and rest for a while when Gabe pointed out a shady spot up the trail.

"It might be coming on fall," he remarked, "but the sun's still hot. Let's rest the horses up there."

But Sky did not want to be tied to the small cottonwood, no matter how hot the sun. He backed up, almost pulling the reins out of Cait's hands and with his ears laid back, stood there shivering.

"What's wrong, Gabe?"

"Cougars always attack from above, Cait, from trees or boulders. Maybe he was under a tree when that cat landed on his back." Gabe took the reins and murmuring softly to the horse, led him over to a large mesquite bush and tied him there. "I think he'll be all right there."

"So he still remembers, Gabe. Even after all this time and work?"

"I don't think he'll ever forget something like that, Cait. He'll carry that scar all his life." Cait knew he didn't just mean the weal on the horse's shoulder. "I suppose that what happens in our past shapes us all," she said thoughtfully as they sat back against a sandstone outcropping. "My mother still dreams about her parents. And my uncle . . . well, look what he became."

They were both silent for a moment and then, before she even knew the question was in her mind, Cait asked: "Why did you leave home, Gabe? Was it just because you had a taste for wandering?"

There was a small, brown patch of needle grass next to him and Gabe pulled at the stems and started looking to see if there were any seed heads left. "My ma died when I was fifteen, Cait."

"I'm so sorry, Gabe," Cait whispered.

"My pa remarried not long after. May was much younger than Pa, and after a year or so, she turned her eyes elsewhere."

"She went after some cowboy?"

"You could say that. She went after me," he said bitterly. "I couldn't face telling him so I had to leave."

"Did Sadie know why you left?"

"May was pretty obvious when Pa wasn't around," said Gabe with a wry grin. "I always felt it was my fault," he added, after a few minutes of silence. "I should have been able to stop her without leaving. Sadie's had too much to carry alone all these years."

"I've been surrounded by my Ma and Da's love all my life," said Cait gratefully. "When I think of you and Sadie and my uncle . . . I feel like a naive and romantic child," she added ruefully.

"I don't see you that way, Caitlin Burke," said Gabe, turning and facing her. "I see you as a fine, openhearted woman."

"Thank you, Gabe," she said, lifting her face to his. "When I said I loved you, Gabe Hart, I meant it. What about you?"

"Oh, Cait, I love you so," he replied, pulling her up so that she knelt in front of him, straddling his legs. She put his face between her hands and kissed him. It was a long and passionate kiss and they were both breathless by the time they pulled away.

Cait sat back on his knees and balanced herself by placing her hands on his chest and then inched forward and very slowly began to undo the buttons of his shirt. "I love how silvery your hair is here, Gabe," she said as she got the last button open.

"What do you think you are doing, Caitlin?"

"I'm just trying to show you how much I love you, Gabe Hart."

"Well, don't be moving up much further," he said, giving her a meaningful look. Cait blushed, but surprised herself by sliding herself closer until Gabe groaned.

"I promised your Da I'd make things right after kissing you in public, Cait."

"And how were you going to do that, Gabe?"

"By marrying you."

"You told my Da before you told me," she said in mock outrage.

"I didn't want him coming after me when we'd finished with Mackie," he said fervently.

"*Are* you going to ask me, Gabe?" she asked, shifting a little more.

"Sweet Jesus, woman, what do you think you are doing? Yes, I am going to ask you, but not like this."

Cait sat back and Gabe sighed with relief. Then he saw that she was unbuttoning her blouse.

"We can't do this, Cait."

But her blouse was open and off and her sweet breasts pressing against the light cotton of her chemise. Gabe reached out and cupped one. "You are so lovely," he whispered.

"Ask me, Gabe," Cait said softly, leaving forward into his hand.

"*Will* you marry me, Caitlin?"

"Tomorrow if you want, Gabe."

"Even if I am just an old horse breaker?" he added, but she could see that he was only teasing.

"I can see I have to kiss you out of your foolishness, Gabe." Her breasts were soft and warm against his chest as she leaned forward to kiss him, and as he felt her weight he grew even harder. Taking her by the waist, he lifted her off him.

"We have to stop, Cait."

"Why, Gabe?" she whispered plaintively.

"Because . . ." He couldn't seem to come up with a good enough reason. They had pledged themselves to each other, after all. "Because the first time should be special and on our marriage night, Caitlin. Because your father trusts me, and I owe him so much," he finally was able to choke out.

"I want you, Gabe," she said simply. "I am a grown woman. And what could be more special than here, in the shadow of the mountains."

She slipped off her skirt and lay down beside him in her chemise and drawers and looked up at him trustingly. After pulling his jeans down, he lay down again, and slid his hand under the soft cotton chemise, running his thumb around her nipple until it began to get hard. She felt him against her thigh and shyly put her hand down, shivering as she felt him pressing against her hand. Then his fingers were against her belly, sliding down to where she felt an aching and a tingling. As he started stroking her gently, and then harder, she couldn't believe the waves of pleasure that washed over her. She was home at last, lying with her love on the red earth of New Mexico, and she thanked God that she had finally found the place where her heart lay.

Gabe was tracing her face with his finger and dropping little kisses on her lips, when he felt something wet against his neck and jumped back. Cait's eyes had been closed in ecstasy but they flew open at his movement. Dear God, was it a snake . . . ? Her fear disappeared with her laughter, as she realized that Sky had pulled the reins away from the mesquite bush and was nibbling at Gabe's neck.

"Oh, it's fine for you to laugh, Cait," said Gabe who had to chuckle at his own sudden terror. "Go away, Sky," he said, swatting ineffectually at the horse. "Well, that's decided it, Cait," he said with a rueful smile. "He's sort of broken into my mood, and I can't say that I'm completely sorry. A bit frustrated, but I want you as my wife before we do this again," he added as he looked down into her eyes and brushed her curls back from her face. "But, Lord, it had better be soon!"

Elizabeth didn't quite know what she had expected after she revealed herself to her brother, but it certainly wasn't the distance he so obviously wanted to keep between them. It seemed that whenever she went in to visit him, he was sleeping, although several times she could have sworn that he had only just shut his eyes when he realized she had come in.

He recovered strength quickly once the fever was gone, and after a few days, Michael was able to get him up and help him onto the porch where he sat in an old rocking chair, watching the daily work go on around him. When she wasn't helping with the chores, Sadie would join him and they would sit there quietly, hand in hand. Those times Juan felt a sense of peace and security fill him and he knew that Sadie's love was healing him in a way beyond the physical, a way he could hardly articulate. Her love, and he had to admit, the feeling of having somehow come home, which Elizabeth Burke gave him.

He wasn't sure he wanted to feel at home. A part of him didn't want to have family, after years of being alone. So he avoided Elizabeth, pretending to sleep as often as he could, not talking to her except with everyday commonplaces as "good morning" or "thank-you" for his breakfast or his dinner when she brought it in to him.

But one afternoon, when Sadie and Cait had gone for a ride and Michael was in town, Juan had gotten himself onto the porch on his own when Elizabeth came around the side of the house, wiping her hands on her apron. "Jonathan, you should have waited for me," she said, hurrying up the steps.

"I am fine," he said, lowering himself carefully into the chair. "I thought I would spare you. You've had enough trouble with me these past few days."

"Let me go in and wash my hands," said Elizabeth, "and I'll bring us both some lemonade. I'll be right back, so don't you even think of closing your eyes," she added with a quizzical grin.

But his eyes were closed when she came back and she put his glass next to him and said almost sharply: "Jonathan."

"Oh, I am awake, Lizzie," he replied, opening his eyes and looking straight into hers. He smiled as he used the old nickname, but she could see that the smile didn't reach his eyes. "It is only that I am not sure I want to be."

"We have to talk, Jonathan," she said quietly.

He almost winced when she used his name. "Do you think you could call me Juan?" he asked. "It has been so long since I have been Jonathan Rush. . . ."

"All right, Juan. If you will call me Elizabeth." They both sipped their lemonade in an uncomfortable silence until Elizabeth said painfully: "I thought that this would be so easy, once you knew who I was."

"In a fairy tale, it would be, wouldn't it?" he said.

"We may have recognized each other, Elizabeth, but we don't really know each other anymore. We've each lived a lifetime in between. And you want to make me remember things I don't *want* to."

"I started having nightmares when you came to the valley, Juan. . . . Of that morning. I hadn't had any for years."

"So I came and brought you bad dreams," he said bitterly.

"No, no, I didn't mean it that way," she reassured him, putting her hand gently on his. "Just that your presence and the memories disturbed me too. It brought back all the horror I thought I'd laid to rest years ago. I think I can understand how hard this is for you. Harder than for me, since I have had Michael's love for so many years. And before that, Thomas's."

"Thomas?"

"He was the officer who rescued me. He brought me to his sister's in Santa Fe. We married four years later. He died in a Navajo raid," she added, her voice low.

"I am sorry, Lizzie," he whispered, turning his hand and holding hers. "So much loss for you."

"Oh, but so much love, Juan," she said with a catch in her voice. "Such a good life compared to what yours must have been."

"I think the hardest part was the first year," he told her after a long silence. "I kept hoping that God would somehow make Ma and Pa be alive again. Then they would come and rescue me," he added. She looked up and what she saw in his face almost broke her heart. His eyes held all the pain of the young boy he had been but he was smiling his almost cynical smile. "Then, when I *knew* God wasn't going to help me, well, I found a way to survive. I buried Jonathan Rush a long time ago, Elizabeth. I think it is too late to resurrect him now."

"Do you remember that morning? It was beautiful, so cool and clear. And Pa was singing that song of his, 'Will you go out West, will you go out West, will you go out West with me?' "

His hand closed convulsively over hers. "Don't, Lizzie."

"Ma asked me to go for water and I wanted *you* to go. If you had, things would have been very different for both of us . . . but I went and all of a sudden I heard a crack and Pa stopped right in the middle of his song."

"Those men did awful things to Ma, Lizzie," she heard him say in a ragged whisper. "I closed my eyes and then one of them grabbed me."

"And flung you over a mule. I saw it all, Jonathan. And I just stayed there, hidden by the creek bank. When they were gone, I finally got up. I pulled Ma's dress down over her legs. I closed their eyes. It was all I could do for them. . . ." Elizabeth's voice broke. She didn't dare look up at him again and the bones in her hand hurt where he was crushing them in his. She began to cry quietly, but continued through her tears. "We buried them the next day, Jonathan. Thomas said a prayer after we laid them to rest. They have been at peace for all these years. You know they would wish for you to be."

"They never came, Lizzie, no matter how much I cried for them."

"I know, I know," she murmured as though she was comforting a boy of seven.

"Dios," he said, his voice breaking. "I haven't cried once since then. What are you doing to me, Elizabeth?"

"I know that you cannot go on until you bury the dead, Juan. That much I have learned."

He sat there, trying to hold it all back: the tears, the memories, the pain. But it washed over him like a flood. When he had been captured, he'd found that he couldn't feel that kind of pain and survive. Even now, he wasn't sure he could make it back to the surface. He wouldn't let himself cry out, but the tears came and the waves of pain broke over him and he held onto his sister's hand for dear life.

When he finally came back to the present, it was

only to say hoarsely: "But it is all too late, Elizabeth. . . ."

"Too late for what, Juan?"

"For me. For us. I can't stay here after all that I've done."

"Like save my husband and Sadie's brother?"

"I could as easily have killed them," he protested.

"But you didn't."

"No, I didn't. Because of Sadie. And because of you and Michael," he added. "I admired both of you for your strength and I didn't want to see you broken."

"Stay in the valley, Juan. Let us get to know each other again. Get to know my family. Raise one of your own."

"So you have been talking to Sadie," he said, attempting a smile. "But I can't stay here with you indefinitely."

"There is plenty of land now that . . ."

"Now that I've scared some people off and Mackie is dead," he said ironically.

Elizabeth had to laugh. "Well, yes."

"I just don't know if it is possible to get back the past. . . ."

"We can't get anything back, Juan. I know that. But we can build something from today on and if we don't try to do that, then don't you think Ma and Pa's deaths are wasted?"

He squeezed her hand again and then looked down as she winced. "*Dios,* what have I done?" he asked, only half joking as he stroked her red-and-white fingers. "All right, Lizzie, I will stay."

Epilogue

It was a cool morning in October that Cait was married in the little adobe church of San Pedro by Father Luis. Both Michael and Elizabeth escorted her down the aisle to where Gabe waited, looking handsomer than Cait could have thought possible in a new black suit. The sun shining in the windows silvered his hair and Cait was reminded of the first time she had seen him. So much had happened since she returned home, and all of it had led her to the man who was waiting for her with a shy smile on his face. "Thank you, Ma, Da," she whispered as they stepped away, leaving her there with Gabe who reached out and gently took her hand.

The ceremony was dreamlike for Cait, with only a few moments standing out: Gabe slipping the thin gold band on her finger, his feathery kiss on her lips, and her parents' faces smiling at her as she walked back down the aisle, arm in arm with her husband. Then they were back at the ranch, greeting all their neighbors who were arriving for the feast.

It wasn't until Ramon struck up a waltz that Cait had any time to herself with Gabe, and she went eagerly into his arms. They circled first, as was appropriate for the new bride and groom, and then Michael and Elizabeth joined them. "What about the not-so-newlyweds?" Jimmy Murdoch shouted, and Juan Chavez pulled a blushing Sadie into his arms.

"I wish they had let us have a party for them," said Cait.

"Given Juan's history in the valley, it's probably just as well they eloped, Cait."

"They look so happy," she said, watching her uncle and new sister-in-law, who had eyes only for each other.

"They can't be half as happy as we are, darlin'," said Gabe, smiling down on her.

Jimmy Murdoch's raucous toasts were aimed at both couples, so it wasn't until Gabe had pulled up the wagon with Night Sky tied to the back that Cait finally awoke to the fact that she was leaving home to begin her new life as Mrs. Gabriel Hart.

As they drove slowly down the road and over to the old Garcia place, she was very quiet. "You're not having second thoughts, are you, darlin'?" teased Gabe. Cait slipped her arm through his. "Of course not, Gabe," she answered. "But I just didn't realize how it would feel to leave Ma and Da behind."

"We're not far away, Cait," said Gabe, giving her arm a reassuring squeeze. "And I'll be over there every day, working the horses. Pretty soon, it won't feel like much has changed at all."

Her mother had prepared a picnic wedding supper for them, but neither did more than pick at the food. Cait finally wrapped it up, saying: "Maybe we'll both have more of an appetite in the morning" and then blushed when Gabe winked at her.

"You go on upstairs, Cait. I'll be right in after I take care of the horses."

She was sitting on the edge of their bed when he came up, dressed in a delicately embroidered nightrail. Her hair was down, framing her face with its dark cloud of curls. She gave him a shy smile and said: "I feel very silly, Gabe, considering how close we've come to making love, but I am nervous."

"Don't worry, Caitlin, we will go slow and easy," he reassured her as he started to undress. She sat back against the bedstead and watched. She thought he might be about the most beautiful thing she had ever seen as he stood there, tall and long and lean.

He sat next to her and began to untie the ribbon of her nightrail and without even willing it, her arms were up around his neck. He slipped his own hands down and under the gown to lift it over her head. Then he pulled her down next to him so that they lay there, bodies barely touching and drew his finger down her cheek to her lips.

"This is the way it should be for the first time, Cait," he whispered, and she nibbled at his finger, drawing it into her mouth as she placed her hand on his hips and pulled him closer. He was hard and soft at the same time and she loved the sensation of him pressing against her belly.

Gabe gave her fingers a last kiss and then linking his fingers with hers, pressed her arm down on the bed and took possession of her mouth with his as he rubbed against her. "I'll make sure you are ready," he whispered as he stroked her gently. And by the time he entered her, Caitlin was near death or ecstasy, she wasn't sure which, the pleasure was so intense.

It did hurt, the first time, but afterward, as Cait lost her shyness, she felt a hunger for more. The second time, which went on a gloriously long time, left both of them limp with spent passion.

After lying there, her head on his chest, listening to his heart resume its normal rhythm, Cait heard a strange gurgling sound. "My stomach's telling me I missed dinner," said Gabe with a laugh.

"You know, I am starving, too," she admitted.

They unwrapped the chicken and bread and cheese that her mother had packed, and ate right from the butcher's paper, licking each other's fingers clean at the end.

Gabe pushed his chair back and took Cait's hand. "It is a lovely night, Cait, come and sit with me for a while." He sat down on their top step and Cait cuddled next to him.

"Look at the sky, Gabe," she whispered. "Isn't it beautiful?"

It was a deep black, so deep that you could get lost in it, thought Gabe. The stars shone cold and clear and as they watched, one streaked across the western horizon.

"A shooting star, Gabe," said Cait, wonder in her voice.

"You should be wishing on it, darlin'."

"I have nothing to wish for, Gabe, for all I could ever want is right here," she said and he tightened his arms around her and held her close as they watched the night sky fill with stars.